I0588938

Also by Doug Richardson

Lucky Dey Thrillers
Blood Money
Reaper
American Bang
The Night is Never Black
Hip Slick and Dead

Other Fiction
The Safety Expert
Dark Horse
True Believers

Nonfiction
*The Smoking Gun: True Stories from Hollywood's
Screenwriting Trenches*

A LUCKY DEY THRILLER
DOUG RICHARDSON

99 PERCENT KILL

los angeles

Velvet Elvis Entertainment
6038 Tampa Avenue, Suite 366
Tarzana, California 91356

More information at www.dougrichardson.com
ISBN: 978-0-9964563-5-7

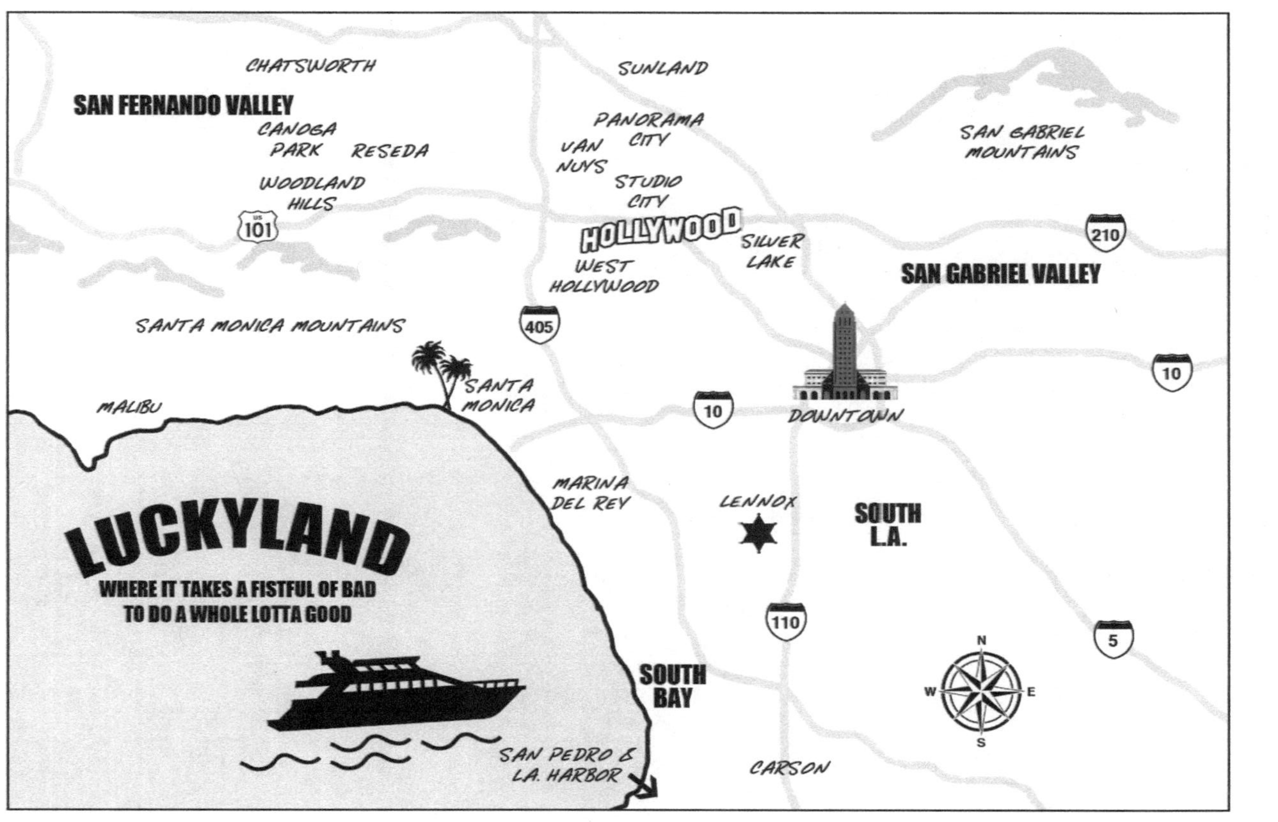

CHATSWORTH
SAN FERNANDO VALLEY
CANOGA PARK
RESEDA
WOODLAND HILLS
US 101
SUNLAND
PANORAMA CITY
VAN NUYS
STUDIO CITY
HOLLYWOOD
WEST HOLLYWOOD
SILVER LAKE
SAN GABRIEL MOUNTAINS
210
SAN GABRIEL VALLEY
10
SANTA MONICA MOUNTAINS
405
MALIBU
SANTA MONICA
10
DOWNTOWN
MARINA DEL REY
LENNOX
SOUTH L.A.
LUCKYLAND
WHERE IT TAKES A FISTFUL OF BAD
TO DO A WHOLE LOTTA GOOD
110
5
SOUTH BAY
SAN PEDRO & L.A. HARBOR
CARSON
N E S W

For my beloved sister,
Carolyn Lee Herbertson
1957-2014

Monday

1

Hollywood, California.

It was so much easier than the old days. Back then, it was closer to a fifty-fifty deal. Half of the investment came from the sheer force of Herm's personality, the other half in pure sweat equity. Herm was fast closing on sixty years old, practically ancient in the flesh game. And with no retirement plan but for the slivers of cash he could stow in his City National Bank safe deposit box, the former pimp was all about less talk and a high-efficiency system for identifying the most commercial girl.

"Just look into the camera and speak your name," said Herm flatly, but in his naturally resonant voice. It was meant to sound as if he'd performed video auditions tens of thousands of times instead of only a few hundred.

"Sandy Smithers," said the candidate through an artificially bright smile.

"That your real name?"

That's when the actress wannabe revealed a sheepish gleam. Innocent. Marketable.

"Stage name," she said. "Do you need my birth name?"

"No," said Herm, interjecting a little of the old charm along with a shiny grill of fine dental work as a pearly contrast to his near-perfect complexion of eggshell-brown skin. "As long as it's the same name on your headshot."

"Oh, good," said the girl, twisting from side to side on the pivoting stool. A sure sign of her nerves.

A pair of umbrella lights on aluminum stands cast a couple hundred watts of soft light onto the subject. The rest of the candle-power bounced off the Sheetrock walls to be absorbed by some low-pile industrial-grade carpet. The videographer's kit looked professional enough and cost Herm less than thirty bucks on Craigslist. Add to that the rental of the fifteen-by-fifteen audition space and advertisements in *Backstage*, and Herm's total monthly investment clocked in at just north of three bills.

"Is this good like this?" asked Sandy, crossing her legs in order to show off her toned stems.

"That's totally fine," said Herm, flicking his eyes up to check the image on the tiny monitor screen instead of actually looking at the subject.

In his bad old days, Herm would have rejected Sandy the moment she'd uttered her stage name. *Sandy Smithers.* Sure, it had a nice double-S sibilance and rolled smoothly and memorably over both the tongue and eyeballs. Just way back then the right girl would've been two to four years younger with an invented stage moniker chock-full of starry ambition.

Like Ashley Apples.

Herm suddenly found himself repeating the name—if only just in his head—freely allowing it to ricochet between his temples as he adjusted the video camera lens, pushing the frame until it was hugging Sandy's curves as tight as her peekaboo blouse.

"Now, I'd like you to please twist yourself about a quarter turn counterclockwise," said Herm.

"That'd be this way, right? Little bit to my left?"

"That's good right there."

"Keep smiling?"

"Probably don't have to tell you that," said Herm.

Little Ashley Apples.

Herm had met the fourteen-year-old in a Sunset Boulevard coffee shop. He could tell from the instant he saw her that she was ripe. As brand spanking new as a shiny penny fresh off the assembly line at the US Mint. She was just off the Greyhound bus and sharing a four-top booth with her hot pink rolling suitcase. And where was she originally from? Was it Washington State or Idaho? Near Spokane came to mind. Man, she was something to remember. A once-every-ten-years find. Herm remembered all the ones who ticked off his top boxes. They were the unicorns. The perfect perfects. Produced by none other than the hand of God for man's earthly consumption. And, if the stars and planets aligned, for Herm's personal profit.

"Do you have something for me to read or do you want me to do a monologue?" asked Sandy, beginning to wonder how long Herm was going to let his video camera linger on her.

"Car commercial," said Herm. "Clients are going for a certain look."

"Any particular kind?" asked the wannabe. "I can do other looks."

"I'll bet you can," said Herm, reverse-zooming the video lens back to the widest angle. "But, hey. Why mess with perfection?"

The actress giggled a little too easily. More tease than surprise. A sure sign she was accustomed to attention.

"Any piercings or tattoos?" he asked.

"Excuse me?"

"Might be some bikini work. Both the agency and automaker are European. I expect the ad will air somewhere overseas."

"Can't they just airbrush out a tattoo?"

"Airbrushing's for still pictures. Digital film is way more expensive," said Herm, easily spilling a little showbiz factoid in the name of veracity. His. Proving that a little truth could go a long way.

"Oh."

"Gotta ask. On the agency casting form."

Herm picked up a clipboard and flipped over the first page to show her. Never mind that it was little more than a copy of an actual casting form he'd printed off the Net. He'd been using the same dog-eared sheet for two years already.

"I have two tiny bits of body art," said Sandy. She twisted at the waist and used a hot pink fingernail to pinpoint the first. "One on my shoulder here. And another cute one in kinda, you know . . . private place."

"So, pink's your color?" weathered Herm, shifting gears and, more importantly, not taking her bait. His game required a professional demeanor. Non-threatening. Entirely devoid of malevolence. That was his job in the food chain.

"I do like pink," answered the girl, revealing a trace of Dixie in her voice. "What about you? You like girls who like pink?"

I just can't get enough of pink.

At least, that's what little Ashley Apples had said to him back in the day.

I like me lotsa pink and just a little bit of gray.

With that, Ashley would gently rub her knuckles up against Herm's spiky salt-and-pepper sideburns, grown just long enough to appear retro, à la some kind of seventies rock star. He'd been about forty years old back then. Ripped like a gym monkey and full of Southern California vitality. Yet the gray around his temples gave him a distinguished streak. When some men of a certain age were spending hundreds of dollars in salon chairs, dyeing their years into blonde or brown submission, Herm found wearing his forties like a badge made the teen girls he hunted feel that much safer in his care. Funny, he used to think. These young women whom he'd chosen to pluck from the runaway tree had all arrived in L.A. with a trunk full of parent issues. Abused. Already halfway down the trail to a future heroin, meth, or crack addiction. Yet it was a daddy sort of lover they still so desired. And hell if Herm wasn't going to be there to provide for them.

I like pink all right. But Herman Bland needs him some green. You wanna help him with that?

And rare was the girl who said no to Herm. At least, not the girls from the bad ol' days.

Why the crap do things gotta be so different today?

"Okay. I think we're good to go," said the finely aged man behind the camera.

"That's it?" asked Sandy, hoping to have been given more opportunity to shine for the lens.

"All I need," said Herm, giving a final once-over to her model consent form. "Now, is this your home phone number or a cell?"

"Cell."

Check one.

"And do you live in town?"

"You mean, here in LA?"

"Exactly."

"Hollywood. Well, I think it's Hollywood. Or is it just East Hollywood?"

"Roommates?"

"Two. I'm sorry. But what does that—"

"Not the best part of town. My guess is you're new to La La Land."

"La La Land?"

"L.A. Hollywood. Tinseltown," explained Herm, his voice reaching down for the tonal mellifluence that lent him such gravitas. His height, smooth yet ethnically confusing pallor, and easy grace reminded many of famed character actor Morgan Freeman. A comparison he used to his advantage.

"You guessed that I was new to California?" she asked.

Check two.

"Good you don't live alone," added Herm.

"That's what my dad always says."

"Might need to travel for the job. That a problem?"

"I love to travel. Where?"

Check three.

"Undetermined. These things change a lot. One day they're shooting the spot in Cancún. The next at an airplane hangar in Lancaster."

"Where's Lancaster?"

"Don't worry. No place you wanna go unless they're paying you."

"Good. 'Cause I really need the money right now."

"Don't we all need the money?" smiled Herm as a way of wrapping up the audition. "Thanks for coming by. If there's a callback, I've got your number."

"Don't call us. We'll call you," joked Sandy. "But I couldn't call you anyway cuzza I don't have your number."

Herm released a polite but still fraudulent chuckle, slipped his six-foot-four frame past the umbrella lamps, and opened the door. Sandy said a faint goodbye, eventually disappearing down a long barren corridor with identical thresholds. It resembled a veterinary clinic more than a commercial casting operation renting audition space by the hour. Once the wannabe had vanished down the stairs, Herm swept his eyes over to the petite young woman in a pair of size-zero Daisy Dukes and bright red lipstick. She was seated in one of two folding chairs that flanked an Arrowhead water cooler.

She was no unicorn. For that matter, neither was Sandy Smithers. But either—given the right circumstance—would still be worth some coin.

"Are you Bristol?" asked Herm.

"I am," said the girl, springing to her feet.

"Well, come on in and let's get you on video."

2

Van Nuys, California.

Lucky Dey loathed stakeouts.

Aside from his longstanding opinion that it was a waste of his time, he had spent enough hours with his ass wearing holes in car upholstery that he'd come to the conclusion that it was also an utter flush-hole of taxpayers' resources. He imagined the cumulative hours of his life lost on what he'd come to call *watch and rots.* He'd imagined the same for other L.A. County sheriff's detectives, then applied salaries, union-negotiated overtime payments, plus the required contributions to each and every health and pension plan. It was a boondoggle, in his undervalued opinion. When cops could have been spending their on-duty time trying to solve actual crime cases, chasing gangbangers with guns, or even the general minding of the public safety, they were often assigned the life-sucking task of watching some empty doorway and cataloguing every innocuous matter of a suspect's comings and goings. Sure, it might possibly, maybe, or eventually lead to a real live hook. But Lucky rued the man hours that would be saved if assistant DAs and the judges who signed warrants would reach into their pants, rediscover their testicles, and allow smart cops to bust down those empty doors and sort out the bad guys from good guys.

What made this Monday stakeout different was that instead of grinding over the waste of his precious time, Lucky was left to ponder the ungodly emptiness that had haunted him from the moment he had woken from his dreamless sleep. Distraction was his only relief from the nearly constant detachment he felt from the human race.

It was December in L.A. and unseasonably cold. Lucky's habit on stakeouts was to leave his car windows rolled down in order to utilize his ears as part of the surveillance. Hearing was key. Be it the throaty fingerprint of a car engine or identifying the direction of gunfire. But the bitter air outside made all those metal pins screwed into his bones just ache, convincing the Los Angeles native to keep the tinted windows at full mast and utilize the late-morning sun to warm the borrowed, mid-nineties model Crown Victoria. It surely wasn't the stealthiest of vehicles. The old Ford reeked of cop car, complete with the hand-operated spotlight mounted just above the driver's side-view mirror. The car was beat to hell, a patchwork of Bondo body repair and primer gray, blending well into the Van Nuys neighborhood that mixed small industry and lower-middle-class single-family homes.

The Crown Vic was parked with its back end up against a Circle K. Lucky, sucking on a forty-four-ounce cocktail of Diet Coke and Mountain Dew, checked the Breitling watch that had belonged to his deceased younger brother, Tony. It ticked in tight Swiss circles, the only survivor of the upturned car fire that had consumed its previous owner.

It was 9:49 a.m.

The Ukrainian bastard Lucky was waiting on should have shown by now. The cop yawned. His eyes autonomically slammed shut as if to demand a power nap just before he forced his lids back open after a bone-shaking sneeze. The ensuing spew left fine speckles on his rearview mirror. With no tissues to clean the misty mess, he tried utilizing the cuff of his jacket, only to leave a horizontal smear across his own blue-eyed reflection. Still, his view was clean enough to chart the deep creases on a face that was less than classic good looks and more akin to a buzzed-cut cage fighter who'd taken one too many cracks to the nose. Considering all the punishment, Lucky was sometimes shocked he could still breathe through his oft rerouted nasal passages.

Personal distractions aside, now was not the time for messing up. He had to get this done and move on to the next item on his never-ending list of duties.

Finally, he spotted the man.

He was hard to miss in the bright yellow Bug. The little damned intel Lucky had was the man's name. Benjamin Anton Kuzmanov. And that nearly everybody, including his employees, five children by three different mothers, and two ex-wives, called him Kuz. The report also expressed that Kuz could best be found driving a newly leased VW Beetle between the hours of 8:00 a.m. and noon on most weekdays. That's when he would leave his fabricating plant for a late-morning meal at Beeps Diner, a local fast-food landmark. Guaranteed, Lucky's female source had claimed. The man apparently couldn't go a weekday without his Beeps' Big Pastrami Breakfast.

The restaurant, famously trimmed in hot pink and turquoise, sat on the northeast corner of a busy boulevard, across which Lucky dodged a variety of cars, their horns sounding like noisy geese chased by a bird dog wanting to play. Lucky ignored the shouts from the annoyed driver of a Wonder Bread truck. The words weren't in a language he could recognize, but they fit well with the middle-fingered gesture the driver used to punctuate his angry, anti-pedestrian tirade.

As the sticky soles of Lucky's boots landed on the opposite curb, he re-directed himself to cut off his target before the man could reach the restaurant's entrance. Lucky was reaching around to retrieve something tucked into the small of his back when he spoke the man's name simply and clearly.

"Benjamin Kuzmanov?" announced Lucky, only to discover his voice swallowed by a cargo jet taking flight at the nearly next-door Van Nuys Airport. So, Lucky waited for a count of three, then elevated his volume with a simple, sharply enunciated, "Kuz!"

The runty man in question glanced over the top of his sun-glasses, gathered in the visage of the buzz-cut cop in boots and Ray-Ban aviators, and reversed his direction with a burst of purse-thief speed.

"STOP!" shouted Lucky.

Son of a bitch.

Before the cop even realized it, he was in a race, chasing the runty rabbit between parked cars and into four lanes of morning traffic. Lucky recalled hearing squealing tires coupled with relief that the sound of high-pitched friction on asphalt wasn't followed by the telltale *whump* of metal crunching metal.

Twenty yards ahead, all Lucky could see were those short damned legs cranking at what felt like double his own pace, a jean jacket flapping, and dark hair trailing as the man called Kuz cut behind the filling station and right-turned himself into the side yard of a transmission repair shop.

Why the hell am I chasing this fucker? thought Lucky.

Once in the yard, Lucky glimpsed the man vaulting over a wooden fence. Disappearing in a flash of curled black hair and denim. Lucky suddenly imagined himself in pursuit of some kind of former Soviet gymnast.

It was as Lucky hoisted himself over the fence that he felt the first significant spike of Monday's pain. A wincing jolt that radiated all the way through his limbs to his fingertips. Yet he continued the pursuit. Keeping his feet underneath him. Driving with his legs and arms down an overgrown back alley that reeked of week-old fry oil before he plowed into an eight-foot-high vertical stretch of chain-link. Lucky climbed as if on autopilot. Got purchase with his feet, but got hung up when trying to sling his body over the top. A rogue wire had punctured through his Wranglers at mid-calf.

"Shit-fuck!" Lucky barked before landing on what felt and smelled like fresh-pressed asphalt.

He spun, scanning for the rat-faced runt he was already blaming for ruining a new pair of dungarees. The radiating pain, though, that was all on Lucky with an extra special mention to the team of docs that had pieced him back together with steel sutures and what must have been yards of orthopedic-grade titanium. The rest of the blame was reserved for an evil former Marine named Greg Beem, who, by some miracle, had survived a car wreck, a bullet to the back, and a rushing river that should have drowned him.

The Ukrainian was dashing across the fresh pavement without an ounce of slowing down. Just beyond was a pair of enormous airplane hangars. Big white elephants set atop an ocean of black asphalt. The short bastard had put some stretch in the distance between himself and Lucky. The running little prick was smaller, faster, and unfortunately blessed with a far more efficient pulmonary output.

That and you're goddamned outta shape, Luck.

A lime green SUV swept wide around the southernmost hangar, cutting off Kuz's angle and forcing him to downshift his stubby legs and make a ninety-degree turn. As he pivoted, his suede deck shoes lost traction, nearly sending him to the tarmac. Then, in no time, his arms were pumping again and his speed was back.

But he didn't see Lucky's fence post of a forearm.

The clothesline move employed by the air-sucking cop instantly turned Ben Kuzmanov from a free-runner into a doorstop. As his back landed on the asphalt, all air left him in a single exhale. Those superior lungs emptied, leaving the small man wheezing for oxygen.

"You're okay, ya dumb runt," insisted Lucky. "Just got the wind knocked outta ya."

Kuz could only offer the slightest up-and-down nod of his

chin, acknowledging Lucky while trying like hell to force his diaphragm to re-expand.

"Now, yes or no?" asked Lucky, astride his captive. "Are you Ben Kuzmanov?"

The tires of that green SUV chirped, driver and passenger doors jackknifing open.

"Yes or no?" demanded Lucky, his right fist unconsciously balled, knuckles pale and prepped to pummel.

"Yeah . . ." coughed the runner, palms open and pleading surrender.

This is when Lucky, in the most accustomed of rituals, reached around to the small of his back to where so many cops stowed guns or handcuffs or both. Instead, he withdrew a short stack of papers, folded in thirds and sealed, then dropped it on the runner's chest.

"You've been served, shit-wad," spat Lucky.

"Whoa . . . wait . . ." hacked Kuz, still seeking inflation to his lungs. Despite the lack of air behind them, his words were clear yet thickly coated with a Russian accent. "I'm getting sued? You're a fucking process server?"

"Got sweat in your ears?"

"Thought you were a cop!"

"I *am* a goddamn cop!" barked Lucky. "Just not today."

"So, you're a cop?" interjected the heftier of the two Lockheed Martin security officers who'd taken up trained positions at ten and two o'clock. Their uniform shirts were the same shade of green as their SUV with brass badges so shiny the sun was glinting off them. Both men were armed, hands placed on the butts of their unskinned weapons.

"L.A. County," said Lucky, finally catching his own breath. "Dude hopped your fence. I'm just the pursuer."

"He's a fucking process server!" said Kuz, finding his feet and dusting off his khakis with the process papers.

"So, which is it?" asked the security officer. "Cop or process server?"

"Both," said Lucky, fending off their looks with a shrug. "So what? Never heard of moonlighting?"

"That means you're *both* trespassing on private property," said the security officer. "Gonna have to ask you to please get in the vehicle."

"How's this?" offered Lucky, snagging his prize by the back of the collar and jerking him as if setting a hook. "I turn around and drag runt-turd's ass back over the fence and we forget this ever happened?"

"If you're really with the sheriff's," said the security officer, "then you should understand protocols."

"We really gonna do it this way?" asked Lucky.

"Lockheed's a government contractor," said the security officer. "Homeland Security writes our rule book. Now, please? Get in the truck."

Though Lucky shook his head in disbelief, he quickly relented for no reason other than he'd ridden down such a road way too many times before. Whether it was the Feebs or just some bullshit jurisdictional beef between county deputies and the jack-booted LAPD, it was sometimes more efficient—let alone easier on the personnel dossier—to acquiesce and let the bureaucrats have their petty procedures.

As Lucky started toward the back of the SUV, the runty runner's tony deck shoes seemed to be stuck in the asphalt. So, Lucky popped him in the back of the head with an open hand.

"The both of us means me *and* you," reminded Lucky.

"I have a business to get back to," demanded Kuz in a practiced protest that Lucky wrote off as that of a habitual shirker of responsibility. "Asshole. You should've left me to my breakfast."

"Next time, don't run, Mr. Kuz."

"Not Kuz. Coooooz. You hear the 'ooooo' sound? Kuz. That's how you say my name."

"Get in the truck, Kuuuuuuz, before I hang you up and use you for a piñata."

3

Universal City.

Thump. Thump. Thump. Thump . . .

Cherry's eyes were closed as she swiveled her hips to the incessant beat. Not that anybody could see that her eyes were actually shut. For that last set of the night, she'd kept her retinas hidden behind a pair of cheap costume sunglasses. White rims. Coffee-grind lenses. The shades were identical to the hundred other pairs that had been handed out to the party guests. Boys and girls. Dressed to their thirteen-year-old nines. About half the young women were wobbling on heels too steep for their young legs to handle.

Cherry danced in her usual spot, at nine o'clock to Marco, the DJ, atop a gray Plexiglas cube with a synchronized strobe underneath. The pulsing light caught the thousands of tiny jewels fixed to her Lycra short-shorts. Each booty shake colored the room in a constellation of ever-shifting rainbows. It was a cheesy effect. But, for the most part, the kids loved it.

Fifteen more minutes, get paid, then a fast elevator to the valet, my shitty car, and a late shift at the Rabbit Pole.

The bar mitzvah had all the bells and whistles of a top-shelf event. The parents of the lucky boy had rented out the event room that sat atop the Sheraton Hotel at Universal Studios in North Hollywood. The space sported two-story, floor-to-ceiling windows with a 270-degree view of the San Fernando Valley. Below, a sparkling carpet of lights spread north and west for miles upon suburban miles. And to the south, a carving streak of car lights cut through the low-lying hills—thousands upon thousands of beams in a constant river that flowed in and out of the Basin and beyond.

"All my friends think you're the hottest dancer," shouted the boy over the ear-bleeding din.

Cherry lifted her eyelids but didn't stop grinding out the song from atop her post. Below her was a thirteen-year-old boy with a mop of black curly hair wearing a nifty, gray tailored suit. Still growing, she sized up. And most likely from serious money. The boy, though nearly six feet in height, was still in full sprout. And only a mom and dad with a bank full of fuck-you cash would hook up their growing child with an Italian custom tailor.

"What's that?" shouted Cherry, wanting the boy to repeat himself. She remembered him, picking him out as maybe the tallest young man at the party and the obvious best friend to the evening's boy of honor. She had even wondered which of the coterie of fawning teen girls attending might be the likeliest to service the young stud—if that hadn't already happened in some darker hotel corner. After all, she had party-danced at so many of these "manhood" celebrations that she'd picked up on the stories. Willing thirteen-year-old Jewish girls—still giggly and seemingly innocent enough—queued up to orally pleasure the bar mitzvah boy and his equally decked-out entourage.

Cherry, who was originally from Sacramento, had written off the sordid accounts as myth, until one Saturday event only a month before, she'd stumbled into just such a situation. Three girls on their knees fellating three equally young boys in the ladies' room's handicap stall.

"You're definitely the hottest dancer," shouted the boy even louder.

"Why, thank you," mouthed Cherry, not caring to compete with the decibels.

"I mean, you can really move," continued the tall boy, venturing close enough that he wouldn't have to scream. "Sure. Like, she may be way prettier than you. But she can't dance near as hot."

Cherry was certain there was a compliment in there somewhere. But the *she* to whom the boy was referring was Cherry's dancing doppelgänger on the opposite side of the stage. Her name was Valerie or Valentina or some damned V name. Whatever the stage name she'd chosen to sell, it for sure wasn't her birth certificate name. That much Cherry could guess. This from a woman whom everyone assumed had her own fake moniker. As if she'd pulled the name out of the air the moment after finishing up her very first strip club tryout. The owner of the club had asked her name. And because she'd already been saying it her entire life, it was easy to remember.

I'm Cherry. Like Cherry pie, you know?

Just like the title of the classic hair metal hit she'd just auditioned to. "Cherry Pie" by Warrant.

So, that's your name? Cherry Pie?

Yessir. That's my name. Don't wear it out.

As for Valerie or Valentina or whatever the new girl's name was. Sure, she may have been prettier, and much, much younger than Cherry. Not yet eighteen, by Cherry's streetwise estimate. But the girl couldn't move nearly as well as her more seasoned counterpart. She was still stuck in ballet class, thought Cherry. Waiting for some mean prima dance instructor to stalk her from behind, grab hold of her bun-head, and yank upward to get the girlie to put some steel in her spine.

The party ended with a final blitzkrieg of disco-pop. Marco, on the turntable, pushed the volume up to an ear-rupturing torment, making Cherry glad she remembered to install her earplugs. For the last set, her job was to venture forth and drag whoever hadn't yet sweat through their Saturday finery out of their seats and onto the dance floor. The new girl hadn't yet mastered the art of luring the unwilling to shake their booties. Out of the corner of her eye, Cherry could see her gesturing and cajoling various middle-aged bar mitzvah invitees to join the dancing throng. That wasn't at all what Cherry had instructed her. The trick was simply to smile flirtatiously, reach out and grab the unsuspecting man or woman, and begin pulling them toward the parquet.

Ask somebody and they'll usually say no. Grab hold and pull and they'll feel obligated to trot back to the dance floor with ya.

Then came the stroke of 11:00 p.m., when, by hotel contract, the boy's bar mitzvah was required to unplug. DJ Marco, who could spot a hotel security phalanx from two hundred paces, turned off the mix and began to strike his audio equipment.

For her part, Cherry wisely stayed amongst the milling adults for a few extra moments, congratulating them, shaking hands, accepting both compliments on her energetic dancing and making herself available for whatever cash tips might come her way. She'd begin with her own twenty-dollar bill folded into her fist as a way of chumming the water. There'd surely be a few more Andrew Jacksons to follow from men who didn't want to be embarrassed in front of their wives or impressionable children. That and there'd always be one or two who would inquire as to her background or even quasi-tease her with their hotel room numbers. And if a man appeared at all cool, she might tell him where he could see her later.

I dance at the Rabbit Pole. Midnight to two. Come see me and I'll dance some more for you.

"Did you really just tell that man you work as a stripper?" asked the new girl.

"I did and I do," said Cherry, toweling the sweat off her face with the nearest unused cloth napkin. In the quiet air following the hours of nonstop dance music, Cherry's voice gave off a throaty tone. Smoky and warm.

"Is that cool?"

"Is what cool?" asked Cherry. "That I dance at a strip club or tell some middle-aged dude where I dance?"

"I guess . . . both."

"What's your name again?" asked Cherry, toweled off and beginning her beeline to the elevators.

"Valeriana," repeated the new girl, following but not nearly as sweat-drenched as her more experienced doppelgänger.

"Valeriana," said Cherry. "You dance for three hours around a lotta these middle-aged Jewish dads and you're gonna find out who's horny and who ain't. Better you have a safe place for them to come watch you finish them. Instead of, you know . . ."

"You know . . ." pressed the new girl.

"Instead of them trying to get you into some hotel room."

The new girl—Valeriana—nodded as if she understood. In Cherry's view, the new girl clearly hadn't the maturity or grasp of the potential side effects or benefits that came with the job of a party dancer.

"You been doin' this a while, huh?" asked Valeriana.

"Party dancing?" said Cherry. "Off an' on for five or so years. Mostly on. It's once a week and an easy two hundred bucks."

"But you also . . . You know."

"Strip. Yeah, so?"

"So nothing . . ."

"Stripping pays for my car and my rent and all my classes. Party dancing pays gas, if I'm lucky."

"Is it hard?"

"Making a living? In this town?" was Cherry's answer, acting as if she didn't understand the question.

"Exotic . . . stripper dancing?" clarified Valeriana.

"How old are you?" Cherry pressed the down elevator button, engaged with the new girl but still moving.

"Eighteen."

"My ass," said Cherry. "More like sixteen or fifteen, or you tell me?"

Valeriana bit her lip like a bad liar. It brought out the pink in her face, flushing behind all the strawberry freckles under a fever of matching blonde hair.

"Don't worry. I'm not gonna tell Marco," promised Cherry. "As long as you don't tell him I told some old guy with bad cologne to meet me at the Rabbit Pole."

"Sixteen this coming Friday," admitted Valeriana.

"And Valeriana's not your real name, is it?"

"Not really . . ."

"That's okay. Think my real name's Cherry Pie?"

"It's not?"

"It kind of is. But that's for another party."

Valeriana laughed. And when she did, her face sparkled like a new day. Cherry would later remember that. She herself was Los Angeles jaded. Had thought she'd seen just about all the city had to give. But Valeriana or whatever the hell her real name was? At that moment, Cherry saw the new girl had something special. Unique. A quality that one could easily see, but not exactly describe. More than just a mix of hair and eyes and preternatural shapeliness.

"Hey," said Cherry. "You wanna come along?"

"To where?" asked the new girl.

"My other job. See how things work."

"But I just told you I wasn't even sixteen."

"Far as I'm concerned, you're Valeriana and you're eighteen and from Shitsburg."

Then it happened again. The lip biting as a tell to the new girl's thinking process. Engaging. Sexy. Telegenic as hell.

"I better not," answered Valeriana. "I'm not ready for . . . that."

"No girl is ever ready for it. Just maybe a little less wanting."

"Wanting for what?"

Man, thought Cherry. What she could do with the new girl. General Ho, the owner-manager of the Rabbit Pole, would probably pay Cherry for an introduction to a girl with such radioactive cuteness.

"There's the elevator," announced Cherry. "Last chance."

"Another time?" asked the new girl.

"Yeah. Another time. You gonna work next weekend?"

"If I'm available. I'm kinda up for another job."

"Ooooh?" guessed Cherry. "Sounds like an acting gig."

"Sorta maybe."

"Well, good luck with it."

"Good luck to you too."

"No luck in shucking your clothes for tips," said Cherry. "As long as the club's ATM machine is working."

Then came the new girl's laugh again. Magical. On the verge of miraculous. With that, Cherry stepped into the elevator and gave an unconsciously girlish wave. Then, just as the doors were sliding shut...

"Wait!" called out the new girl.

Cherry stuck out her hand and the doors slid back open.

"Got nowhere else to go," admitted Valeriana. "Guess it wouldn't hurt if I came along."

4

Reseda.

Lucky's latest and not-too-greatest apartment was a stuffy San Fernando Valley roach motel. There was practically zero air-flow even with all the windows slid wide open. Lucky blamed the brand-new mega-unit building across the alley. It was like a massive, five-hundred-unit stucco and tile buffer that, no matter the direction of the wind, would reroute the molecules of air so that few ever found their way to breeze through Lucky's second-floor windows. That was all the rationale Lucky needed to run the fan on his wall-mounted air-conditioning unit on even the coldest nights.

Suffice it to say, Lucky liked to feel as if the air around him were on the move. Another reason why he pretty much always drove with his car windows partially cracked. And possibly one of the very few reasons Lucky missed the high-desert life he had made up in Ridgecrest; no matter the time or the day or the temperature, there had always been some kind of breeze to tickle the skin.

Tired of both the TV and trying to read himself to sleep from his dusty stack of overdue library books, the former Kern County sheriff's deputy shut off the light and lay there in the dark in hopes his body would succumb to slumber.

Damn it, he thought to himself. *Sleep used to be one of my best tricks.*

It was after 2:00 a.m. when his phone rang. Lucky instinctively reached for his mobile device, only to discover that it was his actual hard line that was ringing. He couldn't remember the last time he'd received a call over a wire or even why he had it installed upon moving into the cramped but furnished one-bedroom rental.

"Yeah, you got me," griped Lucky into the phone after he'd found the cordless receiver plugged into the wall behind an unopened carton of his dead brother's clothes.

"Lucky Dey?" breathed the voice on the other end. Though the voice didn't ring as that familiar, the nearby sound of ice cubes tinkling in a crystal tumbler sparked a name.

"Conrad Ellis?" guessed Lucky.

"Hope I'm not waking you," said Conrad. "It's late for most people."

It must have been a year since Lucky had spoken to the entertainment mogul. He recalled hearing of the man's penchant for pacing about his Bel-Air mansion, running his business after midnight.

"I'm a cop," Lucky tried to joke. "We only sleep on the job."

"Do you really have a job?" asked Conrad.

"Cop job?" returned Lucky. "No. I'm kinda between gigs."

And what a fuckin' understatement, Luck.

Not long after Tony Dey's untimely murder, Lucky had resigned his Kern County job and moved back to Los Angeles. But his reinstatement to the L.A. Sheriff's Department was stuck in bureaucratic neutral. It also didn't help that during those fateful three days when Lucky had tracked down his brother's evil killer, he'd left the LAPD and L.A. County Sheriff's in a pissing match over who would accept liability for all the damage Lucky was alleged to have left in the wake of the eventful chase.

"Still in touch with the lawyer I got you?" asked Conrad.

"He calls, I answer," quipped Lucky. "And when he deposes, I try to show up."

"Good man."

"How are you doing?" asked Lucky.

"Dying slower than my old man," said Conrad. "But that's only 'cause I drink better scotch than he did."

I wonder what he's up to? Half a fifth a day? The whole damn bottle?

Yet who could blame Conrad if he drank until his liver surrendered? While Lucky had lost his only brother to that bastard ex-Marine, Conrad had lost his daughter in the same fiery conflagration. His one and only child. Lucky couldn't imagine that kind of pain. Then again, at thirty-six he felt so used up and empty he couldn't comprehend anything filling the void. At least, anything that wasn't temporary or chemical.

In Lucky's opinion, Conrad Ellis was an advertisement for remaining childless.

"You available for a little private detective work?" spoke Conrad over the phone.

"Available enough," said Lucky. "But for the part where I don't have a license to practice the trench coat arts."

"Trench coat arts," laughed Conrad. "I like that."

"I'm here all week," deadpanned Lucky, sounding slightly more awake.

"The PI license is easy enough to remedy," said Conrad. "Assuming I can arrange one, I have a business pal who needs someone to show him around the city."

"Sounds more like he needs a tour guide than a detective."

"I'd prefer he tell you himself what kind of help he needs."

"Sure," said Lucky without much more thought. "I can meet him."

Of course, Lucky would meet him. And it wasn't out of sympathy for Conrad's loss. Lucky owed him so much more. While Kern

County, L.A. County Sheriff's, and the LAPD passed the responsibility buck like it was some kind of nuclear hot potato, Lucky had laid in a hospital bed in rehab limbo, waiting for someone to please pay his nearly half-million-dollar tab. Without hesitation, Conrad Ellis had stepped in. He had covered both the medical care and the attorney's fees without a single, solitary *quid pro quo.*

"Send you a text with a place and time," said Conrad. "Tomorrow okay?"

"Already is tomorrow," said Lucky, remembering the time of day. "Unless you're talking about, you know . . . tomorrow."

"Go back to sleep," said Conrad.

"Might need a bottle of scotch," joked Lucky. Again, the line landed flat.

"Gimme your address and I'll have my driver bring you a bottle."

"It was a joke, Mr. Ellis."

"You should know, detective," reminded Conrad. "I don't joke about fine whiskey."

"I'm gonna hang up now, sir."

"You do that. And stay in touch, okay? I wanna know how this private eye job turns out."

"I will. Good night."

"Good night, Lucky."

Private Dipshit Detective.

The sheriff's-deputy-in-limbo lay awake for another ninety-plus minutes as the insulting handle pinged inside the boundaries of his skull like an old video game. Not that he begrudged any ex-cop who took to private investigating as a line of work. Lucky believed anything for a buck was fair game. It just wasn't close to the sexy, glam-assed job portrayed in fiction. The PI game was dirty work for fat-assed geeks with an over-affection for computers and writing reports on domestic misery. The job involved little more than divorce cases and, for the occasional kick, workman's comp claims. Setting himself up on stakeouts to video-capture some José or Yolanda out for some beer and bowling despite a debilitating on-the-job back injury. No thanks. In Lucky's universe, the job wasn't worthy of a seasoned sheriff's detective.

Let alone a bona fide Lennox Station Reaper.

But Conrad Ellis wasn't suggesting a career change for the county cop. And if Lucky was going to be snob-up about what kind of work he would do to pay off a few bills, he sure as hell wouldn't have been caught dead serving subpoenas on unsuspecting rubes at fifty dollars per.

When Lucky finally woke from just shy of four hours' sleep, the text containing the meeting spot had already showed up on his phone screen. Conrad must have been extra keen on Lucky's performing the favor because the address was within walking distance of Lucky's Reseda apartment. He knew it too. Manja's Deli and Grocery. If Lucky recalled correctly, it was in a nearby strip mall, sandwiched between Pizza Hut and ACE Cash Express. Outdoor seating. Lucky checked the weather app on his cell phone, then began digging through a pile of unfolded laundry for a turtleneck.

Tuesday

5

"Hey. You must be Mr. Dey."

The stranger stood from his patio seat at the tiny café table and forced a smile. Despite the forty-eight-degree temp, the man appeared comfy enough wearing little more than a simple white dress shirt untucked over designer jeans and a pair of polished black penny loafers. Lucky clocked him at just over five-foot-six and around fifty years old, the once-boyish face now turned as weary as a man carrying the weight of the world. He was also manicured down to his fresh shave and a salon-cut shock of naturally red hair with the occasional streak of white.

More than ten years younger, with his own head shaved for convenience's sake, Lucky carried zero hair envy. It was part of his credo in keeping things simple. And if it was cold, that's why they invented fleece knit caps.

"Lucky," said the cop, introducing himself with a handshake.

"Andrew Kaarlsen," said the stranger, his voice pitched to a tinny height. "You mind sitting outside?"

"Not at all," Lucky lied, lowering himself and his thick, navy wool jacket into the pre-chilled chair.

"I'm from Milwaukee. And we just don't get days like this in the winter."

"Neither do we," joked Lucky. "For us, this is about as cold as we can stand."

"Warm, sunny day like today?" wondered Andrew. "This isn't cold."

"I've seen pictures of it," said Lucky.

"Never been out to the Midwest?"

"Folks out here call 'em the flyover states," jibed Lucky. "The ones we fly over on our way to places like New York and Miami."

"Now, that's pretty funny," said Andrew without actually laughing. "So, you're local? From around here?"

"Born and raised, as they say," replied Lucky.

"So, you know your way around?"

"Mr. Ellis called me at two in the morning."

"Ah, yes," said Andrew. He revealed a knowing smirk. "Always the midnight rambler."

"That's what you call him?"

"Don't know if I made it up or heard it from somewhere else," said Andrew. "But the hours Connie keeps are pretty infamous."

"And you know him how?"

"Connie and me?" asked Andrew. "We go pretty far back. I own a software company. Business applications, mostly. When I was just a start-up, Connie was one of my first customers. Introduced me around to a few fellas. Indebted forever to him."

"Know whatcha mean."

There followed an uncomfortable few seconds of silence. Andrew appeared to be sizing up Lucky. It was not an unaccustomed feeling for Lucky. Street thugs tried to measure a cop's resolve the moment the police car's door swung open. But this once-over from the middle-aged, Midwestern friend of Conrad's made Lucky feel like a horse scaled out before a race.

"Anyway," cued Lucky. "Connie pretty much kept the reason for this meeting to himself. Asked me to do him a favor and meet you. So, here I am."

"Yes. You're an ex-cop, right?"

"Not retired, if that's what you're asking," explained Lucky. "I'm transferring from Kern County back to L.A. Sheriff's. But the reinstatement situation is slow as shit."

"So, you'd be available to do this?"

"Do what?" asked Lucky, his eyes narrowing to a point.

"Right," said Andrew, leaning back as if trying to find comfort in the stackable chair. It appeared to Lucky as if Andrew were trying like hell to keep his composure. "This, right here. Why I'm in L.A. . . . is because I believe my daughter is here."

"How old?" asked Lucky, his arms crossed. The pain Andrew clearly carried and Lucky's own instinct had already informed him where this was going.

"Karrie," continued Andrew. "That's my little girl's name—"

"How little?" pressed Lucky. If the man's daughter was missing, age was paramount when it came to the law.

"She's fifteen," said Andrew. "And, technically, a runaway, I guess."

"You guess? She either ran away or she didn't."

"Okay," Andrew shrugged in difficult surrender. "She ran away."

"From you. In Milwaukee?"

"Well, from Chenequa," corrected Andrew. "It's a suburb. She spends half her time there with me and the other half in town with her mom."

"You're divorced?"

"Not yet. It's an ongoing . . . Well, it's a bloody marathon, if you ask me."

"Acrimonious."

"Sadly, yes. Her mom's just . . ." Andrew stopped the thought as if being polite were more important than sharing his angry divorce grievances. "Let's just say it's been very hard on my Karrie."

"Assuming that's why she ran off?"

"Partly, I'm sure," said Andrew. "Along with the fact that she's just like her."

"Her mom?"

"Yeah. Her mom. She's pretty high maintenance. Then again, I suppose I take the blame for marrying that kind of woman."

"Only child?"

"Yes."

"Is it true, then?"

"Is what true?"

"Old bit of Irish my granny used to say," poked Lucky. "One child makes a fool of three people."

The line was indeed meant to poke Andrew for his reaction. Lucky still hadn't said yes. Or even shown interest.

As for Andrew, he politely considered the Irish adage. And as he thought about it, he appeared to nod with approval. As if he wished somebody had informed him before he and his soon-to-be ex-wife decided to stop after one kid.

"Drugs?" asked Lucky.

"Me?" asked Andrew. "Or her mom or Karrie?"

Lucky shrugged his response. Hands remaining stuck in his woolly pockets.

"Okay. Me? No," said Andrew. "Absolutely not. Not even a beer. My stomach can't take it."

Andrew brought his hand to his solar plexus as if the thought of liquor would give him an ulcer.

"As for my wife and Karrie?" dripped Andrew with sarcasm. "Both, I should assume. My ex . . . or soon-to-be ex . . . I happen to know she still parties. On my dime, of course. And Karrie? For a kid, she's pretty good at keeping her stuff private. So, aside from a couple of marijuana cigarettes I found in her book bag . . ."

"Does your ex do drugs around your daughter?"

"Elise?" asked Andrew. "That's my wife. And that answer would probably be no." Andrew's eyes searched for Lucky's hands . . . or lack thereof. Both were still firmly placed in his coat pockets. "Sure you don't need to write any of this down?"

"What for?" asked Lucky. "I don't know what the job is yet."

"I thought it was pretty obvious," said Andrew, the friendly Midwest pathology showing an edge. "I need you to help me find my baby girl."

"Understood," said Lucky. "You understand I'm not a private detective."

"Connie informed me."

"And if your daughter is underage, there's a lot of other help available to you. There's the Department of Missing—"

"Missing Children and Family Services," finished Andrew, before reeling off the rest of his already traveled dead ends. "The Child Abduction office of the Los Angeles District Attorney's Office. Lemme see. There's Find the Children, California Missing Teens, Children of the Night. I think there might be one more but . . ."

"You've done the tour," nodded Lucky.

"I believe I've reported everywhere a father can report, talked to whomever would see me, and followed up and followed up again." Andrew placed his hands on the tabletop, palms flat, fingers splayed. "I've been here for three weeks already. And I'm flat-out tired of the inside of my hotel room, not to mention dialing numbers I already know by heart, only to be told there's nothing more I can do but check back in another week."

"So?" pressed Lucky.

"I want you to find my daughter for me . . . or with me," burst Andrew. "I'm looking for help, okay? Connie told me you tracked down his daughter's killer. Three days was all it took. You tracked him and you finished him—"

"Didn't finish him. Least, not officially. Nearly killed myself, though. And I was on the job."

"On the job?"

"Was a working cop," clarified Lucky. "With access and support."

"But you're here, right? Talking to me? You must be kind of interested in helping."

"I'm here because Mr. Ellis has been very kind to me over a pretty rough coupla years. I owe him a lot."

"I get that. Really, I do. You don't owe me a thing. But Connie . . . or Mr. Ellis, as you know him. He lost his own little girl. He put me in contact with you because he *knows* what it's like. He *knows* I will do anything not to lose my little girl."

As a veteran cop, Lucky was better than most at reading people and their involuntary tells. When he rode gang duty, he could jam any car full of Crips, line 'em up against any graffiti-painted wall of Compton cinder block, and, by instinct, pick out the leader.

The same was true for victims.

Lucky had gathered that the man from the Midwest was plenty distressed about his circumstances. Maybe somewhat narcissistic in his sincerity. But who the hell had landed his own fortune and not become full of himself?

"Find her and I'll pay you fifty grand," said Andrew.

"And if you don't like what you find?" asked Lucky.

"What do you mean by that?"

"Ain't all palm trees and swimmin' pools out here. Plenty of ugly in L.A. And a lost girl like your daughter doesn't need to go far before landing smack in the shit."

Lucky understood he was still understating the realities. Runaway teens in sunny Los Angeles often wound up drug addicted, working as prostitutes, and/or as targets for predators. The morgue saw plenty of young girls every year, each finding her final rest in what was essentially a meat locker for dead humans.

"I'm aware of the realities of this place—"

"But one more thing," interrupted Lucky. "How do you even know she's here?"

"Oh, yeah. Right here." Andrew fumbled with his phone. He was quick, though, to pull up a recent digital posting from Karrie. "Her last Facebook page."

The digital picture uploaded onto Andrew's smartphone was low resolution and appeared to have been snapped just after sunset. It was a candid self-portrait, revealing roughly half of Karrie's freckled face exploding in an unmistakable smile. Some unseen wind appeared to be swirling a strawberry-blonde mane of a far more appealing color than her father's shock-top red. Pictured next to Karrie was another unknown beauty, equally young, with blue eyes and a rhinestone nose stud. Just behind the duo, anchored in the upper right-hand corner, was the partial neon script of a sign. Somewhat blurry. But the letters could still be made out.

Lucy's El Ado

"Googled what you can see in the neon," pointed Andrew. "It's a place called Lucy's El Adobe. It's in Hollywood across the street from some kind of movie studio."

"I know it," said Lucky. "Mexican food."

"I stopped in there. Showed everybody who worked in the restaurant this picture. Nobody but nobody remembered my girl or the other one."

"Got a date when the photo was posted?"

"Exactly twenty-five days ago, fourteen hours, and . . ." Andrew Kaarlsen pulled up the cuff on his shirt, revealing an antique Gruen timepiece, gold trim with a pearled face. Sleek but not the least bit ostentatious, and oddly strapped to the inside of his wrist. ". . . And sixteen minutes."

Lucky looked past Andrew, squinting through his Ray-Bans in the direction of the morning sun, wishing to hell God would make the day ten degrees warmer.

"I know this is really urgent for you," said Lucky. "But I'd like to think on it. Get in a workout. Shower. Call you after?"

"You're my guy," pressed Andrew, forcing the kind of salesman's smile that opened doors in the world. Only this particular show of teeth was marked with a trace of panic and fear. He was, after all, the parent of a missing child. The man's thin voice cracked. "I need you to say yes."

"Couple of hours." Lucky eased to his feet. "I'll get you my answer."

6

Downtown.

To look at the building from its exterior, the Mayfair Hotel, with its old European-styled awning and red brick facade, hadn't aged much at all in its ninety-plus years of service to travelers visiting Los Angeles. Though not exactly located in downtown proper, its old-school charm at a bargain price consistently lured guests seeking extended stays and a few extra ounces of discretion. It was just far enough off the beaten track that the odds of a business traveler bumping into someone he or she knew dipped from damned remote down to slim and none. Which was just the way Mr. Londale Newton of Atlanta liked it.

"Hello?" answered the voice at the other end of the cell phone connection.

"Hi," said Lon. "I, uh, read your ad on JumpFinder."

"Oh . . . Well, hi. I'm Jodi."

Oh my, how the travel insurance exec cherished his quarterly road trips. Boston and Hartford in the spring. Summer usually brought him to Seattle. Fall was Nashville or Dallas and sometimes Houston. But winter was reserved for Southern California. San Diego and Los Angeles, respectively, where the mean temperature hovered in the mid-seventies and the quality of working girls was undisputed. For the months prior to his getaways, he would squirrel away small chunks of dough, one twenty-dollar bill at a time. The cash stash was hidden in a pocket in the bottom compartment of his shave kit. By the time he eventually hit the road, there would be nearly a grand in unaccounted household cash that his wife hadn't a clue had gone unspent on household necessities like fashion magazines and another decorative display recommended by Martha Stewart.

"Is Jodi your real name?" asked Lon.

"Real enough," flirted the voice. "Did you like my page?"

"Very much," said Lon. "Your pictures sorta spoke to me."

After a business meal, followed by a short digesting nap, Lon had flipped open his laptop and logged in to JumpFinder.com, a website dedicated to selling everything from used cars to furniture to secondhand electronics to local sex services. All anyone needed to do was register a username, click on the escort section, load in a few keywords, then scroll through the individually posted banners.

Jodi's was especially enticing:

♥ — SEXY — BUBBLY — U WON'T
BELIEVE IM OLD ENUFF ♥

And when Lon clicked on the post, the photos he found were conveniently cut off at the neck to conceal a young girl's identity. A barely there string bikini. Six images, each in a different pose. Reclined on a bed and on an apartment rug. In the shower . . . All awkwardly staged, but with a clear and illicit message that the pictured girl was probably close to fourteen or fifteen years of age.

"So, you like my pictures?" asked Jodi.

"I do," said Lon. "Who took 'em?"

"Girlfriend."

"School friend?"

"Yeah."

"I'm kinda a photographer myself," bragged the insurance man.

"You are?" squeaked Jodi. "You wanna take my picture?"

"You bet I do. How old are you?"

"You read my JumpFinder ad. I'm old enough."

"I need to hear it."

"Gonna be sixteen next week . . ."

"Birthday this close to Christmas has to be a bummer."

"You can make it easier for me by singing 'Happy Birthday'."

"Now? Over the phone?"

"Where are you?"

"Mayfair Hotel. Near downtown. You know it?"

Lon began to sweat. Microscopic beads of excitement gathering on his neck into drops, which eventually absorbed into his Geoffrey Beene shirt collar.

"Hey, mister?"

"Yeah?"

"I'm savin' up to buy my first car. If I come over, will you help me with a donation?"

"I'd love to. How much?"

"Two hundred dollars?"

"Cash?"

"Oooooooooooh. I like cash."

"I'll make it rain for you."

By eleven, when Jodi called to say she was downstairs in the Mayfair Hotel lobby, Lon had already scrubbed himself raw, shaved all his body hair, and dressed in fresh underwear, khakis, and a loose-cut chambray shirt. He gave the escort directions to his sixth-floor room then searched for his wallet. He wanted to have the cash folded and ready. The sooner the transaction was out of the way, the quicker he could jettison reality for some role-playing fantasy, the details of which he hadn't yet decided. He'd first need to size up his underage date. See how game she would be.

The knock at the door was weak. Two quick rapping knuckles that would have gone unnoticed if he'd had a movie playing on the Korean-built flat-screen screwed into the top of the bureau. Lon pocketed his cash and swiveled the quick ten steps it took to cross into the tiny corridor that served as an entry. He unchained the door, pulled down the handle and took a step backward as he swung the door inward.

"You Jodi?" smiled Lon.

His first impression was that she wasn't so much a real girl as she was somehow a human in miniature form. Not even five feet tall. A tiny body hanging on to a denim jacket, a lemon-yellow tube top, and a faux leather skirt that hung so loosely the insurance packager wondered how her hips could possibly hold it up. As he instinctively scanned her up and down, he noted her feet were tucked into a pair of kiddie-sized suede Uggs and her head was somewhere underneath a floppy canvas rain hat.

"You gonna lemme in?" asked Jodi.

"Oh, yeah. Sure," said Lon, momentarily thrown off. He hadn't caught a look at her face yet. At six feet three inches tall, it was nearly impossible for him to catch any glimpse of her eyes under that obscene rain hat atop her head. "Raining outside?"

"Cold 'n' dry," she said, slipping past him into the room. Off came both her denim jacket and the floppy hat, revealing bleached blonde hair falling on a single tattoo that stretched between her shoulder blades—five red-headed robins perched on a rose bush's branch.

Jodi's face, though. It wasn't nearly that of a girl approaching sixteen years old. It was world-weary and prematurely aged from smoking too much rock and meth.

"You're not fifteen," announced Lon, releasing a little of the bass in his voice.

"Pictures are me," said Jodi. "And I still look good naked. Anyway, you didn't tell me you were black."

"What's that got to . . ." Lon found himself momentarily stuck, his words locked somewhere between his frontal lobe and subcortex. He had ordered an underage escort and less than an hour later, found himself standing face to face with a pint-sized, thirty-year-old crack whore. "Listen, there's been a mistake, so if you wouldn't—"

Mr. Londale Newton of Atlanta didn't feel the blow to his head as much as he remembered how dark everything had turned in the blink of an eye. Lon was repositioning himself to show Jodi the way out as a matter of punctuating his disappointment. Somewhere between the whore sweeping into the room and removing that rain hat disguise from her head, the hotel room door hadn't shut all the way. In had walked Jodi's black but not-too-genteel pimp. He had greeted the unsuspecting customer with a knotted tube sock full of lead birdshot. The left-handed pimp had struck his victim with a single swipe across the side of the face, sending the big man to the carpet. Before Lon could gather a coherent thought, the pimp had him rolled over, the other sock shoved into his maw as a way of a gag, and a razor-like box cutter only inches from one of his eyes.

"Nowshutthefuckupandlisten," rattled the man Jodi called Romeo. "You gonna gimme yur wallet. Then for da second I'm gonna let you open yur mouth, yur gonna tell sweet bizness here your motherfuckin' PIN numbers. Blink if ya unnerstand."

Lon blinked. His lids fluttered both rapidly and with terrified affirmation.

7

That floppy rain hat of Jodi's was practically swept off her head from turbulence as she hurried down the sixth-floor corridor. *Don't run! Walk, you stupid crack ho.*

She hated the dirty hat. Thought it made her look like a drunken bass fisherman's idea of a joke. But Romeo had insisted, robbing the hat from a homeless man's shopping cart mere moments before they'd turned the corner to the hotel. She initially resisted, afraid of what microbial vermin the bum might be passing on. Lice, most likely. Romeo crushed it onto her head and spat that she should just shut the fuck up and keep her eyes low in order to prevent the Mayfair's security cameras from getting a shot at her face. With that, the pimp pulled his own hoodie over his head and steered Jodi toward the hotel's less-traveled side entrance.

Armed with Lon's wallet and a scrap of hotel room notepad

paper on which she'd shakily scrawled his PIN, Jodi rode the elevator to the lobby. She crossed the expanse, no longer appearing as if in a race but still with a sense of purpose, then exited into the night for the two-block walk to Wilshire Boulevard and the nearest ATM. As per Romeo's barked instructions, she kept the floppy hat brim between herself and the machine's pinhole camera. After punching in the numbers, she was able to remove $1,200 from Lon's debit card and his American Express.

It was only minutes before midnight when Jodi slipped into the bar across the boulevard. There she asked for a glass of water. Not that she couldn't have done with a belt of something eighty-proof and cheap. It might have settled her nerves and, for a moment or two, delayed the craving for a hot pipe full of crystal meth. It was fear that kept the stolen cash in her shoulder bag and water flowing over her tongue. If Romeo so much as whiffed any booze on her, he'd surely beat her into unconsciousness.

Hate that motherfucker.

But Miss Sweet Bizness, as Romeo would sometimes call her, was a thirty-two-year-old prostitute and drug addict. What looks she had left belonged only to her tiny, low-gravity frame. Her face appeared prematurely aged by the years of chemical abuse. So, cutting out on her own and selling herself to cash-carrying johns was a long shot at best. Jodi's rationale was that her best chance at survival was to stay on Romeo's leash. She owed him that. After all, it was his idea to pimp out her high school photos on pervy websites as a way to troll for marks like Londale Newton.

At five minutes after midnight, Jodi slipped out of the bar and headed back to the same ATM. Because it was a new calendar day, the bank allowed her to once again maximize the withdrawals on Lon's cards. With nearly $2,500 in twenty-dollar bills stuffed into her purse, she hustled her way back to the Mayfair Hotel, eased through the desolate lobby, and rode the old elevator back to the sixth floor.

"All good," announced Jodi as she let herself back into Lon's room. This was the blind second before every molecule in her body wanted to scream.

The scene before her was splashed in red. A geyser of arterial spray had redecorated the room in bright swaths of oxygenated blood. Goo was dripping from the walls and ceiling in a Jackson Pollock nightmare of fresh crimson.

"Shut up and close the goddamn door!" spat Romeo as he stripped off his clothes in the bathroom.

"What the fuck!"

"Motherfucker child raper. Deserve to die. You get da money?"

Jodi's face was frozen in horror; only her eyes continued to swerve from left to right and back again.

"He was a pedophiler! Deserve what he get," insisted Romeo. "Now, you gonna help me clean this shit up, so do likes I said and shuts the goddamn door."

8

Hollywood.

Lucky had set his phone alarm for midnight, racking up three hours of solid dozing before his planned hour to rise and shine. He was reclined with the seat of the borrowed Crown Vic at the maximum forty-five degrees, letting his eyes slowly adjust to his surroundings. The gray, streaky glow that hangs over Los Angeles at night filtered through the car windows. He recognized the parking structure, where he'd backed into a corner space. To make certain he wouldn't be disturbed by the security guard, he had left a note on the dash reading:

DO NOT DISTURB
POLICE OFFICER ON THE JOB
VIOLATORS MAY BE SHOT

The sign worked. In the twelve-odd years Lucky had been deploying his handwritten warning, he'd only been awakened once. In East Venice, a brave homeless man had politely rapped on his sheriff's radio car window until Lucky had reluctantly cracked one eye open. The scraggly peanut of a man was undaunted, mouthing the same word over and over again until Lucky lowered the window two inches. Toothless and through lips so chapped they resembled truck stop jerky, the homeless man had wanted to report a rape in progress. Lucky had gathered himself, investigated the homeless man's cardboard village built in a dry storm channel, and discovered a pair of meth-heads having their way with a schizophrenic bag lady of social security age. So disturbed by the sight, Lucky had drawn his pistol, barked at the sick pair, and sent them pantless and scurrying. Lucky had plugged one of them in the right ass cheek and the other through both stems, then, before calling for EMS, had made sure the scene was properly littered with a couple of throw-down revolvers with stolen serial numbers as a way to justify the officer-involved shooting.

"Why din't you kill 'em?" the homeless man had gummed, animated over his afternoon of excitement.

"Find a shelter," Lucky had suggested as his one and only reply before phoning up his pal and Reaper brother, Bledsoe.

Lucky now tightened his aching abdominals, bracing for when he released the seat brake, hoping the weak spring would return the seat to its full and upright driving position. The pain at the base of his spine amped up to a six on the unhappy-to-happy face scale he recalled from the Spine Surgery Center. The Percocet, which had so dutifully aided his recent nap, was already at a rough ebb. Still, he couldn't seem to shake off the grogginess.

Christ, Luck. You were out.

Narcotics had that kind of effect. Since his kamikaze dive through the windshield of an oncoming Volvo and subsequent year of rehab, the former self-confessed Advil junkie had become functionally dependent on prescription meds. The stepped-down opiate kind. Otherwise, the bite from his injuries became so debilitating he had considered swallowing a bullet from his .45-caliber Model 1911 once or twice.

The door to the Crown Vic popped open and out followed Lucky in an attempt to trick his body into a waking state. He moved rearward to the concrete bulwark that kept vehicles from spilling out of the parking structure and crushing pedestrians on the sidewalk below. The landscape that spread out before Lucky was lit up in a panoramic cliché. Over-photographed landmarks such as the Roosevelt Hotel and the electric Christmas tree–topped Capitol Records building sprouted out of the earth like all the other buildings on the porch step of the Hollywood Hills. So many lights, thought Lucky. Uncountable. If each light represented no less than one human being, identifying a singular teenage girl amongst so many appeared hellishly daunting.

And that was just Hollywood.

As an L.A. County sheriff, he'd had the rare occasion to work the zip code, but never felt at all comfortable outside the confines of his radio car. Hollywood and its surrounding areas were a tight mash-up of money, tourists, gay bars, and drug-fueled showbiz lowlifes and elites. It was an absurdly unpredictable territory. Not at all like the triangle of division hubs where he had cut his teeth and thrived for the majority of his cop career. The corridor of Los Angeles badlands that stretched from Inglewood to Compton to Lynwood might have been painfully impoverished and prone to a tyranny of gang violence, but it was also predictable, rich in local color, and devoid of the annoying, entitled elitist class that tended to plague the privileged neighborhoods.

The air was cold enough for Lucky to see his breath, filling his lungs with moist coolness before exhaling it into the night. He could feel his synapses rekindling. Clarity returned and, at that moment, he was back on task.

Opening the rear door of the Crown Vic, Lucky reacquainted himself with the boxes of color copies he'd assembled earlier in the evening at a strip mall copy shop. Two thousand sheets in all. Each identical and two-sided, bearing a photo of Andrew Kaarlsen's missing fifteen-year-old daughter, Karrie. Boldly printed below was the question:

HAVE YOU SEEN ME?

It was followed by a number assigned to the prepaid burner cell phone in Lucky's coat pocket. He wasn't keen on placing his personal mobile digits on the Xerox flyers he planned to paper throughout the Hollywood vicinity.

That's right, Lucky. You're now a private eye.

Lucky hadn't had to think long about the offer. It might as well have been a yes the moment Andrew Kaarlsen served up the fifty-grand guarantee. Not that Lucky cared much for money sniffers. His life had never been about reaching for any kind of gilded ring. Otherwise, why the hell would he have taken the L.A. County sheriff's exam and signed up for training? Kaarlsen's offer was nearly the very same number that had been ping-ponging inside Lucky's head every time he wondered what he would need to bank to sustain himself until his reinstatement came through.

The answer he had given Kaarlsen was a swift text message with a plan to reconnoiter with the Wisconsin business mogul at some juncture the following day. That would allow Lucky a head start on his investigation. He'd been informed by the besieged father that the more obvious chase channels had been run. And with some cursory follow-up, Lucky had found that Andrew Kaarlsen had done his fatherly diligence plus more. Just about every public and private agency associated with teens missing in Southern California had been contacted and followed up to the level of annoyance.

Good man, thought Lucky. Wear the bureaucratic bastards down until they do their jobs just to get rid of you.

The only additional work Lucky had been able to accomplish was some brief conversations with sheriff's and LAPD detectives with whom he had active relationships. They were happy enough to take down the missing girl's information and promised to run it up their divisions' flagpoles to see if anybody took notice.

With those reams of flyers racked like ammo on the Crown Vic's passenger seat, Lucky rolled out of the parking structure and into the misty night. He had no fear that the weather would hamper his mission. It was a Tuesday eve in Hollywood, a zip code where every night was Saturday. Scores of partyers were sure to be clubbing wherever the liquor and designer drugs were flowing. Lucky's plan was to stick the cheap copy paper into as many hands as he could. He had no illusions that he would actually hit pay dirt and pass off the flyer to somebody with an inkling as to where the missing girl was. He fully expected most of the Xeroxes to be barely glanced at and dropped to the sidewalk within mere moments, thus turning the plaintive missive about a runaway teen to litter in a matter of seconds—illegal as hell if Lucky were to spill paper all by himself. He'd be subject to arrest and fines. But if he handed each and every flyer to separate individuals, each of them would become the liable, littering lawbreaker.

And so the bureaucratically sabbaticaled sheriff's detective began a night of crisscrossing the streets of Hollywood on either foot or by wheels, gifting out those flyers to every possible passerby. He was betting that by dawn the damp sidewalks and gutters behind him would be glued with eight-and-a-half-by-eleven rectangles of missing Karrie Kaarlsen. Cleanup wouldn't happen for days. And the streets of Hollywood would serve as one giant billboard for his search campaign.

Just shy of 2:00 a.m. the burner rang for the very first time. The trill was high-pitched and might have been confused for a whistle had it not also vibrated in Lucky's jeans pocket. The initial call of many, Lucky reckoned. Most would be cranks or dead alleys. Still, each and every incomer would need to be logged on a legal pad.

"Hello," answered Lucky, leaning against the fender of the Crown Vic and zipping up his bomber jacket.

"Callin' 'bout the girl," said the young man's voice.

"Whadda you know?" asked Lucky.

"You a cop?"

"Not this month," he said glibly. "Just lookin' for a girl."

"There, like, a finder's fee?"

"If this call leads me to her, there'll be a reward."

"How much?"

"How much you want?"

"Million dollars," said the young man before his voice cracked with a hint of laughter. Lucky heard the scammer's friends busting a gut in the background just a split second before the call was disconnected. Without missing a beat, Lucky reached into the car for another fistful of flyers and proceeded east on Franklin approaching Highland when the burner trilled again. Lucky checked the number, saw it was different from the last call, but still made a bet with himself that it was just one of the previous caller's juvenile pals, dialing from another cell phone.

"Hello?"

"Yeah," said the voice. "I saw the picture of your girl."

"And I'm talking on a phone connected with a GPS tracker. If you're not real, expect a visit from the LAPD—"

Click-beep.

The caller hung up. And Lucky smiled to himself while thumbing off a pair of flyers to a duo of prostitutes who had not so inconspicuously retreated into an archway of flowering Chinese jasmine that shook wet with the rain.

"Ladies," said Lucky. "Looking for this teenager."

"Who you callin' 'ladies'?" boomed a voice so low it sounded like it was rising from a basement.

The shyest of the pair unleashed a not-so-girlish giggle. Lucky hadn't so much looked at the hookers as scanned and profiled them before asking them to accept a flyer. Had he been more discerning, he would have looked past the *Rocky Horror* makeup and plus-sized dresses and clocked their mannish hands and stubbly Adam's apples before mistaking them for ladies.

"My mistake," repaired Lucky. "Take 'em and call the number if you know anything. There's a reward."

"What if my reward involved you and my girlfriend?" guffawed the man balanced on the size-twelve stilettos.

"Not enough Viagra in the world to make that happen," said Lucky.

The quick comeback sent the hookers howling their approval. They gladly accepted ten flyers each, promising to spread them around before hailing him a very merry Christmas. Lucky forced a smile and turned south onto Highland, dead reckoning for Hollywood Boulevard.

The third phone call came when Lucky was papering the nightclubs up and down Vine Street. Lucky was most interested in the groups of obviously underage girls in short black cocktail dresses and the steep heels popularized by strippers. Never married—and childless, as far as he knew—Lucky attempted to imagine himself as the father of one of these young tartlets. Hard as he tried, he couldn't place himself in the shoes of a parent. Any parent, for that matter. The closest he could get was picturing himself face-to-face with a neglectful father, pondering whether to employ a retractable steel baton to send a parenting lesson to his kneecaps.

"Hello," said Lucky into the burner phone.

"Lookin' at the paper you been givin' out," said the voice at the other end. By intonation and the bass in his timbre, Lucky instinctively figured him as a large black man. Possibly one of the linebacker-sized bouncers he'd met guarding the doors at one of the clubs.

"Got something for me?" asked Lucky.

"I might. Coulda seen your girl," said the man.

"Where and when?"

"Dragonfly. Maybe three hours ago."

"What's the address?"

With that, Lucky backpedaled and retraced his steps until he found himself outside a three-story brick and wrought-iron facade of what appeared to have been the entry to dozens of different venues over the years. The most recent incarnation, called Club Dragonfly, sported strips of deep blue neon accents. But after a blunt interrogation with the beefy black man in the size-sixty jacket, Lucky could only be certain that the part-time bouncer had pegged one of many young women who could fit the basic description of young, pretty, blonde, and green-eyed.

By four in the morning, with the streets of Hollywood reduced to a cold winter simmer, Lucky abandoned his walking tour in lieu of slow-trolling in the Crown Vic, handing his last flyers to anyone he came across, including both LAPD patrols and sheriff's black-and-whites whose jurisdictions abutted along lines that could have only been drawn by city politicians.

The eastern sky was showing promise that dawn was imminent and Lucky was down to the bottom of his last box of color Xeroxes. He was calculating in his head the number of times he would have to perform similar paper hanging. Next, he reasoned, would be the Santa Monica to Venice corridor. Followed by the fifteen miles Ventura Boulevard ran from North Hollywood to Woodland Hills. Plus spot checks of the aboveground modeling agencies that serviced the porn industry. Three to four days of gas and shoe leather to accomplish rounds two, three, and four. And Lucky hadn't a clue if any of it would lead to something concretely investigative.

Wednesday

9

West L.A.

The sun-rotted windshield wipers of the borrowed Crown Vic could barely sweep clean the constant downward mist that had settled into the Basin like a soiled blanket. The burner phone, cradled in a console cupholder that doubled as a change dish, had been silent for over an hour when it both rattled and trilled. The detective fished for it and before answering, checked to read the incoming number. The word "blocked" displayed in fuzzy relief, reminding Lucky that he was both exhausted and in need of the folding reading glasses he'd absently left on his nightstand.

"Hello," Lucky answered.

"Yeah," said a man's voice, flat and without affect. "Callin' about the picture of the girl."

"You got the right number," said Lucky. "What do you know?"

"Tell you exactly what I know," said the man. "I know *her*."

"You know the girl in the picture?"

"That's what I said."

"I'd like very much to speak with you," ventured Lucky.

"Thought that's what we were doing?"

"In person," said Lucky. "I can come to you right now."

"Okay then," said the man. "You know where the Norm's diner is on La Cienega?"

"I'm close by," said Lucky. "Can be there in five minutes."

"I'm already here," said the man. "Through the front doors, right turn, last booth next to the restrooms."

"What are you wearing?"

"Don't worry. I'll recognize *you*."

Lucky knew the location, all right. It was a mere mile away, dead in the heart of West Hollywood. And unlike its neighbor to the west, Beverly Hills, the somewhat recently incorporated City of WeHo hadn't yet established its own stand-alone police department. Instead, like some of other independent municipalities within the county, they'd contracted with the sheriff's department for their first responder needs.

Could I be this goddamn lucky?

It was 5:35 a.m.

After a mere five and a half hours of plastering Hollywood with cheap flyers, he'd have been happy as hell to get a twenty on the missing teen and close up his private eye business nearly as fast as he'd opened it. Not all investigations took weeks or months. Some are solved in hours. Others had practically solved themselves just after pushing the simplest and most uncomplicated button.

Two short blocks from the iconic Beverly Center mall, Norm's La Cienega location was already gathering its fair share of early-morning diners while jettisoning the late-night vampires who'd stopped in for a post-party pick-me-up. As instructed, Lucky walked through the diner's entry, made a fast right, and set a straight line for the restroom doors. The two booths flanking the back exit were both occupied—one of them by a trio of off-duty Salvation Army santas. The opposite booth contained a male in a plaid flannel shirt, medium build, the bill of his golf cap pointed at a nearly completed *Los Angeles Times* crossword puzzle.

As Lucky slipped into the booth, the man in the flannel shirt turned his grinning face upward to greet his guest.

"You're shitting me!" sniped Lucky.

"You were expecting somebody else?" answered Andrew Kaarlsen with something less than a grin.

"Jeeezus."

"Thought we agreed we were going to do this together?"

"How the hell did you—"

Andrew lifted the newspaper to reveal one of the two thousand flyers Lucky had handed out.

"Couldn't sleep," admitted Andrew. "Went for a pre-dawn run. Only thing that seems to work with all the stress. Anyway, turned a corner and this was starin' up at me from the sidewalk."

"Been papering local neighborhoods all night long," groused Lucky.

"Thought it was you. But didn't recognize the phone number," pointed Andrew.

"Bad idea to print out thousands of flyers with my own number on 'em," said Lucky, revealing the burner phone from his pocket. "Numbers are attached to this one."

"Anything yet?" asked Andrew. "Leads?"

"Aside from you pretending to be one?" groused Lucky. Aggravated, he sat back in the booth.

"Lemme buy you breakfast," insisted Andrew.

"Why didn't you tell me it was you when you called the friggin' number?"

"Told you yesterday. I'm sick and tired of seeing the inside of my hotel room, waiting for somebody else to do the work." Andrew was leaning forward, practically covering the surface of the table with both arms. "I'm her father. I'm the one who wants her home. I need to be a part—"

"Just tryin' to find your girl," defended Lucky. "My mistake, though. Shoulda let you in on my plans."

That familiar ache in his low back was beginning. The Percocet that hadn't yet been totally scrubbed by his kidneys was losing its mojo.

"Really wish you woulda told me what you were up to," said Andrew. "I woulda helped."

"I didn't start 'til midnight—"

"Like I sleep a lot? Come on. I'm her only G.D. father and she's my only G.D. girl. Sheesh. I'm sitting on my thumbs here. Bring me along. Use me."

Whether from years of practice or because it was just the way he was wired, Lucky gave away so very little as to what he was thinking. For his ability to keep his thoughts and feelings concealed, his old Reaper pals used to suggest that he compete at professional poker. Lucky might even have considered moonlighting down at the Gardena card casinos if he had the inclination to spend hours reading cards, calculating odds, and divining the motives of his opponents. But all of that required patience. Something of which Lucky almost always had in short supply. His idea of poker was assessing a quartet of ghetto teens hanging out on a street corner. Lucky would bet fellow sheriff's deputies that he could divine—based on a mere fifty-yard once-over—which of the boys in question was packing heat, the caliber of the weapon, and what flavor of contraband he was holding.

"Look, man," said Lucky, fingers splayed and gently tapping on the tabletop. "You're paying me to do something for you. And that's what I intend. But some of the way I do things might not require assistance, if you know what I mean."

"Think I give a shit if what you do is legal or not?" pressed Andrew. "When it comes to Karrie, I don't care what kind of chances I have to take."

"I hear ya—"

"I don't think you do," pressed Andrew. "You don't have children, then you haven't the devil's clue what this is like for me. Now, Connie vouched for you. Said you could get things done."

"Best I can do is give it my all," said Lucky.

"Well, that's what it is to be a parent. Giving it your all for every moment your kid is on this G.D. earth. Do you think I'm giving it *my all* by sitting in my hotel room and waiting for the phone to ring?"

"No . . ." said Lucky, reluctant and in a rare breath of compromise. "I hear ya. But Connie informed you I'm not a regular PI. Not up to speed on all the liability issues involved in clients riding along."

"You want a letter of indemnity?" asked Andrew. "Have a lawyer whip up something. Signature and witness. You will be absent any malice that might befall me in the quest for my daughter's return."

Quest. Jesus.

Then again, maybe it was Lucky who didn't have his priorities straight. He couldn't tell if it was fatigue or the spreading pain in his thorax that left him suddenly bereft of argument.

"It's your money," was all Lucky could think to say.

"Not about my money."

"I know," corrected Lucky. "About your daughter."

"Karrie."

"Yes," relented Lucky. "It's all about Karrie."

10

Silver Lake. 10:21 a.m.

For the ten weeks Karrie had been residing in L.A., she hadn't once needed to pay for her room. Though need might not have been the best description. As a fifteen-year-old teen, she'd couch-surfed plenty back home in Wisconsin. The only difference was her parents pretty much thought they knew whose couches she was crashing on. At least, most of the time. From the moment she had landed in sunny Southern Cal, she found it easy to flash her perfect rows of recently straightened teeth, winking dimples, and sea-green eyes to charm her way into enough short-term friendships to borrow a nearby sofa for a night or two. Pretty soon she was receiving invites to share apartments and rental homes from Los Feliz to Woodland Hills. Not that Karrie knew where Woodland Hills was, exactly. She'd been silly drunk on the late-night drive to the West Valley burg and she'd pretty much slept through her free ride to the next comfy couch.

"C'mon, Val. Time to get up and out," shouted Cherry Pie from the bathroom.

Karrie woke for the third time, just as out of it as she was the first time Cherry had poked her. Her eyes tried to focus on the old, cottage cheese–styled ceiling complete with blooms of brownish water stains from roof and plumbing leaks.

Whose couch is this? Oh, yeah. Cherry's. And my name's Valeriana. I'm in L.A. Right . . .

It was the first night she'd crashed at Cherry's. The pale dancer with the purple-dyed hair had taken her on a trial run as a two-night roomie. The Silver Lake apartment Cherry shared with two dancers—conveniently away on tour—was a half mile up the slope from East Sunset, a quarter mile west of Dodger Stadium, and cramped with furniture rescued from neighborhood sidewalks.

"Last call, Val," barked Cherry, her footsteps shuffling quickly across the squeaky old hardwood.

Karrie sniffed her hands and forearms for the scent of men's cologne or manly fluids. It was her only waking routine since landing in Los Angeles. Though she could only recall one actual time she'd consented to sex in her ten weeks, she'd woken up two or three more times, disoriented, not at all sure where she was, and stinking of a man. There had even been some noticeable bruising. All of which was swept into her brain recesses with every other negative thought. Always replaced by a sunny smile. Such was how Karrie was built. Or so it was once explained to her.

"Where we going?" asked Karrie, still recumbent on a corduroy couch the color of Campbell's tomato soup.

"You seriously forget?" said Cherry from the bedroom.

"Foggy," growled Karrie.

"I said yes to this cuzza you."

If Karrie could have slid her fingertips under her skull and massaged her brain, she would surely have rubbed until a memory stirred.

"My audition," reminded Cherry. "Hello?"

"Oh . . ." said Karrie, mostly to herself. "Right. Think I remember now."

"You wanna shower, you got, like, five minutes."

The night before took form in Karrie's mind like a damaged file of low-resolution digital video. Full of contrast and paper-thin voices. Karrie couldn't recall the club as much as the scene. Loads of girls her age, she recalled. Only they were mostly dressed in designer togs, sucking back frothy, alcoholic concoctions from straws, and sounding no more sophisticated than the suburban brats she had left behind back in upscale Chenequa.

"TV commercial, right?" asked Karrie.

"You wanna go all stinky with girl funk, that's your call," said Cherry.

"Don't smell that bad."

"Cold today and I don't wanna have to roll down my windows," said Cherry. "But I will if you smell like dude."

"Wasn't no guy last night."

"Bullshit. Schmo-Joe with the dreads was all over your underage ass."

"Schmo-Joe?"

"His words, not mine," said Cherry, appearing at the center of the tiny living room, the air suddenly fragrant with hair spray. "You said you liked his hair. He said it was 'cause he was half Samoan, half Jewish. Turned his Jewfro into dreads. You said 'Jewfro?' like you never heard that before. He said Schmo-Joe. Everybody laughed."

Karrie shook her head with zero recollection.

"Did I drink that much?" asked Karrie.

"Dunno. You did pop a thizzy."

"Thizzy?"

"X."

"Fuck me. I don't remember shit."

"You need to remember that you said you wanted to come with me."

"Commercial thing."

"Audi commercial."

"My dad drives an Audi."

"No shit?" said Cherry from the kitchenette, where she was doing breakfast inventory of the spare contents in the fridge. "Val's got a rich daddy?"

"I'm taking a shower."

"Hurry your high school ass up, then."

Karrie stumbled to the bathroom, still steamy from Cherry's shower. She stripped off her T-shirt and tatty sleep shorts and climbed under the lukewarm spray.

Don' wanna talk about who I was or where I'm from. Don' wanna talk about who I was . . .

After a quick scrub-over, Karrie toweled off and dug into a Hello Kitty backpack, where she kept all her clothes, makeup, and hygiene supplies. She came up with a pair of low-mileage underwear, leggings, plaid skirt, and her one cable-knit sweater. Cute enough, she decided. Her hair she'd worry about in the car. Lastly, Karrie reached into the front pocket of the pack, using a sharp fingernail to reach the hidden compartment she had fashioned to store whatever cash she collected from the occasional work she had managed to find. She counted out three twenty-dollar bills, which she quickly folded into fourths and secured into one of the cups of her bra.

And what about Cherry Pie?

Karrie unzipped the front pocket once again and peeled off two more twenties. She'd offer both to Cherry for rent and food, insisting she take at least one of the bills. Karrie wasn't a sponge. Nor was any member of the Kaarlsen clan, she reminded herself in a secret moment of pride.

That's right. Daddy would want me to pay my way.

"Are you coming?" shouted Cherry, sounding as if she were already out the front door.

"Right behind you," piped Karrie, re-zipping her backpack and rushing from the bathroom.

11

West L.A.

"So, where we going?" inquired Andrew.

"You? You're going back to your hotel," said Lucky, flat and without compromise.

"Whoa, wait," said Andrew. "Thought we decided that I was gonna ride shotgun."

"Homework first."

Lucky wheeled the Crown Vic left onto Olympic Boulevard and pointed it in the direction of downtown Los Angeles. Even with Saturday morning traffic, Lucky was still calculating a slow commute.

"What kind of homework?" asked Andrew, not-so-comfortably settled into the worn, velour-covered passenger seat replete with cigarette burns.

"Called around yesterday," said Lucky. "Never worked a

missing persons before. But the biggest clues about where your daughter is today are best found back where she came from."

"You mean back home?"

"We're already here and I'm not keen on experiencing Wisconsin in the winter. So, I'm gonna need you to write down everything and everybody she had contact with in the two weeks before she turned up missing."

"She's here," insisted Andrew. "We know she's here because of the photo I showed you."

"All I know is that she *was* here," pressed Lucky. "I'm serious. Wanna help me? Then gimme a detailed chronology of where she'd gone, who she'd been with. Everybody, everywhere. Phone numbers of friends. Anything you can get. Who she talked to, what they remember she said."

Lucky glanced at Andrew to see if he was a man switched into receptor mode. What he got instead was the daunted look of a father who might have all along been struggling to know his daughter.

"Christ," said Andrew. "Not sure I know where to begin."

"Doesn't matter. Just start it and go 'til it's done. Work the phone 'til your ears bleed. And write everything down."

"You know I've pretty much already told you just about everything I know—"

"Then you're gonna find out more," demanded Lucky.

Lucky heard the harshness of his own words. He'd recognized his own chippy tone and momentarily questioned if he had gone over the line with his very first and one and only client. Everything about Andrew appeared relatively genteel. He came off as the picture of a Midwesterner with soft hands. A rich, reserved desk jockey suffering the loss of his marriage and his daughter.

And he also holds the checkbook.

Money, again, thought Lucky. Why the crap did stuff most always come down to dollar signs? He weighed his options—the same choices that usually came down to: *Do I kiss ass or do I kick ass?*

Lucky's factory settings were pretty much always switched to the latter.

"Listen," said Lucky, sounding almost apologetic, hefting the words he chose. "Been a long morning. And now I gotta print up a whole bunch more of these to paper the beach tonight. So, forgive me if I sounded short—"

"Not at all," answered Andrew. "You're right. I wanna help. I wanna do anything I can do to find my daughter. And if digging up more than I already know is gonna help us, then I'm for that."

"Should warn you," cautioned the cop. "You might not like some of the shit you discover."

"I'm well aware of that."

"Can't let the fact that you're her old man color judgment." Lucky was already rethinking his request of Andrew. "Might wanna hire a Milwaukee investigator just in case."

"In case of what?"

"In case you can't stomach the ugly truth."

Lucky would have preferred the remaining portion of the downtown drive be served in silence. And if not for the nerves of his passenger that had been plucked like the strings of a tuneless harp, the twenty final minutes might have passed with little more than road noise. Instead, Andrew fussed and probed Lucky with pro forma questions one might've asked on the first tee of a country club.

Married?

Never.

Girlfriend?

Not presently.

Brothers, sisters?

Nope.

College?

Some.

Football fan? Baseball?

If the beer's cold...

Parked in a cab lane in front of the downtown Biltmore Hotel, Lucky said so long to the bereft father, offering an encouraging, but not quite whole-hearted, thumbs-up before launching away from the curb. As he unconsciously plotted his short route through traffic to the Piper Technical Center, he noticed the slick forming on the Crown Vic's steering wheel. His palms were wet with perspiration.

Jesus, Lucky. Really? You?

He was used to sweat leakage. He was a man. He preferred Gatorade over coffee. And he could barely begin a workout without opening ten thousand pores. The morning, though, was cool. His kidneys, he figured, had probably already scrubbed the last microgram of Percocet from his bloodstream, evidenced by the girdle of pain that currently squeezed him. So, why the hell were his palms opening up in a stigmata of sweat?

Because you haven't seen her in nine months, you dickhead.

As Lucky's subconscious demanded to be heard, he relented without a struggle. Wrestling with himself felt like a waste of time and energy. So, he swallowed his sudden and begrudging case of anxiety, left-blinkered the Crown Vic onto Broadway and finished off the drive in a bit of policeman double-time, weaving between cars and sometimes speeding down yellow-striped dividers until he was at the garage entry to the Piper Technical Center. The supercharged Ford bottomed out and sparked on the ramp to the parking lot, followed by the familiar sound of squealing rubber against years of oil deposits on tire-polished concrete.

Lucky set the brake and swallowed his spit, considered refilling his anti-pain bucket with a half tab of Perc, then popped the console and fished around until he heard the rattlesnake sound of his Advil bottle. The voice in his head recommended a triple dose. Lucky's abused stomach lining might have disagreed. But he planned to split the difference with something stale from a third-floor vending machine. So, he locked the Crown Vic and headed for the corner stairwell.

It was 12:54 p.m. in Chinatown.

The LAPD's Hooper Heliport sat atop the Piper Technical Center. The largest rooftop heliport in the continental US, it was home to the city police department's fleet of nineteen helicopters.

The mid-December sun hung at what appeared to be the sky's apex. Unfiltered and pale, the vertical cast left the faces of various flight techs appear black in the harsh down-shadows.

Finishing off a microwaved muffin, Lucky hung back under a stucco awning, watching her move through the pre-flight inspection of her helicopter. From two hundred feet, she appeared even taller than he remembered. Her wild spray of black hair was pulled back into a tight bun and neatly tucked under a fitted aviator's cap. Her athletic body moved elegantly inside the matching blue-black jumpsuit. Not quite the jeans, boots, T-shirt, and letterman's jacket she was wearing when he had first encountered her in a Pasadena café. She had made a strong impression then. Just the way she was making an impression now as Lucky quietly observed the woman and her Bell JetRanger chopper. A beauty with her beast.

It was when she shouted out to a helicopter tech for an oil rag that she noticed him, half hidden in the shade, licking the reconstituted blueberry off his fingers. After a squinty pause, she gave Lucky a wary wave and began to walk in his direction. With that, Lucky meandered out onto the tarmac and met her halfway.

"Hey, stranger," said Gonzo, at first apprehensive, then braving a hug and a warm kiss to Lucky's unshaven cheek.

"Hey yourself," he said, momentarily lifted by her flashing smile. "Like what you're wearing."

"Yeah?" she said, faking a model's twirl. "Suits me, yeah?"

"That it does."

"So, what brings you over this way? You lookin' to switch from muscle cars to helos?"

"Charger's in the shop again. Drivin' a borrowed Crown Vic. You should see it. Primer gray. Duct tape. Real shit-mobile."

"Sounds badass enough for you."

"It's a beater. But fits my current job status."

"Still in Lucky Limbo?" she half joked.

"Cop union. Lawyers. You know."

"And the pain management?" she asked, arms flexed akimbo.

Pain management. Gonzo's code for Lucky's alleged addiction.

"Well, that didn't take long," said Lucky, mock-checking his watch.

"Honest question," defended Gonzo. "Not like I ever stopped giving a shit."

"Then you know the way it is." Lucky's words were suddenly clipped with a dash of teeth.

"Guess I do."

Lucky's pain management was a sore spot and the unsaid core of the former couple's way-too-civil breakup. If Lucky ever wondered if he truly missed her, the answer came with some bitter truth. The moment they politely touched on the heliport tarmac would sting and linger for days.

"Pain's still there," admitted Lucky. "At least the bullet . . ."

"Yeah, the bullet," she finished with a nervous laugh, welcoming the slight change of subject.

The story of the bullet predated their knowing each other. But it was an endless fascination to Gonzo's curious son, Travis. Years back, Lucky had been ambushed in an apartment corridor and shot in the back of the head. Obviously, Lucky had survived, but the .25-caliber bullet had proved inoperable, lodged in a delicate, but somewhat benign tangle of nerves and soft tissue near the top of his soft palate. The injury wasn't without pain, causing chronic headaches for the sheriff's deputy. There was also the scallop of a scar that remained two inches behind his ear. Gonzo had dubbed it "Lucky's unlucky conversation starter." Unlucky not because he was the rare cop who survived after getting shot in the head, but unlucky because Lucky could usually do without conversations, especially those in which he was the primary subject. Gonzo had confessed that sometimes at night while Lucky slept, she would brush the rim of the intrusion scar with her fingertips and ponder her own mortality issues along with those that plagued their profession.

Then came the "accident." At least, that's what Lucky preferred to call it. It happened exactly forty-one days after Lucky had thrown himself head-to-windshield into the onrushing Volvo wagon. While sharing a physio-rehab unit breakfast with Gonzo and Travis, Lucky had felt something wedged at the back of his throat, setting in motion an awful coughing fit. The result was a bloody, metallic flavor in his mouth. The foreign object briefly wedged under his tongue felt as if he'd loosened a filling. Yet the moment he spit it onto his plate he knew what had happened.

There, on the plate, rested a copper-jacketed hunk of lead. Malformed. But without a doubt, a .25-caliber bullet.

"You know Travis keeps the bullet in a jar on his nightstand," said Gonzo. "But he wants to preserve it forever in a custom snow globe."

"He's a weird kid," smirked Lucky. "Good thing Christmas is coming."

"Told you when my pre-flight was, didn't he?"

"Yeah. What you get for allowing your kid a cell phone."

Gonzo chuckled and nodded, but still had her arms wrapped across her chest. There was a familiar ease to the duo but obvious tension in equal measure. It was as if the natural warmth of affections still lingered behind heavy layers of bulletproof Kevlar. It reminded Lucky that their choice to split up after their brief relationship was far too cordial. Possessed with both love and defense. Why the hell had neither cared enough to fight for it?

A cop in a jumpsuit identical to Gonzo's brushed past her as he hauled a pair of hard cases toward the helicopter.

"We workin' today?" chirped the helo-cop.

"Be right there," answered Gonzo, before cuing Lucky for his windup. "What's going on with you?"

"Side gig," said Lucky. "Missing persons thing. Think I remembered you worked a detail like that."

"For, like, a cup of coffee. Had maybe three weeks in that unit before robbery/homicide called me up."

"More experience than me." Lucky unfolded one of his flyers, giving Gonzo an acquaintance with Karrie Kaarlsen's smiling fifteen-year-old face.

"Young and very white."

"Milk-fed from Milwaukee."

"You've done all the initial stuff? Public and private agencies?"

"Working with the girl's father. He had a pretty good head start before I got the call."

"Did I miss you hanging out a private dick sign?"

"Right. And the joke is I was an a-hole before I went private."

"Okay," she relented. "Peace."

"It's a onetime dealio. The dad's a pal of Conrad Ellis."

"Ah. So, Connie figured the guy who successfully tracked his daughter's killer—"

"Could easily find one freckled teenage runaway."

Gonzo shook her head, easily recalling the three-day descent into hell that had brought her together with Lucky. Back then, he was a sheriff's deputy working for Kern County, trying to chase down a killer ex-Marine and his refrigerator truck loaded with frozen blood. Gonzo, practically free-floating between assignments within the LAPD, had been assigned to babysit the visiting detective and keep him out of trouble.

It didn't quite work out.

"Any tips you wanna give me?" asked Lucky.

"Pretty blonde runaway in L.A.?" quizzed Gonzo. "Like a needle in a haystack of needles."

"What it looks like."

"Gotta hope you get lucky."

"Not a science, huh?"

"Not hardly."

"Suppose if I gave you a bunch of these flyers and asked you to drop 'em from your whirlybird . . ."

"Would if I could," squinted Gonzo. "Anyhow. Gotta get up in the air. So, lemme know how it goes?" And she meant it. Well, sort of. Unless Lucky cleaned the painkillers from his system, the boundaries were clear and concise.

"Will do," was Lucky's terse promise.

And that was that.

A nod from Gonzo and she'd already begun backing away toward her helicopter. The hug and kiss that came with hello was noticeably absent from their goodbye. Tension had clearly crept in and made a home, aided by the visual cues and subtle mental reminders of the gulf between them.

Lucky had turned himself around and was already legging it back to the pilothouse when he heard Gonzo shouting back at him.

"HEY!" she yelled. "FIND OUT WHAT HER DREAMS WERE."

"WHAT?"

"FIND OUT WHAT SHE WANTED TO BE," Gonzo impressed. "THAT'LL SHOW YOU WHERE TO LOOK."

A quick wave goodbye and she jogged the rest of the way to her helicopter.

12

Hollywood. 2:16 p.m.

"Just look into the camera and speak your name."

"Cherry Pie," said the dancer and hopeful commercial actress. She faced the video lens and let her lips slide across her gleaming teeth.

"Cherry Pie," repeated Herm. "That's a good one."

"Long story," shrugged Cherry.

"That so?" Herm tried not to smirk. In his years as a flesh wrangler, he figured he had heard at least three other young women who had used the name. All strippers. He didn't have to guess how Cherry paid the rent.

"Is this okay? How I'm sitting?"

"Perfect," said Herm. "Tell me a little about yourself."

Not that Herm cared a lick. He knew from the moment he'd cracked the casting studio door and read off her name. Cherry had stood as if built out of springs, looked him directly in the eye, and crossed the threshold with far too much confidence. While she rattled on, flashing her perky charm with animated flourishes, Herm continued to ask the same rote questions he had asked most of the other young women, all the while he discovered himself quietly obsessing over the strawberry-blonde sitting outside the door. The pretty thing whose name very clearly wasn't on his list. What had Cherry called her? Val? Not that it mattered. He just needed to get her through the door and parked on the stool and in the warm glow of his umbrella light. Herm's flesh-radar had been more than tickled by the lass with those aquatic eyes.

There was ripe . . . and then there was her.

A unicorn. The first one to cross Herm's path in years.

Karrie was dry-throat thirsty from a night of popping X, clubbing, and scoring drinks off anybody who would buy for her. Seated on a folding chair next to a water cooler, she only wished the cup dispenser hadn't been empty. She had checked for a kitchen, then the women's restroom for a cupboard that might hold a sleeve of paper or Styrofoam cups. She had even considered drinking directly from the cooler. Just a sip to relieve the feeling that her tongue might soon become permanently stuck to the top of her mouth. It was just that the act itself might have proved embarrassing, requiring Karrie to kneel at the cooler and tilt her head sideways while opening her mouth and depressing the spigot release.

Fortuity for Karrie came in the form of a good-looking dude with a red coffee mug. Even funnier, she later recalled, it was the damned mug she had noticed before his sexy rake of dark chocolate hair and trimmed weeklong growth of beard. An audition room door at the end of the thin corridor had squeaked open and out had stepped the man. Maybe five foot ten. Faded T-shirt and jeans. And carrying that bloodred mug.

"Hey," asked Karrie. "You wouldn't know where I could get a clean cup? You know. For the cooler?"

"Wouldn't have a clue," said the swell looker with the red mug. "Brought this with me."

Karrie allowed her butt to return to the seat. She couldn't help but look disappointed.

"But if you're really thirsty, you can borrow mine," said the looker.

"That's okay."

"Seriously. Haven't even used it yet. Right out of the dishwasher."

Through Karrie's fifteen-year-old filter, the looker's face revealed little threat. In fact, everything about the man down to his vintage Chuck Taylors appeared malice free. That, and how many deadly germs could a dumb coffee mug carry?

"Thanks," said Karrie. "My throat's all scratchy and stuff."

The man with the mug approached the cooler, kindly filled the cup, and handed it to her.

"Thanks," she said, sipping the water before letting it openly flow and comfort her esophagus.

"Gabe Roth," the dude introduced himself, offering a soft hand.

"Oh, hey. Thanks," said Karrie, wiping her mouth with her sleeve before accepting the handshake. "I'm Karrie . . . er . . . I mean, Val."

Gabe's head cocked in curiosity.

"Shit," said Karrie.

"I don't need to know your name," said Gabe, letting her off the hook. "Glad to share my mug."

"Really appreciate it."

"Auditioning?"

"Excuse me?"

"Are you here for casting?" asked Gabe with a gesture toward the door across from her.

"Oh, no," said Karrie. "My friend. Just came with her. I'm just waiting."

"So, you're not an actress?"

"No. Well, not yet," she said. "I'm a dancer, though."

"No shit?"

"I really am." This is where Karrie clocked Gabe's knowing smirk. "Oh . . . right. Of course, I'm, like, something, right? Actress or a model or something."

"You're sorta in the Mecca of it."

Mecca?

Karrie's face was all too quick to reveal that she didn't get the reference. The word wasn't yet, nor might it ever be, part of the teenager's somewhat limited vocabulary.

"Los Angeles," clarified Gabe. "Showbiz capitol of the universe."

"Oh. Right."

"Where you from?"

"Wisconsin."

"And you've been here . . ."

"Like, ten weeks is all," admitted Karrie. "Still learning my way around things."

"Found anywhere to dance yet?"

"You mean, like, classes?"

"Yeah."

"Haven't got that far yet."

"I know some pretty good studios," offered Gabe. "Lotta girls get cast out of 'em for videos and stuff."

"Wow, cool," said Karrie, uncertain if the looker was merely being conversational, actually trying to help her, or laying the plumbing for some kind of seduction routine.

"Photographer," said Gabe. "Freelance. Do a lotta headshots and whatever. I know the dance stuff 'cause they hire me sometimes to shoot their shows or help with updated shots on their websites. Actually, setting up for some actor headshots down the hall."

"Oh, really?"

"You have any headshots yet?"

"Never had any," said Karrie.

"Seriously? With a face like yours?"

"I mean, I've had pictures taken. For sure." Karrie realized she needed to step up her game and sound more mature. Otherwise, she'd never pass for a *young* eighteen. "Just nothing official."

"Like a headshot."

"Like that. Yeah."

What followed was the slightly awkward silence that peppers most first conversations. Neither Gabe nor Karrie knew each other well enough to establish a flow. One of her few Twitter posts flashed in her mind.

Oh, how I hate awkward silences.

This was usually where Karrie would resort to girlish flirting. Instead, Gabe let her off the hook with:

"Gonna need my mug back."

"Oh, right," giggled Karrie. "Really appreciate the loan."

"So, how long's your friend gonna be?"

Karrie could only shrug.

"Well," continued Gabe. "I'm set up in there and I got, like, twenty or so minutes before my first session shows. Wanna give it a try?"

"Give what a try?"

"Some pictures. Official ones. You can be my test dummy."

"Test dummy." Karrie laughed.

"Got a high-def monitor set up," said Gabe. "You can see what you look like under a really flattering light rig. Very soft."

"Right now?"

"Right now."

"Don't headshots cost money?"

"Headshots, yeah. Test shots, no. Anyway, maybe you owe me for borrowing my mug."

"Oh. I owe you now?" asked Karrie, officially in flirtation mode.

"Not really," answered Gabe. "But what you got to lose?"

Gabe gestured for her to follow. Karrie, in return, paused a beat, instinctively upping the sexual tension. She smiled, rose to her feet, and followed Gabe twenty paces down the corridor to the inviting soundproof door of his rented unit.

No sooner had Gabe's door shut than Herm's swung open to release Cherry Pie back to the world. The faux casting director tried not to appear so terribly disappointed upon discovering that the young strawberry-blonde—over whom he'd so silently obsessed—was no longer seated and waiting on that folding chair. Cherry looked equally flummoxed.

"You're missing your friend?" asked Herm.

"She was supposed . . ." began Cherry. "Probably in the ladies' room."

"On the first floor," said Herm. "Think she's there?"

"She better if she wants a ride."

"Roommates?"

"Letting her crash with me. Seeing how it feels."

"Okay," said Herm, faking a smile. "Nice work. I have your information, so I'll call you."

"You will?"

"Depending on what the clients say," cautioned Herm. "I have all your contact stuff."

"Sure do," smiled Cherry, encouraged as hell.

"Have a nice day," said Herm, shaking her hand before slipping back into his closet-like interview space and clicking the door shut. Then once he was alone again, he double-checked to make certain he'd kept Cherry's details. Wrong as she was for his flesh-commerce purposes, Cherry had indicated that her friend was, in fact, a roommate of sorts. If Herm was ever going to get next to that strawberry-blonde ray of light again, he'd need to devise some kind of casting callback for the chirpy little Cherry Pie.

No problem, he thought. No problem at all.

13

Downtown. 6:39 p.m.

"C'mon in," invited Andrew, dressed and pressed in denim and a matching long-sleeved chambray shirt. His neat attire and hair were utterly betrayed by a face creased by worry and insomnia. "Just about done with my homework."

Not unlike the man, Andrew's suite at the Biltmore was designer simple—old-school, elegant, and neat to a fault. Yet it wasn't the crispness of the space that struck Lucky. It was the sheer square footage. To his trained eye, the corner digs must have covered eleven hundred square feet. A larger footprint than Gonzo's Pasadena duplex, not to mention the tiny San Fernando bungalow where Lucky first shared a room with his younger brother, Tony. That was before, in a fit of womanly rage, the boys' mother had put a match to the rental home and torched it to the cinder-block pilings.

"Home away from home, huh?" coined Lucky.

"Comfortable enough," said Andrew. "Altogether different view, though. At least, what I'm used to."

Andrew needn't have frenetically gestured like a man cranked on caffeine. The view from the hotel was east-facing and favoring the train yards and industry of old Los Angeles, framed by diffused light, classic hotel art, and hand-embroidered draperies.

"Got my notes right here," pointed Andrew, cutting over to a round conference table burnished to such a high polish that it mirrored the mica lamp overhead. He gathered up three legal pads, each meticulously scrawled in blue and red pen.

"Read 'em to me on the way," suggested Lucky. "We got more litter to hand out."

"Oh, right. Flyers," remarked Andrew, huffing and stuffing his notes into a kid leather backpack, then spinning counterclockwise to find his jacket. "Bedroom. Wait. Be right back."

Lucky felt a ping of regret, wondering if he should have allowed Andrew to deal himself into the investigation. Sure, the Midwestern dad was banking the operation. But the man appeared to be surviving on little more than hope and coffee grounds. A potential liability. Lucky briefly considered offering a few of his precious Percocets along with the suggestion that Andrew nap for the next forty-eight hours.

To his immediate left, Lucky spotted the gourmet kitchenette, replete with spotless cookware that to his eye had never had a flame under them. He did, though, crack open the fridge stocked with bottled beer, soda, and water along with fresh fruit and milk. On a separate shelf were at least three dozen cans of Red Bull, packed in place like ammo. Silver bullets of certain stimulation. No wonder Andrew appeared as if he had been jacked into an electrical outlet.

"Mind if I grab a soda?" shouted Lucky.

"Whatever you need," called back Andrew.

Lucky chose a couple of Dr Peppers, depositing one of the cans in his jacket pocket, then, just before closing the fridge, stopped as he noticed a plastic baggie stuffed full of disposable syringes. Next to that were a pair of medications stacked one on top of the other in the door rack.

Velosulin.

Alprostadil.

The initial med Lucky easily recognized as one of the many brands of injectable insulin. That's because in his years as a cop, he'd encountered nearly as many diabetic needles as heroin. The second prescription he'd never heard of. Though he guessed, based on the name, it was prostate related, making Lucky wonder if Andrew was suffering from the dreaded male cancer curse. If so, it was hardly a front-burner issue compared to finding a beloved and only child.

"Talk to me," cued Lucky, popping open a Dr Pepper with one hand and holding the door with the other.

"Okay," said Andrew. "How far we going back? One week? Two weeks?"

"Gimme three days before she ran away."

"From Chenequa?"

"From home."

"Right, right," said Andrew, flipping the pages on one of his legal pads while backing into the Biltmore's fifth-floor elevator. "The very last night she slept in her bed was—"

"Which bed?" interrupted Lucky, remembering that Andrew and his wife were in the middle of an ugly split while sharing custody of their teenager.

"The bedroom at my house in Chenequa. She didn't like staying at her mom's in the city."

"City?"

"Milwaukee. The Queen Wench is renting a penthouse downtown."

"Queen Wench?"

"My ex . . ." explained Andrew, realizing it didn't quite require an explanation. "You should hear what she calls me."

"And your ex, where is she with all this runaway stuff?"

"Happy to let me do the footwork. Called me just about every hour for the first week. Now I just text her updates."

"Did she ever want to give an assist?"

"Elise reserves the right to blame *and* complain."

"But we're talking about her daughter too."

"How's this? Next time she phones, I'll put her on with you."

Andrew's tone said so much more than his words. Resentment commingled with the resignation of a relationship that had long ago turned malignant. Lucky had seen plenty of that in his first five years on patrol, answering the seemingly never-ending domestic violence calls.

"Go with what you got," said Lucky, suppressing a belch after polishing off the Dr Pepper.

"October seventeenth. Thursday. Saw her for breakfast. Dropped her at school—"

"Anything unusual?"

"Not that I could tell," confessed Andrew. "Must've replayed that morning a thousand times. Looking for some kinda clue. Not that we talked much that day. She always had her headphones on in the car 'cause she didn't like that I listened to my talk radio."

"Your talk radio?"

"'My car. My sounds,' I used to always say." Andrew bit his lip with regret. "Shoulda let her play her stuff. Maybe she woulda thought she could talk to me. Maybe I woulda known more."

"Or maybe you woulda been held hostage listening to a lot of crap music," forgave Lucky, hoping to add some much-needed levity. "But keep goin'."

As the duo cut out of the lobby to the parking valet, encountering a middling rain that had slicked up the city streets, Andrew kept up a fervent recitation of the revelations he'd gleaned from phoning every number he could shake out of what friends of Karrie he actually knew.

"She cut school that Friday around lunch," recounted Andrew. "Was in her biology class but was showed absent for world history . . . Her middle school best friend Jamie remembered seeing her at Dairy Queen with a group she called 'burners.' That's supposed to mean they smoked a lot of weed . . . Yeah, I knew about the pot. Smelled it sometimes when I'd come home. She always denied it and I didn't wanna push 'cause, well, her Mom smokes it. And not every once in a while. She wakes and she bakes. I never minded that she did it. After a while, figured it made her easier to live with.

"Karrie left a message on my voicemail, saying she was sleeping over at Megan's. Gotta admit, she slept over there almost as much as she did at home. Said they did homework together. But when I talked to Megan's mom, she told me Karrie hadn't slept over in months. So, guess I was more than out of the loop. Seems I wasn't even in the same universe. Anyway, she got Megs to ask around. Found out Karrie had been hitting up this club on East Mason. Had a fake ID, which I suppose tells us she was drinking . . . 'Kay. Talked to the owner and one of the bartenders. Says there was a girl who called herself Sunny or Sandy who matched my daughter's description. I've asked one of my lawyers at corporate to see about getting a look at any security camera stuff . . . But nothin' about who she went home with, where she was sleeping.

"Last person I could find in Wisconsin to see her was an old babysitter of hers who called me to say she'd seen Karrie on Monday morning at the DMV. I mean, the DMV? What the heck? She's fifteen. Doesn't even drive, but she's in line. Woman swears it was Karrie too. But didn't try and talk to her. Just wondered if she had Karrie's age wrong. Said she just stood there in another line, staring at my daughter, counting on her fingers how many years it had been since she sat for us."

The thermostat in the Crown Vic seemed to have decided on its own that the floor temp was sub-freezing and blew a sudden wash of heat at Lucky's feet. As his calves began to sweat, Lucky reached for the window controls, cracking both driver and passenger side windows. A rush of Santa Monica sea-infused air, wet and cold, flooded the upper half of the cabin. Only then did Lucky show concern for the comfort of his passenger. He glanced over at Andrew, who seemed hardly conscious of the abrupt change in air pressure. Andrew's face was the picture of fatherly regret, wan and gray with a pair of leaky eyes unable to stem the tears.

"Lord Jesus, what'd I do?" stammered Andrew. "What made

her so G.D. unhappy that she'd want to leave everyone who loved her behind?" The man's jaw quivered along with the words. Bereft. "For cryin' out loud, she's fifteen! I know being a teenager is hard, but fifteen? Running off to some California septic hole?"

"Watch yourself," said Lucky. "I grew up in this septic hole."

"You know what I mean . . ."

"Yeah. I do."

"Fifteen."

"Shitty age."

"What the heck were you doing at fifteen?" asked Andrew. "I remember what I was doing and it sure as hockey sticks wasn't anything close to this."

"Jacked my first car when I was fifteen," offered Lucky, earning him a sideways look from his morose client. "Seriously. Was on a bet from Joey Capponera's older brother that I couldn't. Eighty-one El Camino. All I had to do was jump it, drive it three blocks, collect a case of cold ones."

"You stole a car for a case of beer?"

"Hell yeah," confirmed Lucky. "But at fifteen, I'd probably have done it on a dare. Case of brew was just the icing."

"What about drugs?"

Lucky took a mental moment to ponder. He knew the question was about his teen years. But the conversational query time-warped to present day and Lucky's present obsession with managing his pain. The Percs. A prescription-sized bottle of which could be easily outlined in the front pocket of his denims. He wondered if Andrew would be trusting him with finding his precious child if Lucky's secret addiction weren't such a precious secret.

"Did I do drugs?" Lucky answered. "Here and there. Teenage shit. But mostly it was booze and chasing tail."

"Girls." Andrew silently nodded, remembering.

"What makes teenage boys go round and round."

"Some things never change."

"Back on point," said Lucky. "What about your girl . . . and boys?"

"Right, yeah . . ."

"Or are we talkin' 'bout men?"

"What?"

"Gotta ask. Some men are into younger girls as well as some girls are . . ." Lucky let the inference hang.

"Karrie and men?" asked Andrew, slightly choked by incredulity. "Like eighteen-year-old guys?"

"Or a lot older," cautioned Lucky. "Could bear on where and how we're looking if your girl had a thing for—"

"Men. Yeah. Heard you."

"Hard to swallow?"

"I'm her G.D. father. What do you think?"

"Assume she's also sexually active?" Lucky made sure to take a firm gaze at Andrew with that assertion. He felt the need to see just how much grit the missing girl's father possessed. Lucky had refrained from such questions. But if Andrew couldn't be real with him, what were the chances they'd be able to turn his research into hard leads?

"Her mom took her to get birth control pills," admitted Andrew. "So, you can infer what you want."

Lucky just listened.

"Not like I discovered 'em on the bathroom counter. Elise left a message on my voicemail like it was a reminder to call the tree trimmers. 'Hi. Just thought I'd let you know that Dr. Singh has prescribed Karrie birth control pills. Don't freak out when you see 'em. Don't interrogate her. It's a girl thing and it's sensitive, so just act like it's nothing.'"

Then came the big question. It had been right in front of Lucky since he'd sat across from Andrew at his local low-down Reseda deli-mart. Why hadn't he asked it yet? Instinct? Timing? Lucky had experienced so much as a cop and detective that much of what he did and said while on the job was unconscious.

Only the question wasn't at all unconscious. Lucky no longer wanted to assume. He wanted to know.

"Gotta ask you," began Lucky. "But most fifteen-year-olds like the comforts of home."

"One home," corrected Andrew. "Kids want one home. One family."

"So, you know the question."

"You wanna know why she ran."

Lucky slowed for a stoplight. The patches of mist gusting in from the beach blew across the windshield in brush strokes of pinkish red.

"Suppose she hates the both of us," answered Andrew. The grapefruit-sized lump in his throat swallowed most of his manly bass. "I hate my ex. She hates me. Guess this is how Karrie decided to express herself."

"Think maybe she doesn't wanna be found?" broached Lucky.

"She's fifteen."

"We've established that."

"What are you implying?" angered Andrew. "That she's better off?"

"Not hardly." Lucky shook his head and applied the gas as the light turned the mist into emerald green. "Just stating what you're up against."

"What *we* are up against," argued Andrew. "We have an agreement."

"We do," nodded Lucky.

"I knew what you meant. Just hard, you know. Accepting the truth."

"See the Christmas lights? Promenade's comin' up on the right," switched Lucky. "Shouldn't take us more than a couple of hours to paper the place and move on."

14

West Hollywood. 7:01 p.m.

Liza Witt was barely a week out of rehab and attending two meetings a day. First thing in the morning at St. Agatha's on Wilshire over in the Miracle Mile district—and then the evening AA group on Melrose near La Cienega. This wasn't her first go-around. Her most recent stint in detox and recovery was her third. The charm, she joked. All before the tender age of twenty-five. Higher education had become a washout for her. But at that moment, she didn't need that kind of pressure. For maybe the first time in her sketchy history of sobriety, she was truly taking it one day at a time. Thank Jesus for the trust fund her Nana had set up for her troubled grandbabies. Otherwise Liza would be stressing over rent or a minimum-wage job. Because of the forethought of her loving grandma, Liza could wake up with no pressure or plan to do anything that day but stay straight . . .

. . . and shop.

It had been barely a couple of hours since she had wandered into Marc Jacobs on Melrose, fallen madly in lust with a brown suede quilted handbag, slid her platinum card into the hand of the salesgirl with the super-cute fringe bangs, and walked out feeling like a whole new woman. The dopamine boost she got from the purchase got her wondering if shopping would be another addiction from which she would need a stint in rehab. She quickly forbade the thought and carried on to her next destination, her evening AA meet-up.

The smell of hot coffee hit her before she hit the back door of the old ninety-nine-seat theater. Folding chairs were assembled on the stage in a simple orbit. There was no dais or lectern. No supposed head seat. Equanimity was what the evening group was about. A circle of sharing and trust. A brotherhood of addicts who, as individuals, were helpless against their disease. But as one?

"Somebody's early," said Rodney, his voice slightly reverberating through the space.

Liza dropped her things on a chair and let her Proenza boots carry her toward the voice, her four-inch heels sounding like a pair of toy hammers pounding nails into the stage.

Rodney, the self-proclaimed proud 'n' loud Diana Ross impersonator, stood in a half-lit corner at the foot of the stage-left stairs. Tuesday was his for providing the caffeine and carbs required for any self-respecting AA meeting. Instead of the usual box of Krispy Kremes he'd gotten busy in his own apartment kitchen and whipped up a pile of raisin scones.

"Pure Irish," Rodney boasted of his baked goods. "Sinful with butter, but better with jam."

"Does that line work for you in boy bars?" asked Liza.

"Said it just now for the first time," said Rodney before his eyes mockingly rolled up into the back of his skull. "Least, I think."

Liza couldn't resist a scone and when she picked up the fist-sized confection, felt it was still warm.

"Wow, you really did just make these," she exclaimed.

"Hips don't lie. And neither will yours if you have more than one of 'em."

"That's what I forgot to do today. The gym."

"You still doin' two-a-days?"

"With retail therapy in between."

"Anything I'd like?"

"New bag," said Liza. "Marc Jacobs."

"Just today?"

"Warmer than your scones."

"In your car?"

"Hell no," said Liza, pointing a perfectly manicured nail. "On my chair—"

Rodney's eyes would normally have followed the direction of that index finger. But his gaze was prematurely stuck on the twenty-something's face—her quizzical look, candy red lips slightly parted in confusion.

"It was right . . ." began Liza, then her feet started moving back toward the stage while belting, "Where's my new fucking purse?"

A few other early comers froze in place, wondering what the hell kind of lightning bolt had set the pretty fashionista into her sudden rage.

"I just left it!" she barked, arriving at her chair. "Right here on top of my jacket."

Liza received little more than shrugs from the few other early comers who were milling about, finding chairs.

"Did it have, like, a thick embroidered thing on the strap?" asked the model-type, smoking in her pink-on-pink sweats. "'Cause when I just walked in there was this dude walking out—"

"Was a Marc Jacobs."

"That's why I noticed it!" said the model-type. "Just a minute ago. Right out the back door I saw—"

"Guy with a purse and you didn't think it was weird?" asked another addict.

"We're in West Hollywood?" the model-type defended. "Hello?"

In the meantime, Liza was beelining toward the back door as fast as those designer boots would allow. Attendees were beginning to drag in, each smelling of cigarette smoke or minty-fresh Life Savers. She pushed past each of them, sliding sideways to avoid a head-on collision inside the threshold.

The side alley was dark but for the light splashed from a pan lamp hanging over the stage door. Liza twisted left and right—to the street and then the back alley. She chose the back alley. And was just beginning to run when a hand spun her from the elbow. Rodney was up in her grill.

"You check the street," he said, breathlessly. "You see a cop, wave him down."

With that, the female impersonator dashed into the darkness, hustling headlong toward the back alley. Liza stood frozen for a heartbeat, then switched directions and ran toward the lights of Melrose Avenue.

15

Herm was rarely late. Especially to AA meetings. Since his teen years he'd taken pride in his timeliness. An appointment time was, in his opinion, a contract—an agreement between two or more parties to meet at a predetermined hour. As a pimp, he would brag that his girls were prompt enough to be on television. If *TV Guide* said a *M.A.S.H.* rerun would air at seven thirty, so it would. Herm even began nicknaming his stable after his favorite shows and, in sober moments, could still remember them all. There was *Three's Company, Hill Street Blues, Twin Peaks, Lost* . . .

"Hey, I Love Lucy," Herm used to shout from his Mercedes window, "you got customers waiting at the Sportsmen's Lodge."

Obsessive compulsive disorder. That was the official diagnosis. He'd suffered from the illness his entire life. And once cocaine was introduced, that character defect that proved so rigid turned into a violent, unbendable rod of titanium. What followed were stints in county jail and prison, involuntary detox, and a state-issued membership in Narcotics Anonymous. Sobriety eventually stuck. Which was why Herm was in a bit of a rush to make the Tuesday meeting at the Senior Center on Melrose.

The call to Cherry Pie had gone as expected. Earlier in the afternoon he'd phoned the number she'd left. He'd informed her that the German client had liked what he'd seen and wanted to get her on video reading some recently added dialogue. As Cherry was beside herself, gladly taking down the details, Herm had a suggestion. The Audi people had a notion that, for the commercial, two girls might be better than one. And could Cherry please bring her roommate.

"My roommate?" Cherry had asked.

"Didn't I meet her?" Herm had replied. "Strawberry-blonde, freckles, green eyes? Think the two of you could be dynamite together."

"Oh, Val," Cherry had answered. "She's not my official roomie. Just crashing with me right now."

"But you could bring her?"

"I'd have to ask her, but yeah."

"Wanna put the two of you on tape together."

They agreed on 9:00 p.m. Herm hadn't reserved an audition room, but that was part of his play. Meet the girls out front, feign some kind of secretarial error, then recommend a nearby private studio that he would claim he could borrow. Of course, he would drive. Within the hour, Little Miss Unicorn would be bagged and tagged. The photographs would come next. Plain. No frills. Just the young girl and her untapped beauty against a white wall backdrop.

Ka-ching!

It was barely 7:00 p.m. Time enough for Herm to make an AA meeting. There was the 7:15 group that met in a function room behind Melrose's Sweetwater Café. After eight years sober, Herm's AA attendance had bordered on religious. Two or three times a week, minimum. An hour here and there. The meetings were like a church of meditation. Whether he shared or just closed his eyes and soaked in the sobriety struggles of his addicted brethren, the act of attending took at least twenty points off his diastolic blood pressure.

But Herm hadn't calculated on all the traffic snags with the nearing holiday.

"You can turn right on red, you moron!" Herm shouted from behind the wheel of his new Ford Edge. But with so much sound-proofing in the vehicle's panels, he could practically hear his words being swallowed.

Two cars ahead, the Corolla's blinker flashed and wheels turned, ready to swing a right turn. But the driver was either old or paralyzed or a transplant from New York who hadn't yet read the California memo that it was okay to turn right on a red light.

"Ass clown," muttered Herm while checking his rearview mir-ror. The alley that cut east to west was thirty feet behind him. The demarcation line between Melrose businesses and residents. Better yet, there were no cars stuck behind him.

As if on auto, Herm dropped the SUV's gearbox into reverse. The digital dashboard display flipped into video mode, revealing a wide-angle rear bumper view. Herm checked the image and accel-erated so quickly that his wheels chirped against the asphalt. In a matter of seconds, Herm was back on time, surging down the alley, both gaining speed and, more importantly, beating the infernal traffic.

The potholed strip of back alley was rough riding, but nearly empty of cars and ran at least eleven uninterrupted blocks. Not only was Herm getting to his AA meeting on time, but he'd have time to hit the 7-Eleven next door for a Super Big Gulp cocktail of Diet Coke and lemony sweet Mountain Dew.

As Herm inched the accelerator closer and closer to the floor, the SUV's spanking new suspension absorbed the pitch and potholes so well, Herm might have had the chance to read the addresses posted on the rear of each business. But the alley was barely lit, and only by the rear porch lamps that hung over all the bolted backdoors. Herm kept twisting his neck left, hoping for some street numbers to register against his eyeballs.

Going too fast, you jackass.

He glanced to the speedometer and was alarmed when he read the needle floating between seventy and eighty miles per hour.

"Wow," said Herm to himself, instantly backing off the accelerator.

The engine wound back a thousand RPMs and decided to downshift into fourth. That's when Herm felt the *whump*. Was it a problem in the automatic transmission? Or another impossible-to-see pothole absorbed by the chassis? The car had surely bucked on him. Maybe he'd run over a cardboard box? If so, it would probably be stuck in the undercarriage.

Easing further on the gas pedal, Herm felt the pull. Something was dragging, stuck underneath the SUV. He rolled down the window and his face was smacked by the atmospheric chill. His ears were keen, though. He could hear scraping across the asphalt.

"Son of a BITCH," burst Herm, applying the brakes hard enough to fuss with gravity. The front end of the SUV dipped. Herm heard and felt a slight snap beneath the floorboard. Whatever had been trapped underneath had cut itself loose. Eighty feet later, Herm and his new Ford Edge had finally come to a rest.

With the brake lights in full flare, Herm checked his rearview mirror to see just what the hell he'd run into. He scoured the frame yet couldn't make out even a panel of cardboard. Herm needed more light. He gripped the shift knob and coolly slipped the transmission into reverse gear. The backup lights engaged, blasting the red haze with white while, inside the SUV, the display screen switched to the rear-facing camera view. The wide-angle shot was a grainy, high-contrast image and showed little detail beyond the first ten feet.

Fine, fine. I'll back up.

Herm let his foot off the brake, and the SUV rolled backward as if being guided by the concrete drainage strip that bisected the alley. His eyes never left the screen as he steered the car like it was some kind of video game. At last, a disheveled pile appeared. Some kind of colored, print fabric. This is when Herm figured he had probably run over somebody's suitcase, the lock exploding underneath his car and depositing the clothes into a congealed polyester clump.

With the mystery in his mind solved, Herm should have braked, cranked the transmission back into drive, and carried on with his appointed plan. 7-Eleven. AA meeting. Hook up with Cherry Pie and her young unicorn roomie at the audition space.

But it was something about that backup camera. The super-wide angle. The way with every reversing tire turn, more detail would come into focus while, at the same time, the distant parts of the image fell off into the oddly curved blackness. It mesmerized him so that he wasn't so much paying attention to that clothes pile he inched closer to until his rear bumper was a mere five feet from it.

That's when he jammed his foot onto the brake.

That clump of fabrics was no print pattern. It was a blood-spattered mangle of a person who lay twisted in the middle of the alley. With mannequin arms and legs askew, inhumanly posed.

"Holy fuck . . ." Herm heard himself utter.

The cognitive receptors of his brain couldn't believe what he was staring at. But the limbic region, otherwise known as the reactive frontal lobe, had its own impulse.

Fucking get the fuck out of here!

As it turned out, Rodney had never seen Herm's speeding SUV. One second he was on his feet, fully committed to facing down the purse thief. Then in an eyeblink, he was blindly struck and raked into the car's undercarriage. Unconsciousness came in an instant. Death, though, wasn't as accommodating. It would take Rodney four full days before the doctors at Cedars-Sinai recommended that he be removed from all life support. At the time, there were still no suspects in the hit-and-run crime.

16

Santa Monica. 9:28 p.m.

Santa Monica's Third Street Promenade stretches north and south for three blocks between Wilshire Boulevard and Broadway. A scant quarter mile from the Pacific Ocean, the pedestrian-only mall is a daytime melange of restaurants, retail shopping, show business office space, and movie theaters. But at night, the concrete stretch transforms into a carny-like midway of street performers, teenage clubbers, and enough neon to set the moist evening air into a rainbow of primary glow.

The Christmas and Chanukah lights were the icing on an already frosty cake.

Lucky dropped Andrew off with a stack of the *HAVE YOU SEEN ME?* flyers at the southernmost end, promising to circle back and park three blocks to the north. They would work toward each other and eventually meet in the middle.

The air was getting wetter and sticking to Lucky's ream of fly-ers. All the better, he thought. All those cheap copy pages dropped and left behind would stick to the sidewalk like papier mâché. As Lucky began to wonder how long before his disposable cell phone would begin to stack up with cranks and false leads, it vibrated in his pocket. After last night's conga line of wasted calls, he had half a mind to shuttle all immediate dialers to voicemail and filter through them later. Only the 213-prefixed number in the caller ID box was familiar.

"This is Lucky," the detective answered.

"It's Bleds," replied the caller.

"What the hell?" said Lucky. "Where the hell you callin' from?"

"My drunk-in-laws," joked Lucky's former training officer, Wayne Bledsoe. He'd been calling his wife's parents the drunk-in-laws as long as Lucky could remember. "We're wrapping up our eight crazy nights of Chanukah. You'll never guess what they bought me."

"A gym membership?"

"You're no fun."

"Just figured that out?"

"How's your job status?"

"I'm employed. But you knew that or else you wouldn't have called my burner number. You got the email?"

After his visit to Gonzo, Lucky had set about sending an email blast to every L.A. sheriff's deputy he could find on his contact list. It contained a snapshot of the *HAVE YOU SEEN ME?* artwork and a simple extra message: *Cop to cops. Please help a brother out.*

"Gonna take a week to clean up the mess you made in Hol-lywood last night," guffawed Bledsoe.

"You taught me that trick." Lucky switched the phone to his other hand, not missing a beat to slip a few flyers underneath the windshields of cars parked along Wilshire.

"Christ, I did, didn't I? Whose mugs did we paper Ghettotown with?"

"Whose didn't we?" Lucky's mind shot back to the days of uniforms and nights in the black-and-whites. Bledsoe, tired of rolling miles off their radio unit's rubber to track down a pair of Crips wanted on drive-by charges, pulled into an all-night copy shop and dropped some plastic to pay for a few reams of enlarged mug shots on colored paper.

"Red for Crips. Blue for Bloods. Copy place loved our asses," said Bledsoe.

The duo papered ten square blocks of Compton. Phones may not have rung off the hook, but all it took was one call from a five-year-old latchkey kid who knew how to dial his uncle's kitchen phone and—presto, bingo—the first suspect was bagged. Over the year, they'd repeated the procedure with a modicum of success until a non-local environmental group looking to clean the ghetto of garbage-choked gutters decided the local sheriffs were enemy number one from all the tree pulp they were flushing to garner tips on gangbangers' whereabouts. A memo was generated from the downtown tower: there would be no more littering poorer neighborhoods with the unwanted wanted posters. Deputies Dey and Bledsoe were required to return to their previously proven methods of intel-gathering, a.k.a. cracking gang member heads.

"The bad ol' days," joked Bledsoe.

"Your eight crazy nights not entertaining enough?" pressed Lucky.

"You mean why'd I call your burner?"

"Not that I don't love catching up. But I've got plans to litter in multiple municipalities."

"Right," segued Bledsoe. "DT outta Carson . . . my brother-in-law's second cousin once whatever . . . met him a coupla times. Member of the tribe, you know?"

"He's Jewish?" confirmed Lucky.

"And family. Anyway, somebody on somebody's friend's list posted an email on some kinda social media thing. Says he's seen your girl."

"Wait. My *HAVE YOU SEEN ME?*"

"What you're littering the city and email boxes with. Yeah."

"And the guy recognized my missing girl?"

"Best I could get was, 'Looks familiar,' is what my brother-in-law said."

"Pretty, blonde, and fifteen," deadpanned Lucky. "That's like half the teens in Redondo."

"Your girl," said Bledsoe. "She some kinda dancer?"

Lucky was halfway across Santa Monica Boulevard. He wanted to put the brakes to his Vibram soles, switch ears, and confirm whether he'd heard his old training officer correctly. Then, under a set of flashing headlights, he hustled safely to the other side.

"You ask if she danced?" asked Lucky. "Yeah. My girl's got a dance thing, according to her old man."

"The guy says if it was her, she was working as a party dancer."

"That somethin' like a stripper?"

"Exactly what I asked him. But no. You know. Bar mitzvahs and shit. Birthday parties. Sweet sixteens. DJ brings dancers to pimp the party, get all the fat asses moving."

"Like you."

"This fat-ass stopped dancin' at my *first* wedding," laughed Bledsoe. "Let's say the music hasn't moved me since."

"Got a number for this second-cousin-in-law . . . or whatever he is?"

"Nothin' that close. But if you call the station, I think he's on tonight."

"Thanks, yeah."

"Name's Mikey Blumenthal. Got that?"

"I'm good." Lucky clicked off with the practiced press of his thumb. He pocketed the burner and carried on handing out flyers until Bledsoe's text came through with the Carson Station detective's digits. In those fleeting moments, Lucky quickly calculated the odds that this one tip would lead to a case-closing recovery. A hundred to one? A thousand? Ten thousand?

Higher, you detective dumb-ass.

"Probably," Lucky muttered to himself as he waited five rings until a voice picked up.

"Detectives' desk," announced the male voice, dull and rote.

"Lookin' for Michael Blumenthal," said Lucky, hoping he'd already found him.

"Out chasin' guns," said the man. "Lemme send you to his voicemail."

"You got a cell phone for him?" asked Lucky.

"Who's this?"

"Name's Lucky Dey. Used to work outta Lennox."

"You on the job?"

"I'm in the middle of transferring back from Kern."

"Yeah, man," said the voice. "I heard of you."

"Cool," said Lucky. "What's your name?"

"My name's none of your fuckin' business."

The shift in tone was more than a tell to Lucky. It rose to the level of familiar. As in beef-worthy.

"We met, brother?" asked Lucky.

"Ain't no brother," said the voice. "Least not to no Reaper."

"Right," said Lucky, instantly resigned. But only by habit. Sheriffs inked with Reaper tattoos had reputations. Some deserved. Others lumped into the exclusive club as if they were crack-slinging gang members. No better than Crips or Bloods.

"Got me at a disadvantage," excused Lucky. "You know about me but I don't know dick about you. How 'bout you give me Mikey Blumenthal's mobile and we'll call it even?"

"Shove that evil tat up your Reaper ass," finished the voice before hanging up.

The rebuff could have stung more. But Lucky was, at worst, only mildly aggravated. He had bumped egos with plenty of bullet-headed deputies over nonsense from turnkey duties to crosstown college football picks. Then there were the Reapers. That small cabal of Lennox cops, each inked and numbered and sworn to its own unholy oath. Blood brothers in a war against street cops. Yet Lucky never wondered—had he been able to calculate the antipathy a single tat would inspire amongst fellow officers—whether or not he would have balked at accepting the Reapers' invitation. Truth was, if he were on his deathbed and counting, joining the Reapers' ranks would have been the very last of Lucky's regrets.

He was, though, facing a dilemma. The call had left him still without a cell number to contact the Carson deputy. The solve had three prongs. One, he could dial every cop he knew who worked in the southern Basin to see if they or anybody they knew would have Mike Blumenthal's digits on their smartphone. Two, he could back-burner the semi-flimsy tip Bledsoe had passed along until tomorrow, when the fat man could deliver the actual contact info. Or three, he could cut to the chase, point the borrowed Crown Vic toward the city of Carson, and sniff around for the crew of deputies out chasing around for guns.

17

Hollywood.

Nine o'clock had come and gone. This left Cherry Pie and her new roomie, Valeriana, standing on the sidewalk outside the Franklin Avenue audition space, otherwise known as the Casting Place. Mobile phone glued to her hand, Cherry checked the time again, igniting the screen and using up what little power she had left.

"So, tell me why I had to come?" asked Karrie—a.k.a. Valeriana. "Is it gonna stay this wet all winter? Thought it never rained here."

The December misting had morphed into a steady drizzle. With Cherry's car parked around the corner, both girls were huddled under an eighty-year-old pepper tree that had been planted long before the old stucco apartment building had been converted into a commercial space. The roots, some of which had surfaced in search of water, had made a mess of the sidewalk, cracking and separating the concrete like a stale cookie. While occasionally pinching her dampened sweatshirt from her skin, Karrie kept her twitchy legs warm by balancing her toes at the edge of one of those root-caused fissures and slowly lowering her heels for a calf stretch.

"Give him 'til nine thirty, okay?" said Cherry.

"Your call," said Karrie. "I'm just along for the free coffee."

"Should try the door again," said Cherry. "Maybe he parked in back and is waiting for us."

"You just did that then minutes ago."

"That was ten minutes ago. He coulda parked by now."

"He blew us off," said Karrie.

"I didn't get that kinda vibe from him."

"What kinda vibe is that?"

"I dunno. The blow-me-off kind, I guess. He's a for-real casting director."

"I'll check," said Karrie, finally so chilled she was willing to test anything in order to hurry the process along.

She skipped up the brick steps to a pair of double doors with tin veneer tacked on to throw an industrial spin on the property. The knob, aged and bronze-looking, appeared like it would be cold to the touch. This is why Karrie hesitated giving it a tug. She instinctively paused, rubbed her hands together until she felt the friction, then stretched her fingers for the knob. Inches from her fingertips, beyond her grasp, it was as if the door magically unlocked. Karrie heard a bolt thrown and, without so much as her touching the door, it swung inward.

"Oh . . . hi," said Karrie without thinking, a strangely embarrassed smile spreading across her freckled face.

"You again?" grinned Gabe.

"Yeah, me," shivered Karrie. "Me 'n' my friend down there were supposed to meet some casting dude."

"From the other day?" asked Gabe. "That same guy?"

"Guess so, yeah. Was just checkin' to see if maybe he's inside."

"Just me," shrugged the photographer. "Sorry. Was just doin' a last once-around and saw you."

"Saw me?"

Gabe eased into the threshold, his dark brown mop of hair coming into shaggy relief under the door lamp—friendly dimples in full articulation despite his beard. He snuck a look upward and to the left.

"Right up there," he said.

Karrie tracked Gabe's eyes up into the dark corner of the overhang and the lens of a hooded security camera mounted above and to the right.

"Oh," said Karrie with a girlish giggle.

"Sure he said to meet here?" asked Gabe. "Kinda late."

"I'm just along for the ride." Karrie gestured to Cherry Pie, fifty yards away and finding only mild protection under that sprawling, overgrown pepper tree.

"Again, huh? Just hitchin' along."

"This one's a callback."

"Nothin's scheduled here," said Gabe. "But if you guys wanna hang out inside, I can stick around 'til you figure what's what."

Karrie left Gabe at the door, skipped back down the steps, and relayed the conversation to Cherry Pie. Pissed off at being stood up, Cherry thought she'd had enough of waiting and thought a better use of her time would be to work off her frustration in a late-night dance class before her scheduled spins on the stripper pole. As per her usual generosity, Cherry offered to bring Karrie along to the class or the club or both.

"Think I'll hang out for a while . . ." Karrie tilted her head toward the cracked door of the casting space. "Just in case your casting guy comes by."

"Right, whatever." Cherry rolled her eyes and fished in her purse. "Need any condoms?"

"Shut up!"

"He's cute. You're cute. Shit happens."

"See you back at your place?"

"Remember where the key is?"

"Inside the garden gnome."

Cherry Pie gave the fifteen-year-old a sisterly squeeze, then tried to beat the heavier drizzle to her car around the corner. That's when she felt the first pang of panic. Without thinking, she glanced back over her shoulder to make sure the girl she knew as Valeriana was safe. Karrie had already disappeared inside the building. As for Gabe, she only glimpsed him for a heartbeat, scanning the street before shutting the business door behind himself.

She's her own girl, Cherry thought to herself. Not even a full-on roommate. Yet still, she was young and if Cherry had to pick a little sister to care for, why not the sweet strawberry-blonde teenager whose dad drove an Audi?

Cherry smiled. Maybe she'd inadvertently found herself a new roomie. The idea squelched whatever worry she'd only just contemplated. How was Cherry to know she would never see the girl again?

18

Santa Monica. 10:24 p.m.

"Chasing guns?"

"What it's called," answered Lucky. He'd met up with Andrew somewhere in the middle of the Third Street Promenade. The first thing he'd noticed was that much of Andrew's flyer stack remained intact, trapped beneath his arm. This made Lucky wonder what the hell Andrew had been doing for the past hour.

"But you say this guy saw my Karrie?" pressed Andrew.

"It's a lead. But slim at best," confirmed Lucky. "I don't have the guy's cell number, so what I'm gonna do is get down to Carson, find the guy, and hear what he has to say face-to-face."

"Well, let's go," said Andrew.

"Huh uh," stalled Lucky. "Cover more ground if you stay here, finish up with your stack. I'll get down south, find out what I can, double back and pick you up—"

"You want me to finish my stack?"

"Got some left there, dontcha?" Eyebrows raised, index finger extended with his thumb cocked like an accusatory gun, Lucky left little room for subtext.

Andrew's face flushed. He held out the stack of unexpended flyers, cocked his elbow, and like a spring-loaded pitching machine, fired the sheets of paper into the atmosphere.

"So, how many do I have now?" smiled Andrew.

"That's not gonna help find your girl."

"Here's what *we're* gonna do," insisted Andrew. "Both of us are gonna get in the car and drive to wherever-the-heck and find this gun guy."

Lucky clocked a vertical vein formed in a jagged stripe down Andrew's forehead. When he had spoken, his teeth, slightly yellowed from years of tobacco use, were bared to the gums. But in the past few days, the cop hadn't witnessed a single moment when Andrew had so much as excused himself for a smoke or spit. Lucky found himself pondering if Andrew was a nicotine addict in need of a fix.

If Andrew was committed to riding up front in the big boy seat, Lucky would consent. Hell. He might start to like this guy.

"You ride with me to Carson?" dealt Lucky. "It's what I say and when I say it."

"What's the big deal about this Carson place?"

"Gangbanger Alley," said Lucky. "You'll see."

The task force that "chased guns" was a hodgepodge of detectives who, on random calendar nights, would gas up their unmarked radio cars and hunt for suspicious young black men. Loitering on corners or crowding storefronts. Cruising in groups of three or more. It was acutely profiling. The South County Sheriff's equivalent of "stop and frisk." The "male usuals" were clocked and stopped for one of a litany of violations the deputies had at their disposal. Those young men were searched and their cars turned. It wasn't much work. The cops knew the players and who would usually be holding. Drugs were the entrée. But gathering up hardware was the point of the exercise. Gangbangers with guns were usually trigger-happy and looking for trouble. So, sending a phalanx of detectives out on random nights to vacuum up street weapons was supposed to have a suppressive effect on gang crime.

"Wow," remarked Andrew once he'd heard Lucky's explanation of chasing guns. "Talk about your civil rights violations."

Lucky didn't answer with more than a smirk. The windshield wipers of the Crown Vic were engaged, streaking across the glass in a barely effective attempt to flush it of moisture.

"Ever think of replacing your windshield wipers?" It was more of a comment than a question.

"Not my car," said Lucky.

"It never rains in Southern California," Andrew sang.

"Not true. But not far off. Sun bakes the rubber and wipers go bad quicker than you can say Pep Boys."

The residential streets of West Compton were tree-lined and blanketed in darkness. Streetlights were few. So, what little illumination there was came from flickering porch lamps, the occasional uncurtained window, and the Crown Vic's sweeping high beams, igniting the asphalt that rolled underneath the car's wheels like an ever-moving carpet.

Andrew marveled at the way Lucky was able to navigate the urban grid. He was like a backwoods pathfinder, not caring for street names and stop signs, but using landmarks to carve his turns deeper into this "hood." Mangled mailboxes, tree stumps, buckled sidewalks, a corner liquor store. These were signposts Lucky and every other Reaper had memorized down to the knots on a strip of faded redwood fencing.

Then there were the memories. They rolled past the apartment where Lucky had been blindsided by a knife-wielding granny protecting her son from a domestic abuse arrest.

There was the Circle K convenience store and filling station that had suffered more armed robberies than the diseases carried by the meth-smoking hookers who worked out of the rear bathrooms.

And then there was the intersection of South Normandie and West El Segundo. Once when Lucky had gotten lost, training officer Bledsoe had made his wet rookie shinny up a pole and read the street names out loud for the whole block to hear.

"Driveway right there?" remarked Lucky. "Was workin' alone when I jammed some Crips there. They were slingin' rock down the street and hadda go back to that house for a resupply."

"Jammed?" asked Andrew.

"Sort of a surprise stop."

"What they do?"

"One popped off at me with a nine-mil. Fucked up my windshield good. They ran up the drive."

"And?"

"Knocked one down in the hedge over there. Other one I punched a coupla holes through while he was tryin' to get his key in the lock."

"You shot 'em?"

"Shot at me first."

"And?"

"And what?"

"You kill 'em?"

"Naw," replied Lucky, turning with just the heel of his left palm. "Shoulda. Ass clowns both up and sued me, the department, the sheriff, the county supervisors."

"After they shot at you?"

"Lawyers," Lucky deadpanned.

He spun the wheel in the opposite direction, wheeling the Crown Vic into a residential alley. Another shortcut. With his right hand, he reached back into the small of his back and withdrew his model 1911 .45-cal and left it cradled across his thigh. Andrew didn't miss the sudden glint of stainless steel.

"Expecting something . . ."

"Nope. Just force of habit."

The alley was coming to an end at another street. When Lucky's vehicle cleared the pair of flanking fences, the car would be quickly exposed. So, Lucky re-gripped the weapon, leveling the muzzle at his own door panel while leaning forward and looking past Andrew out the passenger-side window.

It was a tidy bit of tradecraft. And not at all lost on Andrew. He was at once impressed, shocked, and taken aback that there he was, seated alongside this cop who, based on his actions, was prepared to release a torrent of gunfire at the mere hint of real danger.

"That bad of a neighborhood?" asked Andrew.

"Down this way?" said Lucky. "It's all bad."

After ten or so minutes working a square-mile grid, Lucky found what he was looking for—a sheriff's black-and-white carrying two uniformed deputies. The detective waved them down and flipped a U-turn to come alongside them on a north/south boulevard. Lucky identified himself as a cop out of Lennox looking to connect with the Carson crew chasing guns that night. A radio call later revealed the team was 10-7 at Jimmy J's, an all-night taco stand known to give discounts to any first responder with a badge or uniform. Lucky was well acquainted with the joint as a Carson station cafeteria. He thanked the deputies before spinning the Crown Vic's power steering until the muscle car was roughly aimed in the direction of the nearest carne asada burrito.

The original Jimmy J's was little more than a hot cart that James Javier would roll from his Carson hovel to a busy corner. After his day job fixing transmissions on city busses, he'd serve homemade soft tacos and burritos from 5:30 in the evening until he ran out of the fresh tortillas and various fillings his wife, Marta, had prepared. Forty-four years later, Jimmy J's was still a family business. The hot cart had turned into a full kitchen and a walkup window housed in a yellowing shack with a huge awning boasting neon-lit fiesta-colored signage. The illuminated *T-A-C-O-S* sign practically jutted into the intersection, the five blazing letters flanked by the faded cursive *Jimmy J's*. Yet, after nearly half a century, the only seating was the four outdoor picnic tables permanently chained to ten-inch eyehooks anchored in the city sidewalk.

Before Lucky had parked the Crown Vic, he had already spotted the six Carson detectives who made up the gun crew. And there was nothing undercover about them. Each wore jeans, running sneakers, and a leather or rain-repellent jacket cut at the waist for easy access to their weapons. They were packed into a single picnic table like aluminum cans in a six-pack.

"Now, you stay put," ordered Lucky, placing the car in park but leaving the engine running.

"Tagged along all the way down here and you won't let me go the final thirty yards to cross the street?" complained Andrew.

"Something like that," was all Lucky said. He cut short the argument by climbing out and slamming his door shut before Andrew could form another sentence.

Lucky waited on westbound traffic before crossing without the benefit of a crosswalk or green light. In order to beat the east-moving cars, Lucky had to plant a toe and trot to the opposite curb. It was as if a piano string in his back had been plucked with a half-dollar, releasing a shock of pain that radiated down his right leg all the way to his Achilles.

Son of a bitch . . .

The trot turned into a semi-skip better resembling that of a lame street dog. And though he made it safely across the four-lane, he had to pause once he stepped up onto the curb, hug the lamp-post, and let his right leg hang to the toe until the hurt eased. He wondered if that was his sciatic nerve, informing him that early old age was a strong probability if he didn't take on physical therapy with more seriousness than doing curls with a cup of Starbucks.

"Any of you guys Mike Blumenthal?" began Lucky once he was able to ease up on the picnic table without appearing like a complete gimp.

"Who's askin'?" said the detective nearest him. He was the thickest of the sextet, seated at the end of the bench with half a cheek hanging over.

"Name's Lucky. Used to be outta Lennox."

"I heard of you," said the cop with the caterpillar eyebrows and matching mustache. The wire-thin cop was squeezed into the center of the bench, taking up less seat space than the average eight-year-old. "Didn't you shuffle your shit off to some boon-docks backwater?"

"Worked in Kern for a few years," said Lucky. "Now I'm just waitin' for the reassignment to go through."

"You put in again for Lennox?" asked the mustache.

"Soldier where they send me," said Lucky.

"I hear that," said the detective at the end, an average-looking Joe with a strong jaw and his wedding ring on his left pinky. He toasted Lucky with his bottle of imported Mexican Coca-Cola. "I'm Mikey Blumenthal. You the guy lookin' for that dancer girl?"

"That'd be me."

"What dancer girl?" queried the cop with the massive shaved head that looked even more humongous in an Oakland Raiders fleece beanie.

"We talkin' honey-strippers?" chimed the cop with the caterpillar mustache.

"Bar mitzvah," said Blumenthal.

"You went to a bar mitzvah with strippers?" joked the one colored man in the crew. "Sign me up for a conversion to Blumey's tribe."

Lucky graded the darker cop as a Samoan deputy he'd met once before—a former rugby player with cauliflower ears. Probably a Mormon boy, thought Lucky. Part of the department's *good families make good cops* recruitment program.

"You'd have to be circumcised," barked the thick cop to the Samoan.

"What the hell?" said the caterpillar cop. "What's a black dude who can't afford to give a few inches for a new religion?"

"This kinda black dude," laughed the Samoan cop. "Us island negroes don't got no dick to spare."

While the crew guffawed at their own clever banter, Lucky was hanging back, letting the conversation ride. He knew better than to wedge his own agenda into their precious lunch break. And the conversation was guaranteed to come back around to the outsider.

"Forget about Mikey's little dick," said the beefy one. "I wanna know how strippers make the card at a bar mitzvah."

"Not strippers," insisted Blumenthal. "Just hot little dance asses to get the party jumpin'."

"But hot enough to be strippers?" confirmed average Joe.

"Hot enough," corrected Blumenthal. "The young blondie thing? Wayyyy hotter. Ain't that right, Lennox?"

"Just here to find out the when and where," centered Lucky. "Who were the hosts of the party? Maybe I get a phone number?"

"So, why's she on your radar?"

"Runaway," said Lucky.

"And who's got the Lennox boys chasin' little blonde runners?"

"Not on the job," said Lucky. "Side gig. That's all."

Lucky's eyes lifted over Blumenthal's head and sharpened his focus to the walk-up window. That's where he spotted Andrew, right hand stuffed in his khaki pocket and fishing for enough change to pay for a cold bottle of imported Coca-Cola.

Asshole. I thought I told you to stay in the car.

"You check the clubs?" asked Blumenthal. "'Cause with a motor like that little girl's, ten'll getcha twenty she's straddling a pole somewhere."

"Straddling a pole somewhere? Or somebody's pole?" joked caterpillar.

"C'mon, assholes," said the Samoan. "That's somebody's daughter you're talkin' on."

"Shut up. Every gash out there is somebody's daughter," pissed caterpillar. "My fuckin' ex from Hades was somebody's fuckin' daughter."

"You gonna help the Lennox brother out or what?" asked the beefy cop.

"Yeah, yeah," said Blumenthal with a half grin. "Sorry. Just gotta help me out once you find her."

"What's that?" cued Lucky.

"See? Hard to believe, but I was once that young. You know. Thirteen?"

"And Jewish," reminded beefy.

"Yeah, yeah," jabbed Blumenthal before continuing his special query. "Was your runaway girl at the party . . . and, I mean, *if* that was your runaway at the party. Was she just there to, you know, dance with everybody? Or was she some kind of party favor? For all the bar mitzvah boys?"

Lucky recalled seeing all Blumenthal's near-perfect teeth. Both neat rows, his lips pulled back into a broad shit-eater's grin. His eyes were utterly fixed on Lucky's. The stare had a caveat to it. Then, without so much as a blink, Blumenthal's eye sockets suddenly widened to their maximum orbital before his eyelids came crashing downward over a shocking grimace. From the back of the cop's skull came a gravity-defying explosion of fizzy black soda laced with shards of tumbling glass. As Blumenthal's shoulders followed his head to the table, a man appeared in Lucky's field of vision. He looked like a baseball hurler at the end of his pitching motion. Only this hurler was left holding the broken neck of an imported Coca-Cola bottle.

And it was Andrew.

19

Marina del Rey.

"God, don't remind me of my couch-surfing days," confessed Gabe, his fingers already interlaced with Karrie's.

"You're not *that* old," said Karrie, gripping the man's hand a bit tighter.

"Wasn't saying I was old. Saying I don't look back on those days with much affection. I ate dog food."

"You ate dog food?"

"Wasn't like I was starving. It was more like a dare."

"The dry kind or that Spam-looking stuff?"

"Spam. We stir-fried it."

"Ewwww. Really?"

Gabe smiled and sheepishly nodded, those adorable dimples of his showing up even in the thinnest light. Though the sky had dried, the air was still mist-filled. The tide was receding, leaving foam bubbles on the Marina del Rey sand with each lessening wave. Despite the cold, the pair strolled hand in hand, barefoot, and with each step, squeezing off the freshly pancaked sand from between their toes.

"My feet are getting numb," laughed Gabe.

"Pussy."

"I'm a pussy?"

"You wouldn't survive where I'm from."

"Downside of being California grown," admitted Gabe. "I had this girlfriend in high school. Her dad was being a hardass, demanding she go to college somewhere in the northeast. I remember accusing him of being this big snob about East Coast colleges. He couldn't have gotten more pissed at me. I remember him right up in my grill and saying, 'I want my daughter to go to a northeast school because I want her to learn that life isn't sunny and seventy!'"

Karrie laughed. She was trying to imagine Gabe as a high school senior. Somehow she'd pictured the scene with his girlfriend's father taking place around some sun-splashed Beverly Hills pool. Shade palms and a Spanish-speaking cabana boy serving piña coladas.

"But you actually grew up in Beverly Hills?" she innocently asked.

"South of Wilshire," he corrected. "Sub-Beverly Hills. But, yeah. Not quite 90210."

As they continued their stroll, sometimes not talking for what seemed like eternal stretches, Karrie took comfort in the fact that Gabe hadn't once asked about her age. She hated when guys did that. As if they needed to know that she was either under or over some magical age of consent. Sure, Gabe *was* quite a bit older than most of the dudes she'd hung out with.

Most.

Early thirties, she gauged. But somewhere, somehow her old soul and his goofy, almost juvenile demeanor seemed to meet near the happy middle.

And when he'd reached for her hand, it didn't at all feel forced or forward. In fact, Karrie couldn't recall if she'd ever held hands with anybody but her mother and father. She remembered a summer farmer's market choked with customers. She had been, maybe, five. Smaller than small. She could have easily been swallowed by the crowd. But the child was between her parents, holding each of their hands. Secure. Safe.

Since then, nobody. Well, nobody until Gabe. She couldn't help but feel that her hand fit well with his.

"We had money," confessed Gabe. "Then my old man met Stacy."

"Stacy?"

"Coke whore bitch. Least, that's what my moms called her. I just called her Stacy. Anyway, she and my dad snorted the savings, our house. I was on track to go to UCLA but ended up at Valley College and driving a Starline Tours van."

"Poor baby."

"Do I sound like I'm complaining?"

"Just bustin' balls."

"So, you're a ballbuster now?"

"Could be," she teased.

"Maybe you're a wannabe ballbuster," he smiled. "But an actual ballbuster?"

"Like you know the difference?"

"Worked with enough actresses. So, yeah. I do know."

"Actresses are ballbusters?"

"Star actresses." Gabe punctuated his point with a wink. At least, Karrie thought it was a wink. In the barely there light, it was all body language. It allowed her to imagine things the way she wanted them to appear.

"You've photographed famous people?" asked Karrie.

"Nothin' editorial," explained the photographer. "But I've got a pal who works production as a still shooter. Calls me when he needs a sub."

"What's a still shooter?"

"The on-set photographer. Shoot the setups. Behind-the-scenes stuff."

"Actually on the movie?"

"On the set. Right there with everybody else."

"Wow."

"But here's what it is," explained Gabe. "Some actresses? You know, the really big ones? They've got approval over what photos you can use. What you can't."

"No way."

"It's in their contracts. Called a kill percentage. Bigger the name, bigger their kill."

"That's crazy."

"At the end of every day, as the still photographer, you gotta submit all your pics. Every file. They go to the actresses' people and they come back approved or not. All vanity, man."

"Think I'd like that job."

"Sucks, man. Really."

"I'm talkin' about the actress," she giggled. "That kinda power? How people treat you and how you look? What girl wouldn't love that?"

"See what you mean."

"Makes me wanna have a kill list."

"Kill percentage," he corrected.

"Same thing."

"So, what would yours be?"

"My list?"

"Percent. Most of the big stars get eighty, ninety percent kill in their contracts."

"Oh, hell no," zipped Karrie. "Nothin' less than ninety-nine for this girl."

"Ninety-nine percent kill? That's what it's gonna take?"

"Gotta keep my standards, ya know?"

"Way high."

"Well, not too high."

"Ninety-nine percent?"

"I'll make allowances," said Karrie. "Hey. I'm on a date with you, right?"

"Oh," said Gabe. "This is a date?"

"And I'm lowering my standards," she teased.

"Just for me? Wow. Thanks."

They both laughed. Their repartee had been fun. Warm. Full of tease with pinches of substance. All the while, Karrie's hand never left Gabe's certain grip. There was a comfort there. A bit of peace and feeling of well-being that she hadn't felt since . . . Well, after she thought on it for a moment, it was something she'd never, ever felt.

Damn, girl. You are already so into this guy.

"Good place to turn around," said Gabe.

"Sure," said Karrie. "What's next?"

"If you can lower your standards for a little longer, figure we can think of somethin'."

"Ooooooookay," said the fifteen-year-old. "Maybe just for a little longer."

"Well, all right then," grinned the photographer. "Let's see what kinda trouble we can get into."

20

Carson.

The instant the Coke bottle struck the back of Deputy Blumenthal's head, Lucky could have sworn the gig was over. As much as he might have liked the pasty-faced software mogul from Wisconsin, he didn't imagine the business relationship could recover from a visit to county jail. Generally speaking, the brakes on Lucky's patience ran thin on his best days.

Nevertheless, the father of the missing child had taken obvious insult to the lascivious denigration unknowingly aimed at his daughter. And after Andrew had uncontrollably attacked the on-duty cop, the table full of deputies had responded in defense of a brother officer in the blink of an eye. The cops saw the attack as a random act by some anti-cop nut-bucket.

Lucky was the only man besides Andrew who understood the context of the assault. So, despite his damned sciatic nerve, he booted himself up onto the picnic table's top and launched himself over the still-in-shock Blumenthal and horse-collared Andrew down onto the sidewalk. Then with himself between Andrew and the incensed deputies, he held up a stalling palm and shouted:

"HE'S THE GIRL'S FATHER!"

Lucky continued to shout out as he was dragged off Andrew and pinned to the pavement by the Samoan cop and one of his thick brethren. The remaining deputies, including the injured Blumenthal, found enough cause to pummel a few heavy feet into Andrew's ribs while they rolled him and hooked his wrists with handcuffs.

Meanwhile, inside the taco stand, the window girl had already dialed 911. And the officer-in-trouble code went out immediately over the system. In no time at all, seven more sheriff's black-and-whites descended onto Jimmy J's along with a helicopter from County air support. With all the flashing lights, neighborhood passersby were certain there must have been some kind of drive-by shooting or major arrest. Cell phone cameras were recording and uploading images to social media pages in a matter of micro-moments.

All because Deputy Blumenthal hadn't a clue the runaway girl's daddy was standing ten degrees to his stern, his ears not missing a single sexual inference, and needing little to turn volcanic.

While paramedics carted off both Andrew and Deputy Blumenthal to the Harbor-UCLA Medical Center, Lucky remained and made sure to insert himself into the prolonged negotiation between Lennox and Carson sheriff's deputies. Bledsoe was strung in via cell phone. The bottom line was that the event was something akin to a misunderstanding gone terribly haywire. No charges needed to be brought. Blumenthal would assume responsibility for the insult in the form of a written apology and Andrew and his deep pockets would cover all medical and however many workdays the injured deputy might lose due to his concussion.

Still, during the entirety of the attack and subsequent sheriff's-style whitewashing, Lucky was counting the seconds until he climbed back into his borrowed Crown Vic. This would be the moment he, in his own rationale, would be officially excised from the gig. Once released from the hospital, Lucky was sure Andrew could find his way back to his hotel, and with a little phone work, find a proper private investigator to dig up his precious daughter. To put a punctuation mark on Lucky's decision, he removed the burner phone from his pocket, snapped it open, made certain the battery was removed, and dumped the pieces onto the passenger seat.

The end.

An accident on the 405 freeway left the northbound artery crawling. Ribbons of flared red taillights appeared to stretch for miles. Normally, the cop in Lucky would have found the nearest off-ramp and meandered his way back to the Valley via surface streets. It was the shark in him, as if when navigating Los Angeles, he couldn't bear to sit still in traffic. But it was anything but a normal night for Lucky. He'd just gotten into a scuffle with six fellow deputies, then recused himself from finishing a job. To Lucky, sitting in near-standstill traffic perfectly suited the lousy moment. He was in all likelihood unemployed again.

And he was glad for it.

Lucky flicked on the radio. The first station he landed on had Christmas songs on auto-rotation. Instead of instantly scanning for another station, he stalled on Mariah Carey's cover of "All I Want for Christmas Is You." It stirred a memory of a petty dinner table fight between two brothers. Their lymphoma-riddled mother had insisted on cooking up a full-on Thanksgiving meal for her two boys. Tony was in high school and Lucky was already in his second year as a uniformed deputy. The Irish-Italian matron, long divorced from a man who had walked out years before, wouldn't let her boys elevate from their respective seats without the threat of cracking a wooden spoon across their jar-headed scalps. Her cancer had journeyed deep into stage four and would most likely bury her within five months. This would be their last holiday season as what Tony called the Nuclear Super Trio. And hell if Mom wasn't going to cook.

Then came that petty snit of a fight. Was Mariah hot? Or not hot? Little brother Tony insisted the diva was not only hot, but a smokin' looker from the Planet Ten. Lucky, who hadn't really thought too much on the subject, decided to counter with the argument that Mariah Carey was uniquely unattractive. In fact, sometime during his teenage-hood he had heard that she only allowed herself to be photographed from the right side of her face. And unless brother Tony could produce photo proof of her left side, Lucky would continue to insist speciously that any designation of "hot" would have to wait.

It was a trivial scene that never rose beyond the laughs it produced from his easily delighted mom. But it had clearly stuck. And ever since, he couldn't hear more than a few notes of any Mariah Carey song—Christmas or otherwise—without the mental reminder of that special night. The muscles in Lucky's face built an involuntary, if middling, smile that earmarked the memory as pleasant. At least more than the awful reality that both little brother and mother were deceased, cremated, and buried next to each other in a Mar Vista cemetery.

The Mariah Carey tune had already cross-faded into Bruce Springsteen's rendition of "Santa Claus is Coming to Town" when Lucky's cell phone buzzed. Instinct told him to ignore the call, calculating that it was the bruised Midwestern daddy prepping to hurl curses his way.

A pang of guilt trickled over the tiny domes of Lucky's nerve endings but was soon squelched by the pain welling above his hips. He needed to get home and get horizontal as soon as possible. Ease the strain on his back instead of merely swallowing more and more Percocets.

By the time Lucky landed at his Reseda apartment, the pain was such that merely climbing the steps to his apartment was a chore. To make matters worse, upon making the last turn to his front door, he found himself face-to-face with a large black man. No less than six-foot-four, a professional athlete's shoulders, suited in designer gray with his gloved hands neatly folded in front of him.

"Lucky Dey?" asked the man, polite as hell. Lucky had instantly clocked him as a professional-driver-slash-bodyguard.

"Who's askin'?" was Lucky's de facto reply.

"Mr. Conrad Ellis would like to speak with you."

"Look, pal. I just drove over from that side of the hill," said Lucky. "And right now, if you'll forgive me, my back needs me to switch from longitude to latitude."

Lucky was already familiar with the routine. Conrad Ellis, the billionaire germophobe who preferred to keep his communiques over the natural prophylactic of a telephone, would sometimes see the need for actual in-person visits. On those occasions, he'd send a car and driver to retrieve the subject and deliver him or her to and from his Bel-Air mansion.

Easing past the suited bodyguard, Lucky flipped his key ring until the familiar Schlage deadbolt key revealed itself in the dim porch light. He was about to turn the lock when he felt the big man's hand softly grip his shoulder.

"Mr. Conrad is in the car," said the bodyguard. "He'd invite himself in but . . . well . . . Mr. Conrad says you know his preference for more controlled environs."

"Right," said Lucky. It didn't take a professional soothsayer to reckon a visit inside Lucky's apartment would be something less than antiseptic.

"We're right at the curb."

Damning his screaming back, Lucky sucked it up and trailed the bodyguard back down the steps and through the building portico that led to a sleepy street where two- and three-story apartment buildings stretched in both directions. A corner streetlamp flickered and sporadically buzzed, the sodium bulb inside only a few hundred night hours from extinction. Taking up most of the curb space was a Mercedes limousine, custom stretched and freshly polished to a liquid black.

The bodyguard swung a door wide. Lucky stiffly bent at the waist to peer inside. Conrad Ellis waved, his right hand swiveling at the wrist in a beckoning gesture.

"Come on in, Luck," said the billionaire.

Lucky knew better than to shake the man's hand. As he slid onto the rear-facing seat, the custom leather squeaked until he settled. The car's interior was lit as softly as the man's home. Warm and sparse yet comfortable, giving a quiet luster to the mahogany cabinetwork, which housed a minibar and a twenty-inch video screen tuned to Bloomberg TV.

"How are you?" asked Conrad.

"Hurtin' a bit right now," confessed Lucky. "Had a helluva time pullin' your buddy out of what coulda been a nasty beatdown."

"So I heard," nodded Conrad. "As you might expect, Andrew and I spoke."

"Figured as much," gestured Lucky, arms slightly spread. "Otherwise why?"

"I quite like the Valley," said Conrad. "Feels more like normal America."

"But you live in Bel-Air."

"Granted. What I have there they don't have anywhere in Southern Cal." Conrad reached into an ice bucket and refreshed his tumbler with three cubes. Then he twisted the cork from a bottle of forty-year-old scotch. "Join me?" he asked.

"I'm good," said Lucky, already having changed his mind about swallowing a few Percocets before reclining. The pain was too significant. The idea of liquor entering into the decision-making process felt dangerous. "So, you spoke to Andrew?"

"I did. He's pleased with your progress."

"Strange considering I almost got him jailed," said Lucky.

"Andrew's not so easy," continued Conrad. "He's a performative little creature. Type A, like most successful alphas."

"Well, speaking as an *unsuccessful* alpha, I may not be the best-suited guy to find his daughter."

"You found mine," said Conrad, his voice dipping soberly. "Well, you found her murderer. No easy chore."

"I got lucky."

"No pun intended."

"Never heard that one before."

"Don't quit on this," urged Conrad.

But Lucky hadn't quit. Though he'd surely been leaning that way, he hadn't shared that factoid with anybody.

"What do you know that you're not telling me?" asked Lucky.

"Like I said. I had a long talk with Andrew." Conrad sipped at his honey-tinted scotch. The ice in the crystal tumbler made a distinct tinkling sound. "Can't say I know you that well. But I consider myself a helluva judge of character."

"That so?"

"And based on what I asked you to do, what Andrew has reported back to me, my guess is that after this evening you'd be pretty much ready to call it a date."

"Fair enough," nodded Lucky. "Maybe I'm just that easy to read."

"You don't have children," noted Conrad.

"I keep hearing that."

At thirty-seven years old, Lucky barely had been able to hang on to a relationship for two months, let alone fathom raising a child. Aside from playing a brief role as a father figure to Gonzo's son, Travis, the closest thing Lucky had to parenting experience was a failed run as a parks and rec manager of a T-ball team made up of learning-disabled children. His short tenure had ended when an opposing coach insisted on running up the score on Lucky's crew of physically challenged six-year-olds. In retribution, Lucky met the coach in the parking lot and ran up the score of teeth he could knock out of the asshole coach's gums. When the coach threatened to press charges, Lucky left the downed man his card identifying him as an L.A. County sheriff's deputy. After a wink and a "good luck," Lucky retired from coaching.

"Being the parent of a teenager is its own kind of crazy making," toasted Conrad. "It's primal. Your job is your child. And when the teenage years come, well, it can send you round the bloody bend. Especially with girls."

Lucky nodded as if he understood. And, to a degree, he did. He'd had plenty of on-the-job experience wrangling teenage girls. Alone, drunk, and lost, they were manageable. But in groups, most cops knew they would need to call for female backup just for the addition of eyeballs and defense from a guaranteed sexual harassment suit.

"You'd die for your child," continued Conrad. "Gladly lay down all that you are and all you have just to keep 'em from jumping off a cliff. And not just once. Goes on for the whole teenage cycle. Serious father would eat his child's pain if it would make them that much safer."

"I getcha," said Lucky. It was clearly an intellectual response, though. The kind of human connection Conrad was describing was alien. He might as well have been talking about Bigfoot.

"Andrew's in a bad divorce. Lost his wife. Now he's lost his little girl. That's enough to make a sane fella go batshit nuts." Conrad shifted in his seat, then pointed with that tumbler of scotch whiskey. "If Andrew *wasn't* behaving like he'd burned through a few memory cards, then I'd wonder if something was off about him."

Lucky found himself recovering something of his little brother, Tony. Theirs was more than the typical sibling affection. Without a father in the home, older brother Lucky occasionally had worn the man-of-the-house pants. And Tony was the type of teen who often needed protecting. What if he'd up and disappeared on Lucky and their mom? The thought produced a weird flash of anger that left Lucky's face slightly flushed. As the air recirculated inside the limo, he could feel the beads of perspiration form on his stubbled scalp.

"Feeling alright?" asked Conrad.

"Might be coming down with something," said Lucky, knowing full well that his statement meant an end to the germophobe's visit.

"You understand if I ask you to leave then?"

"Of course."

"Think about what I said."

"Already have," said Lucky. "And I hear ya."

With that, any doubt Lucky had about whether or not he was quitting the private detective gig was all but quashed. Conrad had crossed Mulholland and half the Valley just to rope Lucky back in and re-close the deal. Successfully so, he added. And now it was time for Lucky to get the hell out of Conrad Ellis's limo.

Thursday

21

Santa Monica. 3:12 a.m.

Gabe's apartment was a rent-controlled sublet. Five short blocks from the Ocean Boulevard cliffs that overlooked Pacific Coast Highway and the beach, the second-story walk-up was even closer to the Third Street Promenade, where, only hours earlier, Lucky and Karrie's father had been papering the misted outdoor mall with color Xeroxes sporting Karrie's photo with the eerie caption, *HAVE YOU SEEN ME?*

With her fingers still gently intertwined with his, Karrie let Gabe lead her up the paint-chipped steps of a six-unit, '50s-era complex. Inside her skin, she found herself strangely at peace. Maybe it was the walk on the beach. Or the long conversation over fried eggs and chocolate shakes at Rae's. But somehow the dam had broken and, for the first time ever, she had told someone everything. All of it. Her childhood. Her parents. The volatile upbringing and the horrible, never-ending battle over the divorce.

Her loss of virtue.

Her few boyfriends.

Her fewer girlfriends.

Her growing lust for distance from everything she thought she knew.

It was a purge that bordered on impoliteness. Self-possessed, but so full of relief. It was akin to vomiting years of poison. And all the while, Gabe merely listened with an easy patience, asked correct, incisive questions without seeming as if he were prying or pretending to play coffee-shop psychiatrist.

A loosely hung string of twinkling white Christmas lights draped the door of Gabe's place. The leftover eight feet of strand was haphazardly wrapped around the fat paddles of a waist-high beavertail cactus in a cracking terra-cotta pot.

Karrie giggled at the sight.

"Christmas in L.A.," remarked Gabe, his voice barely above a whisper.

"I love Christmas." Karrie heard her own declaration and made a quick correction. "Well, I love Christmas lights."

"Oh, really?"

"Why so quiet?" asked Karrie.

"Old man downstairs likes to complain about my late nights and pot smoking. My New Year's resolution is gonna be not to deal with him."

"It's not New Years yet," teased Karrie, raising her voice just enough to be irritating.

"Close enough." Gabe unlocked the bolt and pushed the door inward with a gentleman's gesture signaling ladies first.

"Anything I should be scared of?"

"Only me," grinned the photographer.

"Oooh. I got the shivers."

The apartment was dark but for the slits of streetlight that muscled past the pair of drop-roll shades masking the living room window. Karrie could feel Gabe gently behind her, not so much nudging, but expecting her to step over the threshold. So, she eased forward, detecting the faint aroma of scented candles intermingled with musk once inside the door.

"You said you like Christmas lights?"

"Uh huh."

Karrie felt Gabe's arm stretching across her back. She heard the familiar flip of a wall switch. Then before her ignited a living room looped in Christmas lights, from colored to icicle style to twinkling, forming a virtual galaxy.

"Oh. My. God," exclaimed Karrie.

"They were on special at CVS," said Gabe. "Think I kinda overdid it."

"No! You totally didn't!"

"I've got beer and . . ." Gabe quickly disappeared into what appeared to be the kitchen. Karrie heard the familiar clinking of beer bottles along with carbon dioxide escaping as he twisted off each cap. She was still marveling at what a warm, glowing feel she got from so many indoor Christmas lights when Gabe returned at her right shoulder.

"This," he said, handing her a bottle, already frosting.

"You know I'm not old enough to drink," said Karrie, soft enough to be a purr.

Gabe laughed and showed a smooth beige tablet gently pinched between his thumb and index finger.

"Just one," said Gabe.

"One what?"

"One oxy. One beer. One dance under my stars."

"Never done oxy."

"As mellow as it gets," assured Gabe, showing her the tablet that was already on his tongue. He washed it back with a single swig.

"Okay . . ." said the teenager, sticking out her own tongue as an invitation for him to feed the pill to her. Then she drank from his beer. "Now what?"

"Now we slow dance until the pills say otherwise."

"Are you one of those goofy romantics?" she asked, allowing

herself to fold into his arms. She pressed an ear against his chest and listened to the shocking speed at which his heart thumped. A telling clue that, underneath his external calm, he was getting excited. She hoped to hell it was all because of her.

"My gawwwwd. Your heart is racing," she revealed.

"It is?"

"S'okay," she said. "Cool on the outside, crazy on the inside?"

"Think you just described most artists," he replied.

"I wouldn't know."

"But you were going to an audition?"

"Only because Cherry was."

"Cherry Pie. Helluva name."

"Better than Herm," joked Karrie. "I mean, what kind of name is Herm?"

"Short for Herman, I suppose."

"Herman. Right. Sounds ancient. But then, if I remember, so was he."

Disregarding the frantic beating of Gabe's heart, Karrie swayed to an imaginary slow song. All the while surrounded by that constellation of Christmas lights. And, as the drug slowly took its morphine-like effect, she experienced an inner warmth that she hadn't known since suckling at her mother's breast.

That's when everything faded into black.

22

Panorama City. 8:23 a.m.

Herman Alan Bland was born in Panorama City, California, and grew up in the shadow of the massive Budweiser brewery that marked the epicenter of the San Fernando Valley. The zip code was two parts small industry and one part modest, single-family homes. Depending on which way the wind was blowing, young Herm would wake to the sour odor of brewing hops. He hated the smell and swore to his mother and two older sisters that once he moved away he'd never, ever return to the immediate vicinity, not to mention the rest of the Valley. In Herm's mind, he'd pretty much kept that vow, keeping his life small and manageable for the last thirty years inside the same two-bedroom West Hollywood apartment.

But, eventually, his immigrant parents died, bequeathing their tiny clapboard home to Herm and his middle sister, Yvonne.

Their elder sibling, Janet, having recently lost her battle with ovarian cancer, would not collect. With his only surviving sis married and living near Baltimore, it was on Herm to liquidate the sole family asset. And so he returned to the Valley and that neighborhood with the yeasty brewery stink. And no, he hadn't missed the smell. The family house, though, was in such agonizing disrepair that he couldn't bring himself to list it in its current condition. He had resolved to make it his weekend project to fix it up. Someone had told him that DIY renovation had become as easy as the internet, with every matter of instruction available with just a click or two. And with the fix-up job only two short blocks from the do-it-yourself nirvana of Home Depot, Herm decided he might squeeze a better profit out of both the house and his geographically handicapped sister.

Who would have known that Herm would come to treasure his weekend avocation? So much so, he began cutting his Fridays short, leaving his girl-hustling biz—not to mention the potential for catching unicorns—around noon so he could be on his site with a Subway sandwich by one or two. If it hadn't yet dawned on him that his old family home had become a refuge of sorts, it became a sure signpost once he had run over that dreadfully dressed little human in that dark West Hollywood back alley. No sooner had Herm recognized what he had done with an audible "*aw, fuck*" than he had pointed his SUV toward the first northbound artery that promised to deliver him north of Mulholland. The entire drive, the sweat had nearly drained him of fluid, and his neck was tight from both checking the rear- and side-view mirrors along with peeking out the moonroof in fear that a police helicopter would be tracking LA's newest hit-and-run driver.

Fuck me, fuck me, fuck me, fuck me, fuck me . . .

It was a mantra, repeated a thousand or more times until Herm had safely parked his car behind his most recent project, a two-piece wooden gate hinged from each side of the tiny driveway with a roller assist for effortless operation. Herm had been waiting for the redwood to dry a week or two more before he planned to add a few coats of forest green paint as a house-matching finish. As he hastily pulled the gate shut behind his rear bumper, his fingers picked up a few painful splinters, an ill-timed reminder that he had better prep the wood with some heavy-grit sandpaper before he started slopping on the Benjamin Moore Bavarian Forest.

Herm next used the flashlight function on his phone to locate the hose he'd been using to keep the backyard plants alive. He dragged the dirty old coil and attached it to the spigot directly underneath the kitchen window. From there, the hose would reach 360 degrees around his vehicle, allowing the aging pimp to wash off every incriminating scintilla of blood, flesh, and DNA.

By the time Herm had finished with the SUV's undercarriage, he was cold and soaked. If there was blood on him, he couldn't tell. Still, once inside the house, he stripped himself naked, sacked his clothes in a plastic garbage bag, showered under a lukewarm spray, then thanked the god of his understanding that he had stayed in the old fixer often enough to leave changes of underwear, denim, T-shirts, and thick socks.

He brewed a pot of black coffee. Then, as he sat at the same kitchen table where his father would lecture him on how that sour smell of boiled hops in the air reminded him of jobs and progress and everything that was great about America, Herm was finally relaxed enough to revise his mental things-to-do list. Yes. The house still needed so much work. Work that required investment. And those dollars grew not on trees, but from the silky white skin of teenage girls. His mind backspaced to his evening plans before his unscheduled accident and subsequent detour.

What the hell was that girl's name? Cherry Pie's roommate? The unicorn. Valeria-something?

"Hi," said Cherry on the other end of the cell phone call. She clearly remembered Herm's mobile number. "What happened last night?"

"Big, big apologies," said Herm. "Had a family emergency."

"I'm sorry. Is everything okay?"

"On the mend," said Herm. "But we need to reschedule your callback because show business doesn't wait for my personal life."

"That'd be great," said Cherry. "I so appreciate it."

"How's later this morning?"

"I can make it work."

"Late morning? Eleven? Noon, even? Same casting place."

"I can do noon."

"With your roommate, don't forget. I still need two girls."

"Oh. Right."

"Is there a problem?"

"If I can find her. I think she's out for the night and she doesn't have a phone."

"Are you sure there's no way to contact her?"

"No," said Cherry. "Unless you have the name of that photographer guy."

"I don't . . . Which guy?"

"Works outta the same building as you. Think his name is Gavin or Gabe or something."

"Gabriel. Yes. I think I've met him."

"Well, after you didn't show, Valeriana kinda hooked up with him. And now it's, what? Ten? So . . ."

"So, we don't expect her home."

"You know what? I'm at the gym. So, she's probably already back. Don't worry. I'll bring her."

"You do that."

Herm could hear his own shallow breath in the earpiece of his phone. It made him wonder if Cherry could hear the same thing. And from there, could she extrapolate that his underarms had begun to sweat with anticipation? Herm hadn't been this anxious in ages. All from the anticipation of getting his practiced hands on that unbelievable little strawberry-blonde.

"Can I ask something?" asked Cherry. "Are there other girls you're considering?"

"It's Los Angeles," said Herm, not intending to sound so bleak, while massaging the bottom of his voice to roll out the gravitas. "There are always other girls."

23

Beverly Glen.

"So, you really are lucky," grinned Andrew.

"Just a nickname. This here happened because sometimes things just work out."

"Divine intervention, maybe," said Andrew, needing to form some kind of compromise to explain the excellent news.

"Whatever," said Lucky. "I've had suspects go from being impossible to run down to having them practically appear in the back seat of my radio unit. All I needed was bracelets. Shit just happens."

"To you."

"If the glove fits," said Lucky, allowing himself a rare smile.

The duo was seated at a small outdoor table under a bank of clicking heat lamps. The tiny deli sat amongst the few other restaurants and storefronts that made up the Glen Center at the top of the Santa Monica mountains, only yards from the iconic Mulholland Drive. The deli and its stepsister eateries enjoyed a mix of hill-dweller clientele as well as a cornucopia of Valley residents and Basin folk who used the destination as a convenient halfway point for meetups.

Andrew sat across from Lucky. He wasn't really touching his weak cup of joe but was remarkably animated considering the bruising that had bloomed overnight across the left side of his face. Swirls of purple and yellow. Lucky could even make out the impressions from where a set of sheriff's knuckles had connected with his face.

Lucky felt sorry enough to offer both Advil and Aleve to the runway's father but refrained from suggesting Andrew try some of his precious Percs to manage a face screaming with pain.

"So?" suggested Andrew.

"So what?"

"You got a phone number?"

From his wallet, Lucky extracted a folded yellow Post-it note. On it was a Valley phone number, scratched out by the secretary for the party company that booked out DJ and dance crews. Deputy Blumenthal's tip had led Lucky to a fortuitously easy rundown. A phone call to the bar mitzvah boy's family was followed by a visit to the West Hills office of the party company's owner. The Russian-born man was not only quick to identify the photo of Karrie Kaarlsen, but had a record to show she had worked two parties, each for fifty dollars cash. She had only identified herself by her first name, Valeriana. But she had left her cell phone number in case they could use her for future jobs.

"Holy moly," exclaimed Andrew.

"All you gotta do is dial," said Lucky.

"I'm nervous."

"Have a right to be."

"What if she sees my home area code and doesn't pick up?"

"Then leave her a voicemail."

Andrew was holding his phone, his thumb sliding from number to number on his keypad without pressing a one.

"I have to acknowledge . . ." began Andrew, "that she ran away for some kind of reason. What if she might not want to talk to me at all?"

"I'd say that's a pretty grown-up thought."

"From me? The actual grown-up? Who attacks cops with bottles of soda pop?"

"I'm nobody's old man. But I know with teens that stuff gets pretty tangled," said Lucky. "Look. She doesn't know you're anywhere local. So, call. It looks like you're dialing from Chinook-wah or whatever you call it."

"Chenequa."

"Leave her a voicemail. Tell her you love her. See if she calls back."

"I gotta figure out what the heck to say."

"And you will. In the meantime, I'll run down the number. See who's been calling her, where she's been calling from. That way, if she doesn't answer, we'll be only a step or two away."

"Okay," nodded Andrew. "Think I'm good with that."

"Take your time," said Lucky. "Call her when you're ready. And don't forget to pay the bill."

Lucky smiled, took his index finger, and used it to slide the Glen Deli's bill over to Andrew's side of the table before easing to his feet.

"Hey, Luck," said Andrew. "Thanks a million."

"Maybe you should text her a photo of your face," joked Lucky. "Let her see the lengths her old man would go to get his little girl back."

Lucky finished with a wink and a wave before crossing the parking lot in search of his car. Somewhere behind him were Karrie's dad and a ten-digit phone number scrawled on a yellow sticky note. By the time he'd gripped the door handle to the Crown Vic, he'd already abandoned trying to calculate just when Andrew would stone-up enough to dial his daughter. The best he could figure was that parenting was full of so many complications, a childless, unmarried cop-in-transition who could barely manage his pain addiction didn't have a hope in the underworld of understanding them. The best Lucky could accomplish was his job. And on that day, it was running down that phone number. With that, he began contacting his cop connections with access to cellular phone data. Hopefully, in an hour or so, whether Andrew had called or contacted his runaway daughter or not, Lucky would know the teenager's network of recent contacts. And surely, one of those would know where the girl was.

Lucky was close to finishing the job. Very, very close.

24

Silver Lake. 12:51 p.m.

Cherry Pie was late, rushing, and hadn't even reached the threshold to exit her apartment when she heard the phone ringing. Nearly three hours earlier she'd promised Herm the Casting Man that she would deliver her couch-surfing roomie. In hopes that she'd still turn up, she'd successfully pushed the call back another hour. Herm had made it clear that he needed two girls with contrasting looks for the job, strongly implying that without the freckled strawberry-blonde, Cherry Pie needn't keep the appointment.

But hell if some irresponsible twat of a teenager was going to stand between Cherry and a possible gig. After all, Herm had already expressed an interest in the girl with the purple hair. To Cherry, that meant she was halfway there. Come hell or high water, she was showing up for the casting. And not necessarily alone.

She'd tripped through her call directory and social media pals for just about any girl who might fit Valeriana's profile. And on shorter than short notice, Cherry had drummed up two candidates, both who promised to meet her at the Casting Place.

Then there was that phone trilling. And it wasn't Cherry Pie's barking Chihuahua ringtone. The sound was cheap and as stock as Radio Shack, easily recognized as that of Valeriana's pay-as-you-go phone. Cherry Pie spun a dancer's one-eighty from the door to her apartment, dropped her bag, and stretched her fingertips as if those delicate digits were equal to her ears in assessing the whereabouts of the runaway's phone.

The second trill was to her right, emanating from somewhere in the shamefully small kitchen. So cramped was the room, there wasn't even space to open the modern refrigerator door fully. Cherry sliced into the deco space, twirling in place before realizing that she was repeating herself. Plenty of times she'd carried in bags of groceries, cradling her phone between her shoulder and her ear, only to say goodbye and leave it resting facedown on the cereal shelf to stow the half-pints of Häagen-Dazs quickly before everything melted.

Sure enough, there was Valeriana's low-budget phone, facing screen-out, leaning against a big, double box of Honey Nut Cheerios. As it trilled a third time, Cherry could easily read the incoming phone number along with the location subhead:

(414)555-3298
Chenequa, WI

Staring at the number, Cherry briefly wondered if it held some kind of importance to Valeriana—or if it was merely a wrong number or some kind of junk call. But the real reason she was interested in finding the phone was the strange compulsion that without her phone, Valeriana had forgotten Cherry's number and had dialed her own in hopes her roomie would pick up.

"Hello?" Cherry answered, her voice a little extra smoky from a constant case of dry throat.

"Uh . . ." began the voice on the other end, high pitched yet distinctly male. "Hi. I'm looking for Karrie."

Because there was nothing at all in the voice for Cherry to recognize, nor reason for her to answer for some stranger named Karrie, she switched back into hurry mode and abruptly ended the call.

"Sorry. Wrong number," pitched Cherry, clicking off without another thought and making sure to leave the phone in plain view on the counter so Val couldn't miss it.

Cherry keyed the dead bolt and scurried down the stairs to the street and her car.

As it turned out, Andrew couldn't wait. That number passed to him by Lucky was supposed to remain undialed until he had returned to his hotel room. Then, in the privacy of his comfortable suite, he could have a moment to breathe, ease his heart rate, and carefully enter the ten digits. How many rings before she'd answer? Or might she see the caller ID and dismissively shunt her father off to voicemail? Still, Andrew would hear her voice at the other end, either live or recorded. One step closer to a family reunification.

Hallelujah.

Only that slip of paper with Karrie's phone number was burning a hole in his shirt pocket. How or why the hell could he wait until the damned hotel? The inside of his rental car was private enough.

Andrew *needed* to hear his daughter's voice. So, he pulled over at the first turnout he could find on Mulholland Drive, switched off the navigation program, fidgeted for the tiny slip of paper, then let his thumb tap out the correct sequence. The pounding in his chest was so great that he heard the percussion trapped between the phone and his ear.

Then he forgot to breathe.

Shouldering the rental car door open, he stepped out into the misty air, felt dizzy on his feet, and staggered to the left rear fender. How many rings had gone by? Two? Three? More, even?

Finally, a click and a voice answered.

"Hello?"

"Uh . . . Hi. I'm looking for Karrie?"

"Sorry. Wrong number."

And there, the conversation ended with whoever had answered clicking off as if the man at the other end were disposable.

"Not my Karrie," Andrew wheezed aloud to nobody but maybe the lizards and snakes in the canyon beyond. The voice he heard had a bit of husk to it. A smoker's voice. Or maybe the woman who had answered was just unlucky with how DNA had installed her vocal cords.

Not my Karrie.

Andrew found himself wadding the slip of paper into a tiny ball, which he flicked away with less regard than a finger full of snot. The anger in him welled and flushed to his skin. His muscles tensed. And without a shadow of forethought, he cocked his arm and hurled his mobile phone as far as he could, spiraling it across the road and deep into the canyon.

The San Fernando Valley stretched before him like a foggy sea of suburban sprawl. He imagined it was a frozen Wisconsin lake and the slightness of breeze smelled like a mix of ice and winter juniper.

Eventually, a calm came over him. His heart slowed. His breathing and heart rate returned to something that a trained medic might concur resembled normal.

"Daddy's here for you, honey," said Andrew to nobody but the air. "Daddy's here and I'll stay 'til I can bring you home."

25

Lucky had no illusions whatsoever that the phone number he had handed Andrew might be a dead-end for the daddy. All cell phones had caller ID. Young Karrie could easily be in the habit of declining to answer calls from unknown numbers. Or worse, IDs that come with area codes that might remind her of home sweet home. The child was, after all, a runaway. And there were always reasons why—all of which might have prevented Karrie from accepting the call from her father.

With the Crown Vic parked at a broken meter on Sepulveda, Lucky waited in the driver's seat a block south of a ten-story glass and steel high-rise with an aviation firm blocked in blue letters across the top facade. With a little patience and $500 cash, Lucky was moments from completing his street transaction for something other than pain pills. And it wasn't even illegal, though it sure as hell felt like it should be.

To access the call and cell tower records attached to that mobile phone number, Lucky would need to secure a warrant or court order, both requiring the signature of a Superior Court judge. Had Lucky not been between L.A. and Kern County sheriffs' gigs, it might have been a shade easier had there been a case number and a crime.

But thank Christ for the gift of technology. As a process server, Lucky had the occasion to use one of the hundreds of data brokers currently mining the personal information most digital consumers gave away for free—or, more accurately, without their own knowledge. Nearly all such companies worked on a mass scale, collating and selling their demographically packaged gold in volume chunks to everybody from major retail chains to ever-interested political parties. Currently, the private detective market hadn't proved scalable or showed enough promise of profit to anyone other than the occasional enterprising computer jockey who thought a few extra dollars might ease the pain of spending forty-plus hours a week as a cog in a sea of corporate cubicles.

Lucky's cog was named Emery.

Emery was maybe five-foot-two max, in her trademark black trench boots, and Lucky guessed her tech-savvy job didn't leave her with enough cash to feed her two addictions: tattoos and Molly, the crystal powder form of MDMA, a.k.a. the street drug ecstasy. Besides her weekend sojourns to any rave within driving distance of her electric vehicle, the twenty-five-year-old was on a mission to cover nearly every square inch of her alabaster skin with artistic ink and, by Lucky's calculation, was just about halfway to achieving her goal. His discovery came on a drunken night that landed somewhere between a weak moment and a mutual act of convenience. Emery and Lucky had agreed to meet up to exchange about $200 worth of personal data on a hard-to-find former hedge fund trader who had so far dodged a myriad of subpoenas. The after-work tiki bar where they conducted business was barely around the corner from Emery's Playa del Rey apartment. One funny umbrella'd drink had led to another and the unlikely pair found themselves between her sheets. Afterward, Lucky had joked that it was just like having real sex with the Sunday comics.

Emery had not only been amused by Lucky's review of their one-night stand but had posted the quote on a variety of her social media pages as something akin to an advertisement.

"Hey, I got a new one," said Emery, before her butt so much as landed in the passenger seat of Lucky's borrowed Crown Vic.

"Sure you wanna show me here?" half-joked Lucky.

"Not on or near any of my gold and treasure," laughed Emery, revealing teeth even whiter than her skin. "Right here."

Emery lifted her sweater to reveal some of the flesh that covered her rib cage. With a shellacked black fingernail, she circled what appeared like a cartoon cat with a Pinocchio-like red nose.

"You don't recognize her?" asked Emery off Lucky's puzzled look. "It's Krazy Kat."

"Right, yeah. So it is."

"You don't know Krazy Kat?"

"Nope."

"From the old Sunday comic strips?"

"Look. I'm older than you. But maybe I'm not that old."

"Well, I did it cuzza you and what you said."

"As long as you didn't do it *for* me."

"You were good, Mr. Lucky," winked Emery. "But not worth permanent ink."

Lucky feigned a look of insult while Emery pulled out a manila envelope she'd hidden between the top of her jeans and the small of her back.

"Your number wasn't attached to a smartphone so I couldn't get a lot of details," said Emery. "But it did geolocate. So, between that and the cell towers, I got patterns enough where I think you can at least intercept her."

"I'll take it," said Lucky. Emery was already pushing her way out the door when Lucky stopped her. "Hey. Dontcha wanna get paid?"

"She's a runaway, right?"

"Yeah."

"On me, then," said Emery. "Think I wanted to be that girl for maybe three years of my life. But I stuck it out and, hey, despite all my body art, my family is really dope about me now."

"Appreciate it. But a job's a job."

"Just lemme know how it all turns out." Emery shut the door with a thunk, twiddled her nails at Lucky, then turned tail back to her building and the cubicle that, by Lucky's account, she owned more than it owned her.

26

Hollywood. 1:41 p.m.

"What the hell am I supposed to do with this shit?" shouted Herm in a rare and honest moment. He waved a black-and-white headshot of a comely blonde actress and, had he not been so tall and intimidating, would have been barking directly into Cherry Pie's face.

"I know she's not who you asked for, but she's right outside the door," fought Cherry, wanting to reach for the doorknob that led away from that closet-sized hunk of white-walled audition space. Her friend Cameron, who had agreed to audition in place of her temporary roomie, Valeriana, was beyond the door.

"I specifically said you and the *other girl*," angered Herm. "Now, you're wasting my time with some—"

"Her name is Cam. And she's blonde and pretty and maybe your Audi people will like her—"

"You want me to meet her?" The question was more sarcastic than rhetorical, but Cherry didn't seem to read either.

"Yes. That's why I brought her."

With that, Herm practically shoved past Cherry as he reached for the knob and yanked the door open. Springing to her feet was a leggy bottle blonde with a Barbie tan and the body of a wannabe runway model in need of three more inches.

"Sorry to waste your time," spat Herm. "But you're wrong for the part." And before Cherry could so much as defend herself, Herm had already spun on her with an index finger inches from the perfect turned-up nose her immigrant mother had bought her for her sixteenth birthday. "And since she's wrong, that makes you wrong! Package deal, I said. You and the unicorn!"

"Unicorn?" quizzed Cherry, wondering if she had heard him right.

"I'm all done here," impressed Herm. "And so are you."

"Well, you don't have to get your panties in a bunch," the dancer defended. "It's just a fucking car commercial."

"Which you're not gonna be in," reminded Herm, as if there ever were a damned Audi spot that he had been hired to cast.

"You know what?" pissed Cherry. "I'm gonna report your shit to SAG."

"Whatever," said Herm, jonesing for a drink as much as he ever could recall since getting sober. Let her call the Screen Actors Guild and complain until she got it out of her system. He wasn't registered as a legitimate casting agent. Herm was sure his name was nowhere in their database because his kind of placement work was off their radar. And they were damned glad for it.

"C'mon, Cam." Cherry grabbed her friend's arm and guided her toward the exit.

"Really sorry," said the blonde, uncertain as to whom she was or should be apologizing. Herm or Cherry?

The casting man watched the pair clip-clop in their stacked heels all the way to the stairwell, vanishing from sight but hardly from Herm's recent memory. He'd be sure to hold on to the anger for hours. Probably until he had escaped the Basin for the deep

Valley and his home-sweet-fixer-home and that loving caress of brewed hops wafting on the air.

But first . . .

Herm latched the door to his rented audition space and retreated to a rear stairwell that fed all the way down to the turnkey complex's basement business office. The manager, a chain-smoking matron who seemed never to age nor gain or lose a single one of her two-hundred-plus pounds of ghetto charm, appeared to know each of her customers by the sound of their descent.

"How ya, Herm?" asked Queenie without looking up from her computer screen.

"Looking for one of your fuck-tard renters."

"I got lots," said Queenie. "Which one you lookin' for?"

"Dude with the end block."

"First floor or your floor?"

"My floor."

"That'd be Mr. Gabriel Roth."

"That's him."

"Always nice to me," defended Queenie. "What you want him for?"

"Personal."

"Now, Herm." Queenie's voice lowered to a mannish growl. She peered up over her rhinestone readers and pursed her lips as if she had tasted something sour. "You know I don't do with nothin' personal."

"Seen him 'round?"

"Not yet today. But he comes and goes when he comes and goes, you know?"

"You're full of information."

"Way it is. He's all artist, that boy."

"Got his number?"

"For personal? Or for somethin' havin' to do with workin' outta here?"

"Business, babe. Just don't wanna have you deal with it."

"Sexy when you lie," teased the marm, punching up Gabe's contact number on her computer screen. She highlighted the digits and turned the screen to face her visitor. "If he calls me to complain, you didn't get the number from me."

"Guarantee he won't," promised Herm, squeezing out a closed-mouth smile that could have leaked saliva at the corners. He quickly copied the number onto his own phone, drummed his knuckles across Queenie's desk, then disappeared up the stairs in three graceful strides.

"You still got it, Herm!" she barked after him.

"Uh huh," was all he echoed back to her before his footfalls faded into nothing.

27

Van Nuys. 4:07 p.m.

As a strip club, the Rabbit Pole was relatively new to the competition for San Fernando Valley men in search of naked women and weak, overpriced liquor to quench their undernourished souls. Sandwiched between a plumbing distributor and a construction equipment rental company sporting a lot stacked with earth movers, cranes, and cherry pickers, the royal blue joint looked like a large, single box.

In neon script that never dimmed read the club's simple credo:

All Nude Girls All the Time
From 11 a.m. to Midnite

The dancers at the club worked in three shifts: the Early Riser, a.k.a. the first shift of the day, grinding it out for the unemployed, the disabled, and men who wanted to put a wrap on their horny minds by the end of lunch hour; the second shift, named by the employees as Happy Ending Hour, ran from four in the afternoon to eight in the evening, primarily attracting the kind of wolf who desired a buffer between the job and whatever he called home; the final work block of the day, from eight to closing, was appropriately called Last Dance.

For Cherry Pie, Last Dance was her most favored shift. It allowed all day to audition, afternoons to attend either acting or dance classes, and early evenings to workout a few extra bucks as a party dancer. Her late nights were left either for partying or stripping for big tips at the Rabbit Pole. And though she wasn't the least bit ashamed of her side gig as a fantasy sex puppet, she figured the odds of her not being recognized increased with the lateness of the day when the business professionals waned in favor of bachelor parties, couples in search of stimulation, and single men fantasizing about a date with a beautiful stripper.

And the girls of the Rabbit Pole, they were so very beautiful. It served as a reminder to Cherry Pie that in a town where shallow was an art, beauty came fast and damned cheap.

"Well, look who's working the Happy Ending Hour," blurted a dancer Cherry knew only as Yolo. Short, she figured, for Yolanda.

"Yeah," acknowledged Cherry, finding an empty stool at the dressing room mirror. "I heard a buncha Persian dudes were comin' in, looking for a party."

"No shit?" asked Yolo. "You sayin' they gonna bring the Benjamins?"

Cherry only smiled and got down to her makeup kit. The Persian line was total bullshit. But it was sure as hell easier to sell than the truth. Which was that she was pissed as hell after her run-in with Herm the Casting Man. She had first tried to laugh it off with an extra sugary caramel Frappuccino. Then she had tried to sweat off the lingering angst with a double dose of dance classes. Yet Cherry still couldn't shake the lousy taste that Herm had left in her mouth. With that, she recalled what so many performing coaches had taught her. Use the painful emotion. Savor it and profit from it. Fine, she thought. If there was a spot available, she'd channel it from the pole. She would set her high beams on a man who closest resembled the casting asshole and bleed every last greenback from him. She would even throw in a lap dance or two if it separated the man from his money any faster.

The owner of the Rabbit Pole, a lanky Vietnamese entrepreneur whom all the dancers affectionately called General Ho, was happy to fit Cherry into the lineup whenever she was willing. She was a cash machine and Cherry knew it. Her sass alone could whip a party of men into a rain-making frenzy.

"Your body bangin' today," grinned General Ho. "Not so tired like when you work Last Dance."

"I always look good for you," defended Cherry. "That's 'cause I'm in my fucking prime."

Prime was an understatement. In show business, where a female performer's shelf life is generally shorter than the average auto lease, Cherry was more than aware that the clock was tick-tick-ticking.

Lookin' real good, Miss Elk Grove.

Cherry examined herself while unlatching the locks on her makeup kit, her deceased father's old fishing tackle box. She had begun using it during her stellar three-year run as the lead in every one of her high school and community theater performances. The local looker who came in third place in Elk Grove High's valedictorian chase and was unanimously voted most likely to become a movie star, had forsaken her mother's wishes for a Catholic college and an MRS degree in exchange for a chance at Hollywood glory. It had been four years since she had last spoken to her Polish-born mom, having long since vowed not to return until her dreams had been fulfilled and there was a bank account with her birth name on it, full of cash, so she could prove she was right about her future all along.

Marcjeri Piechowiak.

From as early as she could recall, all the kids had called her Cherry instead of the phonetic *Mar-chair-ee* that was her given name. And by junior high, the last name was a natural, shortened to *Pie* by anybody with a scintilla of imagination. The name Cherry Pie had stuck to her like a cattle brand. Add to that the easily downloadable tune by the eighties hair-metal band Warrant and the black-haired Marcjeri couldn't walk down a high school corridor without someone singing—or even thinking the lyrics.

By the time Miss Cherry had rejected higher education in lieu of a career in the limelight, she'd made the lascivious moniker her own, practically forgetting how to spell her own christened name when it came to filling out applications for credit cards and driver's licenses, and most importantly, income tax forms.

Perhaps such is why she liked most of her paid gigs, including that at the Rabbit Pole. Both General Ho and the customers paid in cash. A nightly tax-free haul of singles, fives, tens, and every so often, a few Andrew Jacksons. But my oh my, did those low-denomination bills add up.

General Ho had grand boyhood memories of the strip bars of pre-communist Saigon. He had so loved the atmosphere of cigarette smoke and colored lights that he wanted to replicate the same vibe in tobacco-free California. The effect was achieved with a fog machine that atomized a mixture of water and nontoxic glycol into a controllable pea soup. So, when the computer-controlled spotlights swept the room, each displayed a distinct colored beam.

Cherry's favorite part was when a new dancer entered the stage—be it herself or any other soon-to-be-naked hottie. The DJ would pump the mic and growl a fictitious name like Desiree or Brianna, the music would queue, then the lights would automatically spin and rotate with each beam suddenly concentrating on the tinsel curtain. That's when the designated dancer would burst into view with a practiced strut.

And the money game would be on.

"Big tipper in the house!" a passing pole girl announced, sounding disappointed that her time was up on one of the pair of satellite platforms that flanked the main stage.

"Now check it, guys and girls!" announced the DJ. "Coming up on the Star Stage, get out those bills for Miss Cherrrrrrrrrry Piiiiiiiieeee!"

That's me, she said to herself, waiting for her song to play. She really liked to change up her music, often to the annoyance of whichever DJ was spinning that day. The new music files would be on a flash drive that she'd palm over to the DJ before she'd head backstage to change into a G-string and makeup. But that always assumed that the man at the turntable was sober enough to put the correct name, face, and flash drive together.

Which isn't precisely what went wrong. Though it could be described as going sideways.

Instead of the techno beat startup of her expected music, she was struck by the power chord start of that mother-effing Warrant song—the one that bore Cherry's name—the cliched stripperific tune she had always refused to dance to.

"Fuck me again," cursed Cherry from behind the curtain. She more than half wanted to send a Lucite heel flying through the tinsel and into the crowd. And that was just out of spite. But that would have just turned her mood into something so sour she might not be able to retrieve herself. Her better angel wanted to dance. *Needed* to dance. So, with that, she dug the toe of her shoe into the floorboard, let it sync up to the Cro-Magnon beat of eighties hair metal, and let her splayed fingers and nails split the curtain.

And find that big tipper.

If there was applause, Cherry didn't hear it. That's because Cherry never did. Her ears, like the rest of her body, were clued in only to the music while her eyes, on the other hand, were all about making connections with whatever man, woman, or beast might be holding the thickest stack of cash.

But the damned smoke machine!

The air was so dense she might have choked. All because the fogger sometimes infused the air with such an overdose of dramatic mist that it was hard for a dancer to read men's expressions beyond the first row, let alone any appreciative rises in their trousers.

Yet Cherry soldiered on. She sashayed and spun and flexed and contorted herself in the usual man-appealing ways, but always with her specialized brand of sass. Her secret sauce, she would call it. To hell if the air was too dense to eyeball the customers. She'd make *them* see *her*. And the dollars would flow even before she had unhooked a solitary Velcro fastener. Soon, she would ease closer to the strip-lighted edge of the stage. There, maybe she would let a gentle-appearing fellow or two touch the elastic just below her hipbone, inserting a folded dollar like chum for the sharks. After which, she would accept further cash with a personal wink, a flash of teeth, and the pinch of her fingertips, slipping each bill into her G-string until it better resembled a grass skirt with a buzz cut.

A flash of green caught her eye. Just beyond the floodlights. A bill handed from a broad-shouldered man in a bomber jacket to a brood of girls, their butt cheeks lined up like muffins in a tin. More bills were shown and, one by one, the nearly naked dancers skittered away. Singles and fives weren't known to draw any kind of crowd. At least not at the Rabbit Pole. The Big Tipper was doling out no less than fifty-dollar bills like candy.

Eye contact, honey. Make the man see you.

With her gaze fixed on the shadowy figure, she snaked herself to the stage edge, unfolded her body until it was fully upright, then without a musical phrase, found a place within the song to motivate a very un-stripper-like move.

A series of chaînés.

Using the Big Tipper as her reference spot, Cherry's continuous half turns on one foot, generated by a synchronization of arms and hips, drew a spontaneous burst of applause from the customers. Never mind the scowls and jealous looks that classy spin earned from her fellow dancers. The capitalist in Cherry was all about the attention she could draw from a man and his billfold.

At the moment her spin ended, as well as the ridiculous song, the tuning fork in Cherry rang like a cash machine as the Big Tipper turned his attention to her, the girl on the Star Stage. As he approached, his features came more into focus with each progressing step. His eyes seemed business-like. Direct. Nothing close to what she would call aroused. Sure, he was a man in a strip bar with a thick roll of cash he wasn't afraid of revealing to all. If he wasn't trolling for a thrill, a lap dance, or even a blowjob in the next-door parking lot, then why the hell make such a tipping show?

Still, the man eased nearer, boldly peeling off a hundred-dollar bill from his stack. Bait. Her instincts screamed. But for what?

Cherry twirled closer, boldly striking a dominating pose to tell that one high-tipping customer that, for this one moment, he belonged to her. This, her intuition told her, was precisely what this man desperately needed. To be led by the nose and into her pocketbook. All the while, she did her best to avoid looking at the actual currency pinched between his thumb and forefinger. It was about his eyes. The connection. She wanted to make him want her. Need her. Have no other option but to invite her into the VIP room for a private dance and hand all his money over to her.

But it was the actual money that got in the way. Blocking his eyes from making contact with hers. As if he didn't want to be looked upon. As if he needed her to see what he was offering. See precisely what he reckoned she was worth. A deal breaker for Miss Cherry. She was prepared to dance away from him—set her sights on another rube—when over the next indistinguishable tune she thought she heard a question.

"Have you seen her?"

Seen who? Cherry immediately asked herself.

"Look at the picture."

Of Benjamin Franklin? Cherry quizzed. Who hadn't seen a hundred-dollar bill before? Did he assume she was that desperate?

"The photograph," pressed the Big Tipper. "Do you know her?"

Somehow, she'd missed it. Paper-clipped to the creaseless, minty-green hundred-dollar bill was a small high school photo of a pretty strawberry-blonde with freckles and an innocent smile.

Oh, hell, Cherry said to herself. *That's Valeriana.*

The contract between Lucky and Andrew Kaarlsen could have been written on a cocktail napkin. In simple, hand-printed letters it would have read that Andrew had agreed to stay in the Crown Vic or else Lucky would break all his fingers before quitting on him, thus leaving his skinny Midwestern ass to fend for itself.

As the client, Andrew had every right to be shown the details Lucky had gleaned from tattooed Emery, the pint-sized South Bay data broker. The right to ride along while Lucky pursued leads had already been negotiated and, after the fiasco in Carson, renegotiated. The staying-in-the-car-when-Lucky-said-stay-in-the-car part of the agreement had lastly been bargained down to a deal breaker.

Using the tower and other wireless connection info, a map of the mystery cell phone number's life emerged. The initial clues Lucky was looking for were patterns. Locations where the phone was tracked multiple times could show him where Karrie might yet return. Hopefully, a workplace or a residence. For the two months of data provided, Karrie rarely appeared to land in the same spot more than twice. The pattern revealed a teen that was either sleeping on couches or with random partners, frequenting more 7-Elevens than shopping malls, using any old coffee house as her Wi-Fi hotspot, and adept at utilizing both city buses and subways. Most recently she had probably found a three-night bunking situation at an apartment in Silver Lake. For some detectives, X would have marked the spot right then and there. All that would be required was a twenty-four-hour surveillance stand and the patience to wait for the fifteen-year-old to show up.

But there was another waypoint on the map.

A onetime ping in the Valley had dropped a Google Maps pin onto the address of a strip club called the Rabbit Pole. It was a curious location for a fifteen-year-old girl. But not necessarily for a broke runaway who had been making cash as a party dancer. The club, fearing a nightmarish and embarrassing shutdown were they to get caught employing someone so grossly underage, would have demanded no less than a birth certificate before allowing Karrie to strip. Yet the cell tower records showed she had been at the club for two to three hours. It was Lucky's hope that Karrie would have at least stood out and maybe been introduced by somebody.

"I say we stake out the apartment," Andrew had strongly suggested.

"Probably will," Lucky had replied. "But somethin' tells me we might learn what your little girl was into if we run this down first." Lucky's index finger was on the Rabbit Pole's address.

Andrew didn't put up much of a fight. Lucky couldn't tell if it was because he was trying to behave or if he was, as the runaway's father, becoming morbidly curious about the dark side his daughter had begun to present.

"Might need to stop by a bank," Lucky had suggested.

"Why?"

"Cash is king in those kinds of places. And tens and twenties don't impress if you want more than a sniff."

After a bank stop where Andrew was able to withdraw $5,000 in hundreds on his American Express, Lucky pointed the Crown Vic north, navigating deep into the chilled but newly sunny San Fernando Valley until they arrived at the Rabbit Pole.

It was just after 4:00 p.m.

"You're staying in the car," reminded Lucky.

"I know," snapped Andrew. "Our agreement."

"Not just that," explained Lucky. "Like, there's a two percent chance your little girl got herself some counterfeit papers quality enough to fool the owners."

"You're saying I might be risking seeing my baby girl giving some hairy biker a G.D. lap dance?"

"Sayin' some shit you can't unsee," advised Lucky.

The last line was more bull than actual supposition. What Lucky needed was for the client to stay in the car, twiddle his thumbs, spin, anything but start his own investigation inside a strip club. Instead of cops roughing him over, there were sure to be a few oversized men of Samoan or African heritage whose primary function was to unceremoniously, and even injuriously, expel unwanted customers if they so much as appeared to be harassing one of the dancers.

Though Lucky removed his Ray-Bans as he entered the club, he was still fighting the deep blackness as his eyes adjusted from the daylight. He was quick to show the roll of cash as he peeled off enough for the cover charge. Next he followed a hostess in a bikini, heels, and fishnets through a pair of spring-loaded double doors that led into the main room. It was artificially smoky, streaked with enough moving and pulsating light to repel most epileptics, and with music pounding louder than human comfort.

"'Scuse me," Lucky shouted over the volume. He touched the hostess's shoulder to get her to turn and face him. "I'm looking for someone."

As the hostess turned, she saw Lucky holding that high school photo of Karrie paper-clipped alongside a hundred-dollar bill.

"Have you seen this girl?" asked Lucky.

"Yo," barked a bouncer at Lucky's ear. "No touching the ladies, okay?"

Lucky swiveled to find exactly what he expected. A dark, broad-faced black man whose posture was a strong dose of don't-screw-with-me business.

"I'm looking for this girl," said Lucky to the beefy bouncer. "You seen her? Then there's a lot more of these."

Lucky flicked the hundred-dollar bill.

The bouncer clicked on a pen-sized flashlight and lit up the tiny photo of Karrie.

"Too young to work here," replied the bouncer.

"You're legit," agreed Lucky. "She didn't have to dance. But she was here."

"Nope," said the bouncer. "Now, you here to see some titties or you gonna keep asking folks about that piece of jailbait?"

"How 'bout I do both?" Lucky flashed three more hundred-dollar bills, folded them over his thumb, then stuffed them in the bouncer's breast pocket.

"Okay," nodded the bouncer. "But no more touchin' the girls."

With permission temporarily granted, Lucky nodded and eased deeper into the room. He would cruise the bartenders soon enough. First, he wanted to tip his way through the half-naked dancers and cocktail waitresses. Working women, he reasoned to himself, were more apt to talk, give up information, and be sympathetic to the plight of a runaway teen.

Despite the offer of money and more-where-that-came-from,

one beautiful dancer after another—hardened or otherwise—gave the photo a thoughtful turn or instantly shook her head. Nobody appeared to recognize Karrie Kaarlsen. Nor did a single woman comment on the girl's age. It was as if they understood migration as a natural phenomenon. That thousands of beautiful young women, well-adjusted and otherwise, seem to find their way to Los Angeles every year. It was like there was a shipment that landed every hour.

Lucky had tipped the bouncer well. Yet he knew that guaranteed little more than leeway. How long before the manager or owner saw him tipping women for info instead of permission to gawk at their sexual splendors? A bar that doubled as a secondary runway for dancers stretched to the left. To Lucky's right side was the elevated main stage, the source of the smoke and that dazzle of swirling lights. There he clocked a sculpted dancer with a punky purple hairdo. A stunning figure. And just magnetic enough to steer Lucky away from the bar and into her tractor beams.

That's right, Luck. She's lookin' at you.

It was as if the horny men at those tables cluttering the foot of the stage were being totally ignored by her. Or perhaps it was just that the thin smiles of George Washington, which the men waved like schoolboys hoping to be called on by the hot teacher, didn't quite stack up against the bodacious Benjamin Franklins that Lucky was promising.

It was all unsaid. But there was no doubt the stripper was beckoning Lucky to come closer. And as he neared the footlights, he raised that hundred-dollar bill with the affixed high school photo. The purple-haired vixen put her shoulders back, planted a toe, and, as if choreographed, spun a slow-motion three-sixty that delivered her to the edge of the main stage.

This was when the man in Lucky wanted to lower his eyes. If only for a millisecond. Her body was, after all, a flawless specimen of the feminine form. Naked. With curves and skin that usually existed only in men's most lusty imaginations.

Yet it was about the eyes. Critically so. And as Lucky fixed on hers, he carefully tracked her pupils as they ever-so-slightly swerved the slightest of degrees to the right, landing on that wallet-sized photo of smiling Karrie. Next came an oh-so-telling flutter of false eyelashes. The corners of the dancer's smiling mouth flattened as her lips unconsciously pressed tightly together. With that she curved her back and snapped her head forward so the shag of her hair covered her face as she spun away to the other side of the stage.

If there had been a brief spell between the man and the woman, the dancer had somehow lost interest and broken it off like snapping a stick of uncooked spaghetti in her teeth.

<h1 style="text-align:center">28</h1>

"She's our girl."

"What do you mean by that?" asked Andrew.

"She's the one," said Lucky. He settled back into the Crown Vic and pulled the lever under the driver's seat that released the lock. The seat slid fully backward for maximum legroom.

"Who's the one?" insisted Andrew, lost and anxious after having to sit and wait while Lucky waved hundred-dollar bills around the strip club.

"Stripper."

"What about a stripper?"

"Knows your girl." Lucky found the reclining crank and increased the seat back's angle.

"Wait. Someone in there knows my Karrie?"

"I told you," said Lucky, closing his eyes. "Stripper. She's the one."

"Which one? What'd she say?"

"Didn't say anything." Lucky stretched his right arm into the back seat and retrieved a sweat-stained Dodgers cap to shade his eyes from the streetlights and neon spilling from the club.

"So, how do you know?" pressed Andrew.

"I just know, okay?" said Lucky, irritated and not really caring to share the kind of trade tricks and neurologic tells he had learned as a detective. His back ached like hell and he didn't want to swallow another Percocet for that calendar day. "Girl gets off at eight. I'll talk to her after. Until then, I'm gonna nap."

"So, you know she knows because of a hunch?"

"Experience."

"Experience as a cop?"

"Sure. Why not?"

"You know, as the client, I think I have a right to ask—"

"And I have the right to a nap. Headache bordering on migraine."

"So, it was a hunch?" repeated Andrew. "We're staying here because of a hunch?"

"We're staying here because I got the car keys." Lucky jangled the set as a reminder, then returned them to his pocket.

"I didn't hire you because you had hunches," insisted Andrew. "I hired you because Connie said you could find my daughter."

"Getting closer every minute."

"So, let's get even closer by going back inside and talking to this stripper!"

"Said her shift ends at eight."

"And we're all about respecting a stripper's work hours."

"Respecting the bouncer who let me chum the club with all those hundies you set me up with. We struck pay dirt with the stripper. Now we wait."

"Frickin' frickenstein!"

"You wanna huff and puff when I'm not tryin' to nap?"

"This whole situation is . . . torture."

"At last, we agree on *something*."

Lucky hoped he had snapped a lid on the subject. He craved quiet and sleep. With that baseball cap over his face, he relaxed his shoulders into the seat and yearned for silence. It brought him immediately back to his days as a training officer out of Lennox. Half as a test, the other half out of necessity, he would park across the street from a supermarket to catch a fifteen-minute on-duty cat nap. During which he would demand his trainee keep his mouth shut while keeping a keen count of who exited and entered the grocery chain. Afterward, there'd be a pop quiz on the rookie's powers of observation. How many customers entered and exited, their sex, ages, clothing, and distinguishing behaviors. Lucky would claim he'd check the trainee's answers against the radio car's dash cam video later. But he never did. Or had to. The exercise had already served its dual purpose.

As Lucky drifted off, he tried to disregard Andrew's restless movements—his shifting in the passenger seat, sighing as he tried to control his anxiety, the rustling of his windbreaker, even the mild beeping of a game he played on his cell phone to pass the time. After some time, Lucky heard the car door open and felt a sudden change of air pressure in the cabin, the shocks of the Crown Vic readjusting for the change of weight, and the door clunking to a distinct close.

Just as it always had, the relief of being alone warmed him. For as long as Lucky could remember, the sound of a door closing on him was often a moment of welcome. He quickly drifted off.

A sharp twist of acute pain woke Lucky. At least, that's how he recalled it. A trigger point two inches below his shoulder blades and just to the right of his spine had erupted into a knife tip that was slightly relieved with a simple posture adjustment.

And then Lucky smelled the chicken.

Popeye's Louisiana fried chicken, to be exact. The distinctive aroma filled the space. Lucky's nose curled and his eyes adjusted to the dark.

"That drool on your mouth," said Andrew, "from dreaming of strippers or dreaming of dinner?"

"You went out for chicken?" Lucky croaked.

"I was hungry," said Andrew, sinking his teeth into the skin of a chicken breast. "C'mon. Got dinner for two."

"Not a fan."

"A cop that doesn't eat junk food?" mused Andrew. "You disappoint."

The alarm on Lucky's phone chirped. 7:55 p.m. As he came to, calculating that he had five minutes until his target stripper's shift ended, he spotted her already crossing the far side of the parking lot. Between the cars, up against an ivy-covered cinder-block wall, she walked at an athletic pace, a long raincoat, and a woolly cap pulled down low over her purple hair.

His hand switched on the ignition and started the Crown Vic. He kept the headlights extinguished, dropped the auto into gear, and traversed left at an angle that might best intercept her.

"What where?" asked Andrew. "We going now?"

Lucky gestured with his chin, keeping his eyes split between the girl and the front end of the Crown Vic.

"Can't see what you're looking at," said Andrew.

Neither could Lucky. His stripper must have already ducked into her vehicle. Lucky tripped the headlights and turned a hard right toward the back row of the lot. He was looking for a dome light, brake lights, or the telltale white flare of backup lights. Any indication that she might be pulling out of her parking space. Lucky swung another ninety-degree right, his own headlights sweeping and landing on the rear end of a VW Jetta that had just geared into reverse. He sped up. Brake lights flared. The driver of the Jetta waited for the Crown Vic to roll by.

Only the Crown Vic slowed and stopped directly behind the vehicle, effectively blocking the German car from backing out of its space.

"Stay in the car," reminded Lucky. "And hope she doesn't have a gun."

"A gun?" asked Andrew with a burst of surprise.

Lucky popped his door open, allowing the dome light to ignite and possibly reveal some of his features to the girl in the Jetta. He held up both his hands, open and without malice, for her to see in the rearview mirror. Then with a pen flashlight he blazed a beam onto that high school wallet photo of Karrie Kaarlsen, making certain the driver of the car might clearly see his intentions in her side mirror.

"YOU KNOW HER," Lucky shouted. "I NEED TO TALK TO YOU, PLEASE."

He could see her in the mirror's reflection, a dark shadow in a wool cap, motionless. He could tell her foot was firmly on the brakes because of the red flare from the lights.

"C'MON. I KNOW YOU KNOW THIS GIRL," Lucky tried to confirm.

The girl cracked her window open to barely an inch and lifted her lips so he could hear her.

"CALLING 911 RIGHT NOW!" she warned.

"Good idea," said Lucky. "Then you can explain to them what you were doing bringing a fifteen-year-old runaway to a strip club."

Of course, Lucky wasn't certain at all about the assertion. It was a classic bluff. But how the girl played it would answer volumes.

"Or you can give me five minutes and just talk," urged Lucky.

"You're not a cop?"

"Not today." Lucky eased between the Jetta and the car parked next to it, then, as much as it hurt, bent a bit at the waist. "Can you see through your rearview mirror? If you haven't, look . . . Now, see the other guy in the car? Tell me you can see him."

"What about him?" asked Cherry.

"That's Karrie's father."

"Who's Karrie?"

"The girl in the picture."

"You're not gonna hurt me?"

"Just wanna talk about the girl."

Lucky straightened and retreated a non-threatening yard. Took a deep breath. Then was glad to see the Jetta's door crack open and, behind it, the dancer he had met almost two hours earlier. She was tinier than he expected. Without the stage and a pair of spiked pumps, she was barely five feet.

"Valeriana," said Cherry.

"Is that your name?" asked Lucky.

"No. The girl in the picture," she said. "Told me her name was Valeriana."

Cherry shifted in place, peering past Lucky's thick frame at the second man in the Crown Vic.

"That really her dad?" asked Cherry.

"All the way from Wisconsin."

29

Herm needed a girl he could sell. Not just any girl. What he called a Suzy Q kind of girl. American or Canadian. White and assumed to be built from pure apple pie. Classic good looks. From cute to pretty to downright beauteous. A tight body that was already in bloom. Optimal age, fifteen to sixteen. A very simple and profitable recipe. For that, there were always buyers willing to fork over up to fifteen grand in cash.

And in Los Angeles, Suzy Q's grew like leaves on trees.

Without such a girl, though, Herm would soon cease to manage his almost modest lifestyle. After all, he did keep two homes in pricey Los Angeles. The rent-controlled apartment in West Hollywood and his Valley home improvement project. Without a payable Suzy Q, his healthy construction habit would surely stall. This was his precise thinking when, an hour prior, he had stood smack in the middle of the crown molding section in one of the two Home Depots within three miles of his Panorama City address. He paused over his decision to salve his frustration with a little DIY therapy and then left a cart half stuffed with copper plumbing supplies in the middle of the store.

The trek to the home improvement store had begun as a distraction to get his brain off of that young photographer known as Gabriel. After succeeding in acquiring a cell phone number, Herm had called, heard the man's voicemail, and left a neighborly, work-friendly message with his callback digits.

That was hours ago.

And like a spider bite that turns to a nagging itch, the usual distractions were no longer helping Herm shake the urge to redial and redial again until he received a reaction.

My unicorn, he'd begun to say to himself, switching from *the* to the possessive *my*.

Now, Cherry Pie. Were she still fifteen years old, she would have been a ripe Suzy Q. That's assuming there was an appealing hair color under all that purple.

Forget about unicorns, Herm.

Easier said than done. That's because unicorns were just that. Unicorns. Rare. Exceptions to the beauty rule. Some might describe it as having to do with a girl's eyes. Herm had long ago refrained from trying to put an explanation on the unexplainable. Unicorns were unicorns, and that was just that. Measurable only in what the flesh market would pony up. And those numbers could sometimes crack the low six figures if his Triad connection could identify the right Asian buyer.

Forget her, Herm. And start the fuck over.

Start over. That meant acquiring a new target. Herm first wondered if he had the patience to hunt and gather via his most recent scam—the casting call. And the answer came in loud and clear from the planning resources of his brain. A decided no. Herm would backtrack to a more time-efficient plan with fewer moving parts. Sure, there was a bit more exposure. But Herm was a practiced professional. In his career, he had netted countless teenage girls. And in L.A., they were such low-hanging fruit that all a hunter-gatherer needed to do was reach out, grab hold, and snap one right off the ol' Suzy Q tree.

As Herm saw it, the illegal nightclub scene was like the biggest floating craps game in human history. Venues would open and close in a matter of weeks, only to reappear under different names the next weekend. Most importantly, the location would be changed, making it difficult for under-manned and overtaxed police departments to keep track, let alone move in and shut down the nightly extravaganzas of music, dance, drink, and illicit drugs.

Enter the world of social media and it was as if a turbocharger had been applied. Not until the actual moment the venue opened for a one-night-only blowout would the address be revealed to the teeming throngs of teens ravenous to escape the confines of their nuclear families and party until dawn.

As much as Herm understood the bones of the illegal club scene, he wasn't at all clued into the digital side of it all. Thus, he was out of the loop and didn't know the when and where of the operations. No matter, he wisely reasoned. Temporary clubs still demanded build-outs. Lights and sound and cases upon cases of liquor, which required loading into a particular location. He correctly figured that all he needed to do was troll the warehouses on the side streets east of downtown in search of after-hours activity that matched the profile. Once he had marked the spot, he could retire for eight hours, returning at 3:00 or 4:00 a.m. to prowl for a drugged or drunken straggler, lost from the herd and in dire need of assistance.

And it would be Uncle Herm to the rescue.

It surprised the teen-snatching veteran how quickly he happened upon a club in the process of setting up for the evening. The giveaway was the Ryder rent-a-truck backed up to a large warehouse edged by the rail yard. Most commercial trucks weren't normally operated by drivers working rigs with a big, red "RENT ME" emblazoned on the side. Pretending to be a curious security supervisor, Herm learned the rolling venue was known amongst the underground scene as House of Hideous Blue.

Helluva name, he thought. No IDs required, twenty-dollar cover, and miles of ten-dollar Red Bull and vodka cocktails. An ATM on wheels. Nice business. The more Herm thought about the prospects the roving club might bring him, the less he thought of that strawberry-blonde roommate of . . . what's her name? Oh, yeah. Cherry Pie, he finally remembered. Lousy handle. As he surveyed the territory, he found plenty of places to lie in wait, with both easy ingress and egress. Who knows? He might even stumble upon a gem to make him forget Miss Strawberry-Blonde.

The last thing Herm expected was for Gabriel finally to call him back. But just as he was sitting down to a meal consisting of an old favorite—fried eggs, bacon, and grilled sourdough bread at downtown's Original Pantry Café—he recognized the number he had copied off of Queenie's computer screen.

"This is Herm," he answered, pressing his phone to his ear while inserting his index finger in the opposite ear canal, trying like hell to drown out the sound of the restaurant.

"This is Gabe Roth," said the voice. "You called me?"

"I did, yes," answered Herm, trying not to let the surprise to his nervous system play as surprise in his voice. "Thanks for calling back."

"What can I do for you?" asked Gabe.

"Think I have something of yours," said Herm. "Slipped under my door but it had your name on it."

"Really? Don't have a clue what it could be."

"Neither do I," continued Herm. "But it's big and flat and says 'rush' on it."

"Rush?"

"Don't have it in front of me. But I think it was an ad agency envelope," lied Herm. "Recognized the logo."

"Haven't the faintest, but . . ."

"Thought of slipping it under your door but I didn't want to damage it any further."

"It's damaged?"

"Not so bad, I guess."

"You gonna be over there tomorrow?"

"I'm not sure," said Herm, truthful this time. It would depend entirely on his luck later that night.

"How about tonight?" said Gabe. "If it's not too far, I could come to you."

"Don't think it could wait?"

"Might be about a gig," admitted Gabe. "And when they're few and far between, well, you know what that's like."

"Don't I know it," said Herm, his plans already shifting beneath him. "We could meet up at the building?"

"The Casting Place?"

"Not far for me," said Herm. "On my way home, in fact."

"Meet you there in when? You name it."

"What time is it?" asked Herm to himself. Though he didn't need an answer. He had hours before he could begin throwing his net. And meeting up with Gabe was still the priority. If Cherry Pie didn't have a bead on his unicorn, Gabe just might. All Herm would need was a phone number, and he'd be that much closer.

"How about an hour?" asked Gabe.

"Works for me," said Herm.

"Very grateful," said Gabe. "Appreciate this, Herm. I'm gonna owe you."

Owe me? Damn right, you owe me.

"See you in an hour," finished Herm, clicking off with perfect timing. His meal was being served on heavy white restaurant ware. The fried eggs were still sizzling next to four flat strips of crispy bacon.

"Well, all right," said Herm to himself, quelling the excitement within. "Well, all right, indeed."

30

Studio City.

Negotiating the drive back to Hollywood was awkward at best. Thirty minutes earlier, back in the Rabbit Pole parking lot, Andrew was required to remain anchored in the Crown Vic while Lucky continued to ease Cherry Pie's concerns that neither man was a pervert or a threat. That it was for Karrie's own good that Cherry cooperate with the reunification of father and daughter.

"I seriously didn't know she was fifteen," Cherry confessed while navigating her VW Jetta over the winding blacktop that was Laurel Canyon Boulevard. "I mean, maybe not legal and not quite eighteen. But close to, like, seventeen, you know?"

"I get it," said Lucky from the cramped passenger seat. He checked the side-view mirror to make certain Andrew was still in tow, following in the Crown Vic.

"Val's dad's a flippin' tailgater," observed Cherry.

"Karrie's dad," corrected Lucky. "Just so we don't confuse things. And, yeah. He's kinda close."

They were on the downhill side of the canyon that connects Hollywood with the Valley. The destination? Dead reckoning for that casting location where Cherry had unknowingly handed off her care of Karrie to some thirty-ish photographer guy she thought was named Gabe. The light that night had been sketchy. At the distance from where Cherry had been standing under that sidewalk-busting pepper tree, she couldn't shape more of a description of the man beyond Caucasian and maybe bearded.

The snaking road was slick with rain and the muddy leftovers from recent rockslides. The last thing Lucky's aching back needed was to be in a rear-end accident with the heavy Crown Vic at the giving end. He considered having Cherry pull over so he could give Andrew a warning. But because they were merely ten minutes away from the destination, he let it go.

"Kinda feel for him," said Cherry.

"Feel for who?" asked Lucky.

"Val's . . ." began Cherry, before correcting herself. "I mean, the dad . . . Way my mom tells it, my pops wouldn't have crossed the room to check my temperature."

"Maybe we're related," Lucky deadpanned.

"Seriously. He's come all the way from Minnesota—"

"Wisconsin," corrected Lucky. "Not that it matters. Minnesota. Wherever. Still colder than shit there."

"You from here?"

"Suppose someone's gotta be."

"You got the job."

"What?"

"Dunno. Something I heard. Nobody's from L.A. So, when you meet someone from here, it's like they're special or something."

I got the job.

While Lucky pondered the term, he kept allowing his eyes to wander around the interior. With each sweep of the Crown Vic's ever-crowding headlights, Lucky would catch a glimpse of something else. So far, he had figured Cherry's car to be at least ten years old. The leather upholstery was shiny with a couple hundred thousand miles of wear. At his feet, in the passenger footwell, were Power Bar wrappers along with two plastic Frappuccino empties.

"Don't think being from here's a job . . ." said Lucky. "More like an affliction you learn to live with."

Cherry Pie unleashed a tiny laugh and a smile. Genuine. It was the first time Lucky had seen it. Imperfect rows of teeth but still camera-ready. She had shifted from cautious—not even willing to step from the refuge of her car—to nervous but helpful, standing with Lucky in the Rabbit Pole parking lot, recollecting her short history with Karrie Kaarlsen. And now, behind the wheel, personally guided the detective and father to the last place she had seen the fifteen-year-old.

"Anything of Karrie's in here?" asked Lucky.

"You mean, is there anything in here that's not my shit?" joked Cherry. "Sorry. My car's a friggin' garbage pail. Don't usually take passengers. Least when I'm littering it's in my own crap-mobile."

Lucky leaned back and looked over his left shoulder into the back seat, then waited for another turn in the road when he would catch some illumination from the headlights behind them.

"You know, she's much older than her age," segued Cherry. "Not, you know, like she's not fifteen like you said. But like an old soul, you know?"

"Mature," summed up Lucky.

"Girl's been around, 'kay?" infused Cherry. "I feel like I can tell you 'cause you're not her dad."

"Experienced for her age."

"Knows her way up and down the street. Dudes. Parties. Drugs."

"That why you introduced her to General Ho?"

"Told you. Thought she was eighteen."

Lucky thought he'd caught a glimpse of a satchel behind the driver's seat. "Backpack yours?" he asked.

"You mean my shoulder bag? Didn't I put it in the trunk?"

With his left arm, Lucky stretched into the darkness behind

the driver's seat to grab a handful of a nylon backpack. Heavy. Stuffed with who knows what? So, he got hold of a strap and arm-curled it over and onto his lap.

It took Cherry barely a glance.

"Wait. That's Val's," she said.

"Karrie's, you mean."

"Right. That's hers."

"Left it in your car."

"I guess."

As the lights from the road flashed and faded across the car interior, that dull Hello Kitty logo appeared to wink at Lucky as if it were some kind of invitation.

Zzzziiiiiiiiiiiipppppppp.

The sound of Lucky unzipping the bag sounded closer to the ripping of fabric.

"Hey," bit Cherry. "That's not yours to go through."

Lucky ignored the comment, dipping into the backpack and examining items from the top down. Scrunched-up clothes, for the most part. Two bras. Non-matching panties. Candy bar wrappers. Tampons. A sharpie-decorated pair of Chuck Taylors. A Ziploc baggie containing a half-used toothpaste tube, a variety of hotel mini soaps, a hairbrush. Stolen towel. Half roll of toilet paper. Another baggie with marijuana remnants and Zig-Zag rolling papers. A few loose dollar bills and change.

In both side pockets were her makeup stashes divided into more Ziplocs. Some glue-on party glitter. An empty Pez dispenser resembling the Joker from Batman. An old iPod and headphones, the battery dead.

Flipping the backpack around, Lucky found the zipper for the nearly hidden front flap, moved it four inches left, then let his fingers feel around inside until he withdrew a pair of folded white envelopes. Each sealed. Lucky held them up, waiting for a wash of light so he could read the addressees.

"One for 'Mom,'" read Lucky. "And the other for 'Dad.'"

With that, Lucky spun one of the envelopes, looking for a

seam under which to tear it open. This was when Cherry's hand reached over to throttle Lucky's back.

"Look," said Cherry. "I get why you have to look at everything. But those aren't addressed to you."

"Fully aware," said Lucky. "But same rule applies. Letters might contain information that—"

"Isn't that her dad back there?" asked Cherry, her eyes flicking into the rearview mirror. "Think she deserves just a little privacy?"

Lucky stared back at Cherry as he pondered her request.

Privacy? What fifteen-year-old deserves privacy?

Lucky thought better of opening either envelope, refolding them and placing them unmolested back in the pocket.

The last five minutes of driving until they arrived at the Casting Place went by in silence. Lucky had Cherry park her car precisely where she had the night before when she had last seen Karrie. She walked through all her moves and conversation and stood under the pepper tree where she had last waved goodbye to the teen. Lucky paced off the distance to the front door. Thirty-four yards. A hundred and two feet. Even eyes that tested at the top of the optometry scale couldn't distinguish much with a single streetlamp as a source.

"Well, somebody other than Karrie's gotta know him," decided Lucky. "It's late. I'll talk up whoever I can find inside. You might wanna pass on to Andrew everything you told me."

Andrew, whose behavior that day had been nothing short of a Boy Scout's, stopped standing in Lucky's shadow and stepped closer to listen to Cherry.

"Excuse me?" said Cherry. "I said I'd bring you to where I last saw her. I did that. Now I wanna go home."

"So, leave me your address," said Lucky. "Take daddy man with you and I'll get him when I'm done."

It was a woman's instinct to inch a step back and regard Andrew with a glance of distrust. Cherry gave the redheaded stranger a second once-over. Skinny. Sallow-cheeked with a terribly bruised face.

"What happened here?" Cherry used her index finger to circle her face, but was referring to Andrew's.

"I flew out here to find my daughter," answered Andrew. "And it hasn't been a cakewalk."

"Listen," said Cherry. "I'm all happy to help and shit. But seriously. I don't know you guys. And this is getting too weird for me."

"I hear ya," said Lucky, suddenly crossing to Cherry and hooking her elbow. He pointed at Andrew. "Give us a sec, pal."

"I just wanted to say—" began Andrew.

"A sec," interrupted Lucky. "Step back to the car, will ya?"

Andrew threw up an obedient hand before withdrawing a few paces.

"You can let go of me now," hissed Cherry.

"That is the girl's father," reminded Lucky. "And he's traveled all this way to our little corner of the cesspool to find his daughter. A notion, not twenty minutes ago, you described as kinda romantic."

"Didn't use those words."

"Listen. I'm not a cop right now. But I got plenty of badges on speed dial who'd be more than happy to make the rest of your week miserable. Or . . ."

"Or?"

"Get in your car. Take him back home with you. Where do you live again?"

"Silver Lake."

"Take him home with you to Silver Lake, catch daddy up on everything you know about his baby daughter until I come fetch his ass."

"Please?" volunteered Andrew from twenty feet away. "I'd love to hear anything you can tell me about my girl."

Cherry stood with her arms akimbo and an over-confident sense of her own propriety. She stared Andrew down for a good eight seconds.

"You paying him?" she asked Andrew, clearly referring to Lucky.

"'Course I am," said Andrew.

"Then pay me," insisted Cherry.

"That's the ticket," said Lucky. "I'm sure you'll work out something."

Lucky left them with a mocking gesture of hands praying to a God he didn't know. He turned his back and strode headlong up the walkway and the steps to the front door of the Casting Place. Andrew watched Lucky all the way until he disappeared inside.

"So?" cued Cherry.

"So, I'm Karrie's father," said Andrew, at last introducing himself with a polite hand.

"I'm Cherry and, as far as I know, your girl had hella reason to wanna get the hell outta Minnesota."

"Wisconsin," corrected Andrew. "Chenequa, Wisconsin."

"I really don't wanna look like a you-know-what by asking for money," apologized Cherry. "But it looks like everybody's gettin' paid but me."

"How's five hundred dollars, cash?" offered Andrew.

"How's a thousand?" countered Cherry. Her pose was all balls, no bullshit. Then just to punctuate her point, she jangled her car keys. "And the train is leaving the station."

31

Hollywood.

"**P**iss fuck!" griped Herm, discovering that once again the towel dispenser in the lone, single-holer men's room at the Casting Place building was bereft of paper. The cardboard roll seen through the semi-translucent plastic was obviously bare, had been that way all day, and nobody in the building had thought enough to ask Queenie to have it replaced. And now, Herm was left with wet hands and the choice to either allow them to air dry or wipe them on his silk shirt or black linen slacks. Choosing the former, Herm shook free what moisture he could, splattering the mirror with hard water drops, then gently blowing on his fingers.

As Herm was considering cursing the oddly wet winter that had temporarily shoved the normally dry air southward into Mexico, his ears clued in to the familiar hollow clanking of the front entry. The passage mechanism had stopped operating long ago, so Queenie had simply left the deadbolt in the locked position, causing the heavy door to crash, shake the building to its earthquake retrofitting, and echo back a resounding metal-on-metal note.

Herm checked his Rolex. A fake, he would usually acknowledge. But as Rolex knockoffs went, it was an outstanding fake. The time read just shy of an hour since he had spoken to the rat-bastard Gabriel on the phone.

He listened as the footfalls emptied past the bathrooms and receded maybe ten paces down the hall before he reached for the door handle to let himself out. Wet hands or not, Herm sought to walk up behind the flesh-thieving bastard and catch Gabe by surprise before issuing a friendly smile and ushering him into his private interview suite. Once the door was locked behind him, the talk would shift from one neighbor helping another to a more primal, man-to-man summit.

Where is she? You know, the strawberry-blonde? Whatever she told you, don't believe a fucking word. She's the underage honey pot of a well-connected senator. You want a visit from the FBI? Homeland Security? Hey, pal. I'm doin' you a favor, so cut the love song and give her up so I can send her back to where she belongs.

Herm's little speech was yet untested. But certain, he reasoned, to rattle the younger man once the threat was delivered with the appropriate gravitas, something Herm had in plentiful supply. So what if Herm showed a certain possessiveness over the little teenage princess? Once he got his hands on her, she was certain to be wholesaled out of his hair within twelve hours and washed of any of Herm's fingerprints or damning evidence the "casting director" may have left behind.

Cursing his wet hands, Herm pulled the bathroom door open and eased out into the main corridor that accessed those turnkey offices. A mere four paces ahead there was a figure, shorter than Herm, but broader than he recalled. If memory served, the photographer he sought had a full-on mop of hair. Yet the man in front of Herm had a buzzed scalp and the shoulders of a rugby player.

Herm's next thought was to turn back around and return to the bathroom. But what the hell for? His business there was complete but for air-drying his dampened mitts. So, why then was his flight response on full alert?

"Hey there," said the man, pivoting himself. "You work here?"

"I do, yes . . ." stammered Herm. "Well, sort of." Herm had already stalled in the center of the corridor as if he had stepped in wet concrete.

"Well, you sorta do or you don't?"

"Don't work for anybody," answered Herm. "I rent a space right over . . ." Then, as Herm wondered why the hell he was answering the questions as if he had to, he asked a question. "Can I do something for you?"

"Just wanna know if you've seen this young woman."

Before Herm could gird himself for the unknown, he found himself face-to-face with a small, wallet-sized photograph of that strawberry-blonde.

My unicorn.

Herm had faced down both cops and private detectives more than a few times—always after the crime had been committed and long after any evidence could be traced back to him. Maybe that's what triggered his amygdala response. Utter and pure instinct. In a few seconds of self-reflection he realized he had stared at the picture for a moment too long to justify any kind of denial.

"She looks kinda familiar," said Herm. "But around here . . ."

"What do you mean 'around here'?"

"This place is for casting," explained Herm. "Daytime it's crawling with 'em. Actors, you know? Pretty girls like that lined up and down the place."

"This girl?"

"Or girls like her. Like I said. Looks familiar in a generic kind of way," said Herm, hoping to find an opening and turn the tables on the obvious cop or detective or whoever the hell he was. "Can I ask who you are?"

"Yeah," said Lucky. "I'm the guy who's lookin' for a girl."

"Any girl? Or that particular girl?"

"Just the one," said the man. "Anybody else around I could talk to?"

"Not a clue," said Herm. "I just popped in to pick up some files. Building office is in the basement. Could be someone down there."

"Appreciate your help," said the man with an outstretched hand.

Herm gripped it with a manly tension before realizing his hands were still wet.

"Oh, so sorry," he said. "No towels in the bathroom."

The man seemed to pay little mind, pivoted once more, and headed for the stairs.

Like many veteran cops, Lucky felt he had developed his own custom bullshit detector. So sensitive, he fantasized, that with a simple palm-to-palm handshake he could divine criminal intent. It wouldn't be a tingle or heat or hairs on the nape of his neck or any kind of metaphysical passing of matter. It would be a voice with origins that felt sourced from somewhere near the base of his skull—not far from the old bullet wound and scar. It would speak flatly with a plain two-word message.

Good guy.

Or . . .

Bad guy.

Sadly, Lucky needed more than just a handshake.

He had already clocked Herm as at least a generation older than him. Maybe even more. And the long strides with which Herm seemed to lope told of a man whose athletic days might not have been so far behind him.

But it was in another man's eyes that Lucky had his best success. He wasn't keen on reading eye movement or involuntary skyward twitches that might lead a neuroscientist to believe that a subject was accessing cerebral centers for truthful recall or fiction-making. Lucky's favorite tell was in the pupils and whether he could detect changes in dilation in response to questions or certain stimuli.

Like a photograph.

While Herm gave the photo of Karrie a serious once-over, Lucky was squeezing the spheres of his own eyes in an effort to get a clear focus on Herm's pupils. In the dimness of the corridor under the weak strip of fluorescents, Lucky failed to get a read. That and the subject's soft contact lenses appeared to wiggle slightly as he gazed at the photo.

Still, a voice inside Lucky practically barked.

Bad guy!

As frosty as a winter morning. Crystalline. Bell-like and with authority.

Bad guy!

The handshake was just punctuation. Lucky quickly found the stairwell that led to the basement, only to find the office was locked for the day. The handwritten sign on the door had an in-case-of-emergency telephone number, which Lucky snapped a photo of before launching himself back up the stairs in hopes of running into Herm again. It was the TV cop move dramatized time and time again. Just when the subject thinks the questions are over and done with comes a quick surprise encore. The television bad guys were nearly always tripped up by the tack, giving way to sudden fits of anger or stumbling over their own hackneyed stories. In Lucky's true life cases, it didn't necessarily succeed other than further aggravating the respondent. But sometimes that was enough.

Then there was that sometimes . . . every once in a blue interrogation moon . . . the subject would add a morsel of useful information. Almost like a turn signal, indicating whether Lucky should go left or right.

"EXCUSE ME!" called out Lucky, exhuming himself from the building basement. He could see Herm was already halfway through the rear exit leading to a private parking lot.

If Herm slowed, it was imperceptible. He cleared the door and let it close behind him.

"YO!" shouted Lucky, rushing after Herm until he'd stopped the door just before it had fully shut. "JUST HAVE ONE MORE QUESTION!"

Herm was halfway to his Ford Edge when he made his about-face.

"Dunno if I have any more to help you with," said Herm with a shrug.

Lucky covered the parking lot distance with a back-stinging trot, burying a grimace and holding up his hands in polite resignation.

"Just one more thing," said Lucky. "You say she looked familiar."

"In a general kind of way," clarified Herm.

"Yeah. That's my question." Once again, Lucky produced that photo for Herm to look at. "Did you mean she looked like a lotta girls you've seen before? Or does she look like a girl you might've seen?"

"Is there a difference?"

"Well, for one. It puts her in that building right there. Where you do whatever you do." Lucky was pointing at the casting building with one hand while sticking the photo of Karrie only inches from Herm's face. "Take another look. Did you see *her?*"

Herm looked right past the worn wallet photo, making certain he had established direct eye contact with the former sheriff's deputy.

"Can't really say," shrugged Herm again, clicking the unlock-door button on his key chain. "But good luck, man. Really hope you find her."

Lucky excused the tall man with a tacit nod and took a step and a half rearward in order to get out of Herm's way. He waited, though. And watched as Herm started his car, dropped it into drive, and carefully eased out of the parking lot.

Bad guy, repeated the voice yet again.

Whether the voice was accurate or not, the man in the SUV forgot to switch on his headlights until his front wheels had rolled onto the asphalt of the side street that fed back onto Franklin.

When those headlights flared and swept the row of vehicles against the opposite curb, the figure of a man appeared in the space between a Honda CRV and a white panel van. Automatically filling out the report in his head, Lucky described the man as early to mid-thirties, under six feet, dark hair and maybe bearded, denim pants, navy blue or black peacoat, hands in his pockets.

And staring right back at Lucky.

As the headlights disappeared along with Herm's SUV, Lucky had to readjust his focus to compensate for the dark. It was in that instant that the man in the peacoat appeared to have vanished as quickly as he had appeared.

It's just Hollywood, Lucky. Up to its nose hairs in oddballs.

32

9:23 p.m.

It had to be a world record hangover. In her short but somewhat experienced fifteen years, Karrie had been high or drunk or imbibed enough to have experienced the aftereffects of all kinds of binges. Yet before she even lifted her eyelids, she knew she had landed the granddaddy of 'em all. It felt as if her brain had swelled and was straining at the walls of her skull for any kind of exit. That and with every labored inhale, her sinuses felt fuzzy and arid. Her lips chapped and her tongue seemed swollen, unable to leave even the slightest slick of saliva behind on her soft palate.

Sheezus, Karrie.

The teen tried to shock her mind into rewinding to the previous evening. She could easily recall the walk on the beach, the ocean, the conditioned sweet smell of Gabe's soft beard when they danced . . .

All memories seemed to stall right then and there. The music. The slow moving against the fast beating of Gabe's racing heart. The rest had to be a dreamless sleep. Which, in Karrie's wisdom, meant drugs were involved.

When she moved the slightest inch, her body ached. Stiff. Her joints sore as if she'd played a week's worth of field hockey matches. And what the hell was that smell? Dry as her sinus cavity felt, there was an ugly funk in the air. Was it her? Christ, she wondered. If she reeked that bad, what would Gabe think? She reached across the mattress to get a bearing and felt nothing and nobody. Not even a duvet cover. It was then she realized her eyes were open and yet her retinas could still only read blackness. Dense. A place utterly absent of light. What time was it? Sometime before dawn? Gabe must have some kind of blackout curtains in his bedroom. Because it was the most stifling dark she could ever recall.

Karrie slowly rolled to her left, ignoring both the pain in her head and joints in hopes of catching even the slightest of bearings. Anything for a clue, be it a crack of light from a window, the glow-green numbers of a digital clock radio, or even the slight red ember on a ten-dollar smoke detector.

Instead, at the end of a left-hand rollover, her wrist landed with a metallic clunk against some sort of vertical barrier. The sound echoed. Or was that just in the teenager's aching head? Karrie turned herself again, pushing up on all fours. Her fingers stretched wide against a mattress that felt rough, without even a sheet for protection. It was then that she could smell the urine. A putrid mash of ammonia mixed with—what was that—mildew?

"Gabe?" asked Karrie aloud, practically choking out the words across her bone-dry teeth, then hearing her own slight voice reverberate back to her. "Gabe?" she nearly cried again, louder and with some diaphragm to push more air over her tongue.

Without a returned answer, the fifteen-year-old felt her way down to the edge of the bed. Only to discover it wasn't a bed at all. But a rather thin mattress lying atop what felt like a splintery slab of plywood. She rapped her knuckles against it, hearing back a dull connection with wood.

"Gabe!" shouted Karrie, realizing that as trashed and hungover as she felt, better than half her foreboding feelings weren't in her head or abused body. Something about the situation was oh-so-terribly wrong. For a moment she had wondered if she had passed out and been cruelly pranked, left to sleep it off in some kind of basement. Yet as she found her feet, stretched out her arms, and eased forward in the blackness to find out just where the hell she was, her fingertips eventually came to find another vertical span. This time a wall. Rough and flaking. And when she rapped on it, it channeled the sound with even more metal, the reverberations surrounding her but giving a sense of depth and space. The ceiling was low. The walls were close.

Panicked, Karrie pounded on the wall.

"GABE!" she shrieked at the top of her lungs. The adrenaline coursed within her salved the loudness of her own voice. "GABE? WHERE THE FUCK AM I? GAAAAAABE!"

"Shut up!" yelled a voice from beyond, female, not so distant, equally metallic yet still muffled so the words blended into almost a garble.

"WHERE'S GABE?" screamed Karrie.

"I said shut up! I just wanna sleep, you bitch!"

"BUT WHERE AM I?"

"How the fuck should I know? I'm locked in a box, just like you're locked in a box. And I was sleeping until you started the shit fit, so just stop, okay?"

"BUT I NEED GABE, OKAY?"

"I don't know nobody named Gabe. But my bet's he's the one who put you here, so SHUT THE FUCK UP."

"WHAT IS THIS?" Karrie started to cry.

"Just shut up, please, and go back to sleep!"

"BUT I'M NOT SUPPOSED TO BE HERE."

"Like anybody's supposed to? Just shut it, okay?"

Karrie's words evaporated into gasping sobs of freakish fright.

"What's happening?" she shuddered. "What's going on with me?"

Her fingers finally traced the fourth wall, confirming she had somehow found herself imprisoned in a metal box of sorts.

Metal box. Mattress on a plywood floor. Am I in prison?

Karrie slid down the wall to the floor, heaving and so wrought with uncontrolled sobs she thought madness had somehow overtaken her. Her entire body shook, followed by a cold sweat that sprang from every petrified pore.

"Gabe?" she squeaked again, barely forming the words on her lips. "Please. Where are you?"

33

Santa Monica.

"**G**abriel Christopher," shouted the voice in his head.

It was his mother's voice. Clean, without modulation, and piercing through the back of his neck as if he didn't require ears to hear. The tiny woman, all of ninety-five pounds and a hellion mix of Greek and Italian blood, could scare any Christian soul from whatever sin he was about to perform and send him directly to the confessional. When Gabe's mother was alive, she was his conscience. Now, when he heard the voice calling his God-given name, it was his shame that appeared to have roused her ire. As if she were still living somewhere amongst his molecular self. Always there. Omnipresent and ready to crack his skull with her big, wooden spoon.

He had heard the voice the instant he had switched the little yellow Oxycontin pill for a blue tablet, placing it on the back of the girl's willing tongue. She had said her name was Valeriana. But Gabe knew it was made-up. Pretty much like everything else in Los Angeles. Fake. Like a prop or a bit of staged scenery. Only his mom knew different. Dead as she was, she still knew the game Gabe was playing was part of the real world.

And, for that matter, a crime.

She had called his name again after he had bundled the unconscious girl in an old stitched blanket, shouldered her down the back steps of his apartment, and gently placed her in the trunk of a rented blue Nissan. The trunk was vacuumed so clean it might have just been installed at the factory. He had heard the voice again as the trunk lid snapped shut with a thin and metallic click.

Gabriel Christopher!

His mother's voice rang again—berating him when he accepted the tight bundle of cash in exchange for following the instructions. He had parked the car on some dark, industrial street in the Valley and walked three long blocks west to a designated bus stop. It was when the city bus pulled away that the fear hit him. That somehow in the course of driving from Santa Monica to the Valley, the drugged-out girl in the rental car's wheel well had somehow shifted positions and unconsciously smothered herself to death.

Gabriel Christopher!

As the day wore on, his mother's voice eased to a nagging whisper, not unlike a lousy top-forty tune that would sometimes stick in his head, the harmonized hook playing over and over and over. The money also added some sound padding. A $5,000 stack of hundred-dollar bills could do a lot to ease his suffering headshot business. He could catch up on some back rent and utility bills. He had broken out the first uncirculated hundred at a Santa Monica Union 76 station with a Circle K mini-mart. It paid for a tank of gas, two AriZona iced teas, and a fistful of Slim Jims. That was going to be his dinner until his cell phone rattled the loose change in the front pocket of his khakis. The voice on the other end was unfamiliar. The same went for the number, which he would have left unanswered had he not suddenly concerned himself that it had something to do with the blue Nissan rental car and what he had left in the trunk.

The man had identified himself as Herm, a sort of office neighbor from the Casting Place. An overnight delivery addressed to Gabe Roth had been mistakenly delivered to him. Ordinarily, Gabe would have requested for the box or package or whatever it was to be left on Queenie's desk. Only it was after hours, the office was closed, and something he hadn't been expecting had been overnighted to him.

In the end, it was the gas tank, full to the stem, that made the decision for him. With a belly full of chemicals and caffeine, and sticks of spicy Slim Jims looking like a floral array sprouting from his spare cup holder, Gabe found it easy to say *why not?* So, he agreed to meet the kind man called Herm at the Casting Place as soon as he could get there.

Gabe never quite cared for the Casting Place's rear lot. The spaces were tight and after his car had suffered multiple body dings, delivered—he was positive—by narcissistic actors who cared not a glimmer about property that wasn't their own, Gabe preferred street parking. In the dim light that was left from the day, he'd shoehorned his eleven-year-old Honda into a metered space, fed a single quarter into it, then practically skipped his way toward the wrought-iron gate that guarded the rear entrance.

There. Precisely there, across the side-street blacktop is where he put the brakes on all forward momentum. Sixty yards from him, standing in the nearly empty parking lot, were two men. One he instantly recognized as Herm, his tall and distinguished office neighbor. The other was a man unknown. White with a shaved head and a boom to his voice that socked of authority. He measured the space between the men as twenty or so yards, then keenly watched the unknown man cover the distance to the taller gent in a way that appeared to leave Herm defenseless. What—as if it were any of Gabe's business—they were discussing was as unrecognizable as the thicker man. Yet there was Gabe, feet stuck to the concrete as if he'd been bolted to the sidewalk, staring dead ahead at the unknowable conversation as if it mattered.

That is when his mother's voice, relegated to an obnoxious hit tune loop, broke through yet again.

Gabriel Christopher!

Why that pair of conversing men in the parking lot had a rat's ass to do with his mama's shaming voice Gabe didn't know or much care. It was, though, some kind of warning. A mother's warning that demanded to be heard and heeded. Gabe stood on the sidewalk for maybe a minute longer, motionless in the camouflage of dusk, watching the man named Herm climb into his SUV and drive away. That's precisely when Gabe's legs beat their hasty retreat.

34

Silver Lake. 10:45 p.m.

Having grown up in Southern California, Lucky recalled Silver Lake wasn't called Silver Lake unless one lived in Silver Lake. By most locals, it was known as the neighborhood north of Echo Park. West of downtown. Or the easternmost end of Sunset Strip. In the seventies, it was briefly famous for its gay S&M bars, attracting international men seeking like-minded gents in black leather and metal studs. But by the turn of the millennium, the landscape had turned trendy with coffeehouses, alt rock clubs, and art galleries to go along with the south-facing hillsides chockablock with turn-of-the-century bungalows, each ripe for renovation and a real estate killing.

Still, to Lucky and so many other Los Angeles sheriff's deputies, Silver Lake was LAPD land and the zip code known for shortcuts into Dodger Stadium.

The navigation on Lucky's phone pointed him to an address on North Benton and a four-unit stucco apartment building, circa 1947. Overgrown and with large clay pots spilling over in fountains of unrestrained greenery, there were two downstairs apartments and two upstairs, divided by stairs angling in a V from the extremely weathered concrete walkway.

Lucky had taken the one empty space in front of a city fire hydrant, relatively certain there would be no conflagration or that he would be ticketed by some enterprising night owl of a parking Nazi before he had left with his one client. No sooner had he stepped on the sidewalk than he'd heard a shriek, quickly followed by that unmistakable whiskey voice.

"GET THE FUCK OUT!" screeched Cherry Pie.

Instantly, appearing under the one yellowed upstairs porch light, Andrew backed out of a low doorway better suited for a hobbit. His hands shoulder high in the ubiquitous sign of surrender.

"But you asked me for money!" insisted Andrew.

"You called me a whore!" blasted Cherry, her slight silhouette prepared to slam the entry shut.

"I said *prostitute*," defended Andrew. "Not *whore*."

"Like there's a difference?"

"Might wanna hold it down," throated Lucky, noting the downstairs lights flicking on.

"Get him the hell offa my steps," demanded Cherry.

"Awright, you heard her," calmed Lucky. "Let's say good night."

"I didn't call her a whore," insisted Andrew. Nonetheless, he heeded Lucky's advice and pointed his shoulders downhill. He passed Lucky at the bottom of the steps. Lucky was glad to see that Andrew was shouldering Karrie's backpack.

"Got just a couple of questions for her and we're out," promised Lucky ever so quietly.

Cherry was lingering just beyond her threshold as if to make absolutely certain the bruised, gingerbread millionaire was off her property. Lucky kept a wise distance, stopping at the top landing.

"So, what happened?" asked Lucky. "My man get creepy on ya?"

"Nothing I didn't already handle," said Cherry, freshly show-ered with a short pink terry-cloth robe wrapped around her. "I dance. That's it. No tricks."

"So, he propositioned you?"

"Him? Hell no." Water droplets spilled as she shook her head. "No. Probably just a misunderstanding."

"Weird guy, right?"

"No shit."

"Anything inside our teenage girlfriend left behind?"

"Phone," said Cherry. "Gave it back to her old man. Other than that, everything else was in her backpack. He's got that too."

"Sure you're okay?"

"Fine."

"Gonna leave you my number," said Lucky. "She makes con-tact with you. Or that guy."

"Gabe."

"You're gonna call me, right?"

Cherry mustered a nod. She shivered unreservedly. The goose bumps on her legs looked like a colony of mosquito bites.

"Good night," said Lucky. "And thanks. Really."

35

Downtown.

"I didn't call her a whore!" insisted Andrew, his face so flush and rosy it nearly erased the black and blue.

Lucky was steering the Crown Vic through a series of darkened side streets that traversed the low-slung hills just south of Chavez Ravine. He was thinking if Andrew had been a sheriff's trainee, he might have suggested he stick his red face out the window and make siren sounds, allowing for cross-town travel in full Code 3 mode.

"I didn't ask if you did or didn't," reminded Lucky.

"I hate it when people put words in my mouth," Andrew continued to grind. "That's not at all where I was going . . . or what I was implying."

"So, you didn't ask if she was a prostitute?"

"I did . . . but not," explained Andrew. "She dances naked, right?"

"Since when does stripper equal hooker?"

"I'm the father of a missing G.D. fifteen-year-old! I think I have a right to know just what kind of . . . women . . . she was shacking up with!" exploded Andrew, his voice conquering the Crown Vic's eight cylinders. "After I found out if she was a prostitute I was gonna ask about drugs. You think I'da been out of line to ask that?"

Lucky swiveled his neck, dropping his eyeballs squarely on the diminutive dad. And there it was again. Pulsing across Andrew's forehead. That zigzag vein. Bulging, it seemed, this time with as much venom as blood. The man was off the chain. The brow above his nose crimped and his front lips lifted to reveal every millimeter of those yellowing fangs.

"Crap salad!" slammed Andrew. "You're not her father. How the heck are you supposed to know what it's like to lose a child?"

"She's missing. Not dead," low-toned Lucky in an attempt to lower the level of sudden rancor.

"How would you know?" accused Andrew. "Did you stumble over a new clue tonight?"

"We're close. We know where she's been, who she's been with—"

"G.D. stripper!" Andrew hammer-fisted the dash with a thump. "My baby girl is only fifteen!"

"You need to cool your jets."

"Don't tell me what I need. I'm the G.D. father. I'm paying YOU!" Once again, Andrew unleashed another fist into the protective dash panel of foam and composite plastic.

Thump. Thump. Thump!

"Stripping for men. And not young men either. Older men who stare and drool and have fantasies about . . . about all kinds of horrible, evil shit."

The disconsolate dad, both fists balled with a building rage, pounded the passenger door panel with the heel of his right hand.

But that wasn't enough. He went after the dash again, striking it with the toe of his left shoe.

Lucky applied the brakes. Hard. Not only to slow the Crown Vic, but also to shock Andrew out of his billowing rage.

It was a downsloped drag overlooking downtown. The streets were wet with that seemingly unending month of rain. With the wheels slightly locking, the Crown Vic began a skid. To avoid the fishtail, Lucky released the brake, righted the car toward the curb, eased into a stop, and meant to scratch out a mental note to have the anti-lock system checked before returning the Crown Vic to its home.

That note, though, would burn in the next minute.

"My precious baby," growled Andrew. "Living with a G.D. prostitute."

"Are you gonna ease off or what?" said Lucky.

"Whore."

"Enough." Lucky put a firm grip on Andrew's shoulder. A touch that, nine times out of ten, would have resulted in one of two responses: a momentary pause in the uncontrollable outbursts or the manly "don't touch me" shrug. Only Lucky got neither. It was as if he had pressed a button that sent Andrew's right leg into a coil just before he unleashed a hammering heel into the dash.

Lucky wanted to box the little man's ears. Or twist one until he squealed himself back to Planet Reality. But that would have been a dumb-assed move. Smacking the client. The man with the checkbook. Causing actual pain and injury to the father of the runaway teen.

Forfuckssake!

He shouldered the damn driver's door, stepped out into a sudden downpour, and splashed his way onto the sidewalk until he had a hold of the passenger door's handle. All the while, the vehicle was rocking with heavier and heavier kicks from Andrew, unhinged and barking his fatherly frustrations at the world.

"C'mon. Outta the car," ordered Lucky with the rap of his knuckles, preparing to pull the door open for punctuation. He lifted the handle, expecting that feeling of the door unlatching. Instead, there was the impotent sensation from a locked door.

Lucky knuckled the window again.

"Unlock the door, Andrew!"

That's when he saw it. The final blow to the Crown Vic's dash. Andrew's right knee lifted, showing a yogi's flexibility, hinging near his right earlobe. Then came the final crack, followed by a concussive *WHUMP*. The cabin of the car instantly filled with a gassy mist as the airbag's capacitors dumped their electric load. At nearly the speed of light, a servo joined a thimble-sized reserve of sodium azide and potassium nitrate, making for an instantaneous chemical production of nitrogen. The result was an inflating bag with enough protective sock to bust the average adult's nose, or save his or her life.

What it also did was blow a gaping hole in the car's dashboard—one that would require a wallet-denting replacement.

"Sheezus!" muffled Andrew, flailing his arms until he found the inside handle. As the door swung out, Andrew was greeted by Lucky's hand grabbing a fistful of red hair.

"You stupid knob-jockey!" Lucky spun Andrew onto the sidewalk, letting go of the red scruff and leaving his paying client stumbling up against the brick wall of a closed Argentine *carniceria*.

"What you do that for?" asked Andrew before realizing his busted nose had turned into a bloody sieve. "My frickin' nose again!"

"Like I did that?" said Lucky. "I think you'd know if I'd actually been the one to hurt you."

"Your G.D. car."

"Not *my* car, as a matter of record!" pissed Lucky. "And because you had to have your little panty fit. Well, look at it. Now I gotta replace the fuckin' dash. You know what airbags cost? There's a reason why gangbangers boost 'em!"

"My nose is broken again."

"Well, waaaa, waaaa, waaaa," mocked Lucky. "For Christ's sake, grow a pair, will ya?"

"You don't give a crap," cried Andrew. "Not about me. Not about my daughter."

"Know what? You need to walk your shit off." Lucky stepped back and gestured down the sidewalk. "Easy stroll back to the hotel. Get your head unscrewed from your asshole."

"Don't talk to me like that . . . You work for me!"

"Said walk it off, Andy."

"Maybe you don't get how the world works! I pay! And you get done what I need done!"

Steadfast, Lucky's left arm remained a straight directional sign, angled to the sidewalk, strongly encouraging Andrew which way he should beat his feet. Yet the only steps Andrew took were the two between himself and Lucky.

"I bet this is the real reason why you're not a cop anymore." Andrew's finger was accusing, pointing just south of the tip of Lucky's nose. "You have a problem with your G.D. place in the food chain."

If patience were a gas tank, Lucky was already on fumes. Nonetheless, he gathered what wits he had left, inhaled a single cleansing breath, and gave one last instruction.

"You're angry. You're hurt cuzza the airbag. You need time to yourself," advised Lucky. "Walk back to your hotel. Pull yourself together."

"I need. To find. My daughter!"

"Doin' the best I can," shrugged Lucky. "And I don't need you making it any harder."

"Read. My. Lips. Dipstick," pointed Andrew. "You. Work. For. Me—"

If Andrew Kaarlsen let out a howl, nobody but Lucky was within earshot to hear or give witness. At least not when, under that torrent of rain, Lucky grabbed hold of Andrew's accusing finger and twisted it counterclockwise until he detected the distinct diffused snap of a bone. The scream was sharper than that of the actual bone breaking.

"Now," hissed Lucky. "That was me. Hurting. You."

Lucky left the spoiled ass-hat bitching on the sidewalk, the little man winding in place as if centrifugal force would send pain-killing blood to his swelling digit. The Crown Vic with its deployed and flaccid passenger airbag was still humming when Lucky shut one door, climbed in through the other, and fast-drifted into a curb-to-one-eighty U-turn. If Andrew Kaarlsen were calling after him, shouting invectives or even hurling loose bricks, Lucky wouldn't have had a glimmer because he had consciously chosen to ignore both rear and side-view mirrors.

Walk if off, Andrew.

It was strong advice that Lucky would have stood behind. But because of how the argument terminated, Andrew would need to walk it off into the nearest emergency room or urgent care facility.

And if Andrew needed to cool his hot ass down, Lucky needed to lie down, swallow a pair of Percocets, and allow his screaming back muscles to unclench. The extra drug dose would pretty much assure seven-plus hours of deserved sleep. There would be absolutely no need to set an alarm or rise early. He was certain to be sacked by sun up. Relieved of his teenager recovery duty forever ad infinitum.

Friday

36

Panorama City. 4:41 a.m.

It had been a hellish storm. At least by Southern California standards. After the two-hour torrent of downpours, dumping God only knows how many inches of rain on Greater Los Angeles and thereabouts, a nasty wind had whipped up with gusts of about forty-plus miles per hour across the Valley floor.

Unable to sleep, Herm lay in bed, waiting for the sound of drip-drops inside his half-renovated house. When the hard rain finally abated around one in the morning, he experienced a warm glow of satisfaction that his roof repairs had held strong under the severe conditions. But as the moist air gave way to that howling wind, a second worry crept under Herm's skullcap. Then a third. The latter being a nattering pang that involved his surprise encounter back at the Casting Place.

No doubt that officious-looking man flashing a cutesy-pie pic of Miss Strawberry-Blonde was some kind of cop.

Herm's only question about the situation was if he had been set up by his suspicious office neighbor. Or that ball-busting purple-haired skank called Cherry Pie.

Then would come another hard push of wind and instantly, foremost in Herm's mind, his anxiety would shift to his beloved duo of mature eucalyptus trees.

Once a majestic eighty feet of hardwood glory, the pair had become a nuisance to the nearby homes with their forever peeling bark in need of monthly cleanups. Making matters worse, their wide-reaching branches continued to harass city telephone and power lines. So much so, the city had, without Herm's permission, sent in a crew of tree-climbing saw-monkeys to dispatch the problem. One afternoon, while Herm was on the other side of the hill plying his flesh-selling trade, a truckload of Spanish-speaking illegals pulled up to his Panorama City project. A crew of a dozen tree-trimmers emptied out and, in a matter of an hour, had both sheared and topped his magnificent eucs, effectively cutting their height by half and leaving them looking like a pair of bare, white forearms sprouting from the southeast corner of his backyard.

"I grew up with those Goddamn trees," groused Herm to the Department of Water and Power. "How dare the city desecrate property without the owner's proxy."

Soon after, the trees began to grow fat and wide, bushing up like a pair of massive chia pets in a race to overtake each other. A friend who was both an AA member and arborist explained the ugly phenomenon as a kind of ecological panic. The end result was that his precious trees had been permanently transformed into massive shrubs.

They'd also become hazards. With compromised root systems and top heavy from the sudden concentration of foliage, they had lost the ability to allow a stiff wind to sift safely through their branches. This caused Herm to lie awake on more than a night or two, wondering when the hell what was left of his eucs would come crashing through his bedroom ceiling, maiming or killing him in such an unglamorous fashion. He could solve it with a phone call and a personal check to the same private contractor who had gladly cut 'em down. They could haul the wood and grind the roots into pulp until the trees were just a boyhood memory.

Hell no.

The dangerous wind had peaked and diminished sometime just after 3:00 a.m. The eucs hadn't toppled that night. Nor would they ever have a chance again. That's because an idea had stirred in Herm. Something delicious and poetic and more masculine than a lifetime prescription of medical testosterone.

A chainsaw.

A tool with teeth. Shiny, new, and best of all, his. Able to fell tall hardwoods or anything else that might stand in his way.

Like a flesh-poaching office neighbor.

Or a cop bearing bad news in the form of an old wallet photo.

Certain his chainsaw was waiting for him at his nearby Home Depot, Herm lay in his bed, checking the clock, dozing in and out, but all the while lusting for one of those long-bladed bitches he'd seen on so many reality survival shows.

When the digital clock finally ticked over to 5:29 a.m., Herm was up, showering, brewing a pot of dark roast, then in his car by 5:50. He wasn't the first in line at the construction mart. The Mexicans were always there first. Or Hispanics, as Herm would have to remind himself. Brown and barely awakened faces would be milling about, speaking a speedy form of Spanglish, and sucking the straws on super-sized jugs of caffeinated soda and energy drinks.

The doors opened precisely at 6:00 a.m. After the initial rush of contractors—licensed or otherwise—Herm strolled in right behind them. And because he pretty much knew every square inch of the store, he was quick to navigate to the powered tools section. He bypassed both the battery and electric saws and went straight through to the gas-powered machines. If Herm was going to cut down his favorite old friends, he wanted the entire neighborhood to hear it. That, and he couldn't wait to feel what it was like, laying that blade against a trunk, trigger in full-throttle mode, teeth chewing at the fleshy wood exactly the way he had designed.

Yes. It was sexual as hell to Herm. And if asked, he would have fully admitted as much to pretty much anybody. Hell, he might even share about the thrill of the first cut in Alcoholics Anonymous, once he found a new regular meeting.

A Husqvarna quickly caught his fancy. The body was lipstick red and glossy, sporting a twenty-four-inch blade and nearly six horses of trunk-gnawing ecstasy. It was the epitome of lust at first sight. Once Herm had checked it out, he could barely read the other brands and their specs. The Husqvarna was too damn sexy to leave Home Depot with anyone but him. He imagined his credit card was so desperate to buy the monster, it might melt a hole right through the leather of his billfold.

"You're gonna be mine," whispered Herm to the power tool, flagging down a white-haired sales associate. "Need help with a chainsaw."

"Okeydokey," replied the mustached old Irishman in the orange bib. "Know much about 'em?"

"My first," said Herm, certain by the old man's former bronco-breaker look that he knew his way around man tools. "But I kinda got my attention stuck to this Husqvarna right here."

"That's my top model," shadowed the salesman. "On the high side price-point wise, but pretty much can do everything you ask."

"I want it to eat a couple old eucalyptuses."

And possibly a human or two.

"And it'll smell good doin' it," smiled the salesman. "Want me to give you the tour?"

"Oh, please. Do your magic," smiled Herm, feeling not the least bit fatigued after a nearly sleepless night. "I am *all* yours."

37

Downtown.

In his entire fifty years of life on earth, Andrew Kaarlsen had never suffered a single broken bone. While the other boys participated in football and hockey, Andrew was part of the burgeoning wave of young men who were raised on VHS movies, computer games, and Twizzlers. Outdoor sports, healthy or otherwise, were damned in lieu of school afternoons and weekends spent in front of computer screens playing in simulated worlds.

And then, in a matter of days, Andrew had to endure both a beatdown, a busted nose, and a double finger fracture. But rather than wander into a strange emergency room or urgent care clinic, the Wisconsin software mogul called his personal secretary's home number, waking her in the middle of a blizzard with a less-than-polite demand that she rustle up some kind of limousine or town car. Bleary-eyed, she was able to geo-locate her boss via his smartphone and, in minutes, she'd rallied an available car to hustle over to Andrew's downtown location, gather him up, and deliver him once again to the emergency room of Cedars-Sinai hospital next to Beverly Hills. And because his secretary thought to call Conrad Ellis, Andrew was leap-frogged over the waiting sick and injured, x-rayed, his finger expertly splinted, and his nose reset once again by the very same on-call plastic surgeon.

"This is like our second date," joked the plastics doc. "What happens if we make it to a third?"

"Unlucky you, I'm still married," nasaled Andrew.

The good news? Andrew would survive. The bad news? He would have to make do breathing only through his left nostril for however many days he was to remain in Los Angeles.

Nobody knew it yet, but that number was down to less than twenty-four hours.

The town car dropped Andrew back at the downtown Biltmore at around 3:00 a.m. The Vicodin the ER docs prescribed to ease the oncoming pain to Andrew's swollen face and finger had left him sluggish and drowsy. Despite his considerable anguish, he fell asleep on the couch just inside the front door of the suite. He would have remained there for eight or more hours if he hadn't already ordered an automatic room service meal of oatmeal and shaved almonds with milk and espresso to be served every morning promptly at 6:30 a.m. The door unlatched at exactly the bottom of the hour and into the suite entered a uniformed Sudanese transplant carrying a silver-plated tray. The server hadn't noticed the heavily bandaged face of the hotel guest slumped onto the couch until he heard an audible groan.

"Sorry, sir!" panicked the startled server.

"Leave it and go," growled Andrew.

The server left the tray on the desk and made a hasty retreat, quietly clicking the hotel room door behind him. Andrew, in the meantime, just wanted to return to his slumber, but the pain from the swelling on his face eventually proved it impossible. Afraid that another dose of prescription painkillers would result in more wasteful slumber, he padded to his bathroom and found his travel bottle of Advil.

Eight hundred milligrams later, Andrew gingerly gave himself a sponge bath, dressed in fresh sweats, then sat down with his laptop and oatmeal. His right hand worked the spoon and his left the track pad, avoiding his usual clicks on news and sports stories for searches on a website he had only recently heard of.

JumpFinder.com.

He tapped out the word "escort" and quickly narrowed his results filter to "strawberry" and "petite" and "freckles" and "green eyes" and, most dangerously, descriptors designed to imply the illicitness of youth. The results flowed quickly as he scrolled through one personal ad after another, wishing, hoping, praying he would land on something familiar. A limb. An eyeball. A familiar dimple that would identify his Karrie, whom, he had somehow become certain, had turned to whoring as a way to support herself.

The mere idea of it gave Andrew's stomach an uncomfortable churn. Escort after escort, scanned through a cheap pair of reading glasses that couldn't find the true bridge of the man's nose. The specs were askew, but still functional, maximizing the resolution of each suggestive pose.

Slightly less than an hour into the exercise, as Andrew continued to revise and narrow every search, he became overwhelmed and began to tear up. Not from the pain in his face, but from an increasingly fearful heart. Andrew hurt for himself, of course, and also for every other parent who had lost a young girl to the child-swallowing vortex.

Yet despite the private waterworks, Andrew kept clicking through miles of pages. He had made a pact with himself to exhaust the site before moving on to the next and the next until he had either identified his daughter or eliminated her participation in all local escort ads. The images piled up in his brain. Numbed him to the ever-constant parade of young flesh until, past his own bleary eyeballs, he found himself on pause and staring at a pair of youthful stems in a yellow string bikini.

Like so many of the advertisements, the face was obscured
to disguise identity and age. But the features, the skin type, the
Nordic pallor with the recognizable bloom of freckling, struck
Andrew cold and frozen for so long that his screen saver unexpect-
edly kicked in.

Karrie.

Andrew tapped the space bar, instantly regenerating the page
with its very teenage bikini body. The ad message was simple and
clearly penned to attract a man with a certain and perverse predi-
lection.

♥ — SEXY — BUBBLY — U WON'T
BELIEVE IM OLD ENUFF ♥

The mobile phone fumbled in Andrew's dominant yet now
splinted hand. It took him a moment to steady it and punch in the
number with his thumb. He held it to his ear, listened to the rings
at the other end, and waited for a voice to answer.

Karrie's voice.

"Hello?" said the woman at the other end, a tad squeaky with
her voice.

"Oh," said Andrew, not planning to sound so awfully disappointed. "I . . . I was expecting someone, something . . . you
know . . ."

"Someone more girly?" asked the voice, perkier at the smell of
money. "I promise you, I'm just the girly you need. What's your
name, daddy?"

"Listen. I saw the pictures, and I thought you were—"

"Just the right age?"

"Someone I knew," admitted Andrew.

"Well. I'm Jodi. And I'd sure as heck like to know you. You
have a name, sugar?"

"I'm . . . I'm Charlie," fibbed Andrew.

"Hi, Charlie."

"Hi."

"You like what you see?"

"Yes, well . . ." said Andrew. "But the pictures on JumpFinder. They looked like—"

"They're me, Charlie."

"Right. But they look like someone else. And I thought—"

"What's her name?" asked Jodi. "Maybe I know her."

"You don't—"

"Small world, our thing. Wouldn't hurt to ask."

"Her name's Karrie . . . er . . . sorry," stammered Andrew. "Her name, I think, is Valeriana?"

"Val?"

"I think so."

"Strawberry-blonde? Sweet sixteen?"

"Fifteen."

"That's her. Yes. You want me to bring her too?"

"You can do that?"

"I'm sure your Val is my Val," cooed Jodi. "We could do a Charlie twofer."

"Twofer?"

"Twofer one. You. Me. And Val."

"Karrie . . . I mean Val . . . would come with you?"

"If I can rouse her. It is pretty early in the morning. But me, I like men in the morning. More wood from the pile, if you know what I mean."

"Yes. Right." Andrew attempted to fake a laugh, but couldn't because his racing heart was eating too much oxygen.

"Where are you?" asked Jodi.

"At a hotel."

"And does that hotel have a name?"

"Yes. You're right. The Biltmore. Downtown. You know it?"

"Nice. I know it. What time would you like us to come by?"

"Soon?"

"How's an hour sound?"

"Yes. An hour's good."

"Room?"

"Eleven thirty-four."

"We will be there."

"You and Valeriana?"

"Me and Valeriana. Yes. See you, Charlie. Bye, now."

Andrew hung on the phone until he heard the digital click of the terminating connection. He checked the time on the phone's screen. It was only 7:29 a.m. At 8:30, his daughter would be arriving at the hotel.

Might be.

Would be, argued one side of Andrew's brain, accustomed to countering his negative thinking.

Then came a question. An annoying query that stuck under Andrew's bonnet like a stone in a shoe. If Val does arrive at the hotel. And Andrew and his baby daughter are, at last, reunited. What should be done about Lucky Dey? Should Andrew pay him the full fifty thousand? A partial amount as a parting gesture that his friend Conrad Ellis would understand? Or should Andrew man up and stiff that finger-breaking son of a bitch?

Andrew let the answer come to him in the shower. Suddenly, that lousy sponge bath he'd given himself wasn't quite satisfactory if he was less than an hour away from wrapping around Karrie the biggest hug that a father ever gave.

"My Karrie is coming home," Andrew said aloud. "Thank you, Jesus."

38

Reseda. 8:16 a.m.

The way Lucky remembered it, he had trundled into his apartment sometime after one in the morning. After finding the energy to take a quick lukewarm shower, he had stood naked, air-drying at the bathroom sink. He brushed his teeth, flossed his uppers, then unscrewed the cap from one of the unlabeled prescription bottles where he kept his precious tabs of Percocet. It was his habit to shake out one or two tablets, depending on his self-prescribing pain index. Only this time, the number was three. And for some unconscious reason, Lucky never returned the extra pill to its bottle. He swallowed the capsule with the other pair, then dumped the rest of the bottle into the toilet.

Lucky was that fed up.

Once he had slept off the meds, his plan was to tough out the next few days on Gatorade and a mix of ibuprofen and naproxen.

If he were a true addict, the pain of withdrawal would be worse than anything his back could dish out. If he weren't, well, he would still need to get himself back into some serious physical therapy.

Lucky recalled little more of the late hours until he woke a few ticks past eight in the morning to the feeble *clang* of his push-button doorbell. Whatever ringer was left in the mechanism sounded like it was coming from somewhere inside a mason jar full of pickle sludge.

Groggy and unbalanced, Lucky instantly regretted the mild overdosing of the med.

Drug addict? Or dickhead?

His body answered before his brain, already craving an opioid flood to blunt his angry nerve receptors. His back had already re-clenched and in the short walk to his front door, was demanding ten minutes of horizontal traction.

Before his hand even reached the knob, a manila envelope was jacked through his mail slot, skidding to a stop on the dirty shag his landlord had advertised as recently replaced wall-to-wall carpet. Just bending over to retrieve the letter proved so restrictive that Lucky needed to grab a chair back with one hand and knee-bend down to pinch the envelope off the floor. As he rose, he felt gravel pops in both knees. Painless. But a certain red flag that his body would no longer repair itself without a significant effort from the owner.

Note to self: Change lifestyle before it changes you.

Lucky cursed his inane bumper sticker philosophy, hobbled over to the couch, and practically flopped himself onto his back, causing a ripple of nerve pain that began at the small of his back and eventually radiated all the way to his fingertips. He waited for the aching to pass, then examined the envelope that bore not a single scrawl to identify the intended recipient. Still, he had every right to rip it open. After all, mistake or otherwise, it had been stuffed into his mail slot. Yet if he had received it in error, opening a personal note that was meant for a neighbor could prove to be messy and embarrassing.

With a tug on the lanyard controlling a set of mail-order

blinds, Lucky unleashed a yellow blast of morning sunlight so potent it made reading through that manila envelope easier than reading the lettered marks in a teacher's upside-down grade book.

Lucky first noticed the number ten, followed by a comma and three zeroes. A decimal point was next, then two more ovals to reveal a check in the amount of $10,000. Lucky's name was machine-printed about three millimeters above the payable line. He easily recognized that the true ink signature in the lower right belonged to Conrad Ellis.

Severance pay, Lucky bitched. For a lousy job poorly done. A high-society way of saying, *You're fired and don't let the door hit you in the ass can.* Conrad was probably so embarrassed he had recommended Lucky that he had insisted on covering Andrew's expenses.

A billionaire's apology to a millionaire.

"No, thank you," spat Lucky, crushing the envelope into a crumpled sphere before sailing it across the room. It bounced into a corner behind that stack of sealed moving boxes containing clothes that once belonged to his little brother. He'd always intended to give the old togs to Goodwill but, like so many other painful issues, hadn't gotten around to dealing with them. Returning to the ranks of the L.A. Sheriff's was still the priority.

And how's that going, Luck?

Lucky's mobile phone made an electronic chirp, alerting him to a new voicemail. Which was odd, considering that he hadn't heard so much as a single ring.

"Timing," said Lucky, suddenly certain that the missed call was from Andrew Kaarlsen, wanting to tie off the last connection to that goddarn corn hole, Lucky Dey. Obviously timed with the arrival of the check, certifying the message of termination in unambiguous terms.

It was then that Lucky felt the regret creeping in. Despite Andrew's continued awkwardness, he probably deserved an apology. No daddy in search of his missing daughter, whacked out or otherwise, deserved what Lucky had done to him.

Hell, Lucky. You give suspects better treatment.

Fully intending to phone Andrew back—and not with any intent of getting his gig back, but to stand tall and take the hit for his own lousy behavior—Lucky twisted on his sofa until his feet were underneath him and stood slowly in hopes that the blood in his skull wouldn't drain too efficiently back into his thorax.

The phone screen bore various options. One read VOICE-MAIL; the other, CALL BACK. In his less-than-lucid state, Lucky dropped a thick thumb on CALL BACK and brought the phone to his ear, fully expecting to hear Andrew's message playing back. Instead, he heard a single ring followed by a familiar woman's voice.

"So good," brightened the woman's voice. "I wasn't sure you were gonna get back to me so quick."

"I'm sorry," throated Lucky. "Who is this?"

"Cherry," said the dancer. "We had a bit of an adventure last night? This is Lucky, right?"

"Yeah," groaned Lucky. "Same guy. Different headache. I just woke up, so—"

"Really sorry. You want me to call you later?"

"No. I'm up."

"You asked me to call if I thought of anything."

"Right."

"Hit me in the middle of the night and I haven't slept since," said Cherry. "I can't believe it didn't register when I was with you."

"Okay," approved Lucky, not yet ready to admit even to her that he had been dismissed. "Whatcha got?"

"So, you know how I told you about the Gabe guy?"

"Guy who Karrie was last seen with."

"Okay. So, the whole reason we were there was cuzza my audition for an Audi commercial."

"She tagged along with you," recalled Lucky.

Cherry went on to describe how a casting director named Herm had shown only a mild professional interest in her until he had stumbled onto Karrie outside his casting door. Only later did he invite the duo back for a second audition, only to stand them up.

"That's why we were there that night," Cherry explained.

Cherry continued with her tale about Herm calling again, the new appointment when she showed up with someone other than Karrie, only to get a blast of Herm's vitriol and personality.

Then Cherry described the man. Tall, elegant. Salt and pepper hair. Multi-ethnic with half a dose of sincerity in his voice. Clearly the same character Lucky had encountered the night before.

Bad guy.

"That was just yesterday?" Lucky asked.

"The morning. Yeah."

"And you still have his contact info?"

"I seriously do, yeah," giggled Cherry. "So, whadda you think?"

"About?"

"About the guy we just talked about?" insisted Cherry. "Think he could have somethin' to do with tryin' to find Val . . . I mean, Karrie?"

"Unknown," said Lucky. "Listen. Can I call you back?"

"Yeah, sure . . . And, hey. If you talk to her old man? Tell him I'm sorry for being such a little bitch. After all. He's her dad."

The nascent fog from that extra Percocet was still clinging to a few final membranes. Despite that, a plan was forming. Less than that. It was more like a shot in the dark. Not so much to get his job back, but to finish. Lucky hated to leave duties undone. At least, those chores that didn't involve care for himself.

"You have plans this morning?" Lucky found himself asking.

"You talking to me?" asked Cherry. "Uh, not really. No."

"Because I think I'm gonna need you."

39

Downtown. 8:45 a.m.

"C'mon sweet bizness," nudged Romeo. "Time ta get your think workin'."

After the bloodbath at the Mayfair Hotel, Jodi wanted badly to blow town. Only with Romeo hanging on to her cut of the cash score, she hadn't the resources to get further than a one-way Metrolink ticket to the Inland Empire—the endless no-man's-land of a suburb between L.A. and Palm Springs. She had spent the rest on packets of crystal meth. But that didn't stop her phone from ringing with perverse requests from adult men cruising her Jump-Finder ad. It was only at Romeo's command that she answered the next query, a call from a man going by the name Charlie at the downtown Biltmore Hotel.

The plan was the same as before. Gain access to the man's hotel room, get his PINs, and while Romeo held a knife to the mark's throat, Jodi would venture to the nearest ATMs and do what she could to drain the unlucky bastard's cash accounts.

She made Romeo promise not to drain the john's blood this time.

But when it came time for Jodi to don that same identity-concealing floppy hat, second and third terrified thoughts came flooding in.

What about the police?

They aren't even looking for us.

But we were there! You killed a man!

We killed a man. And that man was a baby-raper. And the police don't care about no baby-raper.

"I don't wanna kill nobody no more," Jodi harshly whispered as they stepped off the city bus.

"Just do your part and I do mine," griped Romeo, directing her to start walking the two blocks north to the Biltmore entrance. "And put on dat hat."

"We're not even there yet," she argued, still uncomfortable with the headwear. The wide brim flopped about and obstructed her view of nearly everything over her platform shoe–assisted five-foot-one. That, and the slightest gust of wind was sure to send it sailing God knows where. And hell if she was going to chase the piece of crap hat into four lanes of traffic.

"Camera everywhere," reminded Romeo, already disguised in a woolly cap and dark glasses so overreaching they could have been categorized as goggles. "Put on da hat now!"

On went the floppy hat. During the entire trudge to the hotel—a walk that turned into an extra hike as Romeo circumnavigated the hotel in order to judge the most stealthy entrance—Jodi kept one arm in a hook-shot pose, palm pushing down on her crown to keep those whistling downtown gusts from separating that hat from her head.

A side service door had been propped open to the sidewalk. There was a painting crew off-loading a compressor on wheels and coils of spatter-caked tubing. The stick-up duo slipped by and, in a matter of seconds, had easily borrowed the cargo elevator.

"Ugh," moaned Jodi, complaining about the canned sounds piped into the lift. "Christmas music."

"What wrong wit Christmas music?" asked Romeo. "Who don' like Christmas? You sad little girl who never got present?"

"Oh, I got a gift," said Jodi. "My daddy knocked me up one Christmas. I was twelve."

"I go meet your daddy, I'll show him ma razor," chuckled Romeo. He ran his right index finger across his own neck while, with the left in his pocket, he thumbed the blade of his box cutter—open and closed, open and closed.

Click-clack, click-clack.

"All da baby-rapers deserve to die," insisted Romeo.

The doors slid open to the eleventh floor. Romeo stepped off first, quickly scanned the corridors, then reached for Jodi's hand.

"C'mon," he said. "Same as las' time. You knock, I rock."

"You promised. No more blood," begged Jodi.

"Pervert man no fight me? Then ain' gonna be no blood."

"Your shit gave me nightmares."

"Meth give you nightmares."

"Ssshhh," cautioned Jodi.

"Jus' lemme fine da number, okay?"

There were polished brass plates with directional arrows where the corridors converged. Rooms 1100–1122 to the left. 1123–1144 to the right.

Romeo continued to lead. His pace began to quicken to match his ever-increasing heart rate. The way Jodi figured it, adrenaline was to Romeo's nervous system what crystal meth was to her own. He too needed the rush.

That's when Jodi made a vow. If Romeo spilled so much as a drop of blood in room 1134, she was done with the whole scam. She was going to cut from him, the hotel, and maybe even go right to the cops. She might even offer up her testimony in exchange for some kind of deal that kept her out of jail. While trailing slightly behind Romeo, she found herself fantasizing about a plea bargain for some cushy rehab clinic like the ones advertised in local TV commercials. Shangri-La villas high up in the mountains overlooking Malibu. Ocean views. Paradise for the chemically pathetic.

After a final ninety-degree left, the double suite doors stood before them.

"Do what you do," ordered Romeo. His whisper was served with a little shove just below the sash of her baby-doll dress.

All of a sudden, Jodi's tiny feet felt like leaded weights strapped about her ankles. She swallowed and shuffled forward, aiming that ridiculous hat brim a degree or two below the level of the peephole.

"C'mon!" harshed Romeo, pushing only air across his tongue while letting his face screw into an exclamation point. "Do it!"

Jodi didn't give him the satisfaction of even a sideways glance. She had every intention of following through. She needed to get high. So, she lifted her right hand, curled her fingers into a tense little ball, and rapped three times.

40

"You broke his finger?"

The incredulity in Cherry's voice came with an adorably throaty squeak, all at once both amused and surprised. This came at the end of Lucky recalling for Cherry the events that had followed their parting the night before. Not that Lucky had planned to tell his embarrassing tale. He just had no explanation prepared as to why the dash of the borrowed Crown Vic had a big hole in it, the emptied airbag hastily stuffed back into the compartment.

"Seen some broke bones at the club," admitted Cherry. "Always some dipshit who gets outta hand with one of the girls. Bouncers gotta bounce, you know?"

It was still mid-morning. That seemingly endless shimmer of winter rain had wet the asphalt of Sunset Boulevard, adding to the road noise from all the thousands of rubber tires rolling east and west.

"You don't seem like the 'I'm sorry' type," volunteered Cherry.

"Yeah? So, what type do I seem?" asked Lucky.

"Not sure," she said. "Just not a guy who's got a strong relationship with mea culpas."

"I know how to apologize," said Lucky. "Believe me. Had plenty of practice."

"Preschoolers know how to say sorry," topped Cherry. "Doesn't mean they're sincere."

"Man is missing his one and only daughter. And I was over the line," admitted Lucky. "I can be plenty sincere about that."

Lucky locked the Crown Vic in a parking structure that advertised the first two hours as free to the public. From there they hoofed it across the street to the Biltmore's primary entrance and beelined an angle for the elevators.

"Someday," hummed Cherry, finishing her sentence when she caught Lucky's sideways look. "Someday Miss Cherry's gonna stay in one of these posh-ass hotels."

"So, you plan on making the big coin?"

"I'm not even gonna have to pay. Least, that's how the big stars roll. Hotel calls the paps . . ."

"Paps?"

"Paparazzi," she explained. "Paps shoot the stars comin' and goin'. Because the star is advertising, they get comped by the hotel. It's the food chain for the famous."

"Sounds like you got it all worked out."

"All except how to get there," admitted Cherry. "I know it's a long shot. But, hey. Why *not* me?"

The eleventh-floor elevator doors opened and before either Lucky or Cherry could make a single step forward, the lift was bum-rushed by a skinny blonde in a baby-doll dress. Her ridiculous, ungainly hat practically overwhelmed the doorway.

"Oh," said Jodi once she realized she was being rude. She was clipped and retreating to let Lucky and Cherry off. "Sorry, sorry, sorry."

Once the elevator cleared, Jodi spun back inside and began hammering the close-door button as if she were tap-tap-tapping a Morse code message.

"Ugh," said Cherry once the doors had shut. "Skank had some nasty meth mouth."

"Couldn't tell from my angle," said Lucky, gesturing and mouthing "big damn hat."

According his watch, it was mere seconds shy of 10:15 a.m. when Lucky and Cherry finally arrived at Andrew's suite.

41

"You're a dirty man, ya?" asked Romeo. He was seated on the edge of the toilet in the suite's guest bathroom. Bent at the waist, elbows resting on his thighs, that rusty box cutter in his left hand.

"Told you . . ." wheezed Andrew. The awkward position in which Romeo had shoved Andrew into the dry bathtub made it difficult to breathe. Both his hands and feet were bound with clear, sticky packing tape. "I called the number 'cause I'm looking for my daughter!"

"You a pervert," insisted Romeo. "One of dem fuckin' pedo-peeps."

"I'm not, I'm not."

"Fuckin' hate you."

"Don't hate me, please, I'm not that kinda man—"

"Shut up, ya fuckin' baby-raper." Romeo kicked at Andrew's bare feet. They were awkwardly propped over the porcelain edge. "I know you. All of you. What you really hate are kids. Tha's why you do it."

"My daughter—"

"Said you a baby-raper so shut da fuck up!" barked Romeo, instantly lowering his voice once he'd heard it bounce back off the tile wainscot. "Hey. What happen to you finger? You get it broke diddlin' some little boy's asshole?"

"Just get the money. Leave me alone to find my daughter—"

Romeo lunged at Andrew. If only a feint, it scared Andrew so badly he began to gag and choke on his own spit.

"Yeah, man," smiled Romeo. "Choke on you self. Choke 'n' die. 'Cause all da baby-rapers deserve to fuckin' choke."

"I'm not—" coughed Andrew.

"Listen to me, fucker . . . I said, listen to me!" Romeo half-heartedly stabbed with the blade. Too far. The tip pierced Andrew's khakis, briefly burying a few millimeters into Andrew's skin. "All of you done it to me. My sis. Fucked with us babies, man. Screwed up our heads, ya know?"

"Please, please, please—"

"You don't think you deserve to bleed? After what all you done to da worl'?" Romeo stood, using what little height he had to tower momentarily. "You tink I jus' wan' you money? How 'bout I take your balls, yeah—"

Thump, thump, thump.

At the sound of knuckles on the door, Romeo's arms dropped slack while his eyes practically rolled over into the back of his head.

Stupid whore bitch!

"Don' move, 'kay?" With that, Romeo eased the door shut until the hardware clicked with precision, ran his palms along his jeans to wipe clean the sweat, then tried to appear as if strolling without a care toward the door. He had promised Jodi no blood. As much as it had been a lie, he still needed her to withdraw the money. "You better not forgot the numbers!"

* * *

Lucky's first notion was this: though buffered by a door built from solid mahogany, the man's voice heard from the other side hadn't the whiny tenor he'd come to know from Andrew Kaarlsen. An oddity that might have only caused a minor question mark for the average Joe. But the cop in Lucky had already knocked on a thousand doors with an endless parade of unknowns on the other side. As if on remote, Lucky had shifted his weight to the balls of his feet, tilted his spine to eighty degrees while locking his hips for a collision.

When the door cracked, Lucky's eyes weren't focused at eye level. His gaze was waist high, where a weapon would be. Thus, Lucky clocked the box cutter before the lockset had cleared barely one inch.

And that's when Lucky launched.

All his weight drove upward from his feet to his shoulders, plowing into the doors like a defensive lineman on the hunt for a Sunday quarterback. The hinges helped, allowing all the energy from Lucky to transfer to the solid wood door and then the unsuspecting Romeo.

What Cherry would later recall was the distinct *ting* of metal as the box cutter left Romeo's fingers, spun, and ricocheted off the wet bar. The rest was a revelation of efficiency. Before Lucky pushed through the door, she had thought the heavy-duty bouncers she knew from the Rabbit Pole possessed real-deal skills. Danger management. Out-of-control asshole management. But witnessing Lucky in full badass mode gave her a new definition. The man with the razor was summarily rag-dolled by the former deputy, spun a full three-sixty before all his g-forces were released. The man's body skipped off the marble floor—his head thumping like a melon—before the rest of him connected with that fully closed bathroom door. The impact of man versus bathroom door splintered the jamb at the strike plate, releasing the hinges to creak inward.

The actual reveal was even more of a shock.

Upended in the bathroom tub was Andrew, flopping awkwardly in an effort to get away from the tumult.

"Jesus," cried Cherry, not yet certain what she had gotten herself into.

"Shut the front door," said Lucky, taking an extra beat to touch her shoulder gently. "Please. Shut it now."

Romeo moaned, momentarily disoriented, reaching both arms around himself as if he expected to come up with his rusty razor.

Lucky bent a knee and picked up the box cutter, flicking it closed with his thumb.

"Who the hell is this prick, Andrew?" Lucky grabbed a handful of Romeo's hair and three-hopped him over to the area rug, where he pinned the assailant with a knee while twisting Romeo's elbow into a submission hold. If Andrew had tried to answer, Lucky wouldn't have heard him. He tossed the box cutter to Cherry. "Take care of him, will ya?"

As Cherry hurried into the bathroom, Lucky applied enough weight to make Romeo chirp.

"Can' breathe," complained Romeo.

"My man get lonely? Call for some boy toy spoon play?"

"Not a fag!"

"If I was gonna call you a fag I'd be way less PC about it," said Lucky. "Now, who are you and why are you in my man's hotel room?"

"They're G.D. robbing me!" shouted Andrew from the bathroom.

"Who's with you?" asked Lucky, angling his knee sharply into the dimple of Romeo's low back.

"She's got all my cards and my PIN numbers!" Andrew stumbled out of the tub, peeling what packing tape remained on his wrists.

"What's the girl's name?" Lucky pressed harder.

"Calling 911!" announced Andrew. He was spinning in place until he sighted the suite phone on the lamp stand. "How the heck do I get an outside line?"

"Hang up the phone," ordered Lucky.

"Hang up the . . . They were robbing me at knifepoint!"

"I said, hang up the phone before I break your other finger!" burst Lucky.

Andrew stood momentarily frozen. Phone receiver in one hand. Splinted finger on the other, jutting like a gauze-wrapped phallus.

"Call 911 and you get LAPD," explained Lucky. "It's a crime at the downtown Biltmore so they flood the place. Lotta uniforms, detectives, statements. Then there's the hotel security. After that their insurance guys'll show up and want taped interviews, statements. You dial that phone and we're here all day handling this shit instead of looking for your daughter."

"Thinkin' you didn't get the memo," griped Andrew, not thinking while pointing that fractured finger at Lucky. "I cut you loose. Fired your butt."

"I'm here because she called me," argued Lucky with a nod toward Cherry Pie. "She remembered something."

"Might be, you know . . . somethin' important," stammered Cherry, unconsciously pressed with her back against the bathroom doorjamb.

So, there stood Andrew, half shirtless, whiter than white, broken finger, bruised face, small droplets of blood streaking to his navel, room phone dangling in his left hand. He looked like he had been thrown by a roller coaster.

"Yeah, yeah, I'm fired," admitted Lucky. "And I don't care if you pay me or not. Just lemme find your girl. I gotta finish this. Please?"

Andrew's sallow chest heaved up and down. The wheels behind his eyes spun.

"Then what do we do with him?" grimaced Andrew.

Lucky smirked. "What do you wanna do?"

Andrew straightened—as if a simple posture adjustment had added a rod of steel to his spine. He searched left until he spotted a pair of penny loafers he'd left parked half underneath the sofa. Andrew twisted his bare feet into the shoes, then made an about-face, squaring himself to Lucky and the immobilized Romeo. He eased nearer, flicking his eyes to meet Lucky's. A nod was exchanged. An understanding between men. And with that wordless agreement, Lucky released Romeo and took a half step backward.

Romeo saw it coming. He had only enough time to react defensively, folding himself into a fetal ball before Andrew's first foot landed. The toes of the leather loafers were sharp, driving past his forearms and finding ribs, his solar plexus, and chest plate. Air wheezed from him with each blow.

To prevent Romeo from spinning away from Andrew's punishment, Lucky kept his own boot secured on the assailant's ass. It also allowed him a referee's view. He carefully observed every blow while holding his index finger up to his lips as a reminder to Cherry to keep her lips shut. It was clear this wasn't Lucky's first controlled beatdown. Though Andrew was the man swinging kick after kick into Romeo, Lucky was still in control.

Drips of spittle were forming at the corners of Andrew's mouth when Lucky finally stepped in, calling the bout.

"Enough of that." Lucky had a long stiff-arm jammed into Andrew's collar bone.

"He was gonna kill me!" bit Andrew. "I know it."

"Eyes on the prize," reminded Lucky. "Let's get back to finding your girl."

Andrew was sucking air, gassed and exhilarated after the beating. Yet he nodded. He felt better. Satisfied for the first time in weeks.

"Yeah," said Andrew. "Let's go."

With every twenty-dollar bill the downtown ATMs spit into Jodi's hand, the more forgiving she became. Romeo had easily extracted the four-digit PIN from that pasty-faced john. The numbers—1108—were so easy to remember and, as promised, worked on just about every plastic bank card in the wallet.

Pasty-faced john had beaucoup credit cards.

Carefully employing the floppy hat to shield her face from the rain and the lenses of the ATMs' cameras, she moved from machine to machine, half humming and half singing an old No Doubt song that had somehow stuck in her head.

Jodi maximized the withdrawals on each card, the pile of twenties tucked away in the extra roomy D-cup bra she'd bought at a thrift shop for such occasions.

To hell with rehab. I'm gonna get so high.

Jodi guessed she had collected something around $6,000 from the nine bank cards and five ATMs. Her turnaround back to the Biltmore came within a tight thirty minutes from the time she had first knocked on the door of Andrew's eleventh-floor suite. Wet but so damn giddy she no longer cared a whit about the weather, Jodi hurried back, nearly wiping out when her platform boots made contact with the polished tiles in the lobby. She accidentally skated, half-spun while losing her balance, and was heading for the deck when a sure-footed security guard interrupted her fall with a helping arm.

"Gotcha," calmed the security guard.

"Oh, my. Thanks," answered Jodi.

"Ma'am," asked the security guard after getting a better look at her disfigured face. "Are you a guest with us?"

Jodi wanted to lie and say yes. After all, in her thrift-store D-cup she certainly had the money to afford a room. But the serious gaze from the security guard melted every last line of her resolve. She collapsed cross-legged onto the floor in a heap of sudden tears, confessing all in a punctuation-free fusillade. The robberies. The murder at the Mayfair. And the poor pasty-faced SOB who was probably in the process of bleeding to death in room 1134.

A quick radio call and the guard had marshaled all other hotel security personnel. Five men in all. As the front desk direct-dialed the nearby LAPD, the beefy security team piled into an elevator and expressed themselves to the eleventh floor. There they found Andrew's suite door cracked and inviting. With zero force required, the crew entered, armed only with heavy flashlight batons and a pair of unholstered Tasers.

"What the Christ—" uttered the security guard.

Where Andrew was last seen dropping foot after penny-loafered foot into his assailant's doughy midsection lay only the pimp called Romeo. Alone. Gagged. Bleeding. Motionless. Hogtied with the very same clear packing tape he had first used on Andrew. Laying beside Romeo was that rusty box cutter. Inches from his grasp. Useless as hell.

42

Santa Monica.

On a normal day, Gabe would have awakened sometime shy of noon and walked to his corner convenience store, where he would tank up on a brunch of Skittles, spicy Slim Jims, and a liter bottle of Dr Pepper. After a shower, he would migrate east down Olympic Boulevard until he landed in Hollywood. Hopefully, he would have booked an afternoon's worth of shooting headshots. Cup of hot joe, flip on a power strip, and let the photography begin.

On this day, though, Gabe wasn't feeling it. After a fitful night's sleep, he had awakened at seven and spent the next two hours in bed, barely snoozing, all the while hoping sweet slumber would return. Eventually, he succumbed to the temptation of checking the messages on his cell phone. In doing so, his brain would engage and commit himself to the rest of the day.

While still in bed, Gabe found his glasses on his nightstand and began scrolling through texts. The fourth message piqued him. It was forty minutes old from an unknown mobile number.

> Looking for sub still photog for soft p mopic shoot in SF Valley. Ur # came recommended. Noon to midnight. $300 cash. CB only if interested.

It had been nearly a year since Gabe had pulled down a movie gig. Still photography was usually easy money but for the lousy, non-union long hours. When the offer had finally arrived for Gabe to join Local 600 International Cinematographers Guild, he had shifted his trajectory to more independent work. He was an artist, damn it. And getting paid to photograph prickly actors rehearsing movie scenes was duller than lead poisoning.

If only the indie world pay were consistent. He had taken to shooting actors' headshots as a way to pay rent. Even the occasional real estate gig, photographing homes for brokers who uploaded his work to electronic listing sites like Redfin and Trulia.

And now the movies are calling me again.

Gabe laughed at his own joke. Some movie. A soft porn gig over the hill. That meant dim but pretty performers, naked and simulating sex with the hopes that what little dialogue they garnered would eventually look good on a demo reel.

But $300 cash was $300 cash. Plus, it also gave him an excuse to avoid the Casting Place for one more day. He wasn't sure who or what was waiting for him there. Dangerous or otherwise. The drive to the Casting Place the night before had spooked him silly. Was the invite a trap? Or had Gabe just stumbled onto some unrelated conflict? As he had driven back to Santa Monica, he had practically peed himself every time he glimpsed a cop in a black-and-white.

"Hi. My name's Gabe. You're looking for a still photographer?"

"We are, yeah," said the voice on the other end of the mobile call. "You available for this afternoon?"

"I can do it," answered Gabe. "Cash, right?"

"Paid at the end of the day," said the voice. "You okay with naked grown-ups?"

"We all got one," joked Gabe.

"Text you the address. Hope to get our first shot off by twelve forty-five, so don't be late."

The location was a warehouse in Chatsworth. No surprise there, thought Gabe. For as long as he could remember, Chatsworth was the porn capital of the planet. The sleepy north San Fernando Valley suburb was famous for more X-rated production than Bangkok, Thailand. Even funnier, he surmised, was that he had been told that since Los Angeles County had passed the mandatory condom law, adult films had moved their production locations just to the west to Ventura County, where male sex performers weren't legally required to wear prophylactic protection. This left Chatsworth and thereabouts with an abundance of empty, non-revenue-producing soundstages. Maybe that partially explained the unheralded return of soft-core porn, the shy baby sister to the triple-X stuff found on a thousand internet sites. Softcore was cable TV fare, chock-full of beautiful bodies nearly as exposed as standard pornography, but with prettier production values and no actual coitus.

Longer lenses, thought Gabe. Tighter angles. With the primary emphasis on skin tone and women's gorgeous, orgasmic faces.

I can do that.

As Gabe's car breached the top of the Sepulveda Pass, the most popular artery that joined the Basin with the Valley, he fully expected to see more rain clouds and darker skies. Instead, for what appeared to be the first time in weeks, he witnessed the sun breaking through the storm layer. Shafts of lemonade-streaked light cut through the mist, each lamping the Valley floor.

"So, where's the rainbow?" mouthed the photographer. He scanned the horizon, certain that the confluence of bright light and atmospheric moisture would surely produce an arching cliché of color. And pretty much when Gabe thought it wise to stop searching in lieu of returning his eyes to the road, he spotted a color of ribbon so expansive it appeared to draw a crescent-shaped bridge that cleared the entirety of the Valley below—from Burbank in the east all the way to the infamous Kardashian enclave of Calabasas.

Holy moly.

Gabe fumbled for his smartphone, seeking to snap a pic of the über rainbow through the raindrops that slapped his windshield.

BEEEEEEEEEEEEEEEEEP screamed a car horn blasting from his starboard blind spot. Gabe re-gripped his steering wheel and righted the Honda back between the lines. In his zeal for the photo, the car had drifted dangerously to the right into the next lane.

"Oops, sorry!" said Gabe as if the angry driver in the gray Lexus could read lips at seventy miles per hour. He dropped the phone in his lap before waving apologetically. Too late, he reckoned. He'd already seen the Lexus driver's expressively thick middle finger pressed against the windshield.

The better weather didn't last. By the time Gabe arrived at the warehouse-turned-soundstage, the clouds had closed ranks on the sun and the drizzle had returned. Gabe parked, shouldered his camera bag, chirped the alarm on the Honda, then began a quick counterclockwise circumnavigation of the warehouse in search of a stage door.

WHEN RED LIGHT IS FLASHING, FILMING IN PROGRESS. DO NOT ENTER!

The paint-chipped warning sign was in scarlet red. An extra glance upward and to the right revealed an electric rotating beacon that was both extinguished and still. Gabe reached for the handle and pulled the door open. As sudden darkness enveloped him, he unconsciously flashed back to only seconds earlier when he had failed to notice the empty parking lot, the lack of trailers or electrical cables or diesel generators or any of the other telltale signs that some form of film production was in full gear.

The word *whoops* came to mind.

Gabe felt a slight rush of air from behind and to the left. He heard the high pitch of plastic teeth strung quickly through a loop, followed by what felt like instant pressure on his windpipe. His hands instinctively reached upwards to his neck. But he was jerked backward as if on a leash. He lost his feet. He felt the concrete slab as his shoulder blade connected first, then his skull.

The last thing Gabe remembered was a star field of light erupting from behind his optic nerve in a kaleidoscope of mental fireworks.

Beautiful.

43

West of downtown. Around noon.

"What the hockey sticks am I doing?" pissed Andrew. "I fired you. Not for nothing, either. For reasonable cause!"

Lucky flicked a look into the Crown Vic's rearview mirror. Andrew was in the back seat, angled with one of his legs up on the upholstery, using up the entire bench as his own angry throne. Outside, the cityscape that flanked Olympic Boulevard receded behind him in shades of mid-morning gray.

"You're on a quest to find your lost daughter," waxed Lucky. He had witnessed shock before. Though Andrew didn't technically fit the description, he was clearly experiencing a sort of existential crisis. *And why the hell not?* thought Lucky, considering what he'd been through. "And when we lose somebody we love, we will do anything to get them back. Even the wrong thing."

From the passenger seat, Cherry stayed clear of the conversation.

Not without investment, though. All along, she watched Lucky, trying like hell to read the apparent yet stoic pain behind his eyes.

"Big bald jerk, you broke my finger," bitched Andrew.

"I did," replied Lucky flatly. Then he winked at Cherry. "And I apologized."

"You're not sorry at all," said Andrew. "I can read faces."

"Don't believe me? How's this?" asked Lucky. "When we're done and Karrie is safe and sound, I'll let you break my finger."

Cherry expected to see a smirk on Lucky's face. Any sort of giveaway that betrayed the silly promise. Yet there was none to be detected. The game on Lucky's mug appeared as serious as heart surgery.

"I almost died back there," said Andrew, still trying to convince himself that he wasn't just experiencing a nightmare. "Can crap just get any worse?" Then, before Lucky could respond, Andrew pointed his bandaged digit. "Don't answer that. I know there's worse. There's my Karrie and . . . I'm not crazy, you know. I'm just really, really freaked out."

"We're gettin' her back," Lucky had assured.

"Based on what evidence?"

Cherry had stood right between the men as Lucky explained his thinking. All of it revolved around the casting man named Herm. There were Cherry's meetups with him and his undisguised obsession with Karrie. Then Lucky's encounter with Herm that set his short hairs to attention.

Bad guy, Lucky had said.

If Andrew hadn't bought Lucky's rationale, Cherry surely had. She knew nearly nothing about the former sheriff's deputy. Not a lick about his life, his stop-and-start cop career, the dark nights as a Lennox Reaper, the brief move to Kern County, let alone his brother's subsequent murder and the bloodlust revenge that followed.

But what Cherry did know was this: were she to vanish suddenly, she hoped that someone like Lucky would be charged with doing the looking.

"A hunch," complained Andrew. "Like you're G.D. Columbo."

"Who's Columbo?" Cherry found herself asking.

"TV show from before you were born," answered Lucky. "Actor with a glass eye . . . hell if I know his name . . . played the detective."

"Who always had these hunches that turned out to be right," blasted Andrew. "But look around, dipstick. This is not a TV show."

"Know what?" said Lucky, allowing his patience to wane. "Startin' to think I shoulda left you back in the hotel with Mr. Box Cutter."

"And leaving the scene of a crime?" muttered Andrew. "Gotta be some kinda law we broke back there."

Lucky switched lanes without signaling and braked at the nearest curb. The Crown Vic idled.

"What?" said Andrew.

"Welcome to step out if you don't like where I'm headed," growled Lucky.

"Just drive, okay?"

"Stop pissin' in my ear."

"You work for me." It was a weak reminder that was even more weakly delivered.

"You fired me," said Lucky. "So, I don't work for anyone. Now, you're with the program? Or you're not with the program. Your call, daddio."

Once again, it was just Lucky and Andrew, trading hard looks through the rearview mirror. Nothing more was said as Andrew moved nary a muscle fiber.

Lucky checked his side-view mirror and eased back onto Olympic.

Queenie really liked her job. She liked the basic nine-to-five hours. She liked that there was no expectation to put on the fraudulent face of a front-office personality. She liked the isolation of the windowless basement workspace. It was cool, slightly damp in the air, and she liked being able to hear somebody approaching down the metal steps of the stairwell a good five to ten seconds before they landed in front of her desk. That meant whatever she was doing on her computer—be it trolling YouTube for cute cat videos or ogling the newest batches of tattooed lesbian pornography—all she had to do was coolly close the screen and greet whoever or whatever issue was descending.

Most of all, Queenie liked the building management job because it was a big step up from her old post managing apartment buildings. No longer was she on 24/7 call to deal with every color and matter of tenant fracas, from middling to major crime. As it turned out, her uncanny ability to keep rent checks rolling in while protecting her slumlord boss from all nature of city, county, and civil liability was eventually rewarded when her boss expanded into commercial real estate. Once his deal for the Hollywood property— an old Presbyterian church and primary school—had closed escrow, he handed the keys to Queenie and instructed her to turn it into another money maker. It was her idea to create a turnkey operation, renting space on a daily or monthly rate to casting agents, photographers, or anyone else needing a temporary office. She painted it antiseptic white from floor to ceiling, re-keyed and re-wired every old closet and classroom, and called it the Casting Place.

Queenie was not only back in business, but her employment agreement called for her to receive an equity stake if she could turn a 17 percent profit in the first two years. That anniversary was a mere month away. January 15th. Queenie planned to celebrate with a tattoo-decorated hooker and a bottle of twenty-year-old Macallan.

"You're not one of mine," said Queenie, forgoing to extinguish her cigarette in the presence of the stranger. Something about his affect informed her that he wasn't an actor and he simply didn't give a shit. "You read about us in *Casting Call* or do you just want to look at a rate sheet?"

"Not lookin' to do business," said Lucky. "Lookin' for one of your tenants."

"Which one?" she squinted, realizing she had just left her glasses on the sink in the ladies' bathroom.

"Guy named Herm or Herman," said Lucky. "Tall. Sixty. Mixed race. Salt 'n' pepper hair?"

"Oh. You're a cop." Queenie was as certain as the saccharin in her old-school can of Tab. Lord knows she had answered her manager's apartment door to plenty of police. For years it seemed that half her renters were engaged in some kind of criminal act. "City? County? What can I do you for?"

"My man's room is locked," said Lucky, not letting on that he was between police assignments. If she wanted to believe he was the poh-lice, then who was he to argue?

"I'm not the keeper of Mr. Bland's calendar," said Queenie. "Or any of my customers, for that matter. You have his business number?"

"His mobile," said Lucky. "But I think I might need a home address."

"Other than Mr. Bland's business number, I'm not really required to give out anything else—"

"Not without a warrant," completed Lucky.

"Yes, sir," said Queenie.

"Well, I'm not requiring you," said Lucky, leaning over and placing both hands on her desk. "I'm just asking really nicely."

"Can I ask really nicely for your badge and ID?"

Lucky reached into his jacket and, instead of withdrawing a wallet or business card, he held that small snap of fourteen-year-old Karrie Kaarlsen pinched between his thumb and forefinger.

"Guy I'm looking for appears to have an eye for the young ones," said Lucky. "This one in particular. You seen her?"

"Casting place," said Queenie. "Lotta girls come through here. All ages."

"This one," reminded Lucky.

"Nope." Queenie shook her head.

"This Herm guy. You say his last name is Bland?"

"Mr. Bland, yes."

"He real bad wanted to get next to this," said Lucky, flicking the photo like a playing card so it made a sharp snapping sound. "You want your other tenants . . . or the neighborhood or anybody else knowing that you might be renting space to a potential pedophile?"

At first blush, Queenie didn't give a rip. She'd rented to worse. And she believed it was her constitutional, not to mention fiduciary, duty not to inquire. But still, that January bonus date stuck in her head. The fifteenth. The day she at last would have equity in a business. Her business. Whatever protective mother that was in her felt the need to protect it.

"You're not a cop, are you?" asked Queenie.

"You wanna find out?" asked Lucky. "Or you wanna just gimme what you got?"

"Left my glasses in the ladies' room," said Queenie. "You mind if I?"

As Lucky stepped aside, he hadn't an inkling as to whether or not Queenie was planning to return and read off whatever he needed. Or if she was simply heading off to use the bathroom run as a ruse to rabbit on him. It didn't so much matter as long as he had access to her computer. The moment Queenie began thumping her heavy hams up the staircase, Lucky slid in behind her computer and began a simple search:

HERMAN BLAND

44

Chatsworth. 2:12 p.m.

Herm's initial plan was just to talk. It was going to be a basic man-to-younger-man chat with his workplace neighbor. Simple enough. Look the photographer directly in the pupils and inquire as to what the hell he had to do with the strawberry-blonde unicorn.

Where is she? What'd you do with her?

But as potential conversations ran inside his head, Herm wasn't pleased with the results. No matter the imagined circumstance—be it a happenstance bump in the Casting Place kitchen or an appointed sit-down at the nearby Denny's—Herm heard only denials and obfuscation. In no semi-social scenario could Herm imagine Gabe handing over any more than a clue. If Gabe had anything to do with Miss Strawberry-Blonde's sudden vanishing, he sure as hell wasn't going to volunteer it.

Therefore, a plan B needed to be realized. And in what seemed like no time at all, the simple scheme had turned so elaborate that Herm had almost tossed it out altogether. Only later did he cobble the plot back into action once he had realized that his only other option was to flat-out forget about her.

My unicorn.

Herm began by browsing Gabe's website and resume, choosing to exploit the photographer's experience as an occasional still photographer for movie shoots. The rest fell like dominoes. The out-of-service porn soundstage owned by an old flesh game pal. Herm had already purchased an ax and the industrial-sized zip ties to bundle all the eucalyptus logs he was prepping to harvest. And then there was that honey of a cherry red Husqvarna chainsaw he had been jonesing to put to work.

"I don't have a clue what you're talking about!" barked Gabe, squirming against his bindings—zip ties securing his ankles and wrists behind his back.

The photographer was centered in the middle of the soundstage, bound and prostrate on a double layer of one hundred square feet of reinforced plastic sheeting. Ten mils thick, tear and puncture resistant. Home Depot's priciest.

"Her roommate said she left her with you," said Herm. So calmly, in fact, he surprised himself. Inside he was aching to smash the SOB's kneecaps with the ax handle, letting it swing like a hitter measuring a baseball bat's lethal heft.

"I wanna help you," begged Gabe. "Seriously, I do. Just tell me what she looked like."

"You know what she looked like," said Herm. "Otherwise you wouldn't have taken her from me."

"She was yours?" shifted Gabe, nearly admitting to the deed once the concept of ownership entered into it. "I didn't know. Jesus!"

Herm lurched closer in a feigned strike. The chirp of fright escaping Gabe was high and piercing and would have carried far if not for the industrial soundproofing covering the three-story-high walls.

The yawning space looked so much larger from the inside. Lit with a dangle of incandescent lights hung from miles of Romex electrical cables, the stage was swept and empty in hopes of appealing to a buyer. Upon entry, Herm had recalled its former glory as a virtual city of porno sets—from the ubiquitous living room couch to the office settings to all matter of bedroom combinations. Kind of like an IKEA built for sex acts.

No more.

The soundstage had but one last purpose.

"What. Did. You. Do. With. Her?" asked Herm again.

"Listen, man. I'd never ever done this before," cried Gabe. "It was just money."

"How much money?" asked Herm.

"Sure, sure," realized Gabe. "You deserve your cut, right? Since you saw her first?"

"How much?"

"Five grand. And I'll give half to—"

Gabe wasn't able to get the next thought out of his gullet. His words were replaced by a scream as Herm inexplicably stepped in and swung. Low. The ax handle connected with the apex of the photographer's bent left leg. The knee gave way under the crushing blow, the man's calf, ankle, and foot flopping as if suddenly unhinged.

"You piece of shit!" angered Herm. "She was in bloom, for Christ's sake."

While Gabe continued to wail, Herm circled clockwise.

"Five grand, you dumb shitheel!" bitched Herm. "I was gonna get a hundred! You know why I was gonna get a hundred? Because that's wholesale on a unicorn!"

Herm punctuated the point with another cut with the ax handle, this time glancing off the meat of Gabe's skinny forearm, which had been instinctively trying to block the next painful blow.

"WHO?" shouted Herm. "Who'd you sell her to?"

"A guy . . ." whimpered Gabe.

"WHO?" Herm feigned another blow.

"Armenian."

"Name!"

"Just a guy I know."

"Name!"

"Jake, I think."

"You *think* Jake? Or you *know* Jake?"

"I know Jake!" cried Gabe. "Please. She just fell into my lap."

"Unicorns don't fall into your lap," pissed Herm. "You wait for them. Then you thank the god of your understanding when they appear in your orbit."

"So, so, so, so sorry. I didn't know what I was getting into. Please. I won't do it ever again."

"Like I give a damn what you do next?" said Herm. "I just wanna know how to get in touch with this Jake. Okay? 'Cause unless that motherfucker has already moved her, I want back what was mine."

"Look, look, look. Get me my cell phone. Left it in my car, okay? I can call him for you."

As Herm moved closer, Gabe winced as he fully expected more violence. Instead, Herm rolled him right, fishing into his front pocket until he came up with Gabe's car keys.

"Don't go anywhere," snickered Herm.

Stepping from the soundstage, the daylight forced Herm to squint. He was halfway to Gabe's car before his eyes properly adjusted. An error, Herm suddenly recognized. What if somebody was nosing around? Real estate speculators? Crack abusers seeking refuge or a place to smoke some rock? He did a languid 360 degree twirl and was relieved that nobody appeared inside the corrugated fence topped with galvanized razor wire. The only two vehicles in the lot fronting the property were Herm's SUV and Gabe's Honda. Herm chirped the Accord's lock, opened the door, and easily discovered the mobile device, an extra-large smartphone that bordered on unwieldy. Herm was pocketing the device when his own cell phone buzzed. He switched hands and answered.

"This is Herm."

"Hi," said Cherry. "Guess who I got?"

"Sorry," said Herm, not recognizing the voice despite its familiarity. "Who is this?"

"Cherry . . . Cherry Pie."

"Thought I told you not to call me—"

"Unless I came up with my friend Val," chirped the dancer. "You remember Valeriana? She came up for air late last night."

"Your little friend?" asked Herm, slightly askew. "The strawberry-blonde?"

"Yes. That Valeriana," answered Cherry. "Anyway, you wanted us both, right? I found her. Is that Audi job still open for casting or are we too late?"

A muscle twisted in Herm. Just below his diaphragm where he'd had a hernia surgery just three years earlier. It was almost like a bowel kink, registering a sharp involuntary pain.

"You still there?" asked Cherry.

"Yeah . . ." grunted Herm before recovering his wits. "The Audi spot. Right. No. Nope. I don't think that's closed yet."

"Swell," she said. "Sorry about that other thing with that friend I brought. Just trying to make it in this town, you know? Makin' my own thunder every day."

"What you gotta do," said Herm.

"But I got the right girl this time. The one you met. So, when do you think?"

"When?"

"The callback?"

"Listen," said Herm. "Just so I don't waste your time, let me first check with the agency just to make sure the gig hasn't totally gone another way."

"You still got my number?"

"Sure, I do," said Herm. "Call you back later?"

"Make sure I'll keep my ringer on."

"Hey. And don't lose your girlfriend again, huh?"

Herm kept up a straight face for himself and nobody else while he listened to Cherry serve her best serviceable giggle before clicking off the call. Meanwhile, that knot of tension behind his navel cinched even tighter. His eyes fluttered from the pain, his brain shuttered backward to the day before and the stranger he had bumped into at the Casting Place. The man with the cop posture had flashed him that wallet-sized snapshot of Miss Strawberry-Blonde.

Aaahhhhhhhhhh.

All of a sudden, Herm could see the strings—the tripwires to a trap that some unknown authority was itching to spring. The lies were flying. And as Herm saw it, he would be the designated victim if he didn't get wise. And quick.

That fuckhead photographer said he had sold the unicorn.

Liar.

Then Miss Stick a Finger in Her Cherry Pie claims her teen pal Miss Strawberry-Blonde has resurfaced, ready for their collective car commercial close-up.

Liar.

Herm marched across to his SUV and threw up the rear hatch. The brand-new chainsaw sat on a protective double layer of Hefty garbage bags. Gassed and oiled. But without ever having been sparked. The single piston machine was practically begging to be fired up.

What better time than the present?

In the short walk back to the soundstage door, Herm wondered how loud the two-stroke action of the engine might be. He hadn't a doubt the soundstage would sufficiently muffle most sonic waveforms. He just wondered which would make the most noise. The screaming of the chainsaw? Or the screaming from the asshole photographer?

45

2:34 p.m.

Karrie Kaarlsen calculated that her time inside the cargo container might have been anywhere between twelve and thirty-six hours. The constant darkness, interrupted only by bathroom breaks, the occasional shout or scream, and the tiny bits of daylight that leaked into her prison cell, might have been reasoned into a tighter timeline. But Karrie found herself sleeping and waking so frequently that any sense of a twenty-four-hour cycle had been erased.

She did get hungry. And thirsty. She was quenched by sixteen-ounce bottles of water stacked just inside the steel door. Next to the bottles was a gallon-sized Ziploc baggie stuffed with chalky-tasting protein bars.

"Doctor break!" announced the voice outside Karrie's door,

followed by the now-familiar squeaks of the swing-arm lock as it came undone.

She wondered if she'd heard right. Every so often there had been a double knock followed by a heavily accented voice shouting, "Bathroom break!"

Doctor break?

The container door swung outward, letting in a blast of filtered daylight. Karrie's hand came up with split fingers to shield her eyes. She glimpsed the usual guard, a foreigner of average height in a tracksuit with a nylon stocking pulled down just past his nose. The man's heavy beard was shiny and already sprouting after a recent shave. Maybe it was morning, she thought. A new day and with it all the possibilities of a fresh deck of cards.

"The doctor," said the guard with an impatient gesture.

With a grip that circled her entire biceps, the guard guided her past the other cargo containers—eleven, by Karrie's count—over to a warehouse corner where an unmasked Asian man of grandfatherly age sat on a folding chair. A standard set of general practice medical equipment was on a plastic buffet table.

"Sit," said the guard.

There was an empty seat across from the Asian man. As Karrie sat, she realized the plastic seat was damp.

"Need to ask you some questions," said the Asian man. "Basic medical stuff. Nothing to worry about."

"Why?" Karrie pleaded. Though her question had more of a global interest to it than the micro of the moment.

Why me? Why here? Why now?

"How old are you?"

"Are you a doctor?"

"Yes," said the unsmiling man. "How old?"

"Fifteen."

"Any illnesses?"

"Like colds and stuff?"

"More serious," he said. "Hepatitis, mononucleosis, cancers."

"No," shook Karrie. "Why am I here?"

"Do you know your blood type?"

"No."

"STDs?"

"Please," she begged in a shivering whisper. "What's gonna happen to me?"

"Herpes? Gonorrhea? Sexual disease?" he ignored.

"No."

"Drugs?"

"Sometimes?"

"Addictions?

"No."

"Ever had a full pelvic?"

"Like, with a lady doctor?"

"Gynecologist, yes."

"Once," she said. "My mom let me go on the pill."

"So, you have been sexually active?"

"Yeah."

"How many men?"

"Men?"

"Boys?"

"Dunno," paused Karrie, not caring to think about it. "Five?"

"Men?"

"Young men," she shifted. "Boys, I guess."

"When was your last cycle?"

"Dunno . . . two weeks?"

"Regular?"

"I guess."

"Will need to examine you now," said the doctor, turning to the table. "Please get undressed."

Karrie found her own arms holding herself tighter. She tried to will herself to stop shaking. But her body wouldn't obey.

"Nothing to worry about," said the doctor. "It's just like home. Wherever that is."

"Chenequa," released Karrie. "It's in Wisconsin."

"Cold this time of year, huh?" said the doctor, still not making eye contact.

Yes, thought Karrie. Cold as hell. And for the first time in her months in Southern California, she yearned for home. She undressed and, throughout the physical exam that was never beyond the pulse of perfunctory, she tried to concentrate on her memories of Chenequa at Christmas. If there wasn't frost or sheets of ice, it was the snow. The trees with no leaves. But always with the inviting warmth of an electric candle in practically every house window. Inviting, friendly. Home.

God, if I could only be there now.

"B-12?" asked the doctor.

"What?" asked Karrie, her voice relegated to a helpless monotone.

"Have you ever had a B-12 shot?"

"Huh uh." Karrie just shook her head.

"Goes in the tushie," said the doc. "Little sting but that should go away in a few minutes."

"Whatever," cried Karrie.

"Some people say it gives them a little boost."

"Sweet," she said, barely the bemoan the moment deserved. "Just tell me this will all be over soon."

"I'm just the doctor," said the old Asian man. "Do what I'm told. Best you do the same."

Karrie barely felt the needle penetrate her flank. The message of pain finally registered in her brain when she saw the doctor disposing the needle and syringe.

Pain, she thought. What she'd give for something to dull it all. Not just what hurt. But the whole of it. So Cal. Life. Her family. All of it. Karrie wished she could make it all just disappear.

46

Studio City. 3:16 p.m.

Andrew's mobile phone wouldn't stop buzzing. The hotel was calling him. As was his assistant in Wisconsin, leaving voice-mails, emails, and text messages. There were also numbers that went unrecognized. Local area codes. Lucky suggested that those were most likely inquiries from law enforcement. LAPD and the Biltmore's private security contractor.

"They can all wait," reminded Lucky. "What happened back at the hotel's not goin' anywhere."

"The only diet drinks they had was Coke," said Cherry, awkwardly balancing a flimsy drink caddy while climbing back into the car. "And I had them use provolone on your meatball because they don't have mozzarella."

While waiting for Herm to call back, Lucky had parked at a

random meter along Ventura Boulevard. It was Cherry's idea to order lunch from Subway.

Uncomfortable with just the one investigative string, Lucky had phoned a few of his old Lennox pals who were still on the job. What information he was able to pass along regarding Herm he expected would return with the significant blanks filled in, such as possible aliases, social security digits, and the all-important last known addresses.

"Diet Coke is fine," said Andrew, comfortable and semi-reclined in the back seat of the Crown Vic.

"Bottled water works," said Lucky. If he could've gotten away with the truth, he might've added, "with a Percocet chaser." His back wasn't yet completely howling, but the tension ran all the way down both his hamstrings.

"What if he doesn't call back?" asked Cherry, distributing the sandwich orders.

"Then we spooked him good. So, I follow up on other stuff," said Lucky. "Corner the asshole and press."

"What if he gets a lawyer?"

"I'm between cop jobs. I can't arrest. Which means he can't lawyer up on me."

"What you're saying," monotoned Andrew, "is that you can be convincing. Hey. If that happens. Break one of his fingers."

"That'll make you feel better about it?" asked Cherry.

"Won't know until it happens."

Lucky didn't feel he needed to engage. In fact, with Andrew he felt the less he said, the better. He was banking on his short reserve of patience, old law enforcement connections, and some plain luck.

Luck never hurts, Lucky once reminded Gonzo while she tended to him in his rehab bed. He couldn't help thinking of her every time he saw or heard an overhead helicopter. He wondered if it was her inside the cockpit, piloting the whirlybird. Looking over him as he continued to adventure upon the earth's surface. He sucked back on that bottle of Dasani, nearly draining it to the bottom when Cherry's cell phone rang with a retro hip-hop tune.

"'Gangsta's Paradise.'"

Instantly, Andrew was sitting up. Lucky, meanwhile, slid the device from the dashboard to face Cherry.

"Jesus. That's him," she read.

"So, what's this mean?" asked Andrew. "He doesn't know anything about her?"

"We don't know anything," said Lucky as he readied to keep Cherry on task. "Whatever, wherever he wants to meet you? Just agree."

Cherry cradled the phone and delicately clicked both ANSWER and SPEAKER before easing it back down onto the dash.

"Hello?" she said.

"Yes," said Herm, his voice low and with a deadened resonance. "So, you're saying you have my little unicorn?"

A question mark formed on Cherry's face.

"I'm sorry," she saved. "Who is this?"

"You know very well who this is," said Herm. "As well as whoever else is listening. Perhaps that police officer I met the other night at the casting building."

Andrew flicked a glare at Lucky, quick to assign blame if the plan were to go sideways.

"I'm alone," choked Cherry.

"Please don't play with me," said Herm. "I know you have no intention of meeting me with your young friend. That's because you don't know where she is."

"But she's right here next to—"

"I'm not a police officer," interrupted Lucky, sending a shift in the rules of engagement. "Just an interested party looking to recover a lost girl."

"And so very lost she is," confirmed Herm. "But though I had nothing to do with her disappearance, I may have an inside track as to her whereabouts."

"As in where she is now?" asked Lucky. "Do you know where that is?"

"I have information I would be willing to sell," said Herm.

"How much do you want?" burst Andrew into the conversation.

"Oh," said Herm. "A third person. Great. How many there am I dealing with?"

"How much?" demanded Andrew. "Since it's my darn daughter we're talking about!"

"An actual daddykins," answered Herm. "My day just got that much brighter."

"Where can we meet and how much do we bring?" said Lucky, attempting to keep his tone even.

"Fifty thousand dollars," said Herm.

"For what? Just some information?" angered Andrew.

"Fair number," said Herm. "It doesn't cover my losses yet shows me you're serious. Cash."

"When and where?" said Lucky.

"Call me when you have it," said Herm. "Oh. And if you or anyone is recording this, then by listening you should know we are only discussing a transaction. Cash money for information. A legal exchange. No extortion whatsoever."

What followed was a double beep, signifying the end of the cellular connection. Herm had made his demand and clicked off the call, leaving Lucky, Cherry, and especially Andrew utterly hanging.

47

Chatsworth.

Herm didn't think of himself as a murderer. Sure, he'd killed before. But mostly in the bad old days of too much testosterone and too little sense. A rival once met his end. As did a backstreet thief who had failed to estimate Herm's quickness when he had been a lanky pimp. Herm ended the fight when he took the knife-wielding robber to the ground and snapped his surprisingly weak neck, proving four years of high school wrestling weren't for naught. There was also one of his working girls. She had kept OD'ing, so it was only a matter of time before she killed herself. Herm had only helped her along by fixing one of her needles with a lethal cocktail of heroin and the pain sedative fentanyl.

Not one of his killings could be described as fulfilling. In fact, each had come with measurable regret. Like the way a business was forced to write off failed investments. And that included the poor sap who had stepped in front of his speeding Ford Edge just forty-eight hours before. A significant part of Herm's business plan was making his AA meetings. If someone or something got in his way, well, the folks in the military would call that collateral damage. The price that came from the business of war.

The accident victim had paid the price of Herm being Herm.

But that asshole photographer was different. Not that he wasn't business. For sure, Herm would write him off as an expense. It's just that he felt zero regrets. Herm would later wonder if it was due to the kind of man Gabe was, the personal affront that was the actual indiscretion, or merely the basic human pleasure that was returned from the musical pitch of that honey of a chainsaw. Having never operated an actual gas-operated zombie killer before, Herm found the weight of the machine intuitive and the intense vibrations it delivered exciting all the way down to his loins.

Yes, he surmised. It was like good sex.

After Gabe had given up all the relevant information regarding Missy Strawberry-Blonde, the rest could have been described as puerile pleasure.

Too damn bad recess had to end.

Herm wrapped the individual body parts in the plastic sheeting, only noticing afterward that he'd painted well beyond the lines. The concrete floor had been misted over with a fine pink hue for maybe fifty feet in most directions. Thank goodness for the three-dollar disposable poncho Herm kept in the SUV's wheel well in case of emergencies. When the photographer's remains were stuffed into three separate Hefty bags, Herm weighted each with a decorative masonry block shaped in a cube pattern reminiscent of something Franklin Lloyd Wright would have liked.

Born an artist. Died an artist.

Herm chuckled at his own twisted thought, slammed the hatch of his SUV shut, and climbed into the driver's seat. The digital clock on the dash read 3:38. Right on schedule. Just enough time to sink the body's remains into the oft-ignored Monteria Lake in Chatsworth and make his big meeting.

Finally, it appeared things were working out for Herm.

48

Santa Monica Mountains.

For twenty-one snaking miles, Mulholland Drive is a two-lane ribbon of blacktop loosely strung across various ridgelines of the Santa Monica Mountains. Though made famous in Hollywood films and TV shows, the mountaintop road is primarily known by locals as the dangerously winding stretch that separates the Basin from its less popular sibling, the San Fernando Valley.

On most days, Lucky would find himself preferring to traverse Mulholland over some of the more efficient motorways. In a town that was always in a hurry, a cruise along Mulholland was akin to a vacation from the myopia that came from living in ground-level traffic. The views were usually spectacular. As were some of the properties owned by so many of Los Angeles's overlords.

The rains, which had temporarily abated, left the air clean with a visibility that went for miles on end. Yet the picturesque quality of the moment appeared entirely lost on Andrew. He preferred to speechify from the back seat.

Cherry Pie thought the man was having a nervous breakdown.

"Seriously," droned Andrew. "It had to be the parties. When you were thirteen, did you go to parties?"

Cherry glanced leftward at Lucky—as if asking whether she should answer Andrew's question or not. The roughed-up dad had practically been on a stream-of-consciousness rant since consuming what was left of his meatball sub.

"I said no to the parties. Flat out no way," continued Andrew. "She's just thirteen, right? It's not like these are birthday parties anymore. But my G.D. wife. Was a pushover from day one. Day one! Whatever Karrie wanted. Can't deny our baby Karrie. Oh, no. She might not love us when we're older."

Andrew drew in a calming breath. But his brain switched back into rant mode.

"But these parties. They were party parties. Big house. Parents that are away. It's always like that. Path of least resistance. Parents that go away and leave their homes to their kids are asking for it. Kids are instinctive. Know when there's no supervision. So, that's where the parties are. And that's what kind of parties they are."

"I didn't get invited to those kinds of parties," offered Cherry.

"Well, my Karrie did, and I said no," argued Andrew. "Her mother? What didn't she say yes to? Yes, yes, yes, yes, yes, yes. So, dad says no. Mom says yes. That, we know, turns into 'I hate dad. I don't wanna be around dad. I don't wanna be in the same area code as my dad.'"

"Teenagers are complicated," defended Cherry.

"What kind of parent lets their thirteen-year-old baby girl go to parties with Jesus knows what goin' on? Go ahead. Say it. A lousy G.D. parent. Which, translated, means her lousy, crappy permissive mother who, when she's not letting her one and only daughter smoke whatever or screw whatever, fills her with poison about her one and only father."

Lucky thought Andrew sounded drunk. Pain drugs, he surmised. No doubt he was given a handful of edge-easing parting gifts from the Cedars-Sinai pharmacy. The lizard part of Lucky's brain wondered what kind of drugs. Brand? Chemical functionality? It filled his mouth with saliva and made his back molars grind.

"You're a good father," Cherry tried to save.

"Bullshit," insisted Andrew, most likely as a way to beg for more compliments.

"Look how far you've come," argued Cherry. "What you've done. What you're doing for her."

"Don't see her mother here, do you?" argued Andrew.

"That's right," agreed Cherry. "I'll bet when she sees you she runs right into your arms. Cries, even. I sure would."

Lucky was impressed. Cherry had somehow steered the conversation away from Andrew pissing on about what an awful chore parenthood was and converted it into an ego-building exercise. She was turned in the seat, peeking around the headrest. Coyly. Like a stripper working a lap dance for tips.

Lucky found himself stealing looks. He was terribly entertained by Cherry's show. He noted how her teasing upper lip would slide back into a comforting half smile. Mature as hell for someone just twenty-two. Her customer, the broken dad in the back seat, allowed her cooing voice of reason to blow some much-needed air into his weakened chest. The amazing power of belief. Cherry was infusing Andrew with her confidence. And a man who believes in himself, or his manhood, is warm clay. A potential customer ripe for the plucking. Rainmakers, the strippers called them. With ego and coin enough to order thousand-dollar bottles of champagne and slip Benjamin after Benjamin into a girl's sequined G-string.

Lucky reminded himself of the package. In the footwell right behind Cherry rested a FedEx envelope clamped with a binder clip. Stuffed inside were five $10,000 stacks of green, courtesy of the Bank of Conrad Ellis. Lucky was wondering if there would be any cash leftover. And if sweet Cherry Pie was working Andrew in hopes of receiving the biggest tip of her life.

Herm had demanded they meet in a public space, choosing— strangely enough—the sporting goods aisle inside the Van Nuys Costco. Only after agreeing to a time and place did Lucky recall that an ID card was required to enter the big box retailer. As it turned out, neither he nor Andrew were members. Around the time Andrew was calling American Express to see if his Platinum Card might extend them entry privileges, Cherry produced her very own membership card.

"One of the perks for workin' at the Rabbit Pole," smirked Cherry. "Don't ask me why. Not like I'm buyin' Velcro bras in bulk."

After six miles of traversing west along Mulholland, Lucky steered the Crown Vic north and downhill through a hillside residential enclave known as Woodcliff Estates. The single-story homes were all modest, built mostly in the sixties, well-tended, and adorned more with expensive European cars than Christmas decorations.

Showbiz folks, thought Lucky.

Lucky pushed on the gas, instinctively wanting to get out of there and get on with the plan. It was a quick swivel onto Ventura, then up Sepulveda Boulevard into Van Nuys. In minutes, they were cruising the acres of parking at Costco for an available space.

"I'm carrying the money," announced Andrew.

"Remember," said Lucky. "We're paying him for information. Not your daughter."

"My money," moaned Andrew. "And I'll know if he's telling the truth or not. If it leads to my little girl. Might be some leftover for you and Stripper Girl."

"'Stripper Girl,'" grinned Cherry. "Like that. Kinda like a superhero in stilettos. Do I get to wear a cape?"

Inside the warehouse store were miles of bulk retail, stacked high and dry on industrial racks. The canned Christmas tunes warbled off the concrete floors and walls into an indecipherable musical mush. And the damn crowds. It was Friday, yet the building seemed as gagged by bodies as a supermarket on Thanksgiving eve.

Cherry led the way to the sports and fitness aisle, showing the trio down along a wall passage alongside pallets laden with fifty-pound bags of discounted dog food.

"My favorite aisle," Cherry pointed out as she moved beyond the housewares.

Delightful, laughed Lucky to himself. Underneath the tattoos, purple hair, and that teacup body, Miss Cherry Pie was a wannabe Suzy Homemaker.

The sports and fitness aisle was wide yet jammed with products from bicycles to backpacking equipment to the newest elliptical trainers. Christmas shoppers browsed, but compared to some other causeways in the warehouse, there appeared to be some breathing room.

"Now what?" Andrew impatiently bounced.

"We wait," replied Lucky with a glance to his watch. He spun slowly until he spotted a security camera mounted on the ceiling. From there he could follow the looping cabling that linked other cameras, one dedicated for each aisle. Herm most likely knew as much in advance. He had set the meeting, the time, and place, and that spoke volumes about the kind of control he needed to exert. He wasn't scared of the police, otherwise he wouldn't have chosen a locale where authorities could so easily blend in. That in itself confirmed he had nothing more than information to exchange.

Then again, the meeting itself could just be part of a con. And Herm could have nothing substantive to offer but hope and bullshit.

"How long do we wait?" asked Andrew.

"We'll know that when it happens," said Lucky. He tapped on Cherry's shoulder blade. "You did good. But you don't have to be here."

"But I'm the only one he knows," said Cherry.

"Not about you anymore," said Lucky, hushed. "About dad over there and what's in the envelope."

"Kinda need to stay," explained Cherry with a shrug. "I wanna find her too."

"All right," ceded Lucky. "Just keep to the background. Don't talk."

Cherry, arms folded, retreated to a random post in front of cartons of tennis balls. She exchanged nods with Lucky, inhaled heavily. She was clearly involved. Nervous. And uncertain about the outcome.

"Anytime now," sing-songed Andrew.

Exactly, spoke Lucky to himself. Anytime.

49

Van Nuys.

Herm had arrived early. Parked in the far northeastern corner of the lot, he had grabbed an oversized cart, flashed his membership card to the pimpled employee working the door—and simply shopped. Mostly for groceries. Because that's what Herman Bland did every week. Along with Home Depot, Costco was one of Herm's post-sobriety discoveries. He especially enjoyed Saturdays, when endcaps of nearly every food aisle were manned by sales clerks hawking all matter of tasting tidbits. Food pimps, he called them. And because there was so much free chow to graze, he didn't even mind when it seemed like the entirety of a living ancestral tree would clog the main drags. As if weekend marketing qualified as a family getaway.

Once Herm had filled his cart, he continued to stroll as if he were still seeking one last item. All along, though, he kept his activity to three food aisles, the center one being directly opposite the sporting goods aisle on the other side of the warehouse. Between was the clothing section, most of which was spread out on tables, making it rather easy for a tall man such as Herm to peer over other shoppers with minimal visual obstruction.

Despite his bulging cart, it was on Herm's tenth or so trip down the cereal aisle that the double-box deal on Special K became too much to resist. He'd only just found a place to rest it in the cart when, by rote almost, he'd given another glance across the store. His first read was a glimpse of Cherry Pie's purple hair. Nearly instantly, Herm picked out Lucky's features, easily recalling him from those two quick encounters at the Casting Place. The unknown was the third man. Average, red-haired, abnormally pale, and hugging what appeared to be an overnight envelope.

The unicorn's daddy.

The man with the package appeared as unremarkable as his daughter was remarkable. Proof that in some families good looks skip a generation or two. Herm would have to reserve judgment until he saw evidence of what the mother looked like.

Next, Herm shopped a loose but ever-constricting noose around the trio, his every sense sniffing for any kind of police presence. He detected none. In fact, it appeared 90 percent of the men there were short, ethnic, and possibly possessing their own wants and warrants for arrest. No, surmised Herm. Cherry and her two men had come unaccompanied and without an ulterior agenda. There was money to be exchanged for information. Nothing more.

The big man entered the sporting goods aisle from the south, nearest Cherry, and steering the laden shopping cart as if it were a natural barrier.

Cherry unconsciously chirped her surprise.

"Once again," said Herm. "It's just you but noooo blondie."

Lucky spun toward the encounter, shortening the distance between himself and Herm by three quick steps.

"Close enough," warned Herm, swiveling the shopping cart. Herm's eyes shot a look at Andrew. "You the daddy?"

Andrew nodded and started to speak at the same time. But

nerves grabbed his words somewhere at the back of his throat, causing a spasm of coughing.

"Sorry, yes," Andrew finally choked out.

"She looks nothin' like you," said Herm.

"Where's my daughter?" forced Andrew.

"Never said I knew a thing," defended Herm, his hands casually held out, palms facing the ceiling. "Just know who's got her."

"How would that be?" asked Lucky.

"Because I know the young man who grabbed her," said Herm. "Photographer. Beard. Asshole named Gabe." He gave a knowing look at Cherry as if it were her role to rubber stamp what he said.

Cherry nodded at Lucky.

"And what'd Gabe do with her?" pressed Lucky.

"Sold her to the Armenians," said Herm. "Not what I woulda done. But they paid."

"Armenians?" quizzed Andrew. "What's that mean?"

"Organized crime racket," monotoned Lucky. "Trafficking, right?"

"Stole her for peanuts," added Herm. "Tragedy."

"So, that's what you got?" asked Lucky. "Just some bullshit story?"

"I got more," aimed Herm. "You got the cash?"

Andrew held up the FedEx envelope.

"Lemme see?" said Herm, hand reaching out.

The nervous father merely unhinged the clip and tilted the envelope so Herm could see the cash. One of the bound $10,000 stacks spilled out and onto the polished concrete. Andrew scrambled down to the floor to snatch it up.

"It's for real," said Lucky. "Just need to know what you know."

"Like I said, grabbed and sold to the Armenians." From his pocket, Herm produced Gabe's cell phone. He wedged it betwixt two extra-large bags of frozen mixed vegetables, then gave the shopping cart a push toward Lucky. "Name you're looking for is Jake. Everything you need to know is on the phone."

Lucky's first instinct was that the phone was a mere prop in a con—the magic item that possessed secrets worth paying for.

It was a ruse as old as civilization. But as Lucky braked the cart and reached for the phone, his eyes tilted to Herm's pink tennis shoes—an odd color on a debonair man who looked stylish wearing just Dockers and a black T-shirt. Lucky brought his attention back to the phone and, while scrolling the contacts for "Jake," couldn't help but sneak glances back to Herm's pink sneaks.

Only the sneakers weren't pink.

They were white, spattered with a fine coating of red. Most might have suspected paint. Only Lucky, the Lennox cop, had seen way too many gangbangers in white sneakers accidentally colored by blood. As if bloody footwear were the one item a killer would forget to double-check.

"So, how do I know this is the guy?" asked Lucky. He'd found "Jake" in the contacts list. He showed Herm the phone. "Just a name and a number. Could be anybody."

"Believe me, it's not," smirked Herm. "Straight from the asshole's mouth."

"How about this? I talk to the asshole," said Lucky. "Just to cover my bases."

"Assumes the asshole can talk to you," replied Herm with the same satisfied smirk. "But sadly, he can't."

"Pay him," Lucky said to Andrew.

"What?" shot Andrew.

"I said, give him the package," demanded Lucky.

"In exchange for what?" asked Andrew. "So far we don't know squat."

"I know enough," said Lucky, approaching Andrew. "The money."

"No," posed Andrew, indignant as hell.

That's when Lucky reached with both arms and snatched the FedEx envelope from Andrew. He placed it in the shopping cart and rolled it back toward Herm.

"Nice doin' business," said Lucky. "Now, go."

"Screw that!" spat Andrew. "We're not done with you—"

"Lemme ask daddy man somethin'," asked Herm. "Why'd your little girl run away from home?"

"Why do teenage girls do anything?" Andrew fired back.

"See? That's the problem," said Herm. "You mommies and daddies say you never know. Least, that's what you always say."

"You don't know crap!" angered Andrew.

"Oh, but I know these girls," smiled Herm. "That's 'cause when I get 'em all warm and cuddly and trusting, they tell me all of it. And you know what?"

"Shut up!" Andrew spat at Herm.

"Let's go," ordered Lucky.

"Always a good reason," finished Herm. "Always."

Lucky had Andrew by the shirt and was walking him backward. Andrew bucked, pointing his broken finger.

"Walk away!" hissed Lucky, manhandling Andrew into a one-eighty turn. He was trying to get the seething parent out of the sporting goods aisle. Cherry quickly followed without saying goodbye or making eye contact with Herm.

"What'd you just do with my money?" demanded Andrew. "That bastard's the bad guy! I know it!"

"He's a bad guy," answered Lucky. "Just the wrong bad guy."

"I just paid him fifty thousand dollars! For what?"

The trio exited Costco without a purchase. Lucky would go on to explain that it was all about the blood on the shoes. Fresh, he said. Still bright, oxygenated, with some drops having soaked into the fabric.

"How the hell do you know it wasn't my Karrie's blood?" pressed Andrew.

"It was all about the other guy," remarked Lucky. "It was his blood. He's probably dead or hurt real bad after Herm back there tortured him."

In the back of his mind, Lucky was already onto the Armenian connection and that one name on the phone. *Jake.* As he maneuvered the Crown Vic out of the Costco lot, he was on the phone to his old pal, Bledsoe. The division captain's phone went directly to voicemail.

"It's Lucky," he began. "You know that guy I asked you to run the dogs on? Herman Bland of WeHo? Add him as a suspect in a one-eight-seven. Just met. Shoes covered with blood so you're gonna need some kind of PC before you bag 'im. Call me back. I got a lead and a phone number I need help with."

"What's next?" asked Cherry.

"Taking you back home."

"And if I don't wanna go back home?"

"What you do with the rest of your day is your business," said Lucky. "You and Mr. Kaarlsen can work out something between what you deserve and what he thinks he owes you. Isn't that right, Andrew?"

"He'd pay you out of his end," lamented Andrew. "But I already fired him once."

"I'd like to help," shied Cherry. "More than I have, you know?"

Lucky didn't have an answer for her. At least, not yet.

50

Woodland Hills. 3:54 p.m.

"Hagop Aram Tobarian," repeated Jake, knowing that in a matter of seconds he'd have to spell his birth name. At thirty-one, he had long since been accustomed to the routine of repeating his name twice, maybe three times, then having to spell it for whomever was on the other end of the phone call. In this case, it was someone in the Fraud Department at American Express.

"H as in Henry. A as in apple," recited Jake by rote. Sometimes while going through this all-too-familiar exercise, he'd curse his Armenian name, wishing he'd bucked his parents' wishes and married his Taft High School sweetheart, Jamaica Blume. He'd even fantasized about taking her last name in lieu of his own while legally switching his first name to the easier-to-spell Jewish form, Jacob.

Once Jake had identified himself as the primary cardholder, the Pakistani-sounding customer service rep read off the series of suspicious charges on his account. He leaned back in his tilting office chair, feet up on a Korean conflict–era gray metal tanker desk, nodding instead of scribbling down each financial indiscretion. He was more certain with every line item that there was no charge card theft involved. These online items were most likely the result of one of his wife's buying binges. Having to listen to each and every impulse buy was like another tiny shoe kicking at his testicles.

Ah. His buxom Ana Sofia with her raven hair, sleepy brown eyes, and old-world curves. Jake truly loved her as any Armenian-blooded man would love the mother of his children. Four in all, ages two to eleven. Three girls and a baby boy. All but the toddler already enrolled in a West Valley private school. Add to that a mortgage, the two leased cars, utilities, insurance, and all the groceries that were required to fill his progeny's pie holes—the bills were entirely unmanageable on his salary as an overpaid tire salesman. Since high school he had toiled at his father's Woodland Hills business, working his way up to manager and sales chief. Yet as generous as his father was, Jake had still managed to accrue more debt than tangible assets. What he would do without direction from his cousin Zagreb—better known as Ziggy to his peers—was a mystery he didn't care to unwrap.

Ziggy's game was girls.

In fact, Jake knew, Ziggy's business was lots of things. Most of them illegal. Back in high school, Jake had tagged along as the lookout on a few burglary jobs, eagerly accepting the easy cash he would later spend on weed and cocaine. Whispers in the Armenian community of Jake's extracurricular activities eventually reached Jake's father's ears. After that, most contact with cousin Ziggy was severely curtailed. For at least a decade, Jake kept his associations with Ziggy to tilting shots of *oghi* at family gatherings.

On one such holiday, Ziggy, who was also married with children, listened to Jake's complaints about his wife and her sometimes unhinged shopping addiction.

"You need money, cousin?" Ziggy had inquired. "I might have some easy work for you."

Cash, like the old days. Only in rolled hundreds instead of the crumpled twenties Ziggy used to feed Jake after a job.

"I'm brokering girls," Ziggy had told him. "Prostitutes destined for work overseas."

White girls. Young and fresh and the type who sell for big dollars to buyers with a particular taste.

Jake caught on quickly. Ziggy had been talking about human trafficking. A repugnant crime, especially when he thought of his own young daughters. Ziggy thought he could use Jake's tire trucks as camouflaged transportation, moving his human cargo from one San Fernando Valley depot to the next.

Of course, Jake kindly declined his cousin's offer out of hand. Soon, though, after a marathon night crunching the numbers on his household's expenses—and seeing how Ana Sofia didn't seem to mind at all that her husband had slept for two lonely nights on the den couch of their Canoga Park home—Jake rung up his cousin and simply said:

What do I gotta do?

This is how Jake began straddling two different worlds: the legitimate retail tire trade of his father, and the illicit sex-trafficking game that was making his cousin a very tidy sum.

It wasn't long before Jake had graduated from carting drugged young women from warehouse to warehouse in his father's tire trucks—to playing point man to the various stringers Ziggy employed. Once the girl was vetted by Ziggy, he'd turn the action over to Jake, who would supply the stringer with enough flunitrazepam—a.k.a. Rohypnol or Narcozep—to incapacitate the target; instructions for preparation, use, and transfer; plus cash for the final exchange. Jake would then drive the tire truck to one of Ziggy's warehouses, where the girls were kept in cargo containers until they were ready for their overseas journey.

Imprisoned, Jakey. You're a modern-day slaver.

The guilt that sometimes shamed Jake was usually flushed by a concentrated dose of his immediate family. A reminder of the voraciousness of their daily needs. And those fat envelopes stuffed with hundred-dollar bills he received every week.

Jake was just finishing up with one of his repeat customers—an Encino housewife whose run-flat tire rims kept getting bent out of shape every time she parallel parked. Her sob story was redundant as hell.

"It can't be my driving," the housewife insisted. "The wheels are just defective."

Jake's phone buzzed, the vibrate function practically sending it skittering across the desk's surface. Where the telephone number should have been displayed, it read NUMBER BLOCKED.

"Will you excuse me just a moment?" asked Jake. He picked up his mobile phone and slipped out the door and into the five-stall garage, where the constant hydraulics would be sure to cover most of his conversation. Jake answered, "This is Jake."

"Need a delivery tonight," said a voice that Jake knew as his cousin Ziggy's.

"No can do," answered Jake. "Wife's got me locked down for a neighborhood thing."

"You're so pussy whipped," argued the older cousin.

"Is what it is, dude."

"What's the thing?"

"Neighborhood watch meeting. You know. Where some cops come by and tell everybody what they can do to keep the 'hood safer."

"So, it's bullshit, then."

"We're hosting. I'm dead if I don't show."

"How late does it go?" asked Ziggy. "'Cause I don't need my delivery until ten."

"Might be tight," said Jake. "Where's the stuff get to?"

"San Pedro."

"You're trying to get me divorced."

"You will never be divorced," laughed Ziggy. "Not from Ana Sofia. She'll kill you first."

"So, you're trying to get me killed," corrected Jake.

"Delivery's gotta happen. We're committed and I'm a truck short."

"Then get a U-Haul."

"It's you, cuz," pressed Ziggy.

Jake did a slow turn, eyeballing the activity in the shop to see if anybody was eyeballing him. Four of the five stalls were filled, three cars up on lifts. Business was good. Jake imagined that if he were the boss, he'd have been able to pinch off the pressure from Ziggy with an efficient *lavet kunem*, the Armenian catchall for *fuck off*.

But he wasn't boss. At least, not yet.

"What's on the truck?" resigned Jake.

"Thirteen full sets new," said Ziggy. "Everything from off-road to all-terrain to mud."

To defend against anybody who might be listening in—electronically or otherwise—Ziggy and Jake had devised a simple code. *A set of tires* was a kidnapped girl. The genus of road rubber defined that category or quality. *All-terrain tires* was code for an average, pretty girl. *Mud tires* defined a girl of African-American extraction. *Off-road tires* equaled any Hispanic or brown-skinned girl. *Snow tires* were, of course, white girls. A petite girl was a *low-profile tire*. Tall girls were *truck tires* and the larger, more zaftig girls simply categorized as *heavy-duty*. Young girls versus the still attractive but over twenty-two-years-old women were described simply as *new treads* and *re-treads*, respectively.

And lastly, but most profitably, were the special girls with unusually beautiful features. These girls were almost always younger model Caucasian teens with a classic, scrubbed American look of naturally blonde hair, blue or green eyes, fertile but slim bodies, and a fresh bloom of freckles dappling pairs of rosy cheeks. The code for these pricey young lasses was the rare but still manufactured *whitewall*.

"Oh," added Ziggy. "Got one set of whitewalls. So, handle with extreme care."

But for the short notice and delivery hour, everything else appeared normal. San Pedro or Long Beach harbors were the typical destinations where the human cargo would be loaded onto foreign freighters. Daytime was favored over night because deliveries during normal business hours were so much less suspicious.

Concerns for random discovery were also minimized due to fears of terrorism being so high that few federal inspections ever took place on vessels *leaving* American ports.

"Kinda weird delivery time," remarked Jake. "Sure you got your a.m. from your p.m. sorted?"

"Is what it is, cuz," said Ziggy. "Text the deets. You just make sure the truck is on time."

51

Studio City.

"Contrary to popular belief, there's not much substantial data on it," said Naomi Sanchez, the lieutenant in charge of the Los Angeles Sheriff's Department of Human Trafficking Unit. "On average, it's something like seventy-two or so hours. But that's the FBI national average. It changes depending on who's moving the cargo."

"I told you," chirped Lucky, damning both the distracted driving law that banned using a handheld cell phone while operating a motor vehicle on the road, as well as the all too frequent red traffic lights. He was eventually freeway bound on the 101, topping the Crown Vic out just south of eighty-five miles per hour, weaving when he could between the slower traffic. "This is the Armenian mob."

"Time from abduction to leaving US jurisdiction?" she asked

herself. "Twenty-four hours, a hundred hours. Without under-standing how they have set up the pipeline, it's anybody's guess."

"You've got zero CI's inside the organization?" queried Lucky, fishing for the unit's confidential informant.

"As a former sheriff, you must know all assets are protected," said Naomi. "I'm only talking to you as a courtesy to one of your former colleagues."

Cherry had been alternating her view from the serpentine track Lucky was picking down the freeway to the man himself with the cell phone glued to the side of his granite face. She lent an ear to his half of the conversation as he seamlessly switched from leaving terse voicemails for men named Bledsoe and Lopes, to some woman called Emery.

Then her eyes shifted to the rising slopes of the southeast end of North Hollywood and the familiar architecture of Universal City. The movie studio seemed more amusement park than old Hollywood dream factory. In addition to all the rides and attractions, a destination called City Walk had been added, offering a nightly neon mix of shopping, dining, and movie-going as a way of keeping its greedy fingers in to the pockets of visiting tourists. Finally, towering over the park were two high-rise hotels, the Hilton and the Universal Sheraton.

Suddenly, Cherry's heart felt an uncomfortable squeeze. Like some cold hand had reached inside her chest and laid claim to it. It had been on the top floor of the Universal Sheraton where, only days earlier, she had met the adorable girl who introduced herself as Valeriana. Even worse, Cherry admitted to herself she had known at first glance that the new party dancer was under-age—sixteen at the most. Yet Cherry had extended an invitation to show the girl around that Valley sleaze den, the Rabbit Pole, where women like Cherry lost their clothes and a good chunk of their self-esteem in exchange for tips.

"That's where we met," said Cherry, gesturing past Lucky to the Universal property. "Top floor of the Sheraton."

Andrew answered with a resounding snore. After Costco, he'd complained of pain in his hand, so he'd popped some of his prescribed Vicodin before stretching across the back seat of the car. He'd fallen asleep moments after Lucky had ramped the borrowed car onto the freeway.

In the meantime, Lucky was dialing police sources for assistance and information, leaving gruff voicemails and his callback number. Cherry reached into the cup holder and removed the smartphone they'd purchased from that bogus casting man, Herm. Everything about that recent encounter had crept under Cherry's skin. The man seemed so smug and without a scintilla of morality. Cherry wondered why the hell her instincts hadn't served her well when she first auditioned for the scumbag. Or even at her second encounter. Was her own, personal ambition so great that she had completely shut off her creep detector?

The phone in her hands appeared new, well cared for, with a hard rubber protective case. Cherry knew more about Herm than the mysterious Gabe. Perhaps the smartphone would provide an answer. Then she recalled Val . . . er, Karrie . . . excitedly expressing that Gabe was a photographer. If such was true, then the smartphone might contain photos he had taken. Or even pictures of . . .

The phone was unlocked, so Cherry expertly opened the menu and found the icon for photo albums. She clicked the most recent stream. The first saved picture she saw was a simple snap of a tray of gourmet muffins. It had been attached to a text sent to "Queenie" and captioned, "Choose your poison." Cherry swiped to the right, bringing up the very next photo. The image injected her with an all-over chill.

The photo was of Karrie Kaarlsen—eyes shut and most likely sleeping. It was a tight image, above the shoulders and a bit washed out due to the blast of artificial light from the smartphone's flash.

Swiping again, Cherry gasped at the next picture of Karrie, still asleep, but stark naked except for her panties. The young girl was displayed on a rumpled bed, posed just as she was for her close-up, only pornographically exposed. There was also an attached text message to the aforementioned "Jake." The message read:

What do u think? 15 yrs n ready for u.

Cherry hurriedly switched into the text function, seeking the rest of the conversation. She quickly discovered Jake's reply:

Same as las time. $$$ after deliver.

Gabe had written back:

2night 2 soon?

To which Jake had replied:

4 am. Same spot.

Quickly shifting back to the photo album, Cherry swiped through five more photos of the young teen, each of her sleeping—drugged, guessed Cherry—in progressive states of undress.

"Jesus," she whispered.

She turned her head slowly, sneaking a look into the back seat. The snoring had subsided as the father had rolled to his side and pressed his face into the crease between the bottom and back cushions. Then, swinging her look back to the front, she caught Lucky staring down at her with a furrowed brow as if to ask, "What the hell did you just find out?"

"When we get to my place," Cherry whispered. "I promise to show you." With that, she pressed an index finger to her lips with a silent hush and a gestured glance back toward Andrew.

52

5:43 p.m.

The guard instructing her to wash was armed. Before that, when Karrie had found a chance to peek, she hadn't seen any guns whatsoever. That didn't mean she hadn't been scared. Or obedient. The situation alone was enough to crush anybody into compliance. But seeing the butt of his short pistol sticking out of the back pocket of his saggy jeans practically made her pee. As if the seriousness of her circumstances had somehow escalated. Until that very moment, Karrie had instinctively thought she would make it out alive.

After the armed guard swung her door open, he had disappeared for a few seconds and returned with a bucket of cold soapy water, a torn sponge, a half-empty jug of bargain shampoo, and an unopened roll of paper towels.

"Clean up," he said in a plain and unambiguous American

accent. He was slight and, like the other guards, had been wearing a nylon stocking over his head to obscure his facial features. Only he had clearly tired of disguising himself and had it pulled up to his forehead, revealing a youthful, clean-shaven face.

Karrie reached for the bucket handle, intending to haul it back into the darkness of her cargo container.

"Nope," said the guard. "Sorry. But you gotta do it right there."

Karrie released the bucket and stared back at the guard as if to say, "With you watching me?" The guard withdrew a few steps and answered with a shrug.

"You're going to a party tonight," said the guard, practically as an afterthought. "So, I'm supposed to remind you to do a good job."

"Where's the party?" asked Karrie.

"Just wash up," he said. "I gotta do all you girls."

For the first time, Karrie thought about running. Just flat-out barefoot in any direction. Would she find a door? Where was it and would there be more men with guns? How far would she get before she felt a bullet strike her in her back? It was a liberating notion. Somehow, in that flash of time, Karrie imagined death would be better than the humiliation of scrubbing herself clean before an armed thug no more than nineteen years old.

Karrie's feet felt cold and made of stone. She even wondered if her body remembered how to run. Though imprisoned for mere hours, it had already felt like eons.

Karrie modestly turned herself around and began to disrobe, nearly certain that at any moment the guard would order her to turn back around so he could satisfy his eyeballs. Yet no order came. She stripped until she was naked, then squatted before the bucket and, using that old sponge, washed herself. The water was cold and smelled of cheap dish soap. Yet something about it felt good. Like progress.

"Don't forget your hair," nipped the guard. "Once you got it soaped, I'll bring you a fresh bucket to rinse with."

As instructed, Karrie washed her hair last, wetting it then pumping the pink shampoo into one of her palms before rubbing the goo deep into her scalp. It smelled like a mix of bubble gum and mouthwash. And when the suds crept into her eyes, the stinging of it made her mad enough to bark.

"I could use the fucking rinse water," she snapped.

Her eyes were shut, and she was still squatting when she felt him rub next to her and remove the soapy bucket. He was walking away from her. To where? And how far? If there ever was a time to bolt.

But you're naked, Karrie. With soap in your eyes! You can't see shit!

"Hey!" she shouted bravely. "I could use some conditioner!"

"What fucking conditioner?" echoed a female voice from inside a distant container.

Tired of resting on her haunches, Karrie decided to sit with her butt against the freezing concrete. It felt like ice. But her burning quads thanked her. Moments later, she heard footsteps and the slopping of a fresh bucket of water placed in front of her. Her hands were reaching forward to find the bucket when she felt her right wrist pulled into a man's grip.

"Next time, ask nicely," said the guard. He slipped a tube of hair conditioner into her hand. It was smooth and full and felt brand new.

"Thanks," Karrie said, her voice turned meek but appreciative.

"Get to it," said the guard. "I got other girls."

Karrie knelt and used her cupped hands to ladle the clean water into her hair. It was painstaking, and she doubted that she'd ever rinse all the cheap shampoo away. Nevertheless, she globbed the cream rinse into both palms and was grateful for the rosy fragrance. She shivered as she rubbed, hoping to reach every follicle. Cold as she was, she realized that she preferred to be seated naked and near freezing on the cement rather than locked inside the stinky container. She massaged her roots slowly, hoping to make the moment last. Karrie didn't realize the guard had, once again, disappeared.

"You'll need this," he said upon his return. In his hand was a gallon-sized Ziploc baggie containing a plastic hairbrush and a collection of makeup samples cosmetics counters give away at

Christmastime. "Pick something to wear out of the box. Make yourself look fuckable, you get to party. If you don't, it's back in the container."

With his foot, the guard slid over a cardboard container over-stuffed with trashy clothes. Lingerie, mostly. Some with the tags remaining. There was also a garbage bag laden with random sizes of women's high heels.

Whoo-hoo. A party.

He might as well have said they were going to Marie Callender's for apple pie. What Karrie heard was the chance to exit the warehouse. Leave the container behind. Hope swelled in her. A chance at freedom.

Freedom?

Once she had it again, what the hell would she do with it?

53

Silver Lake.

Andrew's medicated slumber lasted the entire ride, all the way to Cherry's Silver Lake apartment. His snoring had switched into a softer yet still audible gear. Lucky cracked the windows as if he were leaving a dog in the car and followed Cherry up the steps.

Cherry showed Lucky the shocking photos of the unconscious Karrie. He examined each and the accompanying texts along with the date and time stamps. If his math was correct, it had been less than seventy-two hours since the abduction.

"Can't let her dad see these," said Lucky.

"No shit," said Cherry.

Lucky knew of whiz nuts who could crack the phone, download everything—all data, hidden and otherwise, as well as recorded geolocations. The other options were to wait for his calls to be returned or, more proactively, hand the evidence over to units at either the LAPD or the sheriff's department. Lucky could lay out precisely what he knew and hope they moved faster than the bureaucratic behemoths they were. Every option pinging inside his skull took time. Too much time. Precious time. Lucky understood that his next move was . . .

Critical.

The phone was key. Lucky regarded it as he sat himself on Cherry's corduroy couch, cradling the item in his left palm as if it might speak and give him the answer.

"Wanna Snapple?" asked Cherry. "Snapple 'n' water's pretty much all I got."

Lucky heard her. But didn't answer. His next move was right in front of him. Like scrambled letters floating in the air. All he had to do was order them correctly to get his answer.

"What are you going to do?" Cherry finally asked.

"I'm gonna text the SOB," said Lucky, finger pointed at the phone. "This Jake guy. He doesn't know Gabe got the shit tortured out of him. Doesn't know we paid anybody off."

"You pretend you're him," finished Cherry. "You play like you're the Gabe guy?"

"Like he's got another honey to sell." It was as if Lucky was speaking the plan before he was thinking it.

He switched on the phone and pressed the text icon. His fingers hovered above the keyboard, composing his query.

"You liked the last girl?" said Lucky as he tapped out the very same words in the dialogue box. "I've got another one for you."

Lucky reread the text to himself. Nodded his own approval. He was preparing to send the message when Cherry stepped forward, jazz hands waving.

"Wait!" she said.

"What?"

"Just wait," she repeated, her head clearly swirling. "You want the guy to respond, yeah?"

"That's the point," said Lucky. "Start a dialogue."

"Then you need to do it like Gabe would."

"Something wrong with what I wrote?"

"You need more," said Cherry. "You need something to *sell*."

"I just need him to text me back."

"Then what? They might know each other. How long before he knows you're not him?"

"I need a shortcut and this is it."

"You need more," said Cherry, doing a sudden about-face and heading for her bedroom. "In here."

Lucky paused, stood, then curiously followed her into a darkened box. Under a window draped with an old quilt was a bed nearly as large as the room itself. To navigate, one needed to crawl over the mattress. Only Cherry wasn't on her hands and knees. She was standing and stripping off her clothes. Instantly, Lucky wanted to say *whoa* or *stop*. Instead, he was more straight to the point.

"The hell are you doing?" he asked.

"I'm the picture you're gonna send with the text."

"I didn't ask you—"

"Take my clothes off for tips. I can do it to help you find Karrie."

As quick as Cherry could strip off her T-shirt, she was pulling down her yoga pants, kicking them away, then bouncing into a horizontal pose reminiscent of the cell phone snaps he'd only just seen of young Karrie. She closed her eyes and parted her lips to appear unconscious.

"Don't act uncomfortable and weird," said Cherry.

"I'm just thinking," said Lucky, unwilling to admit that he was indeed taken aback. The countless list of crazy acts he had witnessed hadn't quite prepared him for her brazen act of volunteerism.

"C'mon," she said. "Stop acting like you haven't seen a naked girl. 'Cause you're a hot cop and women get all wet over that kinda shit."

It finally clicked for Lucky. Cherry was dead right. The best and most efficient way to elicit a response from Jake—whoever or wherever he was—would be with a series of images just like the last. A drugged girl. Young. Attractive. Just like Cherry, who, without makeup, could have passed for seventeen. Younger, even, if the pitch was just right.

Lucky switched on the phone's camera function. He climbed onto the bed, kneeling over the motionless and naked girl. He framed the first picture and after pressing the shutter button, a blast of white light blanketed Cherry a split second before the picture was recorded.

"More," said Cherry. "And do I look drugged?"

"Maybe some drool," offered Lucky.

Cherry shifted, worked up some saliva, turned her head back into the previous position, and let it drip from the corners of her mouth.

"Good," said Lucky, snapping a closer shot. "Stay right like that. Don't move."

He stood upon the massive mattress, making it sag and squeak, straddling the petite dancer while rotating the phone to get a full body shot.

"One more," said Lucky, recalling the order of shots Gabe had used on Karrie. Different girl, but the same vibe. Drugged. Alone. Vulnerable as hell.

54

Canoga Park.

I *hate Christmas.*
I hate Christmas.
I hate Christmas.

Jake was wondering if he was developing Tourette syndrome. Because the closer he got to December 25th, the more the three-word phrase would involuntarily repeat like a loop in his head.

Hate's too strong a word.

In fact, the young father of four had fond memories of Christmas. In Armenian tradition, his mother would clean the house from floor to rafters. They would also put up two trees. One in the more modern American tradition with lights and tinsel and flashy ornaments. And a second in the old-world style decorated with fruit, golden bows, and white doves constructed from papier mâché. The same was true for the day itself. December 25th was celebrated as well the Armenian-Orthodox Epiphany on January 6th.

Not many boys he knew were blessed with two Christmases. It made Jake wonder why his opinion of the holiday had fallen so far down his list of likes.

Pushing a shopping cart, Jake worked the aisles of the Canoga Park supermarket, trying not to miss any of the items on Ana Sofia's list. It was delivered via a smartphone app that made Jake curse the day he'd ever volunteered to do the lion's share of the grocery shopping. Every other day, around three in the afternoon, his phone would begin to ding with each addition. More carrots. Ding. An extra box of Frosted Mini-Wheats. Ding. Two gallons of nonfat milk. Ding, ding. Jake had actually tried to figure out how to turn off the sound, only to discover it left his phone quiet to all comers—an option he couldn't afford.

He worked the market west to east. Hoping not to miss something and needing to double back to an aisle he'd already travelled down. That would take more time. And before Jake pointed his car home, he still needed to post two large care packages to relatives back in the old country, stop by the pharmacy to pick up a refill of an allergy prescription, and swing by the pet store for the special cat chow for their fat fucking feline, Galinda.

Jake was leaning over the cart, forearms resting on the handle, rechecking the grocery list as he eased through the frozen foods section, when his phone chirped with a new text. It was from Gabe, his old buddy from his club soccer days. His brain instantly shot backward to the summer between ninth and tenth grade, playing soccer on the Westside, and scrimmaging while high on the weed good ol' Gabriel would amply supply.

He answered the text and, as if his feet had landed in concrete, froze as the first image appeared. Instantly, Jake turned the phone over, straightened, and checked his surroundings for any nosy-nobs hiding over his shoulder. He waited for a polyester-swollen nanny to move beyond the frozen meals before he returned to his screen. He quickly scanned over the photo of the unconscious girl with the purple hair. Swiped through the four additional pictures,

as both a matter of habit and judgment, automatically approving
of her drugged-appearing attractiveness.

Jake answered:

> *uv been bizy*

To which Gabe quickly replied:

> like what u see?

> *ur timing sux*

> is there a prob?

> *no can do 2day*

> thought u liked what u see?

> *i do but not set for incoming product*

> seriously? she's here n ready to go

> *that's not my prob*

> make me an offer

A weird chill traced up Jake's spine. Yet he quickly attributed
it to having backed himself up against one of the supermarket's
freezers. It hummed with sub-zero potency. Again he checked his
perimeter to make certain that he was unwatched. Or that some
security camera wasn't reading the incriminating texts over his
shoulder.

> *if I can pull it off, u cash back half 2 me.*

> half? Really?

hey. u txted me. Xmas and i need the $$$. we do each other favor.

There was a pause in the conversation and Jake remembered he was threading a time needle. He pushed on, returning his smartphone's screen back to the grocery app and the next item on his list: Carnation Instant Hot Cocoa. That's when his hand vibrated as the text returned:

kk

Jake tapped out:

Hold tight. Chking with my cuz.

Blocking entry to the frozen foods aisle, Jake held up a quick finger to a shrunken old man whose shopping progress was stalled by Jake and his smartphone.

"You young people and your damn devices," grumbled the old man.

"Really sorry," monotoned Jake, more out of habit than from actual regret. He finished punching out his text to Ziggy and pushed on. By the time he made the left turn into the next aisle, he had practically forgotten about the interruption, his old buddy Gabe, and the four incriminating photos of the purple-haired girl that were still open in his text feed.

55

Silver Lake. 5:32 p.m.

Lucky thought about Andrew's narcotic slumber in the back seat of the borrowed Crown Vic, front windows cracked open as if he were a pet waiting for his owner to return. As Lucky found himself craving the taste of any painkiller, he wondered what Andrew had been prescribed. He was reclining on Cherry's big bed to ease the throbbing. From his horizontal position, he had sent those faked photos of Cherry and the subsequent texts. Cherry had assisted, propped up on an elbow, reading the stream as the conversation unfolded. She had even suggested a brief stroll through Gabe's other text conversations as a way to better assume the photographer's voice. And by all appearances, the ploy had some traction. Jake was running Gabe's new find up the sex trafficking ladder. All that was left was the waiting.

"I hate goddamn waiting," Lucky admitted in a rare confessional moment.

His eyes were tired and shut—trying to blot out the bedroom light and the pain he was wrestling with. He recalled Cherry's smoky voice asking questions. Softly. Innocent, but probing. How and why he'd begun talking about his dead brother, Tony, was beyond him. Lucky had told her about Tony's dreams to become an L.A. County sheriff. The failed tests and academy rejections. Then the move to Kern County, where Tony's application had been accepted. This led to Lucky explaining how he had resigned from his post at Lennox Station and re-upped as a Kern deputy in the hinterlands east of Bakersfield.

Bumfuck, he called it.

"I like that name," giggled Cherry. "Bumfuck."

Cherry listened as the backstory took a dark turn. Lucky told of Greg Beem and his refrigerated truckload of stolen blood plasma. The deadly encounter with young Tony on the high-desert two-lane. The subsequent triple murder. Followed by Lucky's seventy-two-hour odyssey of bloodlust and vengeance.

Lucky's eyes remained closed during the entire recitation. The kind of shut-eye that might normally lead to slumber. If not for the pool of pain holding like meat hooks in his low back, he might have actually nodded off. Gabe's cell phone, with its quarter-charged battery, lay safely on his chest. It was sure to alert him the moment the mysterious Jake replied. Soon, he hoped. Yet not too soon. Because while he was fully reclined, the strain on his lumbar region was somewhat eased. The hurt temporarily curbed. A brief cessation in a footrace that was leading him Lord knows where.

Was it the way Cherry smelled that reminded him of Gonzo? Something in her hair? She had to be more than ten years younger and a near foot shorter than his Amazonian ex. Aside from gender and maybe an affection for leather accessories, there was practically nothing the two women appeared to have in common. Yet there it was again. A mild whiff and Lucky could easily imagine Gonzo lying next to him.

"You're still naked, aren't you?" Lucky found himself asking.

"Got a problem with that?" teased Cherry.

"If you don't . . ." Lucky let his voice trail. He was still picturing Gonzo. Half of it was memory. The other half was fantasy, imagining his former lover in the very same bedroom and on the very same extra-large mattress.

The lips, though, were not Gonzo's. Nor was the taste of her breath. The twenty-two-year-old had pressed herself to him without invitation. Nor was she rebuffed; Lucky appreciated the instant distraction from his pain; from the missing teenager; from the teenager's annoying, me-first father.

"Just tell me to stop," warned Cherry, working her way down to Lucky's belt buckle. She pulled his denims loose, lowered his zipper, and reached inside.

"I'm not resisting, officer," chuckled Lucky.

"That's not the first time you've said that," suggested Cherry.

"If it could only talk."

"It would have its own YouTube channel," joked Cherry seconds before taking him into her mouth.

And in that instant, the pain ratcheted back to a negligible number as an autonomic release of dopamine injected into Lucky's brain. Yet it wasn't all pleasure. A caution flag was waving. He didn't really know this girl. She was young and vulnerable and had obviously gotten swept up in the hunt. Such circumstances often led to some kind of sex. Be it in a strange apartment, bathroom stall, or the back seat of a radio car. Cops justified these moments as everything from stress respites to job perks.

"You don't really know me," Lucky said.

"Ditto," said Cherry, sliding up to straddle him. "Box of condoms in the nightstand. You mind?"

Lucky twisted, reaching across himself to the old pine nightstand with top and bottom drawers. In doing so, Gabe's smartphone spilled from his chest. He felt it vibrate beneath him. As if the phone were there to save him from himself, Lucky grabbed for it and checked the screen to read the text from Jake.

Ur good. Same exact routine.

"What routine?" asked Lucky aloud. Cherry laid across him, reading over his left ear. "He musta got instructions before."

"Check his email," suggested Cherry.

Lucky handed the phone off and began pulling up his pants. Meanwhile, Cherry was madly searching through the phone. Like most her age, her agility with technology seemed second nature. She blew through email, texts, applications.

"Here. He made a voice note," she said before pressing play and turning up the volume. There was a brief crackle, then the hush of a man's voice making a memo for himself.

"Rent blue Nissan. Park. Take bus."

That was it, but for the half-sigh recorded at the end. Cherry replayed the voice memo three more times as if she expected to hear something new or nuanced. Lucky, though, had heard enough. He was already mentally building two roadmaps. The first was the cop move. Work the phones. Call in favors. Find somebody within the authority system to run wants and warrants on blue Nissans involved in crimes or that might have been impounded in the past seventy-two hours. Next, he'd request access to cell phone records from which he could have an account of Gabe's calls and approximate travel over the time period. A warrant would be required to search the photographer's Santa Monica apartment—which was in a city apart from Los Angeles—not to mention the bureaucratic nonsense that came with multi-jurisdictional police searches. Add to that more delays, which would come while waiting for returned phone calls, and the time concerns were stacking up.

Sure, thought Lucky. The photos of Karrie were possibly evidence enough to trigger an Amber Alert. But runaway teenagers could sometimes be a tricky loophole. So many were lost in L.A. that it could gum up the system.

No. If working Lennox and South L.A. had taught Lucky one thing, it was that despite the legal morass created by short-cutting procedure, lives could be saved by flushing protocol and employing the following principle: the shortest path between two points was always a straight line.

"Rent blue Nissan," he pointed out to Cherry. "Not a red one or a green one. A blue Nissan. Specific by color. These guys move their cargo like drugs. Car trunk. Park the correct make and model at the dead drop, walk away, somebody shows up after to move the merch."

"Merch?" she asked, before connecting the dots and answering her own question. "Oh. Merchandise."

"Check the guy's GPS," said Lucky. "Maybe we can match an address with a rental car company."

Cherry skipped from the bed, returning seconds later with a laptop, wearing a wrinkled, lemon-yellow T-shirt silkscreened with a faded Endless Summer logo. She was quick to match the few addresses in Gabe's GPS app's history.

"Speedy-K Rental Car in Van Nuys," read Cherry.

"Next address will be the drop," believed Lucky. "Isolated. But no more than a few blocks from a bus route."

"Valley again." Cherry's voice raised an octave from the sheer thrill. She pasted the GPS address into a Google Maps bar. The program quickly animated, dive-bombing into Southern California and locking in on ten square industrial blocks north of Burbank Airport. "8463 Tujunga."

"What's there?"

"Looks like a cement plant."

Lucky guessed that both the car rental joint and the cement plant were owned by Armenians in keeping with crime family traditions.

Cherry scooted over to the edge of the bed and her closet.

"What does a girl wear if she's gonna be left in a car trunk?" she joyfully asked.

"You're not going anywhere," said Lucky. "Let alone in some car trunk."

"But you need me to be the girl."

"I need you to take him back to the Biltmore and pretend you don't know squat about what I'm doing," imparted Lucky.

"Think there's still cops back at the hotel?"

"If they're on the ball there'll be somebody. Answer their questions. Tell the truth," said Lucky, suddenly looking around for . . . "Where's your car keys?"

"To my shitmobile?"

"Assuming Sleeping Beauty is still out in the back of mine, I suggest we switch."

Cherry plucked her car keys from the bottom of her bag. As she traded with Lucky, she gripped him with both hands.

"I helped, right?" she asked, her face smattered with a childlike wish for praise.

"Yeah," said Lucky. "You did good."

"And if I want to help some more?"

"Take care of Daddy and I'll make sure he takes care of you," promised Lucky, escaping toward the door.

"Hey!" she called after him. Lucky stalled, nearly halfway out of the apartment. "Unfinished business."

Lucky shrugged.

"I owe you a blow job."

Right, thought Lucky. But as for words to reply with, he was a syllable short of nothing. The best he could do was leave her with a sort of partially gobsmacked smile before he shut the door behind himself.

56

Van Nuys.

Those old enough remember Van Nuys Boulevard as more than a fat strip of blacktop bisecting the San Fernando Valley. It used to be an iconic landmark. A reminder of those bygone days of Beach Boy tunes, surfboards, Jan and Dean, and the lost art of car-cruising. For two decades, the boulevard hosted the famous to the infamous, and more importantly, their magical muscle cars. On Friday and Saturday nights—or even summer weeknights—the north/south strip was choked with chrome and the throaty echoes of internal combustion. Then came the eighties and the influx of guns into the gang scene. Cruising became less of an expression of car affection and more about turf. Gang muscle over muscle cars. The boulevard eventually became so dangerous to cruise that the LAPD deployed a phalanx of radio units to deter all shades of car enthusiasts and their showy, slow-rollin' fun rides.

The only remnants of those days are reflected in all the car dealerships, car washes, and auto shops that flank the sidewalks. One of those establishments was Speedy-K Car Rentals, which turned out to be little more than two offices in eight hundred square feet next to a sheepskin upholstery shop. The dated stucco exterior was painted white with red racing stripes and was seemingly getting little attention so close to Christmas.

Lucky noticed that but for the colored lights and miles of plastic garland employed by a nearby car dealer, nobody waking from a coma would have known Christmas was so damn near. He twisted the rearview mirror of Cherry's VW Jetta to get a look at himself. By his own account, he looked appropriately scruffy, both unshaven for days and sleep-deprived. A dead ringer for a drug addict.

Because that's what you are.

He swallowed his guilty conscience and unfolded himself from the driver's seat. Hours without any meds had left him wrecked with an added stiffness that crept all the way down his legs to his Achilles tendons. Perfect. He sickly knew that the best acting performances were the most real. He recalled hearing about an undercover cop who needed to affect a limp on the spot. Afraid that his untrained fakery might put the sting at risk, he simply took off his shoe and embedded a sharp stone in the foam arch. The limp became real the instant his body weight was applied.

The door to Speedy-K Car Rentals swung outward. Lucky instantly felt a rush of warm dry air meeting the cold wet from which he'd come. He entered, automatically scanning for exits and security cameras. The only other route of egress he could determine was the door behind the desk leading, he imagined, to a back office or a storeroom. The counter was a gray, chipped laminate that matched the equally monochromatic walls. To the right was a glass case with model replicas of German cars.

"May I help you?" asked the woman behind the counter.

Lucky hadn't seen her at first. She was squat, dark, and matronly, hidden behind a large countertop display advertising aftermarket vehicle insurance. She wore a hair-matching knit black cardigan over a champagne-colored blouse and a floor-length plaid skirt.

"Yes," said Lucky, clearing his throat with a cough. "Sorry. Guy I know recommended I rent from you."

"Do you have a reservation?" she asked with an accent strong enough to reveal that English wasn't her first language.

"No," said Lucky. "But the guy said I should ask for a blue Nissan."

As if cued, the woman's eyes lifted to greet Lucky, like she was viewing him for the first time.

"What's your friend's name?"

"Jake," replied Lucky.

The woman gave the slightest nod as if she'd heard the secret pass phrase. Onto the counter she placed a clipboard with the appropriate paperwork.

"Driver's license, proof of insurance, and a credit card," she said dryly. "Oh, and we don't take American Express."

Lucky had an impulse to ask why. If the car was designated for dead drops, it would clearly be returned right back to the rental company. It would have been entirely in character for a sketchy fellow to complain about payment under the circumstances. But then again, Lucky felt he had already passed the sniff test. He was inside. Recommended by Jake. About to rent a blue Nissan. So, he pulled his driver's license and a Visa card from his wallet along with the slip of paper provided by his insurance carrier.

"Fill this out and I'll be right back," she said. Upon rising from her chair only inches were added to her height. She swept up the cards Lucky had left on the counter and disappeared into the back room.

The hairs on the back of Lucky's neck turned stiff. As far as he knew, she was back there either calling or texting somebody a quick pic of his driver's license. Lucky swiveled his view over his shoulder to check the entrance before returning to the clipboard. With his left hand he picked up the pen and began to fill out the rental agreement. All while his right hand moved inside the tail of his jacket to the butt of the .45-caliber pistol he kept snugly holstered at the small of his back.

Just in case.

By Lucky's mental count, she was gone anywhere between thirty seconds to a minute, at last returning with a photocopied piece of paper on which were duplicate images of his driver's license and proof of insurance.

"By initialing here, here, and here you are declining insurance and agreeing to return the car with a full tank of gas."

But I'm not returning it. It's a dead drop car. I'm supposed to leave it and take the bus.

"Understood," said Lucky, scribbling every place the woman pointed her cheaply manicured nail.

The woman ran the credit card, charging a flat seventy-five dollars. Lucky signed the receipt, accepted his copy of the rental agreement, and stepped to the side as the blunt little woman rounded the counter, jangling a set of car keys. She pushed her way out into the early evening mist and, after a hard left turn, vanished out of sight.

She'll either return with a blue Nissan or I'll never see her again, thought Lucky. Then before his imagination could run through the hundreds of other possibilities, most of which involved him ending up dead, tossed into some rushing sewer with a bullet lodged in his cranium, the one-woman-rental-car-agency pulled up to the door in a sparkling clean Nissan Altima glazed in a metallic cobalt blue. She left the car door open as well as the shop door as an invitation for Lucky to accept the rental.

"Thanks," said Lucky, expecting and receiving no reply whatsoever. He slid into the sedan, quickly adjusting the seat and mirrors. With the engine already running, he needed only to buckle his seat belt and shift the transmission into drive.

But it wasn't until the front rubber left the pavement and touched the asphalt of storied Van Nuys Boulevard that Lucky truly felt that overwhelming pull he had been missing for some time. Not since he had bolted out of Kern County like a rocket out of Hades had he felt such a visceral sense of commitment.

Lucky was, at last, all in.

57

Silver Lake.

All dilemmas came with horns. At least that's how Herm remembered it.

You're stuck on the horns of your dilemma, Herm's old man once said. He could only recall his dad using the metaphor the one time. Twelve-year-old Herm was playing both Pop Warner Football and soccer when he also joined the local Boy Scout troop. Refusing to drive the boy another quarter mile until he whittled the after-school activities down to a simple pair, his mother demanded that Herm make a choice. Choosing vexed the boy. He didn't want to pick between his friends. Plus, the extracurricular activities kept him out of the house where his bipolar mom would pound orange juice and vodka and throw screaming fits so terrifying Herm would lock himself in the garage with his AM radio and headphones.

Herm reluctantly chose to abandon Boy Scouts. And from

that day on, he had looked at all dilemmas as sharp and pointed and grown from a raging bull that could easily disembowel a man with the unlucky flick of his head.

Such was the case of his newest conundrum. To follow that cop fella? Or Father Unicorn (as he'd somehow labeled Andrew Kaarlsen)? From the big box store's parking lot, he had quietly tailed the primer gray Crown Victoria from the Valley all the way back to Silver Lake. Once near Cherry's hillside apartment, he had plugged his car into a curbside space some eighty yards up the slope. From that spot, he could fully eyeball the four-unit apartment building. Shortly after arriving, he watched Cherry and the cop fella step from the Crown Victoria, where the cop fella followed the purple-haired spinner up the steps until they disappeared into an apartment. As for Father Unicorn, he hadn't seen him exit the car or noticed them dropping him off anywhere. And with that strange absence, Herm began second-guessing his plot, half-baked as it was. Once cashed in with the $50,000 in the FedEx envelope, he should have been satisfied, not to mention mentally spending the payday on further home improvements. Yet another idea had formed as quickly as it had taken him to clear the Costco exit and walk to his Ford Edge.

Father Unicorn.

Trading the photographer's mobile phone for the envelope of cash, Herm felt an odd warmth. He felt a surge of confidence in the strange duo of the daddy and his hired gun. They might successfully land that elusive strawberry-blonde, thus rescuing her from the evil clutches of white slavery only to return her to Whereversville, USA.

By the moment Herm had settled in his driver's seat, that weird warmth had turned jealous. He'd been paid. The transaction was complete. He should have wheeled the car out of the parking lot and driven back to his unfinished domicile in Panorama City. Instead, he waited and watched. Until at last he had picked out the three amigos exiting Costco and trudging to a primer gray Crown Victoria.

But she's my *unicorn.*

The ugly emotion gathered again. The same as when he had discovered that young Gabe, the neighbor photographer, had pounced before he had his chance. And why should Daddykins get a chance to bring his little girl home? A little girl who'd already chosen between family and running away. Hell, figured Herm. Until the girl was walking down the ramp to her return flight, she was still game for the kill. Huntable as hell. And worth, possibly, another envelope of green if Herm could bag her.

That's when Herm decided to put a stalk on the Crown Victoria and its three occupants. It had led him to that dated little apartment in Silver Lake. And yet, upon arrival, he'd only been able to mark the cop fella and the purple-haired spinner. Where the hell had Father Unicorn gone? Unless he was still in the car. Sleeping? Or even dead?

After an hour spent chewing on the possibilities, Herm dared himself to get out of his SUV and give the situation a look-see. It was raining again and water ran past his SUV as if he were parked in the middle of a stream. He grabbed a large, golf-sized umbrella from the back seat, popped open the canopy, and started walking toward the apartment building. He kept the umbrella low for cover. The Crown Victoria was ahead, windows oddly cracked given the lousy weather. Then it struck him. The windows were cracked because Father Unicorn was *still in the car.*

But Herm wouldn't find out just yet. Because the moment he neared the left front bumper, he heard voices from the apartment's upper landing. He dared not lift the umbrella and reveal himself. Instead, he kept his course. He heard man-sized footfalls splashing down the fifties-era concrete and steel steps. At any moment, Herm expected the cop fella would jump the curb and round the corner of his Crown Victoria, putting the two men face-to-face once again. Herm lowered the umbrella further and his eyes to the pavement. This is when he noticed his shoes. His not-so-clean running sneakers, finely speckled with Gabe's blood and now, in the wet air, the red was dissolving into a pale pink.

The cop fella was big. But Herm was bigger. And he had an umbrella that, if tilted forward, he could use as a battering ram. If recognized, Herm imagined charging with the umbrella, pushing the cop fella off his feet before turning and running back to his SUV.

It was a half-assed plan. And Herm cursed himself for getting out of the car.

Only the cop fella never appeared in front of him. The footfalls turned and cut behind Herm, interrupted only by the chirp of a car being unlocked. Herm twisted in time to see the weary man with the buzz cut waving back to the purple-haired spinner on the landing before ducking into an unmanly, red VW Jetta. Still walking, Herm returned his eyes forward just in time to glimpse Father Unicorn's red-headed mop. Daddykins was supine in the back seat of the Crown Vic. Herm could hear the snores escaping the cracked windows as he splashed his way past.

That is precisely when Herm felt the stab. A dilemma had been established, and he was already feeling the horns. The trio was splitting. The cop fella was about to drive off in a very non-cop-like car, leaving Father Unicorn to continue his respite in the big sedan's back seat.

Who the hell do I follow?

Who the hell, indeed. After the cop fella in the Jetta quickly U-turned and sped the car downhill past Herm, the casting man did an about-face and hustled back to the SUV. Sharp horns or otherwise, Herm knew he only had between where he stood and the driver's seat of his car to make his decision.

58

Sunland. 6:29 p.m.

On Google Maps, 8643 Tujunga was the address to a cement plant. In all directions, the terrain was industrial. Construction suppliers, gravel wholesalers. There were no streetlamps. The only illumination came from beyond the razor wire security fences and the ambient reflection provided by the omnipresent, low-flying cloud ceiling.

Lucky parked the rented Nissan and switched off the lights. He sat for a few minutes, scanning the landscape. He could see the pathway west. He wondered how many flesh traders had hoofed it until they had landed at the bus stop. He was also curious if there were eyes on him already, waiting for him to slip from the car and walk the walk. At least, that's what he would have done. It was a heartbeat shy of 6:30, making Lucky a full thirty minutes early. His initial plan had been to park, leave the car, stride west just far enough to slip from sight and then double back to some kind of dark corner where he could lie in wait for whoever might come to collect the vehicle. It would be no less than a pair of confederates. At least one to drive to the drop, the other to operate the blue Nissan out of the industrial area to its final destination.

But where to hide? Lucky's 360-degree accounting left him with the simple conclusion that there would be no place where he could properly conceal himself. At least, no place close enough where he could surprise and hold two suspects.

Crap-sandwich!

He clearly hadn't calculated far enough ahead. Yet there he was, ass glued to the seat of a rented target. And a pair of someones would be arriving shortly to fetch the damn thing. Would they be checking the trunk? If so, they'd be sure to find it disappointingly empty.

Unless . . .

Lucky landed on his answer and moved without a second thought. He fought the pain in his back and extracted himself from the Nissan quickly enough, circling to the dirt sidewalk side of the car. After a last once-over of the landscape, he popped the trunk and climbed inside. The pain was excruciating. Yet he found his knees, reached upward and pulled the lid closed on top of himself. The locking mechanism sounded with a distinctive click.

Darkness overtook him. He felt for and produced both his cell phone and pistol, making certain one was set to silent and the other ready to rock and roll. He angled himself so that if and when the trunk was opened, he would merely need to extend and elevate both arms to be guaranteed the very first shot. But the position created a secondary problem. He was unable to unfold his six-foot frame into a position that offered any kind of relief to his herniated back.

"Fuck!" cursed Lucky. His voice reverberated hollow and hard.

Lucky wriggled his torso until he seemed to find the least painful pose, then checked the clock on the phone. It was 6:36. In the sustaining quiet, he could hear the rain tapping on the Nissan's trunk lid. He swore his nostrils were picking up traces of cosmetics. Women's lipstick or maybe a deodorant stick. Was it Karrie Kaarlsen's? Had she been the last girl to occupy the trunk?

Was she even still alive?

To battle the pain, Lucky shut his eyes and attempted a meditation. He'd never actually practiced the craft. But during his last stay in the hospital, a practitioner in the art of mental pain management had stopped by to give him a half-hour primer. He remembered that it began with slow breathing—in through the nose and out through the mouth—and a simple visualization. He had been asked to mine his memory for a moment of tranquility. He'd easily chosen the only image he could recall—a trip when he was twelve and Tony was eight. They were visiting distant cousins who owned a farm somewhere in Northern California. It was summer. Dry and hot. And there was an open field behind the ranch house that sloped to a slight peak. The grass was thigh-high and as pale as ripe wheat. At the highest point stood a lone oak tree. Old and gnarled, its branches spreading up and out against a cloudless blue sky. Lucky and Tony had climbed up there, sat under the tree, chewed straw, and imagined their lives if they could move there. The sheer pleasantness of the moment had been tattooed to Lucky ever since.

The memory proved so profound that Lucky's meditation lasted barely sixty seconds. The pain, too, had been blunted just enough for sleep to overtake him. It was an unexpected lights-out for Lucky. Then, as suddenly and seamlessly as he'd tripped off into slumber, he was awakened by what first felt like an earth tremor. A shift in equilibrium. His eyes popped open and before he could ascertain exactly where he was, let alone how long he'd been asleep, he both heard and felt the vibration of the Nissan's engine smoothly turning over.

Instantly the car was moving forward. Driving away with the surprise cargo in the trunk.

59

Silver Lake.

When Andrew finally woke from his back seat nap, the sun had already dropped and disappeared. It was the lightning blue light of a streetlamp blasting through the rain-streaked windows that was forcing him to squint and think it was still daytime. Immediately uncomfortable, his first cogent thought was how he craved the bed in his posh hotel room. That brought back the images of Romeo—the hoodlum bound and left bleeding for the police on the suite's marble floor. The idea of returning to the hotel repulsed Andrew. So, before he even sat up, he dialed his assistant's mobile number, caring little at all if he interrupted anything important, and demanded she book a new suite in a new hotel, then have all his personal items delivered before his return. Oh, he added, make sure the suite has two bedrooms. He was somehow optimistic that soon he would be reunited with his daughter.

As Andrew shook his grogginess, it slowly dawned on him that the day had been extinguished and he was in fact surrounded by darkness. How long had he been sleeping? Where the hell was Lucky and what the G.D. had transpired in the past few hours? Only after he had wrenched himself from the back seat did he recognize just where he was. Silver Spur or Silver Lake or some stupid L.A. locale. Outside that Cherry girl's apartment. Lucky Dey must be doing what? It was still less than twenty-four hours since he had fired the former cop. Much had transpired since then. Ground had been gained. Yet it was all without a formal sit-down and discussion as to where to the men stood. Maybe now was the time.

He knocked at the door of Cherry's apartment. And while he waited for an answer, his stomach churned with an instinctive distrust. As he knocked again, this time with his fist for a louder, more resounding *thump, thump, thump*, he could feel the reflux gathering to singe the bottom of his esophagus.

"Lucky!" Andrew barked through the door. "How long were you gonna let me sleep?"

He thumped the door again, harder and lower for maximum acoustic resonance. Loud enough to announce himself to the other three apartment units.

"It's open," shouted a woman's voice from well beyond the door.

Andrew pushed into the tiny apartment, warmly lit with candles and a hanging Chinese paper lamp courtesy of Pier One Imports.

"I'll be right out," said Cherry from behind what Andrew surmised was the bathroom door.

The last time he had been there she had kicked him out for implying she was a whore. He hadn't gotten past the threshold—a strong disappointment because he had wanted to glimpse where his daughter had been crashing. His eyes landed on the corduroy couch.

"Where's Lucky?"

"Following up a lead," Cherry called back.

"Without me, of course," Andrew groused. He could feel the elevating burn from his stomach.

"We figured out this really cool shortcut," claimed Cherry.

"Shortcut?"

"Yeah. We, uh . . . Well, he pretty much did most of it."

"Did what?"

"Texted the Armenian guy."

Andrew listened. Beyond the door, amongst the rushes of water and the sound of the squeaking tap, Cherry recounted the events that Andrew had missed during his afternoon slumber. The texts. The faked photos. The simple sleuthing that had led to the car rental company and the meeting spot across from the San Fernando Valley cement plant.

With every little factoid, Andrew's muscles clenched. Once again, he had been left behind by the man who had agreed to side him all the way to the payoff. He felt like a preteen ditched by his older, more powerful sibling. A rube, ripe for the mocking.

"What the crapola am I paying for?" spat Andrew.

"He said you weren't paying him," corrected Cherry from the other side of the door. "Did you really fire him?"

"We had an understanding," insisted Andrew. "For criminy sakes! She's my G.D. daughter."

"Dontcha just want her back safe and sound?" asked Cherry, her voice ticking up in frequency as she swung the door open.

Andrew turned toward her, a half-formed thought frozen in his mouth as his eyes widened. Cherry was wearing a short neon green robe. She was rubbing a towel against her wet, now strawberry-blonde hair.

"Oh," said Cherry. "The hair, right? Was planning on a change but then I thought, hey. No time like the present."

What followed was a frozen and awkward beat. Andrew's strange stare unnerved her.

"Maybe it was the picture, you know?" she continued. "Didn't want some Armenian gang to come lookin' for the girl with the purple hair."

"But it's . . ." began Andrew. "That's Karrie's hair."

"The color? Then I got it right," she smiled. "First thing I noticed about your daughter was her hair. Such an amazing color. And all natural. I was like, wow. Gotta do me that hair sometime."

"Wow," repeated Andrew with a sad mutter.

"She's coming home," salved Cherry. "To you. Don't ask me how, but I can feel it. Lucky's gonna do it. Lucky's gonna bring your baby back to you."

"I should get to my hotel."

"And I'm going to drive you," Cherry insisted, after noting that Andrew had a slight wobble in his equilibrium. "What did the doctors give you, anyway?"

"Vicodin," admitted Andrew. "I can take a cab."

Cherry picked up and shook Lucky's key chain.

"Lucky left me with instructions," said Cherry. "Plus, I'd kinda like to be there when he brings Val . . . Jeez, I keep . . . Sorry. I mean, brings Karrie home."

"Home is Wisconsin," reminded Andrew.

"You know what I mean."

"I do, yes," said Andrew. "I really do."

60

Sunland.

G*oddamn Christmas carols.*

If ever there was a time when Lucky didn't want to hear the seasonal sounds of jingling bells intermingled with melodies strung into happy harmonies, it was while he was an unwitting passenger in the trunk of a cobalt blue Nissan Altima. Yet the unknown driver had gone right for the radio before shoving the transmission into drive. The channels must have already been pre-programmed. Either that or the driver just wanted noise, immediately settling on a station playing an around-the-clock stream of candy-coated sounds of the season.

The pain had returned with a vengeance. And somehow, when Lucky tried to shift his awkward position, his low back appeared to have locked up. Frozen. Not cooperating without causing something excruciating.

What made it worse was the friggin' potholes. The many times Lucky had cursed the L.A. city government for failing on one of its most primary responsibilities—paving and maintaining the roads—didn't matter. The shock-inducing condition of the industrial areas was far worse due to lousy drainage and the metric tonnage of heavy equipment that frequented the North Valley. Every sickening displacement of axle and tire sent shock waves across the trunk floor, the bumps and chunks across the road inflicting even more stabs of pain into the addict without his Percocet.

Great day to go cold turkey, moron.

The rear-mounted speakers made Lucky feel like he was curled up inside a kick-drum. If he had thought of calling out, the warble of sound was so overwhelming, no one would have heard him. Instead, he sent a group text to his old Lennox pals Bledsoe and Lopes:

> if no txt in 2 hrs geolocate my phone n hope
> i'm not dead

He braced his arm up against the trunk lid, trying in vain to protect himself from further bumps in the road. Then, nearly as quickly as the drive had begun, the pavement underneath him seemed miraculously smooth. Lucky quickly calculated that he couldn't have driven far enough to have left Los Angeles's vast city limits. There had been no high-speed travel. No freeways or obvious changes in elevation. The Nissan had also slowed, Lucky guessed, to under twenty-five miles per hour. There came a series of low-speed turns and even more braking, then the final hundred feet felt as if the car had left the asphalt and was driving on smooth concrete.

The car stopped. Lucky felt the weight shift as the driver stepped from the vehicle, yet the engine was still running, as were the Christmas songs. Lucky felt the car door slam, a shift back into drive, then a very slow roll and long, arcing sweep to the right. He pressed his ear to the mat and over the music thought he could hear the tires squeaking as if against a slickened surface.

Oh, shit. I'm here.

Wherever the mystery destination, Lucky quickly realized he had arrived. Now what? Any moment, he expected, the trunk would most surely be lifted. The lid would spring up. And some person—or persons—would get his first look at the surprise cargo. They would expect to see an unconscious—or even semi-conscious—young woman. Purple hair. No more than a hundred pounds. Just like in the photos. Instead, they were sure to be shocked.

And then what?

Lucky planned to draw down on them. Shock them into submission with the gaping muzzle of his .45 auto. But without his lower extremities cooperating, springing out, planting his feet firmly on the ground, and taking command of whatever situation he was facing would be difficult, if not impossible.

Idiot! You have no plan.

In the short seconds in which he prepared, Lucky tried to run the options through his mind. Yet none came. His back was locked. He was half crippled, supine in a cramped trunk, with his singular defense—let alone offense—being the large bore pistol.

The Nissan's engine was switched off. The radio blare silenced. Lucky heard chains moving, then the rumble of a large warehouse-style door rolling downward. Next came a single set of footsteps at an unhurried pace, beginning from Lucky's left and rotating counterclockwise toward the rear of the car. He gripped his pistol in his left hand, arm outstretched, the edge of the muzzle barely touching the fabric on the underside of the trunk lid.

Lucky would later recall the release of the mechanical latch sounding as loud as a cannon and the near immediate report from his .45, virtually silent.

The springs engaged. The trunk lid elevated like the jaws of a hungry crocodile. A silhouette stood before Lucky. Skinny, slight. Male. Wearing baggy jeans and a black leather jacket over a vintage rock 'n' roll T-shirt. Before any kind of recognition, before Lucky could even register on the young man's eyeballs—he instinctively leveled the pistol at the man's right shoulder and let loose a single, 230-grain copper-jacketed missile. The bullet struck leather, then cotton, before beginning its deformation once it penetrated skin. By the time it exited just north of the young man's right shoulder blade, it had fully mushroomed and nearly doubled in diameter.

A nasty punch.

The young man spun off the impact and his knees turned to oatmeal. And before the trunk lid had sprung to its full and gaping tensile, the one and only man in Lucky's range of view had been dropped.

Lurching from his midsection—failing first—then engaging his core muscles until he jackknifed, Lucky threw himself to the trunk's edge, pistol racked and ready to speak again. Lucky's target—that young man in the leather jacket, baby face shriveled in agony—was sprawled on the concrete floor of a dim warehouse.

"Think that shit hurts?" wheezed Lucky. "Try what I been doin'."

"*Ow, ow, ow, ow!*" cried the young man.

"Stop bitchin'," said Lucky. "Just meat 'n' bone. Now, look at me!"

"I'm shot!" complained the young man.

"Want one more in your melon?" barked Lucky. "Now, look me in the eye and tell me who else is here."

Lucky was met in the eye with the pained and terrified face of a young man no more than twenty years old. Most likely of Armenian extraction. If not, then from some other part of the world Lucky liked to call *Bumfuckistan.*

"Just me," said the young man.

Gazing out into the dimness, Lucky made out the shapes of cargo containers—maybe eleven or twelve in all—scattered in no particular order.

"Don't fuckin' move," demanded Lucky. He gritted his teeth and forced his hips to pivot over the empty trunk. The pain that shot up his spine and into the base of his skull nearly overcame him. He imagined he could have easily blacked out if he weren't deathly afraid the young man was going to reach out and take hold of the .45's muzzle.

Some relief followed as his back unfroze and his hip flexors engaged. On his knees, he threw one leg over the edge of the trunk, uncertain if it would even operate, then balanced on the single peg until he had swung his other leg out.

He wobbled. Dizzy. His face flushed with sweat. Yet he felt relief that so far no other men had appeared. His only immediate danger seemed to be the man curled up on the deck—a fellow more concerned about the amount of blood slowly leaking onto the concrete.

"I'm dying!" squeaked the young man.

"Shut up," said Lucky. "What's in the containers?"

"Girls."

Not that Lucky hadn't already guessed. But as his eyes swiveled over to the containers splashed by the Nissan's headlights, he could make out that each door was wide open.

"And where are the girls?" asked Lucky.

"All gone. Least the ones that were here."

"When?"

"Just tonight. Maybe half an hour ago. Thought I was done, then they just told me to go to the cement place and pick up the car."

"This car?"

"Yeah."

"Nobody's here?"

"Everybody's gone."

From his jacket pocket, Lucky produced that dog-eared photo of Karrie Kaarlsen. He lowered it to the young man's face.

"Her?" Lucky asked. "C'mon! Open your eyes and look at it."

The young man rolled out of his nearly fetal ball and focused on the tiny photograph. His pained face filled with immediate recognition.

"Yeah," said the young man.

"She was here?" Lucky confirmed.

"Yeah."

"Where?"

"I dunno."

Lucky eased lower, aiming his knee into the young man's ribs while allowing the gun muzzle to make an imprint against his cheek.

"Last time," hissed Lucky. "Where did she go?"

61

Interstate 405. 9:30 p.m.

The Valley's Best Service Tire truck crept along the choked thoroughfare. Its diesel engine pinged in low revs as Jake eased on and off the clutch. Traffic was so slow he had stopped checking his watch. He was resigned to be missing the Neighborhood Watch gathering. He toyed with the radio, undecided between playing music or listening to NPR. Whichever he chose, it was about staying awake. It was all he could do not to lean on the steering wheel and close his eyes. He was so damned exhausted and bored he had nearly forgotten about his illicit cargo; in the box only ten feet behind where he sat were thirteen teenage beauties. Each of them young and tarted-up with heavy makeup in barely there lingerie.

At least they had stopped with the racket.

Shortly after he had pulled out of the warehouse, one of the girls had started banging on the side panel with both fists, screaming for anybody to help. Most of the others joined in immediately, forcing him to pull over and swing around the backside of the cab to a two-inch ventilation and electrical port. He yelled into the hole for the girls to shut up or risk returning to the cargo containers, where they were promised no food or water for a week. The girls piped down in short order and had remained relatively silent ever since.

Jake checked his GPS device. He had twenty-two more minutes before he arrived at his San Pedro/Port of Los Angeles destination. Then he had to drive back to Woodland Hills to return the truck and drive his own car over to the warehouse so he could tag-team the blue Nissan back to Speedy-K's. Jake estimated that with a little luck he would get home just shy of midnight.

Oh man, he sparked. That wouldn't even account for Ziggy wanting him to stick around in San Pedro. Jake saw his job description expanding once again while his cut of the profits remained static.

Come Christmas dinner, he and his cousin were going to have to have a heart-to-heart on the status of their business relationship.

Karrie was seated at the rear of the dark cargo box on one of the stiff new moving blankets that were draped over stacks of car tires. She had experienced a moment of mild elation as she was finally, but not formally, introduced to her fellow kidnappees. Each teen-age girl was attractive in her own way, none appearing to be much older than she. They were a mixed bag of ethnicities and types. And some looked almost too thin, as if in the beginning ravages of serious drug addiction.

Karrie held hope that as a group, something might be accomplished. Perhaps the overpowering of a guard followed by a stiletto-heeled rush for freedom. Yet closer inspection of the other girls' eyes revealed a desolation of loss. Almost all their postures screamed defeat. In all those awful, trollop-like outfits, the group looked about as powerful as a bouquet of young but dying roses.

As instructed, no words had passed between them as each had been helped aboard the tire truck. And once the door was rolled down and bolted shut, the darkness they were left in felt as imposing as an armed guard. Wherever they were headed felt like certain death.

That's when Karrie stood, felt for the wall of the cargo box, and started pounding her fists into the sheet metal. The wall rippled and reverberated with each impact, making an awful and obnoxious noise.

"HELP!" she screamed. "WE'RE BEING KIDNAPPED!"

Almost instantaneously, most of the other teenagers joined in. Because of the darkness, she couldn't tell who. Maybe it was every one of them. Each with her fists pounding like jackhammers against the cargo box. They joined in the screaming, sounding like a ruckus inside an old tin outhouse.

Karrie didn't even feel the change in direction. The sudden braking. The vehicle stopping entirely on the road's shoulder. All she could hear was the racket she and her fellow kidnapped teens were making. At least, until that booming male voice scared the lace off of them. The man told them to pipe down. Demanding they stop chanting and banging for help. Afterward, Karrie couldn't even remember the specifics of the threat. Just that it was said, and it frightened the piss out of her and the other girls. Once again, silence overtook them and they rode on without incident for a period of what felt like a second lifetime.

Karrie's imagination was the worst part. She was desperate for any matter of drug that could vanquish her excruciating thoughts. Most had manifested at one time or another while she lay across that smelly mattress inside the cargo container. But sleep would win and she would eventually wake to discover she was in the same hopeless place.

The physics of it all had changed, though. There was movement. And with movement came a destination. And with destination there would be new circumstances beyond her control. That was what scared her. With the bathing and the makeup and the slutty costumes, she could only surmise it would involve sex of some flavor. Forced? Photographed? An epic snuff film, perhaps? Good, she figured. Kill us all. Put us out of our teenage misery.

Jesus, Karrie. Stop with the dark scenarios.

But stopping wasn't possible. Not with the box truck inching ever closer to wherever it would land to unload its human payload.

Then she recalled Gabe. She had thought so little of him in the past forty-eight hours; not even assigning him blame for her predicament. Somehow, Karrie wanted to leave him out of the equation. As if he hadn't slipped that mickey into her mouth and shuffled her off to her current captors. She played back their walk on the beach. She had talked and talked and explained her dreams in lush detail. And he had regaled her with his stories of shooting stills for movies, famous actresses and their superstar demands.

Ninety-nine percent kill.

The words flashed in front of her as if scripted in neon. How had she arrived at that number? Oh yeah, she thought. That would be her superstar demand. Ninety-nine percent control over how she was depicted. What an incredible fantasy. Having an iron grip on nearly every possible outcome. Ninety-nine percent. Wow.

Ninety-nine percent bullshit.

There came a stir from the other girls. Their hushed sounds busted Karrie out of her spell. The truck had shifted direction. It was in a slow reverse. The distinct *beep, beep, beep* of the backup warning system droned on for what sounded like forever. The tire truck was inching toward a final destination. That's when an idea flashed. There were maybe a dozen girls. When the doors opened, if they all charged the exit, they might be able to overrun whatever or whoever was waiting for them. Yet the words to her plan got stuck somewhere between her brain and tongue. She swallowed, feeling only dryness on the back of her palate. What spit she had didn't have the volume to flow. So, she forced a cough, setting off an explosive hacking fit. Her lungs convulsed so bad she feared it would set off a gag reflex. She didn't want to vomit. She so hated the feeling of her stomach involuntarily emptying. Let alone there. In the dark. On the truck with the other unfortunate teens. She feared if she soiled herself it would mean an instant return to the cargo container.

Then *clang!*

The sound startled her. And like a fright that scares away the hiccups, Karrie's hacking was abruptly halted by the metallic clattering of the tire truck's door rolling upward. A tuxedoed man stepped up onto the bumper, his arms spread wide as he snapped his fingers.

"Eyes up this way!" demanded the man in the tux, slightly taller than average. He appeared rather young with a clean, trimmed beard to match his equally short hair. A nearby streetlamp reflected off the small bald spot at the peak of his scalp.

This was Jake's cousin, Ziggy.

"I'm only going to say this once, so listen good," continued Ziggy. "You are going to a party. At this party will be powerful and important men who expect to be entertained. So, that's what you will be. Entertaining. Whatever a man wants, you will provide. My people will be close. My people will be listening. If you complain, beg, or cry about your situation, then we will think nothing of cutting your throat and throwing your body overboard. Oh. Did I tell you the party is on a boat?"

Ziggy gestured to Jake, who joined him on the bumper.

"Now, I don't want any of you getting seasick. So, Jakey here is going to give each of you a capsule that we expect you to swallow before you step off the truck."

"What happens after?" squeaked one of the girls. She was so beautiful, thought Karrie. An ethnic mix that was impossible to decipher. She had teased her inky hair into a spiky display. Her makeup and choice of slutty garb looked almost by design. For a heartbeat, Karrie wanted to have been the girl brave enough to speak up.

"After?" repeated Ziggy. "After you're done with your work tonight, my man here will give each of you two thousand dollars in brand new hundred-dollar bills. But only if you promise to never talk about how you got here and who brought you. Now, who's in for a party? Raise 'em up."

Initially, not a single girl held up a hand. Then two girls at the rear weakly lifted their skinny arms. Then three more followed. As did most of the rest. The only holdouts were Karrie and the exotic girl who had asked the question.

"Really?" asked Ziggy. But it was less of a question and gilded by threat. "You either get 'em up or face the consequences."

Karrie felt tears leak from the corners of her eyes. She was shaking so badly it felt as if she were vibrating. Yet she finally lifted her hand. She never once glanced over to see if the spiky-haired girl had complied. She just wanted the ordeal to end.

Ziggy had the teens form a line. He examined them one by one, working a high-powered pen flashlight up and down. Jake would hand him a capsule that Ziggy would place on a girl's tongue. After she swallowed, Ziggy would ask her to open wide so he could examine the inside of her mouth to be certain she had swallowed.

Karrie counted. She was seventh in the queue. As she neared the front, she wondered if she would have enough spit in her mouth to get the pill down once it was her turn. She had taken Dramamine many times before when as a family they went sailing on Lake Michigan. The waters could get rough and Karrie once got sick. Ever since, her mother would keep the box of little yellow tabs in her purse. She would snap them in half before feeding them to Karrie with a sip or two of whatever drink was handy.

Little yellow pills.

As Karrie's examination neared, she kept glancing at the clear baggie from which Jake was distributing the motion sickness capsules. These were two-tone red and gray. Nothing at all like the pills her mother used to feed her. Instinct kicked in. The pills, she reasoned, weren't for preventing sea sickness. They were to ensure compliance. Something designer, maybe. Molly or MDMA or something feel-good like oxy.

Where only moments earlier she had been wishing for a drug to take her mind away from the mess, she was now afraid. Terrified that whatever was in the capsule would numb her wits, Karrie wondered what they would do if she refused to swallow.

"Swallow it or I will get someone to shove it up your asshole!" angered Ziggy to a teen just three girls ahead of Karrie.

Jesus, she said to herself. She thought it and he answered it. She was going to be forced to imbibe. Why so hard? By fifteen, she had swallowed all kinds of pills. Always trusting that they would give her some kind of ride. Then came the pill Gabe had offered. She had taken it without the slightest question.

So, why not one more, Karrie?

The flashlight beam caught her by surprise. Her turn had come. She was in those ridiculous heels, teetering at the edge of the cargo box like it was some sort of cliff. Six inches below her, on the bumper, stood the man called Ziggy. She could smell his aftershave. Thick and sweet. He seemed to pause when examining her. He even stepped from the bumper and backed up a few feet so he could take in all of her, the flashlight beam crawling across her skin like a spider's legs.

"Wow, Jakey," said Ziggy as if she weren't even there. "This one's really somethin'."

"Too good for the party?" she heard Jake ask.

"No," said Ziggy. "But some lucky prick's gonna get way more than his money's worth."

Ziggy held out his hand, into which Jake dropped one of those red and gray capsules. He climbed back on the bumper.

"Open, close, swallow," ordered Ziggy.

Karrie opened her mouth and let her tongue slide forward. Ziggy placed the pill on it. Karrie drew her tongue back in and closed her mouth. A wave rolled across her neck as she obediently tried to swallow. But the dryness in her mouth was foiling her.

"Swallow," demanded Ziggy.

Karrie lifted an index finger as if to say *wait one moment*, looked to be gathering her last quarter ounce of saliva, then once again forced herself to gulp. She nodded in the affirmative, then opened her mouth for examination. Ziggy moved in closer, swept her mouth with the flashlight, and gripped her wrist as he guided her off the truck.

The moment her heels hit the pavement, she knew where she was. For the first time in days, Karrie had her bearings. They were at some kind of private wharf or marina. The unmistakable smell of the ocean tickled her nostrils. Beyond, against the sky, stood erector-like cranes decorated in safety lights. One, though, had a tiny Christmas tree attached. Complete with the star of hope on top.

Hope.

Yeah, thought Karrie. Whatever the hell hope was, she was quickly running out of it.

She gathered with the other teen girls and they were herded by fishermen in black peacoats down a wooden ramp to the wide stern of a trawler. Their collective heels made the noise of a flamenco troupe out of sync with the music.

Jake and his cousin, Ziggy, hung back.

"Suppose you're gonna need me here to haul 'em to the usual spot," said Jake, trying but failing not to sound pained.

"Nope. You're pretty much done for the night." Ziggy patted his cousin on the back. "Got a Christmas bonus comin'."

"The girls aren't comin' back here?" Jake wondered.

"Same boat's gonna pick 'em up," said Ziggy. "Then they're gonna meet up with the freighter outside the harbor."

Jake was curious enough to ask where the freighter was bound. The Emirates? Qatar? Indonesia? But he thought better than to ask his cousin a question Ziggy might feel too compromised to answer. Better Jake play the part of the good soldier and hope his bonus envelope was thicker than last year's.

As for those thirteen girls who had just been promised $2,000 cash and their freedom after a night of forced prostitution? Jake wasn't going to lose any sleep. They were no different than a set of high-priced sports utility rubber.

62

Hawthorne.

"911 operator."

"My name is Lucas Dey. I'm a former L.A. County sheriff's deputy working as a private contractor," began Lucky, knowing the operator would be best served if he was calm, clear, and correct. "I'm currently in pursuit of a medium-sized box truck carrying juvenile sex cargo."

"Spell your name, please, for sheriff's."

"D as in David. E as in Edward. Y as in Young. The vehicle is a tire truck."

"Did you say 'tire truck'?"

"Yes. I don't have a company name. Just a witness description. I believe the vehicle is southbound on the 405. Destination, San Pedro. Please alert CHP and all South Bay authorities."

"You say you are in pursuit?"

"Driving a blue Nissan Altima. It's a rental so I don't know the tags. I also don't know how far behind I am. I just need you to run this on all data bands."

"Are you able to stay on the line?"

"Yeah," said Lucky, switching the cell phone from his right hand to his left. He was on hold. A 911 emergency hold. So, why did it feel no different than if he were holding for tech support from Microsoft?

Traffic was bad. Holiday traffic, no less. And it was getting worse.

So callers would know they hadn't been disconnected, the line played piped-in holiday music. No doubt, the choices were all the secular songs, filtered by some bureaucrat shrink to slow the panicked caller's sky-high blood pressure.

Lucky had initially gunned the rented blue Nissan down the 405, weaving through traffic in hopes of catching up with the tire truck. He applied less tension to his grip on the steering wheel to keep the car nimble while steering with just the one hand.

That dim and desperate warehouse chock-full of empty cargo containers was further and further behind him. It had taken little effort for him to glean what he needed out of the bleeding warehouse caretaker. Lucky had quickly learned that Jake was driving a tire truck full of kidnapped girls to some unknown locale in San Pedro. There were thirteen teenagers onboard and Ziggy—a.k.a. Zagreb—Jake's older cousin, was in charge of the operation. Cash payments were dispensed to a variety of young Valley-raised compatriots—all of Armenian extraction—in exchange for assisting his sex trafficking operation.

Lucky had found a few rolls of bargain paper towels and quickly packed the caretaker's wound before duct-taping the young man's hands to a city gas meter.

That was forty-five minutes ago.

Lucky was holding his tongue from cursing out loud at the tightening holiday traffic. Brake lights were beginning to flare across all lanes. Cars and trucks reduced their speeds in a stop-and-start symphony until, a mile south of LAX, forward momentum had wound all the way down to a negligible three miles per hour. More vehicles packed in from behind, leaving Lucky and that blue Nissan a nearly immovable spec in the ugly and sudden gridlock.

"Fucking cunt hell!" Lucky pounded the steering wheel. The outburst stemmed from a stew of frustration and chronic pain.

"There's no cause to curse me out, mister!" spat the 911 operator, her rise to anger betraying her cultural roots.

Compton, Watts, or Inglewood, guessed Lucky. And he'd stepped right in the middle of it.

"Jesus," said Lucky. "Thought I was on—"

"And you just called me the C-word?"

"Really, it was something else—"

"Hey, Mr. Ex-Sheriff's Deputy. You can go fuck yourself! ASS-HOLE!"

There was a soft click as the 911 operator disconnected from the call. Lucky unlocked his shoulder from his ear and let the cell phone drop to the seat.

"Can I just . . . please, God . . . catch a break?" he muttered to himself.

His mind shot back to his days as a sheriff's trainee—fresh on the job after a year working the county jail, something required of all rookie deputies. Bledsoe, his training officer that first day in the radio unit, had uttered his favorite phrase:

Work the damn problem, rookie.

63

San Pedro. 10:22 p.m.

Thirteen scared and half-frozen teenaged girls tried like hell to balance on the rear deck of the slow-rolling trawler. It was an oversight that they were wearing next to nothing and had zero protection against the elements. The best the crew could muster was a large, blue plastic tarp with grommets on the corners. The girls huddled, each barefoot, holding her heels in one hand and hanging on to her piece of the tarp with the other.

Karrie had been cold before. Wisconsin cold. Jumping out of the hot tub and rolling naked in the snow cold. Yet nothing in her short life had raised such gooseflesh on her skin. She was beginning to shudder from her marrow and wondered how long it would take them all to manifest symptoms of hypothermia. Yet instead of complaining about the temperature, girls were beginning to chatter about the effects of the capsules they had swallowed.

"I'm getting so stoned," volunteered one girl.

"Seasick bullshit," claimed another. "That shit's gotta be, like, close to heroin or somethin'."

Karrie was feeling nothing in the form of pharmacologic dysfunction due to the fact that she hadn't swallowed the capsule. As fast as the pill had landed on her tongue, she'd expertly swept it into a hole in her gums left by an early wisdom tooth extraction. It had never quite fully closed. She had gotten used to nervously playing with it, letting the tip of her talented tongue slip inside, nervously sweeping food in and out. The moment she spied the pills she knew they weren't for motion sickness. And when the man they called Ziggy inspected her mouth with a flashlight, he didn't catch the tip of the pill poking out from the divot in her gums.

She had spat the drug out the second her feet touched the pavement after climbing down from the truck.

Unlike the marathon-like trip in the tire truck, the boat ride turned out to be relatively brief. In no time at all, the tarp was removed to reveal the tall white hull of a luxury yacht. At first glance, the boat looked massive. Its curving brow dwarfed the fishing boat as it came around and idled at the stern, where a low and inviting diving deck jutted out. Crewmen tossed ropes and attached a gangway with cable rails. One by one the girls were ushered across as Karrie hung back. With her mental and physical wits about her, she was in a constant search for a way out. Were they counting the girls? What if she kicked up the lid to one of those fishy holding tanks and disappeared inside? Would they miss her? How hard would they look? Perhaps they would assume she had fallen overboard. For certain, they wouldn't look for her. Nobody would expect a spindly teenager in heels to survive the black water.

Yet they were only thoughts. Fantasies, even. In no time, Karrie discovered she was the last to be beckoned to cross the gangway to the warm, glowing superyacht. Inviting as it was, she knew what would be waiting for her once onboard. A party. Men. And all their illicit expectations.

"What if I say no?" Karrie found herself asking as Ziggy offered her a hand of help.

"Girls who say no have to swim," answered Ziggy. "Look at the lights over there. The shore. Ask yourself, 'Could I make it?'"

Karrie gazed across the harbor as directed. Those massive container cranes covered in colored lights looked miles away. The black water that roiled between sparkled with all the distant reflections. She knew the answer immediately. If she were tossed overboard, she might make it halfway before the harbor swallowed her.

So tempting.

Dying, she thought, would be such a middle finger to the world. To all she had left behind in Chenequa. It stirred the rebel inside of her. But it couldn't crush the hope for the life ahead of her. If she could only survive the night, she reasoned. She might yet get her chance at the future.

64

South Bay.

There may not have been a workday that went by that Lydia Gonzalez didn't want to pinch herself. Comfortably strapped in at the controls of her Bell JetRanger helo, state-of-the-industry noise-cancelling headphones cupping her ears, she might as well have been a gull riding waves of air above all the blood and acrimony that defined a cop's life on the streets. And to think of all the times she had thought about quitting the LAPD. It hadn't been an easy career, bouncing around between divisions like a foster child. All the while, she had the even more difficult job of being a single mom. Then there was the accident that had shattered her jaw and left it wired shut for six months. She had fought for, but had been denied, a retirement disability—the PD claiming her injuries were sustained while off duty.

The decision not going her way was the best thing that could have happened. Her vigor to train and transfer into the Air Support Division had paid off with a raise and a flight suit with her name permanently embroidered over her heart. She was a pilot *and* a woman. A rarity in the local law enforcement ranks.

She found outright joy flying the mechanical dragon. One of the secondary thrills was the autonomy of the gig. The primary function of air support was just that—providing support from the air when ground patrols requested assistance. The rest of the time allowed her or her observer to monitor all calls. And that included a patch into the 911 exchange. It was during one such respite—after spending twenty minutes in close support of two ground units hunting down a fleeing armed robbery suspect as he hopped one backyard fence after another—that Gonzo switched her radio over to what she called the mash-up channel. When tuned, her headphones would be flooded with nearly every call on the cop band. While listening, she would elevate the chopper to five thousand feet and wait for a plea for help that struck her fancy. Once the call and location were identified, her observer and navigator would call out a coordinate. Gonzo would then spin the helo in the precise direction, tilt the nose downward, and, using both gravity and the twin turbojet engines, sled her way to the desired destination.

"Anybody out there know an ex-LASD named Lucas Dey?" asked a dispatcher. "Got a 911 report on juvenile human cargo in a tire truck, southbound 405 headed for San Pedro."

And that was it. All and everything Gonzo had heard on the subject. Yet it was enough to tickle her ears, just hearing his name. The rest she had put together in the summation of the call. Juvenile human cargo? Tire truck? The way Gonzo heard it, Lucky had found his missing teenager and was in pursuit.

Already at her ceiling of five thousand feet, Gonzo rotated the helicopter clockwise until the coastline was ahead of her. The familiar band of red and white lights indicated the 405 freeway was a few miles inland. By her account, the artery was at a practical standstill in both directions. She imagined Lucky stuck down there. Gridlocked. Unable to proceed. Sure as hell, he would be cursing up a blue streak.

"Let's find that tire truck for him," smiled Gonzo.

As she pitched the helicopter toward the highway, her observer flipped down his gyro-stabilized binoculars. In a matter of moments, they were flying a line parallel to the southbound cars and clocking the business logos on every truck and panel van. When that turned up nothing, Gonzo pitched in a slow arc along the trucking corridor that led to the freight docks of San Pedro and the north end of the Port of Los Angeles.

"We're out of bounds," said the observer.

"So what?" said Gonzo. "I wanna find that truck."

Keeping her altitude, they scanned the docks in one direction. And when she made the slow one-eighty to turn about, the observer spotted the box truck backed up to a commercial slip. Closer inspection revealed the truck door was wide open. Flipping to infrared, they were unable to locate any humans but for the driver of the vehicle as he circled back to the cab.

"What about that boat?" asked Gonzo, looking down over her left shoulder. She saw harbor lights reflecting off the outline of a small wake.

"Looks like a trawler heading out to fish," said the observer. But when he caught the odd heat signature of what appeared to be a huddle of humans standing on the stern, his tone changed. "Lotta fisherman on that boat."

Gonzo put the chopper into a slow ascent. She kept the trawler in view while gathering the bigger picture. She unplugged her headset from the radio and re-jacked it into the cell phone. She was grateful she still had Lucky on her list of speed dials.

"Lucky, dear?" Gonzo said the second he answered with his standard sotto voce, *Yup?* "You better still love me because I just found your tire truck."

The superyacht was named *Lost Enigma*. Built in Perama, Greece, it was 211 feet of pure oceanic luxe. It sported a spa, massage room, gym, movie theater, and most importantly, fifteen private staterooms. In full seafaring motor, it demanded a crew of thirty-one. But for a simple party cruise around the Los Angeles harbor, a skeleton crew of fewer than half was required.

After boarding, the teen girls were allowed to warm themselves briefly in a rear salon. The man called Ziggy reappeared with a cardboard carton containing headbands with fuzzy attached reindeer horns. Each girl was ordered to wear a pair. Karrie chose a red set but didn't put hers on. Ziggy gave his final instructions, which when boiled down were twofold: the answer to every man's request would be *yes* and there would be absolutely no negotiation or solicitation for tips. Once again, he promised that at night's end they would each receive a cash payment of two grand as well as permanent release from servitude.

Karrie looked at the faces of her indentured cohorts, wondering if any of them believed the ploy because she sure as shit didn't. Instead, she read each girl as glassy and hopped up on whatever was in those red and gray capsules. Some were already grooving, getting pumped to the music thumping in from above.

"Any girl I catch refusing a request," insisted Ziggy, his voice raised over the walloping bass, "will be severely punished." His last instruction to have fun was swallowed by a man's voice shouting down from above, to *Bring on the girls!*

Placing herself roughly in the middle of the line, Karrie followed a wobbly teen in fishnets and a faux leather skirt up a tight circular stairwell that emptied out into a large creamy living room with plush sofas, pillows, marble pillars, and a mirrored ceiling. The music was practically deafening and dampened the appreciative applause from the male guests. Each man, by her measure, was no younger than forty. Suited. Some had doffed their neckties for the evening. Others were polished and pressed as if they had dressed just for their evening aboard the party boat. Karrie counted maybe twenty men. Though she was too young to scan for wedding rings instinctively, had she cared to she would have noticed quite a few and wondered just how many of those smiling jacks had daughters the same age as she.

There was a huge, black lacquer grand piano upon which was a small, elegantly lit Christmas tree. Over the toxic mix of cigar smoke and men's cologne, Karrie could still catch the occasional whiff of fresh-cut evergreen. As a tear stuck in her eye when she pined for home and her mother, a black man in a red vest carrying a tray of filled-to-the-brim champagne flutes steered into her.

"Merry Christmas," he said thickly, his accent reminding Karrie of Caribbean vacations.

She didn't see a tray of champagne glasses as much as she saw crystal stemware poured full of liquid courage. Karrie thanked him for the offer, downed one glass in three successive swallows, then picked up a second glass. Still holding her reindeer horns in her opposite hand, she decided to deposit them onto the crook of the waiter's arm.

A man from behind touched her elbow.

"What's your name?" the man asked. He was thickly mustached with a full head of silver hair. Not too tall but powerful in the shoulders. A life in the sun had left his skin leathery and cracked, yet his eyes betrayed a rather youthful sparkle.

"Karrie," she answered simply, not realizing she'd all but jettisoned her stage name of Valeriana.

"Pretty name," said the man with the big mustache, though Karrie was certain he would have made the same remark had she said her name was something like Turnip or Ass Crack. "I'd ask where you're from, but that's against the rules."

"Rules?" Karrie asked.

"The less any of us know, the better," he said. "I'm sure you understand. Is that your natural hair?"

"I guess."

"It's got just enough red to make me wonder what you keep under the hood."

"I'm a little seasick," lied Karrie. "Would you mind if I get some air?"

"Take my arm," he offered. "And I'll be honored to show you topside."

"Is this your boat?" she asked, her voice quivering as she cautiously looped her arm in his and followed his steps.

"No, no. Just a guest like you."

"Bet you're not at all like me," she nervously teased.

"Inside we are. Flesh and blood and beating hearts."

Karrie saw three upward steps ahead and a door leading to an outer deck. Beyond she could see the moon attempting to break through the clouds. And then nothing else but the blackness of an ocean. She briefly fantasized about running headlong until she flipped herself over the railing. Would they stop the boat to rescue her? Or just let her sink and be kindly forgotten?

"You know I'm just fifteen?" Karrie found herself saying.

To that, the man with the silver hair and mustache stopped on a dime. He squeezed her hand and grinned so wide she could see his white teeth were capped.

"I know you're fifteen," he said. "Which makes you one very special Christmas gift."

65

Los Angeles Harbor. 11:02 p.m.

As a general rule, L.A. cops could depend on the domino effect. The various jurisdictions of authority—from the sheriff's department to the LAPD as well as the variety of independent authorities and bureaus from Santa Monica, Culver City, all the way down to Long Beach—were practiced at passing the baton to one another. A crime beginning in Redondo Beach that wound up as far east as Glendora was hardly uncommon. Dispatch operators passed calls to each other like blackjack dealers throwing down cards.

Logic and experience informed Lucky he could count on his report of the juvenile sex cargo in transit going wide. Gonzo had already connected with the Los Angeles Port Police, the independent agency that covered all harbor crime from San Pedro to Long Beach. Import/export taxes made for a well-funded maritime PD with copious equipment and officers. Plenty of manpower to take down a large party boat engaged in underage sex trafficking.

Yet Lucky, who preferred leaving little to chance, chose to add fuel to the fire by hijacking a sixteen-foot outboard from the Cabrillo Beach boat launch. The small rental boat was one of two marina runabouts waiting to be winched onto a trailer by a crew of one. The curly-mopped Guatemalan man, who by Lucky's guess spoke little to no English, put up zero resistance as the ex-cop parked the blue Nissan's front wheels in the ocean water at the bottom of the ramp. Haltingly, but still forthright, he waded to the boat, climbed in, found the electric starter, and engaged the rather weak sub-fifteen-horsepower engine. It whined and frothed just below the surface.

"Call the police!" shouted Lucky. Then, recalling his lousy, C-graded high school Spanish, "*Llame, llame!*" he said, making a phone gesture at his ear. "*Llame a la policía!*"

Lucky reversed the little engine, backing the boat out another twenty feet before switching gears and throttling the outboard fully forward. He was soon charging full speed at about nineteen knots—barely twenty-three miles per hour. Hardly the speed he was accustomed to back in the day when he owned a twenty-one-foot ski boat. Those twin six-cylinder Evinrudes could skim him along the smooth top of Kern County's Lake Isabella at fifty-plus miles per hour.

Swell, he thought. He'd just stolen the pokiest watercraft short of a paddleboat. It would entirely defeat his purpose if he were grabbed by the harbor cops just short of his destination, the luxury superyacht Gonzo had reported was named *Lost Enigma*.

All he had to do was find it first.

There was an annoying chop in the harbor. The slow runabout would slap about every third swell. The shock of each impact was painful—wincingly so. Lucky's eyes would slam shut and the wind and mist stung his eyelids. He would reopen them and repeat, every so often checking his trajectory. Gonzo's last message indicated that the yacht was slow-going it up the harbor channel near the World War II relic and museum, the battleship USS *Iowa*, and headed toward the Vincent Thomas Bridge. The channel would be smoother going than the open water. And faster. He controlled his breathing, flexed his knees, and eventually steered the outboard between the two container cranes that flanked the nearly half-mile-wide channel.

It was close to 11:40 p.m. when Lucky finally caught up with the *Lost Enigma*, nearly a full mile beyond the bridge and easing along at a scant six knots. The massive yacht was splitting the channel, its wake rippling behind it in triangular precision. To say Lucky was disappointed to have neither seen nor heard the faintest whisper of police presence would be a gross understatement. The pain in his low back had crawled up his spine, pooled between his shoulder blades, and was shooting spikes into the base of his skull. He would view the apprehension of the yacht as a victory as long as the end result involved him ending up horizontal and connected to a morphine drip.

Yet here he was. Hours into a chase. Having reported the dispatch and transportation of thirteen underage girls to what would appear to be a high-class sex cruise. Lucky had even stolen a boat in his pursuit. However, the superyacht in his sights remained unmolested and sans any detention.

Shit.

For a brief moment, the sinking disappointment acted as a nerve block. It wasn't quite rage he felt. More so that he'd seen this gambit more than once before. Ahead of him and displacing hundreds of tons of sea water with entitled grace was a maritime masterpiece that must have cost its owner tens of millions of dollars. Sure. It was still just a boat. But were it parked on local terra firma, it would have borne an address such as Bel-Air or Beverly Hills or San Marino. *Lost Enigma* was a rich man's plaything. And rich men who partook in tabooed behavior often did so under the protection of authority.

The fuckers.

As Lucky sped the outboard forward, he kept left and in the shadows of the channel wall. This gave him a side view of the yacht. In the ambient light it looked nearly ice blue with every glassed porthole aglow with an inner warmth. Over the whine of the outboard he could hear the unsophisticated thump of hip-hop music. He also made out shapes along the upper decks, mingling silhouettes, and the occasional squeal and manly belly laugh.

Karrie was in there. Lucky knew it like he could feel his pain. Only fifteen years old. Alone. And probably only existing at the disgusting whim of some insider fat cat or pervert politician.

The cops weren't coming either.

Not to that particular party. There was a class war going on aboard the yacht. The protected versus the disposable. Even if one of those teenage girls were able to get her hands on a phone and dial 911, the distress call would probably be buried and all records of it destroyed.

"Stop," Lucky mouthed to nobody but the wind. "Stop it now."

He leaned the steering wheel to the right and eased the outboard back to the center of the channel. The runabout swam over the top of the superyacht's dual wake and eased into the edge of the spill light from the vessel's stern. The figures of two suited bodyguards were easy to spot. Both were on the diving deck, a custom tongue at the yacht's stern, low to the water for easy access after swimming and scuba diving. One bodyguard stood, and the other appeared to be seated on an equipment box, a constant curl of cigarette smoke swirling around him.

Lucky throttled forward, moving up on the yacht and revealing his presence. As the seated guard found his feet, Lucky threw back a friendly, attention-seeking wave. He eased the boat closer, the outboard's fiberglass bow only fifty feet from the exposed diving deck. The boil from the superyacht's propeller fizzed from underneath.

"I'M LOOKING FOR ZIGGY!" shouted Lucky from the outboard.

The shorter of the two bodyguards, trench-coated in a long windbreaker, cupped his ear and gestured for Lucky to come again.

"ZIGGY!" shouted Lucky. "I NEED TO TALK TO HIM."

"PRIVATE PARTY!" shouted the taller bodyguard. He was

well over six feet, built, slightly thick in the middle, and wore no weather protection. The misty rain was collecting like tiny gems on the worsted wool shoulder pads of his navy Italian jacket.

"ZIGGY!" reminded Lucky again.

Both bodyguards began waving Lucky off, demanding he back off.

Lucky returned with an oversized shrug.

"JUST GET ZIGGY AND I'LL GO, OKAY?" pressed Lucky.

It was the taller bodyguard who was first to reveal a weapon. Lucky instantly pegged the pistol as a Sig Sauer 9mm. The casual stance of the bodyguard told Lucky that the bodyguard had no immediate intention to shoot. He was merely brandishing the gun to elevate the warning. The stout guard in the long windbreaker joined in, shouldering a nifty little Beretta ARX assault rifle with an extended clip. No doubt filled with some thirty hot loads of 5.56mm ammo.

Lucky kept one hand on the wheel while the other shot up in open apology and surrender.

"HEY, SORRY!" Lucky shouted. He throttled back into neutral, retarding the outboard's momentum while the superyacht eased further ahead.

Then Lucky saw him.

The man called Ziggy stepped out onto the diving deck. He was shorter than Lucky imagined, in a tuxedo no less, groomed but still carrying the swarthy and overtly cocksure ambiance of an Armenian gangster.

Lucky shoved the outboard back into gear, waved toward Ziggy, and smiled broadly. His entire appearance calculated to appear friendly and without malice. He could see Ziggy talking to the guards, shrugging broadly. The throttle ticked a notch forward, bringing the outboard fully back into the light. Only Lucky didn't back off the power this time. He gripped the lever and shoved it fully forward. The outboard whined and the bow pitched upward in a sudden surge of speed.

Next, Lucky crouched.

Below the useless windshield, lowering his head under the

dash. He expected and heard a series of sharp pops as the body-guards unleashed a volley of bullets at the fast-approaching boat. He heard bullets snapping into Plexiglas as well as the sound of the hull being penetrated. Lucky could taste the fiberglass dust.

Barely two seconds into the gunfire, it stopped as both body-guards and Ziggy needed to dive out of the way as the bow of the outboard kicked off the slightly elevated diving deck. Teak splinters spun away like bits of shrapnel. The sixteen-foot runabout neatly mounted the stern of the superyacht, force-fitting itself into the pleasure spot in a slight sideways cant. The spinning prop of the not-so-mighty outboard engine screamed like a dentist's drill.

The impact sent a shudder all the way up to the superyacht's bridge. The captain instinctively cut the engines and ran down the emergency checklist, the first of which was to deploy his crew to inspect for damage. He couldn't imagine what could have caused the vibration. By his book, the superyacht was riding the center stripe of the channel. The only logical explanation was that they had run over some kind of debris floating just below the surface.

As for the party participants, nary a one seemed to notice a disruption in forward progress. Down below, it was game on: the team of middle-aged sex predators versus the forsaken underage girls. The later the hour, the more those fifteen staterooms were occupied by middle-aged men taking their Viagra-fueled turns on the Christmas carousel.

Karrie wanted a shower. The silver-haired man with the mustache had been kind enough. Not to mention mercifully quick and apologetic.

For what? Raping me? Or finishing on my thigh?

Her first instinct was to ask if she could use the bathroom for a shower. But something about needing the pervert's permission repulsed her. As if she had no self-respect left to her soul. So, without inquiring, she faked a smile and crawled out from underneath him, escaping into the bathroom of walled marble. The fixtures gleamed chrome and stainless and the water was instantly hot. Karrie scrubbed herself from head to foot, dried off, and brushed her hair back into a slicked mane.

"Next?" she mouthed to the mirror.

She asked herself if she regretted not partaking in the capsule. Maybe it would have numbed her or helped flush any memory of the sick ordeal. The night was young. How many more rapes would she be able to endure before finding a heavy object and bashing in some old bastard's skull?

While slipping back into the bedroom, she first noticed the door was open and there was a commotion in the corridor. The man with the mustache had somehow already dressed and disappeared from sight. It took seconds for Karrie to pull on her nothing-sized garb. She was just about to step into her heels when the door filled with a uniformed crewman bearing an armload of neon-orange life vests.

"Are we sinking?" was Karrie's first verbalized thought.

"Just a precautionary," said the baby-faced crewman. His leaden Baltic accent sounded like he had marbles in his cheeks.

Damning her heels, she hurried ahead and accepted one of the yoke-styled vests, putting it over her head and slipping past him into the corridor, where she nearly ran headlong into another, more senior crewman. This one looked equally young, but was red-faced and shouting a string of angry Slavic. Karrie couldn't understand a single syllable, but could tell the baby-faced crewman had made some sort of error because his superior was gathering up the few life vests that had been handed out. Fearing the vest might be taken away, Karrie hustled up the first set of steps she saw, not knowing where they led or what might be at the other end. That's because the floatation device had somehow injected her with hope. Maybe if she could make a surreptitious leap overboard she might actually fashion some sort of survival.

That's right, Karrie. Jump!

But from where? And to where?

Lucky was no longer trying to ignore the pain and the stiffness of his movement. The adrenaline coursing through his veins had pulled off another miracle. The naturally occurring drug was shielding him from the feeling of hot blades cutting through his core from the shock when the little outboard had impaled itself into the superyacht. Once forward momentum had fully stopped, he uncurled himself from his impact position and climbed over the gunwale. The uneven ground his feet found was actually the taller of the two bodyguards, pinned and in a death spiral underneath the outboard's skewed hull. Expecting the other guard to have met a similar fate, Lucky edged forward and crouched under the skiff's bow. Ahead, in the rich glow of incandescence, he could see the man called Ziggy on hands and knees, trying to climb the stairs.

His .45 unsheathed, Lucky approached until he was able to place the muzzle on the back of Ziggy's skull.

"Roll over," coughed Lucky, already having frisked Ziggy from behind. Ziggy rolled mostly to his back. Lucky checked his tuxedo jacket, discovering a sleek, hammerless five-shot .38 revolver in the inside pocket. Satisfied, Lucky took the lengthy snout of his pistol and jammed it deep down Ziggy's tailored waistband.

"What the fuck—"

"Call it a testicle tickler," hissed Lucky. "And I will blow holes in your junk if you don't get up right now and do exactly as I say."

It was awkward for Ziggy to find his feet while Lucky kept most of the pistol shoved inside his pants. But both men managed and began the ascent up the stairs.

"You know the girl I'm looking for," said Lucky. "Blonde. Fifteen. Green eyes. You need to see her picture?"

"No," choked Ziggy, shaking his head. "All you want is her?"

"*All* I *want?*" repeated Lucky. "You caught me. Christmas and she's all I got on my goddamn list."

The stairs emptied into that creamy living space with the plush chairs, pillars, and grand piano. The music remained just shy of ear-splitting. There were a couple of teenage girls dancing closely together while a circle of five gray-haired men in $5,000 suits toasted their sultry moves. Despite Lucky's attire and his strange conjoined twin, they entered and left unnoticed, steering left and up four steps to one of the side decks.

"Which way?" pushed Lucky.

Ziggy had to think about it, appearing to have lost his bearings. With his free hand, Lucky cracked the little revolver into Ziggy's more-than-sufficient nose. Blood issued from his nostrils in a matter of microseconds.

"Fucker!" whined Ziggy. "You broke my nose!"

"Where is she?"

Ziggy hobbled right and forward, crossing by a row of outdoor couches where three more of the powerful party men were ensconced and smoking what Lucky guessed were aged-to-perfection Cuban cigars. Their faces appeared shocked at the sight of Ziggy bleeding all over his pressed white tuxedo shirt.

"Mind your own business," ordered Lucky.

The trio of men stood as Lucky and Ziggy passed. With a glance to his rear, Lucky surveyed that none of the men were a threat.

Lucky shoved Ziggy through a doorway and down another set of steps that led downward into a corridor flanked by staterooms.

"She in one of these?" asked Lucky. "Open 'em."

One by one, Ziggy threw open the bedroom doors. Most were occupied by naked men of various shapes and fitness, positioned above or below some poor teenaged girl. Each scene sickened Lucky deeply—images he'd never be able to unsee. It was all he could do not to pull the trigger on the .45 and forever decapitate what there was of Ziggy's manhood.

"Still don't see her!" angered Lucky.

"This way." Ziggy was weakly pointing to another set of steps at the end of the corridor. As they neared, Lucky spied two sets of tactical footwear on a descent.

More bodyguards.

Keeping his own pistol shoved into Ziggy's pants, Lucky used his left hand to extend and level the revolver.

"Don't!" shouted Lucky at the beefy duo. Both bodyguards were identically suited like the pair Lucky had smashed into on the diving deck. Only their training betrayed them, each man uniformly reaching for his weapon.

The range was close. Maybe fifteen feet. Lucky snapped two

quick shots into the face of the bodyguard on the left. Then, before the other guard could clear a .40-cal from his shoulder holster, Lucky unleashed three quick trigger pulls on the man's hard-to-miss body mass.

Pop! Pop! Pop!

Both men crumpled down the last two steps.

"Fuck!" shouted Ziggy.

"Keep moving," pressed Lucky, using the muzzle of his own pistol to steer Ziggy around the fallen bodyguards and up the stairs.

Despite the unremitting music, Lucky could feel a sudden swarm of activity. Gunshots had that kind of magic. Between the pounding beats, Lucky heard screams and scrambling footsteps.

They cleared the top of the stairs, which opened up to a swanky outdoor dining area on the forward deck. Twinkling white Christmas lights had been strung, glowing against an ever-mounting mistiness. And underneath them stood a singular girl, wet, cold, and barefoot, and holding tight to the orange life vest that hung around her neck.

"Okay," said Ziggy. "So, that's her, right? She's the bitch you want?"

Lucky felt a presence to the right. He swung Ziggy around and saw three more crewmen and another bodyguard armed with a sub-machine gun.

"Please don't!" squeaked Ziggy. Lucky couldn't discern if the begging sound was a plea to the armed bodyguard or another plaintive call to save his cock and balls.

Then time froze. An old Reaper he knew had once referred to it as a slow-motion requiem. A brief and surreal calm before the final storm of bullets was unleashed. Memory was enhanced as if each and every molecule of air and flesh were being recorded in ultra-high definition. Thoughts were clear; sense of smell, acute.

Lucky swiveled his head briefly. Something in him wanted a look at Karrie. She appeared so thin and tiny. Only twenty feet away, shuddering, with wide and unblinking eyes. In those mesmerizing green orbs, Lucky felt the sadness. And abuse. And he knew then and there and all the way to his marrow what had been done to her in the past forty-eight or so hours.

Somebody would have to pay.

Without another scintilla of reason, Lucky squeezed on the .45. The weapon bucked and slid out of Ziggy's waistband, the bullet ripping downward through Ziggy's masculinity before notching a neat hole in the perfectly polished decking.

If Ziggy screamed—which he certainly did—Lucky never heard it. While witnessing faces stood in momentary shock, Lucky bolted for Karrie. He covered the distance in quick strides, gathered her and the life vest into his arms, and pitched both of them over the railing.

There was gunfire. The bodyguard with the machine pistol hadn't switched off the safety, so Lucky and Karrie were spared a certain stitching. As he leaped, he heard the familiar whizzing of spinning bullets cutting the air. But by then they were on descent and, before either could suck in a full breath, they splashed headlong into the black ocean water.

Saturday

66

Downtown. 1:12 a.m.

The Crown International Hotel—a.k.a. the Downtown Crown—shared an architectural pedigree with the Biltmore, dating all the way back to their twin birth in 1923. The eight-story "little sister" was designed as a boutique destination, offering and advertising to its out-of-town patrons the ultimate in privacy— meaning a traveller visiting Los Angeles with his wife and family would have a nearby suite where he could stash a mistress or shack up for a few hours with a high-priced call girl.

When Andrew's Wisconsin assistant phoned to move her boss to another hotel, the front desk suggested the nearby Crown. As a matter of an apology for whatever lapses in security had led to the awful assault Andrew had suffered earlier in the day, the Biltmore management had secured the Crown's presidential suite— one of two top-floor, two-thousand-plus-square-foot apartments decorated with antiques dating back to when they had first dug out the foundation. Above the suites was a rooftop pool that required a penthouse room key for admittance.

As Andrew stepped off the private elevator, Cherry nervously followed. Check-in, as it turned out, had been an unpleasant revisit with the events from earlier in the day. The LAPD and the Biltmore both had detectives who required statements. Andrew and Cherry were briefly separated into downstairs function rooms and questioned about their run-ins with the hotel robbery duo of Romeo and his girl, Jodi. Cherry had dutifully recalled the events as they had unfolded for her. She even tried to answer for Lucky, whom she promised would be along soon, once he had finished running down the recent lead on Andrew's missing daughter.

With their stories appearing to match, Andrew and Cherry were released pending further investigation. It was there in the quaint and retro Crown International lobby that Cherry thought it would be best to bid farewell to Andrew.

"Will you please call me?" she asked. "I'd love to know that you and your daughter reconnected."

"You're not gonna hang out?" Andrew asked, sounding edgy. Like it was a bad time for him to be alone. "Don't you wanna see how things turn out?"

"It's not my party," suggested Cherry.

"Nervous as a cat at a dog show," admitted Andrew. "Swear to Jesus, if he doesn't come home with my little girl, I'm gonna jump off the roof."

"Well, don't do that," half-giggled Cherry.

"Keep me company?" insisted Andrew. "You've been a huge help. Lemme at least write you a check for your time."

"Are you calling me a hooker again?" joked Cherry.

"Heck no!" laughed Andrew. "I may be stupid, but at least I don't make the same mistake twice."

There was, between the two, a new air of hope.

"You like Diet Coke?" asked Andrew. "'Cause my secretary makes sure my hotel room is stocked with all that aspartame crap."

"Too much caffeine makes me vibrate," said Cherry.

Despite that, she accepted Andrew's invite and followed as he inserted the room's key card into the slot. The door opened and Andrew led the way into the sumptuous yet homey penthouse suite. The ceilings were high with glossy white crown molding. The windows were equally tall and ornate. The wall-to-wall carpet was well-cushioned and easy on Cherry's stockinged feet.

"Hungry?" asked Andrew. "We could order up some room service while we wait."

"That's me. All about the free grub," she quipped.

"Good," he said, looking for and disappearing into what looked like a bedroom. "I'm starved. Do us a favor and order whatever you like. Then double it for me."

"Sure. Where's the menu?"

"Somewhere," he echoed back. "I'm taking a shower."

Cherry heard a distant bathroom door close. She turned in place, scanning the big living space for the desk. She found the leather-bound hotel guide under a reproduction Tiffany lamp. Inside she found a dinner menu. The pictures of the pasta looked tasty; she ordered two penne Bolognese dishes and a large Caesar salad to split.

Wondering if there was anything besides Diet Coke, she opened the refrigerator in the kitchenette and hoped to find something that wasn't a stimulant.

"Red Bull," she groaned, disappointed that the primary option was what the girls at the Rabbit Pole called liquid rocket fuel. The backstage mini-fridge was always fully stocked with energy drinks like Red Bull and Monster. Some would chug a can just before their turns on stage. Others would pour out half and tip the bartender to refill the can with vodka, turning the drink into a poor man's speedball.

Cherry chose one of six eight-ounce bottles of water that lined the door. She was briefly startled by the baggie of disposable syringes. Was Karrie's dad a diabetic? Absentmindedly, she read aloud the label on one of the medications.

"Alprostadil . . ."

The mouthful-to-say medication was difficult to pronounce.

But the brand name Caverject rang a bizarre, but recent bell. One of the Rabbit Pole dancers—a black vixen named Tania—would sometimes regale her stripper compadres with her tales as a former Las Vegas escort. She once told a story about a "client" with erectile function so lousy that his only way to achieve a working hard-on was to inject his member directly with a medication called . . .

Caverject?

This smacked Cherry as odd. Not that Andrew would suffer the same dysfunction as some purveyor of Las Vegas escort girls. By her reasoning, there had to be scores of men who required similar prescriptions, otherwise why the drug?

That's not it.

It was more about why the father of a missing teen girl would think he would need to pack his prescription of dong dynamite.

Whatever, she said to herself.

Cherry swung the refrigerator door shut and twisted the cap off the bottle of water. Seeking a garbage pail to toss the lid, she saw what looked like a pile of research that had been scooped up from Andrew's Biltmore Hotel suite and delivered. The hodgepodge of notes and reading materials had been piled onto a corner table in no discernible order but for size. The scribbled-upon legal pads were at the bottom. Standard printed 8½ by 11 sheets such as letters and fax copies were in the middle. And on top was everything from message slips to Post-it notes. The single, odd piece in the pyramid-like pile was an opened envelope that Cherry instantly recognized as the same one Lucky had found in Karrie's pink Hello Kitty backpack.

Pinching a corner with her thumb and forefinger, Cherry inched the envelope from the stack. Yes. She was correct. Karrie had block-printed "Dad" on the front flap in blue ballpoint ink.

Don't you read it, Cherry Pie.

She could have kicked herself for not returning the envelope to its spot in the stack. But then again, that curious itch she needed to scratch might never be answered. Cherry was already deeply emotional in the quest to find Karrie. She had given of herself and hadn't yet asked for a red cent in return. Well, she had indeed asked. But had seen none and hadn't thought of her own wallet in hours. The least she could expect was an answer or two.

Privacy be damned.

In Cherry's mind, she deserved to know what was in the letter. She slipped her fingers into the slot and removed a tri-folded sheet of lined paper that looked as if it had been ripped from a spiral notebook. In the same colored ink was a handwritten note in a mix of rudimentary cursive and lowercase printing. At the top left read a simple and straightforward, "Dear Daddy."

A quick reader, Cherry's eyes were charging through the initial lines of the first paragraph when she was startled by a voice.

"What the G.D. are you reading?" asked Andrew, his voice demonstrably flat—and monotone.

Cherry snapped her head to see Andrew standing in the center of the living room, hotel robe engulfing his way-too-skinny frame and using a hand towel to mop at his flame-red hair.

He's right, Cherry. What the G.D. were you doing?

67

Los Angeles Harbor.

They had hit the seawater in a human tangle and briefly sunk before being buoyed back to the surface by the life vest yoked around Karrie's neck. Both had first gasped for air before noticing how damn cold the water was. Despite the shock, there was an immediate unity to their actions. Lucky instantly fell into a half-breast stroke, his other arm hooked onto the life vest. Meanwhile, Karrie was on her back, assisting by kicking her feet. With every stroke, she watched the superyacht recede, shrinking to a more manageable and far less menacing size.

The swim was in total silence.

The tide was going out, carrying them backward and nearly under the Vincent Thomas Bridge. The span was lit in arcing blue lights. Against the misty black sky, it glowed in an ethereal sort of majesty. Karrie imagined it as a gateway to heaven.

The Catalina Sea and Air terminal was on the south side of the bridge. There was a pair of boat launches, a double-slip dock, a helipad, and a forty-yard strip of beach and rock. Twenty feet shy of the shore, Lucky felt his feet squishing into the bottom silt. It might as well have been his final ascent up Mount Everest. After the more than half-mile swim, it felt as if all oxygen had been depleted from his system.

The teenager helped, crawling herself to safety before slumping on a patch of sand.

"So cold," she shivered.

"C'mon," urged Lucky, helping her back to her feet. He gripped her wrist and they climbed the forty yards to the terminal parking lot. He scanned the half-dozen or so parked cars and quickly went to work in the light of one weak flood lamp angled off the eaves of the one-story building.

Karrie, barely clothed and dripping wet, dumped the life preserver and hugged herself while observing her unknown savior. When she had first laid eyes on him, she had only noted his bulk, buzzed scalp, and leather jacket. He had caught her attention because he stood out from the well-dressed guests and crew on the boat. In barely a bat of her eye, he had met her gaze with an unsettling recognition. She thought she recalled gunshots. But what did those really sound like? The rest was like streaks of color being hurled at her. Then black followed by the enveloping splash of the cold ocean.

Lucky snapped the antenna off a nineties-model Jeep Wrangler and used it to fish between the window and doorframe until the door unlocked. He climbed in, shoved the passenger door open, and called for Karrie to climb in. She obediently complied, stepping up in time to see Lucky had already torn the shielding from the steering column. His hands were shaking from the early stages of hypothermia. She watched him find a clump of wires, strip them with his teeth, and twist them together into a copper point. He paused as if reciting a quick prayer before touching the red ignition wire. The starter turned and, with a touch to the gas pedal, the engine turned over.

"Shut the door," Lucky said while adjusting the buttons marked HEAT and MAX.

"Who are you?" coughed Karrie, her lower jaw vibrating from her frozen core.

"Friend of a friend," he whispered.

The answer seemed to satisfy her. She took a moment to splay her fingers in front of the heating vent but looked disappointed that it hadn't begun to blow warm air.

Only then did she ponder his answer.

"But I sorta don't have any friends," she said.

"You're safe now," said Lucky, gunning the engine in hopes it would begin sharing some heat byproduct. "All you need to worry about is getting warm."

Tears welled in her eyes and she began to convulse with relief. As if the shock of the past fifty or so hours was just beginning to catch up to her. Safe, she thought. What the hell was that? When was the last time she'd felt cared for?

"Friend of who?" The words came out sounding like she was gulping at air.

"I work for your family," said Lucky. "I'm a former cop and I've been looking for you for about three or four days now."

"My family," cried Karrie. Her eyes squeezed shut and, for that instant, she became a toddler. "I miss my mommy so much."

Ahead, the sky appeared to ignite with a blast of lights. From the Vincent Thomas Bridge, a phalanx of police vehicles aimed their floodlights into the channel. The Harbor PD helicopter swirling above unleashed a scorching beam onto the suspended superyacht.

"Good," breathed Karrie. "For the other girls . . ."

"Buckle up," warned Lucky, grinding the Jeep into gear. Either the clutch was stiff or Lucky's knees were turning arthritic, because the Wrangler lurched forward with a jolt. "Sorry."

"I'm okay," said Karrie, sounding more like she was trying to convince herself.

In a matter of minutes, Lucky had swung the Jeep up the ramp onto Seaside Highway. He shifted lanes, making sure to be fed into the 110 freeway north headed for downtown Los Angeles.

"Gettin' warm," Lucky announced, directing the center vent towards the soaked teen.

"Wow. This isn't even your car," realized Karrie after sucking back some emotion.

"Borrowing it. Don't worry. I'll make sure the owner gets what's coming."

"But you stole it."

"Your dad can afford it."

"My dad . . ."

The question in Karrie's voice sounded like a cork had been jammed into her windpipe. The words just stopped. Lucky glanced to his right only to see the teen staring back at him, her eyes round and unbelieving.

"I work for your father."

"No . . ."

"Yes, I do," he clarified. "And he came all the way out here for you."

"He's here? My dad is here?"

"Taking you to him right now. Should be there in give or take twenty minutes—"

Karrie pushed her door open, producing a profound rush of wet air. Lucky was sure, had it not been for her seat belt, she would have leaped right out, staining herself on the fast-moving asphalt. Without a second thought, he had a hold of her wrist. But she tried like hell to shake him free.

"Stop your—"

"I WANT OUT!"

"WHOA, WHOA, WHOA!" Lucky shouted, his vocal cords hoarse from swallowing saltwater. He clutched quickly and nudged the gearshift into neutral and let the Jeep drift to the shoulder, where he braked. The passenger door flapped as the Jeep crunched to a stall.

"LET GO!" she screamed.

Lucky's free hand went to Karrie's mouth, if only to protect his ears from the extreme pitch of her sudden feral screeching.

"Shut up!" he hissed. "I'm not going to hurt you."

"You *are* hurting me!" she was able to muffle.

"Listen to me!" he urged her, tightening down on her mouth and wrist just enough to cause a pinch or sting. "I made some dead men back there just so I could bring you home! Whatever your shit is, it has crap hell to do with me, okay?"

Her eyes. So young and doe-like. Big as saucers and all of a sudden more terrified than anything he had seen in their brief encounter. Slowly, Lucky removed his grip, leaned across her, and shut the passenger door to trap the warmth from the car's heater.

"Now . . ." said Lucky in his best, most calming tone. "Your father . . ."

Karrie's eyes closed. He watched her draw her elbows back into her body and her fists clenched into tiny balls of ivory knuckles.

"I meant it when I said you're safe with me," he continued. "That means safe from everybody. Including . . ."

"But you work for him," she barely whispered.

"Not entirely true," conceded Lucky. "The only thing I care about at this moment is you."

She began to convulse again. But the tear-filled tremors were smaller, deeper, and far sadder than moments ago when she had shown relief from captivity.

The air left Lucky. The cabin was beginning to warm him and so the pain was returning. Though it somehow felt deserved. Like he had it coming.

"Your dad," Lucky cued again. "You ran away . . . from him?"

Karrie's chin dipped to her chest and she slowly nodded.

"Because . . ." he said, even though in the cold of his bones he knew the dark answer.

Karrie inhaled, but the air sucked back in a halting staccato. Hardly cleansing. Barely worth a breath.

"Because . . ." she said. "No matter how much I begged, he wouldn't stop fucking me."

* * *

Lucky wasn't so keen on promises. The word *promise* itself sounded so very loaded to him. And juvenile. A promise, after all, was a bond between grade-school chums. Or something a child held his or her parents to. Promises were not for adults. Instead, grown-ups had their *word*. They had agreements. Contracts. Guidelines. All for a world that, with every step toward old age, was revealed as more gray and fuzzy than idealistic black and white.

Yet, on the subsequent drive to Pasadena and between the sobs, Karrie had whispered her litany of sex abuse suffered at the hands of her father, Andrew Kaarlsen. In response, Lucky could only repeatedly promise that he would do all he could to keep Karrie safe and from him. That's if she, in fact, was telling the truth. Teenagers, he knew, could lie. He'd heard some whoppers from the mouths of fifteen-year-olds. Witnessed pregnant teen girls shed cascades of believable tears just to keep their daddies from discovering they'd been sexually active since middle school.

Karrie was a runaway, after all. Technically a street kid. She might say anything at all to keep Lucky from hand-delivering her to her father.

Maybe it was the way she recoiled. After all the trauma she had endured at the hands of her slave-making captors, the mere mention of her father made the teen appear as if she would have preferred to be back on the yacht than be delivered to her daddy's arms.

So, Lucky promised.

As schoolboy as it sounded coming out of his adult lips, he pledged to Karrie that despite his tenuous relationship with Andrew, he would keep her safe and far away until he had checked into the veracity of her claims. He bypassed downtown and steered the stolen Jeep north until the freeway dumped to an end in Pasadena.

The timing was fortuitous. Gonzo had clocked out of her LAPD Air Support shift at midnight. So, at around one thirty, when Lucky knocked on her cozy little duplex door, she was awake and folding laundry to reruns of *Gossip Girl.*

"Is this her?" was all Gonzo had to ask. The six-foot Amazon of a cop opened her arms and heart and folded Karrie to her breast. "Do what you gotta do. We'll be safe and sound right here."

What Lucky had to do was as easy as it was complicated. It was a short drive back down the 110 to the Downtown Crown. Before he had dunked both cell phones and lost his gun in that frozen swim to shore, he had seen a text memo from Cherry Pie with the simple details of Andrew's new hotel digs. Crown International Hotel. Penthouse 2. Instead of calling from Gonzo's, Lucky thought a person-to-person confrontation might be his best solution. Hand-deliver to Andrew the good news of his daughter's rescue. And then, while looking straight into the father's elated pupils, drop the hammer about the sex abuse claim. It was Lucky's experience that in such a fractured instant, he would be able to see the truth in a man's pupils. Either a shudder or a minute change in dilation. It was gut science. If Lucky remained unsatisfied, he would simply request that Andrew take a polygraph. After all, what self-respecting, non-sexually abusing daddy desperate for the return of his precious teenage daughter would deny the chance to vindicate himself?

Lucky's name was rung up to the suite and he was cleared to ride the private elevator car. The antique ride was slow and not the smoothest. It emptied out into an equally dated top-floor corridor. There were two sets of double doors for the east and west penthouse suites and a single stairwell exit marked in glowing red in case of fire.

The door to the suite was cracked with the swing-bar latch purposefully positioned to keep the heavy door from shutting completely. As Lucky pushed his way inside, he heard Andrew's voice bark loudly from the bedroom.

"IN HERE," called Andrew.

Lucky keyed on Andrew's two words and set a course for the back bedroom. He glanced around, half hoping for signs of Cherry Pie, yet was relieved she appeared to have wisely returned to her Silver Lake apartment. If Lucky was going to unfairly accuse Andrew of sexually abusing his daughter, it would be best to have it just be the two men.

Still damp from the swim—and fighting the returned pain with nearly every step—Lucky felt a slight chill when he first felt the breeze. A window of some kind was open and it was coming from the master bedroom. He turned the corner to find the door propped open with an antique copper garbage pail. Beyond yawned a large bedroom brightly lit and white from floor to ceiling, including the goose down comforter covering the king-sized, four-poster bed. At the foot of the bed was Andrew, naked and seated on a towel as if he had just showered.

Only Andrew's hair and pale skin were dry. In his hand was what looked like the handwritten pages from a spiral folder.

"Did you?" asked Andrew.

"Find her?" completed Lucky. "Yeah."

"She well?"

"That would be a matter of perspective," said Lucky. "But for right now, she's okay."

"But she's not here. With you."

"No."

There was a pair of French doors that led to a balcony beyond Andrew. The doors were open and the sheer curtains billowed into the room with each breath of wind. The lateness of the hour, the lights, the temperature, and the naked father seated on the bed. The scene reeked of wrong.

"Like the room?" asked Andrew.

"What's going on with you?" rebuffed Lucky. "Your daughter's safe and okay. But you don't seem so good?"

"Oh. I'm just awesome."

"Wanna put some clothes on?"

"I'm hot," said Andrew. "Why I got the window open. Swear, all you people from here are G.D. pussies. Should see what we put up with in cheese country."

"Cherry go home?" Lucky asked.

"Cherry Pie," sparked Andrew, shaking the letter at Lucky.

"She's one nosy little whore. Not here five minutes and she's sniffing through my stuff. Private things. None of her business."

"Where is she?" worried Lucky.

"She was really keen on this letter my Karrie wrote me. Left it in her backpack. Just in case, you know?"

"I'm aware—"

"It's a real stake through the heart. A serious dear-daddy-go-fuck-yourself. And after all I've done for that ungrateful little cunt."

"Where is Cherry Pie?"

"Last time I saw her she was in the bathroom," said Andrew. "Hey, girlie! You done in there? Your ride's here. Time for you to go home."

Lucky followed Andrew's eyes to the bathroom on his left. The door was mostly shut.

"My guess," continued Andrew, "is you care a whole lot more about that purple-haired skank than my baby girl. Who, I might add, I've been paying you to recover."

Using the knuckle of his left middle finger, Lucky gingerly reached out and gave the bathroom door a gentle push. It swung inward like it was on hinges of air. The recently remodeled master bathroom was as white as the bedroom, the walls plated with large rectangular subway tiles. At the far end—past the toilet, sink, and sit-down vanity—was a step-up tub with a gold brocade shower curtain pulled fully aside.

Lucky felt a sudden flush warming the skin on his face. This while his eyesight wobbled briefly before regaining focus on the twisted little body contorted over the edge. Her pupils were fixed and her eyeballs slightly hemorrhaged. Her neck was already ash gray and bruised from manual strangulation. Her mouth was agape, tongue limp between her teeth, all under a fresh colored mop of strawberry-blonde hair.

The girl was very, very dead.

"Now that you know where your girl is," angered Andrew. "Maybe you can tell me where I can find mine."

Lucky might have heard Andrew's voice, but little if anything he said registered. That's because he was still staring at the dead body. He must have seen at least a hundred or so in his career. Strangers. Compadres. Fellow Reapers. But none had ever quite hurt him like Cherry.

"I ASKED YOU A G.D. QUESTION!" shouted Andrew.

When Lucky finally twisted back toward the voice, Andrew was rushing at him. A full-on naked banshee charge with a face corrupted in bloody rage. Lucky's reaction came without a concrete thought. It was all chemical as he leaned, stiff-armed with his right, and gripped a single hand around Andrew's throat. With Andrew's limbs flailing, Lucky forcibly walked the smaller man backward, across the bedroom and out onto the balcony. Though Andrew kicked and fought, it all felt to Lucky like one swift move. That was until the second part of the act, when he released the begrudging father after his weight had tipped over the rail and beyond the point of no return.

There was no scream. Only the sound of sucking air as gravity took over. The last anybody ever heard from Andrew Kaarlsen was the loud slap of his body colliding with the pavement. It was sharp, distinct, and echoed briefly through the corridors of downtown.

Lucky took the stairs. As he tripped down each flight and then drove north back to Gonzo's in Pasadena, he was cataloguing the dominoes of his own making: the kidnapper he'd shot in Sunland; the stolen and destroyed outboard, the damage and dead men onboard the superyacht, the hot-wired Jeep that led to the parking structure underneath the Crown International Hotel. There would be found a dead stripper in a penthouse bathroom and a millionaire guest from Wisconsin having fallen eight floors before spreading himself on the sidewalk. Once the evidentiary pieces were put together and the bodies tagged, all roads were going to lead to Lucky.

He was going to need a good lawyer.

But before that, he needed to finish caring for Karrie. As a witness to uncountable crimes, the various police agencies might take a month at her before returning her to her mother. Lucky wasn't going to let that happen. He would see to it that as soon as he could manage, she would be on a flight to Milwaukee. That very day, if she was amenable. Once in the care of her only living parent—and one with more than sufficient means—she would be protected and defended. If the So Cal authorities wanted her statements, they could visit her in Chenequa.

It was nearly dawn.

From Pasadena, Lucky pointed the Crown Victoria west toward Reseda and his lousy little apartment. Karrie—warm, dry, and curled up asleep in some oversized clothes Gonzo had gifted her—was seated next to him. The teen looked even smaller—and younger—and that much more precious. Lucky didn't have a glimmer how to tell her about her father. He just figured, considering what she had been through, the less information he volunteered to her, the better for her fifteen-year-old psyche.

Halfway to the West Valley, Lucky pulled off the freeway in Burbank. At the nearest convenience store, he purchased a pay-as-you-go cell phone and afterward continued on surface streets. The streets were slicked with another dousing of rain, glowing red, green, and yellow from the ever-changing streetlights.

Using the new cell phone, he called and began collecting his voicemails. All the calls from the days prior were finally getting returned. Nearly all of them moot, considering the outcome of events.

And the outcome to come.

After the trail of havoc he had left behind—heroic or otherwise—he would be lucky to find a cop job in Alaska, let alone repossess his beloved L.A. Sheriff's badge. Hell, he thought. He'd probably end up in jail.

The last message on the voicemail was, strangely enough, from a Milwaukee PD detective named Crutcher. Lucky was going to wait to return it when he realized that, with the time difference, such an early morning call wouldn't be a nuisance.

And since when do you really care?

Anything to take his mind off the pain. Lucky was curious as well, so he dialed the detective's number.

"This is Crutcher," answered the detective by rote. All cop, thought Lucky. This was, at worst, going to be efficient.

"My name's Lucky Dey. Callin' you back."

"Oh, hey," said Crutcher. "Thanks. I've been having a little trouble reaching a fellow from around here. Andrew Kaarlsen? Somebody told me you were working for him?"

"What about it?" asked Lucky, not so curious anymore.

"We've been wanting to speak with him regarding the recent discovery of his wife's body."

Lucky wanted to ask, *"Body?"* Instead, he flicked his eyes over to Karrie. He was instantly grateful that she remained sleeping. Or at least appeared to be.

"Come again?" asked Lucky.

"You're a police officer, are you not?" asked Crutcher.

"I am."

"Then I can be frank with the details. Mrs. Kaarlsen hadn't been seen in weeks. Just a few days ago, at the request of her sister, MPD did a welfare check at her condominium. She was deceased, I'm afraid. I don't have the full coroner's report yet, but by all outward appearances it's a homicide."

Lucky's eyes squeezed shut. And he wasn't even thinking of Karrie yet. It was more like his mind was in a sudden whirlwind rewind of the past few days. Everything about Andrew Kaarlsen was adding up in a speedy and obvious equation.

"LOOK OUT!" squealed Karrie.

The teenaged girl—whom Lucky thought was dead asleep—had awakened just in time to see the taillights swerve in front of the Crown Vic, only to flare with blazing brake lights.

Lucky stomped on the brake, practically pushing his right foot through the floorboard. The Crown Vic's wheels locked, and the tires begged for traction. The car, though, slid as if on a sheet of glass. The SUV was at a dead stop in front of them.

The airbag!

Lucky's mind went straight to that emptied inflation device, sprung and useless in the passenger's dash. He couldn't remember if the child had remembered to buckle her seat belt.

On impact, Lucky's airbag deployed with a loud pop that, when married with the crunching of sheet metal, was as loud as anything he could remember. The disposable cell phone sailed from his hand and shattered against the safety glass, which buckled and spider-webbed.

As Lucky pushed the dead airbag away, he first looked at the still-intact windshield, fully expecting to see Karrie bloody and gasping for life on the Crown Vic's distorted hood.

"Ow, ow, ow!" was all she said, stunned yet safely still strapped in by her restraints.

Thank God, thought Lucky. It was as close to an actual prayer as he had said in eons. And he meant it.

Then he smelled gasoline.

"Jesus, I think I know him!" shifted Karrie, her eyes suddenly fixed through the cracks of the windshield.

Lucky's eyes swiveled first, followed by his chin. Looming in the mist and headlights was a familiar figure. Tall and graceful. But with eyes that looked wired with electricity.

"GIVE HER TO ME!" boomed the voice.

Herm threw open the back seat doors of his Ford SUV. From there, he withdrew what Lucky instantly pegged as a chainsaw. Cherry red with an extended blade. Already stained with what Lucky guessed was the young photographer's blood.

"REMEMBER. I FOUND HER FIRST!" shouted the pimp.

Herm pulled the starter cord. In one swift yank, the chainsaw sparked and screamed to life. It was a terrifying, ear-splitting pitch that practically drowned out young Karrie's screams.

"C'MON!" yelled Herm, barely audible over the din. He trigger-revved the machine from its pistol grip, more as a threat than an actual weapon. He waved the blade back and forth.

"Stay right where you are!" Lucky shouted at Karrie.

"Think I'm getting out?" pitched the teen, locking her door for good measure.

Radiator steam was spewing from under the Crown Vic's

mangled hood. As Herm continued to wave the roaring chainsaw, it looked as if he were cutting through a mist.

"GET OUT OF THE CAR!" shouted Herm.

Then, to punctuate his point, he let the blade dip and skip off the top of the mangled fender. Sparks issued.

"Fuck me," said Lucky, before reaching across and unbuckling Karrie's seat belt. "Get in the back seat. Now!"

While Karrie scrambled, Lucky unhooked himself and prayed again. This time for his hips to work. Because everything below his waist was feeling locked up again.

"ONE. LAST. TIME!" bellowed Herm. "OR I WILL CUT YOU THE FUCK UP!"

With both hands, Herm steadied the chainsaw, winding up the engine to a full threat before setting the blade to Karrie's door.

The sparks again. They trailed behind the saw as the teeth bounced and chewed at the Crown Vic's primer gray skin. There was a beauty to the picture. Like fireworks close up, sailing in a shimmering arc back toward Herm's SUV.

Lucky knew what would happen next. And he didn't need to see it. The moment he began his climb into the Crown Vic's back seat is when a single microscopic spark touched off the gasoline that had been pooling beneath his car's engine. The conflagration was instantaneous. It overwhelmed Herm in a fireball. If he screamed, nobody heard it over the continued wail of the chainsaw.

Though the front doors were buckled shut from the impact, the back doors were free to swing open. Karrie was first to spill out to the pavement, followed closely by Lucky, who lifted her to her stockinged feet.

The pair continued their retreat. Hand in hand. Easing clear of the street and onto a nearby curb. In a matter of seconds, the flames were eating up both cars and spewing clouds of black smoke into the just-waking sky.

"What just happened?" cried Karrie.

Lucky had nothing for her. At least when it came to words. All he could give her was his hand, his fingers tightly interlaced with hers. Any plans or promises were suddenly in the wind. All that there was, it seemed, was the permanence of the pain that lived in his body and the tenderness of the girl's hand in his.

Lucky knew nothing more of the future. But for that.

About the Author

Doug cut his teeth writing movies like *Die Hard 2, Bad Boys,* and *Hostage* until sharp enough to pen the Lucky Dey crime thriller series. He lives in Southern California with his wife, two children, and three mutts.

You can learn more about Doug at www.dougrichardson.com and drop him a line at bydougrich@dougrichardson.com. You can also follow him at www.facebook.com/bydougrichardson, on Twitter @byDougRich, and on Instagram @bydougrich.

REAPER

1

Tarzana, California. 10:41 p.m.

Frosty checked his phone screen. It was an unconscious act and only three slow-motion minutes since his last glance. Every passing second felt as if it were creeping like a caterpillar on a tenuous twig. It wasn't the waiting that chapped the twenty-two-year-old. Waiting was what he did. Waiting for Julius to hand out his next instruction. Waiting at the bodega to cash his Gran'nana's social security check. Waiting was process. After all, what was life? As his Gran'nana always say, all to livin' was about waiting to die 'n' meeting her lord and savior, Jesus Christ.

No. What bothered Frosty was the San Fernando Valley zip code. He would generally call his comfort zone anywhere south of Interstate 10 and east of the 405. Crossing north of South Central Los Angeles might as well have been a snowy slog across the Canadian border. Only Canada would at least be predictably opaque with white people. Frosty could handle white people. They'd take one look at his skinny black ass and his yellowed, alien-like wide-set eyes and be afraid. Either that or they'd overcompensate with their polite white guilt. White folk were so goddamn easy that way.

It was the mixed bag outside South Central that caused Frosty's anxiety. The ever-growing polyglot of ethnic minorities and the assimilation from the old known demarcations of black, white, and brown—it was all too confusing to keep current.

Frosty's Gran'nana said it best:

"Used to be able to tell who was who. Now all the mixin'

makes you wanna start ev'ry conversation with, 'What the heck kinda race is you?'"

Up until that Monday, the summer had been cooler than the usual swelter. If only it had stayed cool for one more twenty-four-hour sweep and the Santa Ana winds had held at bay. Then Frosty might not have had to worry about his perfectly functioning sweat glands. Perspiration contained DNA. And everybody knew DNA was what got even the best bad guys caught. In his Jordans, black Wrangler jeans, and a thin, navy blue hoodie, Frosty needed to fit into character, otherwise known to law enforcement as a "black male usual"—an African-American man in his late teens to twenties—a descriptor that, in America, fit tens of millions.

That's right. Try and pick me out of a lineup, motherfuckers.

It was the second day of July. And Frosty had made sure to ride the most obvious transit routes. The Blue Line to downtown. The Red Line to North Hollywood. The Orange Metro bus to some Valley neighborhood called Tarzana. On that route he'd be certain to pass plenty of security cameras and, depending on their operational status, each was guaranteed to capture his image. But the average lens would record little more than a five-foot-ten-inch black man's silhouette in a ubiquitous dark hoodie. Daylight would soon be waning into a dusty twilight. If any enterprising LAPD cop had figured Frosty would be worth a stop 'n' frisk, they'd have come up with little more than a few crumpled dollar bills, a nearly empty container of orange-flavored Tic Tacs, and a stick of CVS-brand lip balm. But the gig itself would be flushed. A new plan would have to be formed.

Near the corner of Reseda and Ventura, Frosty slipped into a supermarket parking lot. Keeping his gaze just south of level, he easily marked the four security cameras, each boxed in what looked like a tin-covered birdhouse and mounted high on a light post.

Sweet. I like me lots of cameras.

Knowing that every captured move would be recorded and eventually catalogued by detectives, he slid up and down the aisles of cars, pretending to test for unlocked doors, only showing interest in the more expensive luxury brands—Lexus, Cadillac, Mercedes-Benz. The exercise lasted less than two minutes. But it was guaranteed to super-glue an easily digestible motive to the crime Frosty was designed on committing.

Frosty crossed Ventura Boulevard near the old Taco Bell and soon melted into the dark and forested residential streets of the Tarzana hills. His path was circuitous. Yet all the while he was precise about his destination. The address was locked in his head. That, and he'd already visited the house on three previous occasions—the last time to conceal his murder weapon of the moment, a .22-caliber Taurus pistol, which was nearly as small as the palm of his hand. Frosty had double-Ziplocked the pistol with a pair of blue surgical gloves before burying the bag four inches deep in the freshly mulched flowerbed that fronted a Tudor-style house two driveways to the west.

It had been some twenty or so minutes since the sun had dropped below the crest of what locals called the Santa Monicas— a low-lying mountain range that bordered the Pacific Ocean, stretching east to west from Bel-Air to Point Mugu. In the gray before night—and more importantly, before the streetlamps had fully sparked—Frosty recovered the weapon, made sure to stuff the baggies in a front pocket, and did his best to make himself comfortable in a concealed corner of the empty home renovation site across the street from the target driveway. The clock on his phone read 8:43 p.m.

There was nothing left to do but wait.

At half past ten, perched on a short, sawed-off chunk of two-by-six, Frosty's bony butt began to ache as he kept shifting from one weak cheek to the other. What he'd have given for the "high motor" his track coach had so valued. So many of his school homies were built with popping gluteus muscles that not only made for fast legs, but also made baggy jeans a cinch to hang low. Somehow Frosty had been born with an ass as slight as the rest of him. For a while in middle school, he was even nicknamed Plank until Frosty shut up the instigator with an after-the-bell beatdown. Though the nicknaming perp ended up in the hospital with three broken ribs and a concussion, he never ratted on Frosty for the simple fear of getting capped by any one of Frosty's compadres—the Palmer Blocc Compton Crips.

Superiority through extreme violence, one of his O.G.s used to say.

That's right, Frostman. Superior violence always comes out on top. Like that Hiroshima and Nagasaki shit. Boom-boom and it's good-night war in the Pacific.

A pair of headlights swept up the hilly curve. From just under an eighth of a mile away, the lights flashed across the neighborhood trees—a mix of eucalyptus, ancient oaks, and reaching cypress, with not a leaf wiggling in a non-existent breeze.

"Fuck all, it's hot," moaned Frosty to himself, slightly surprised to hear his own voice before he whispered back to himself, "Shoulda brought you some bottles of water, dumbass."

The car attached to the headlights—a freshly waxed white Range Rover—accelerated past the address.

Thirst was becoming an issue. Somehow, Frosty had journeyed to the Valley already dehydrated, then marched from mass transit to mass transit before trudging into the Tarzana hills. His throat was dry and when he swallowed, his tongue stuck to the top of his mouth as if it were coated in Jif. He thought to leave his perch, search for a garden hose or a waterspout or even a half-supped bottle of Arrowhead, and quench his thirst. Only the thought itself was overruled by his wiser, quieting brain centers. He'd made personal admonitions to touch absolutely nothing on which he could leave a trace—a single solitary skin cell. Despite his thirst, leaving no trace was Frosty's governing thought. Patience would be rewarded. Just wait it out, do the thing Julius asked, and get back to life south of the 105.

Then came another flash of headlights, only these were the whiter, more ethereal shade of halogen. Yet despite the oncoming presence of a moving vehicle, there was zero sound of a surging gasoline engine propelling the car up the hill. If Frosty's ears were keener, he'd be able to hear the slight hum of an electric motor and the rubber-on-asphalt friction of four performance Pirellis.

But will it be my *Tesla?*

The battery-powered car—four doors and sleek as a Maserati sedan—softly wound down to almost perfect silence as it neared the address. The corner streetlamp threw a blue-gray cast, making the car's skin appear like a fish darting into the shallows.

Yes, sir. That's my *guy driving* my *car.*

From that moment until the ugly deed was done, Frosty's movements could almost be described as robotic. Each step had been thought through days in advance. All Frosty need do was execute his most simple plan. The Palmer Blocc Crip quickly rose and skipped in the direction of the street with speedy deliberation. As the Tesla slowed and pulled up to a residential gate, the driver's window rolled down so the gray-haired man behind the wheel could punch in a code he knew as well as his own name. When his brake lights flared, he wouldn't think to peek cautiously in either his rear- or side-view mirrors. It was getting late on a Monday night. The driver was probably buzzed or even drunk and, only yards from his bed, barely aware of little more than his next task—pressing the four numbers to engage the motor that would swing the gate open.

Frosty noted the seersucker sleeve stretching for the keypad and a pricey timepiece glinting in the glow of the nearby streetlamp. His Jordans made little sound as he covered the short distance across the asphalt. So far, Frosty had touched nothing besides the pistol, an item he'd be certain to take with him. He passed the pistol to his left hand, confident he'd switched the safety into the off position. Next, he automatically quickened himself as he counted out the telephone tones chirping from the tiny speaker box below the keypad.

At the open window, Frosty hooked his left arm inside the doorframe, bending sideways at the waist to make certain the muzzle of the .22 touched the Tesla driver's bristled temple. He pulled the trigger twice, releasing a pair of high-pitched pops. The skin contact and the acoustics of the car behaved as baffles, disguising the sounds to little more than finger snaps.

The driver jerked and lolled. His body barely had time to

slump when Frosty cracked open the car door. It was when he reached across the seat to unhitch the man's seat belt that he was assaulted by the scream.

The unholy howl came first as a blast of unwelcome air from the maw of the woman passenger. A hooker or a secretary, Frosty would later surmise. She'd been both unexpected and had already thrown the lock on her own door. She was in the process of hurling herself toward the driveway when she had realized that she was still restrained by her own seat belt. Nearly forty years old, redheaded, and her blouse unbuttoned enough to show off her new pair of surgically minted double-D breasts, she was sucking in her first breath to unleash a second howl when she discovered herself facing the small-caliber muzzle.

Again Frosty squeezed on the trigger. The microsecond flash of gunpowder afterburn camouflaged the actual bullet penetrating the colored contact lens in the passenger's left eye. The woman slumped four inches, threw a quick spasm, then fell away with her legs kicking. Without the safety belt, she'd have spilled completely out of the car.

With the driver's seat belt unhitched, Frosty tugged the male victim from the car. Next, he climbed in behind the wheel and popped the lock on the dead woman's seat belt, allowing her to crumple into a polyester pile outside her open door.

Frosty pressed down on the brake, geared the Tesla into reverse, and carefully backed onto the street. The passenger door shut itself once Frosty had shifted into drive and tested the electric car's well-advertised acceleration. In less than two minutes, Frosty was on the freeway, pointed out of the Valley, and finding himself cooled by the comfortable breeze provided by the Tesla's electric-powered air conditioning.

"Thank Jesus for motherfuckin' air conditioning," shouted Frosty to nobody other than himself.

2

Compton Station, L.A. County Sheriff's. 11:03 p.m.

The pain wasn't quite excruciating. Yet the muscle memory of how debilitating it had once been wanted to convince Lucky that popping a pain pill would be more efficient than the twice—sometimes three times—daily sessions of self-induced traction. The prescribed series of stretches, contortions, and exercises were designed to build core strength and relieve the stress on his surgically repaired back. Lucky could only suppose they did as advertised, but simply recalling the old pain would trigger Percocet cravings every time he unrolled the foam rubber yoga mat he kept in his locker. He'd lie in the most remote corner of the Compton station's locker room, its permanent mildew smell filling his nostrils. He'd set a thirty-second timer on his phone and once again begin breaking through the adhesions that always seemed to have reformed since his last horizontal bout with himself. Lucky would generally top off the session with eight hundred milligrams of ibuprofen chased by a can of Red Bull.

It was week two of Lucky's reassignment as a Los Angeles County sheriff's deputy. And the next check mark to address on his return-to-duty list was a name on a slip of thin, hand-cut paper. As if to save the environment, all four of the trainee assignments had been printed on one sheet of cheap white copy stock, then quickly quartered with a guillotine cutter. Pretty archaic, thought Lucky, for a modern, urban police department. But this was both County Sheriff's *and* Compton, where they hadn't changed the bolted seating in the lobby since it had been Compton City PD in the 1970s.

Deputy Lucky Dey flicked the slip of paper, folded it into his shirt's buttoned pocket, and performed one last check in the locker room mirror. As usual, his own handsomeness evaded him. Aside from his mother's blue eyes, he saw only wreckage. Scars. A nose permanently misshapen from collisions with both cars and fists. He checked his equipment to make certain he hadn't forgotten something important, like spare magazines for his SIG Sauer. Carrying either a nine or a forty was standard for uniformed deputies. Not quite what Lucky had been used to packing back in the days he'd worked as a detective for both L.A. County and then up north in Kern. A Model 1911 .45 was his preference. It was heavy as hell, which absorbed the recoil. It was also louder and generally smacked a target harder both wherever and whenever Lucky aimed. In other words, a bad guy spanked with a .45 slug generally went down and stayed down.

"Uniform looks good," said Watch Commander Lieutenant Eugene Torres. The stout ex-Marine with a throwback mustache slapped Lucky's shoulder as they squeezed past each other in the tight corridor that shortcut through the dispatch room. "Betcha you were surprised it still fit ya."

"Desk jobs are ass-spreaders," replied Lucky.

"Same with a seat on patrol," warned Torres. "Had this one TO who told his rooks that traffic stops were the best way to supplement the cardio. That, and watching the greasy lunch breaks."

How many years had it been since Lucky had manned the wheel of a black-and-white? No matter. That was the deal he'd agreed to for the sheriff's department to take him back. As well as the responsibility of working as a training officer saddled with two trainees a year. It wasn't quite detective grade. Yet it would have to do.

Lucky stuffed Torres's unsolicited advice with a sideways wink and stepped out into the night. The motor yard was rectangular, a hundred yards deep, and cast in a yellowish blaze of sodium street lamps. Sheriff's patrol units were parked like soldiers waiting for orders. Ford Interceptors, Suburbans, and the old standbys, Ford Crown Victorias. The rumors were that all the sedans would eventually be replaced by roomier, all-wheel-drive SUVs. Swell, thought Lucky. The modern-day cops' black-and-whites were simply a bunch of supercharged mom-mobiles.

His assigned black-and-white was already backed up, wheels touching the curb, gassed and ready to roll. The exhaust was smoothly belching downward in the direction of Lucky's squeaky new tactical boots. The passenger door swung wide and out stepped Lucky's trainee. Despite her own new boots and a lousy-fitting uniform cut to erase any essence of what might be considered feminine, Lucky guessed the young deputy couldn't have weighed more than 110 pounds naked and blown dry.

"Deputy Dey," the trainee spoke up, assuming a strong-spined stance. "I'm—"

"No, no," interrupted Lucky, holding up a single index finger, then using it to fish that slip of paper from his shirt pocket. "Lemme see if I can get this on the first go."

Lucky cleared his throat and again snapped the piece of paper. He remained on the curb, using the extra five inches to accentuate his own six-foot frame over the trainee's five-foot-four.

"Deputy Mequashia Saint George," read Lucky. "I get that right?"

"Shia," corrected the trainee. "That's what I go by. Been that way since kindergarten."

"Mequashia, though," grinned Lucky. "That's pretty fuckin' exotic."

"Grew up in the West Valley," said Shia, unblanched by Lucky's f-bomb describer. "Nothing exotic about that."

"'Less you live in Pacoima."

Shia offered her open palm. Her fingers were delicate, like a hand model's, with a tinge of peachy-pink on her palms to contrast her flawless ebony skin. Shia's nails were short but manicured; her teeth, perfect rows of enamel, the probable work of a gifted orthodontist.

A real beauty, thought Lucky. Slight as she might have been beneath her Kevlar vest, even with the lowered physical bar for women recruits, she'd most likely be able to surprise most males with power well beyond her stellar looks.

As for what Shia saw in Lucky? The training officer didn't much give a rip how she viewed him. At first glance she could have seen him as a muscle-head whitey with a buzzed scalp. Or at almost forty years of age, too old for the uniform. Was he a closet racist after too many ghetto-serving years as a sheriff's deputy? Or an overreaching apologist?

Whatever I am, she'll have to figure it out for herself.

All that mattered to Lucky was that she saw him for who he was: her TO—or training officer. For the next five months, he would be her boss, sensei, guru, and closest ally on earth were she to get herself into a shit storm. And working out of the Compton station, there was guaranteed to be plenty of opportunity for that.

"What do I call you?" asked Shia, her head slightly cocked into a question mark. It was as if she were really asking, *Did you really forget to introduce yourself?* "TO Dey?"

"Lucky," he answered in a simple monotone. "Luck if you want to save on the syllables."

"Lucky works," said Shia, taking her cue as he circled around to the driver's side door.

"You up to speed on the Box?" asked Lucky upon his slide behind the wheel. The Box he referred to was the touchscreen laptop that was standard in every patrol car and mounted on a swivel for both the driver and passenger to operate.

"Top of my class, sir," answered Shia.

"That's good," said Lucky. "Because I'm a moron with machines."

The comment earned him a sideways look from his trainee.

"Been fourteen years since I was in a patrol unit," volunteered Lucky. "So in a way we're both rookies."

Shia, her whip-smart brain beneath efficient cornrows pulled neatly into a decorative knot at the back of her skull, appeared wisely skeptical at Lucky's rookie remark. She'd likely heard tales of training officer shenanigans, hazing, and the general head wrecking of trainees. And this Monday night would be day one of a nearly half-year journey to full street-cop status.

"No reply," grinned Lucky. "Smart girl . . . But I wasn't lyin' about how long since I'd been in a black-and-white. Wouldn't worry, though. Seat belt?"

"Oh, yeah. Right," said Shia, slinging the belt across her torso until the tongue clicked into the receptacle. However, as Lucky gassed the unit forward toward the steel-reinforced gate leading out of the motor yard, she noticed her TO hadn't made a move to secure his own restraint. Nor would he as he eased the Interceptor onto South Willowbrook. Shia's eyes briefly landed on the yellow and black warning decaled on the dashboard of each and every sheriff's patrol car:

**ALL VEHICLE PASSENGERS
MUST WEAR SEAT BELTS!**

"Something wrong?" asked Lucky without even glancing at her. With his right hand he double-clicked the power button on his tactical flashlight, testing the penetrating beam before resting it between his legs. The phallic appearance of the gesture wasn't lost on Shia.

"No, sir," braved Shia. "I'm good to go."

Join Doug's mailing list
for sneak previews, exclusive content, and
news on the release of the latest Lucky Dey Thriller.

visit www.eepurl.com/cRe5-v